Forgiven

Sunny Serafino

Double Edge Press

Scenery Hill, Pennsylvania

Double Edge Press

ISBN: 978-0-9819514-7-8

Forgiven

Cover Artwork: Original artwork design by Double Edge Press. Elements contained within the original design include the following images in its composition:

The following images are royalty paid via dreamstime.com:

Elderly Man in Rocking Chair by Jarenwickland
Baby by Rsargent
Car Chase by Philcold

The following image was via Wiki Commons – royalty free:

Bridge over Ob River

Acknowledgments and Thanks

John Donne once wrote "...no man is an island..." While some may think writing is a solitary occupation, nothing could be further from the truth. Authors are not islands either. We may sit in a sea of make believe but there are facts and truths which must be learned. Yes, we closet ourselves with thoughts, ideas and challenges, but it takes more than just one mind to create a book. In developing the plot, characters and doing the research for *Forgiven,* I called upon many sources.

Not knowing much about the unique medical situations *Forgiven* covers, I fortunately had a wealth of friends with medical backgrounds who generously helped me. Thank you Jamie Steeds, RN, Marian Myers, RN (ret.), Maureen Murphy, RN (ret.), Jan Calso, LPN (ret.) and Sharon Weatherhead, MBA, MT (ASCP). Your collective help was priceless.

Thanks go to Sally Fradette, Dot Pansius and Lynn Ullin who churned through page after page of raw manuscript, catching the little things that writer's often overlook; helping me to improve and grow with each chapter. Special thanks go to Bette Crosby, a fellow author who has always been a deep well of encouragement and support. I apologize if I have left out the names of anyone who also aided me in the exciting adventure of completing this novel.

A simple thank you seems so inadequate for Rebecca Melvin of Double Edge Press and her staff, for their measure of confidence in me and my book and for the time and help they have offered.

I couldn't end my list of thanks without mentioning my husband, Lenny who encouraged and supported me from the very first time I said, "I want to write." His love and support have kept me writing, fulfilling my life-long dream. I love him and I love what I do.

And, of course, none of this is possible at all without my Lord and Savior who guides and sustains me.

Forgiven

Sunny Serafino

1

The troubles of my heart are enlarged;
O bring thou me out of my distresses.
Psalms 25:17

Karen's hand clutched the phone so tight her knuckles turned white. "What do you mean 'sell the house'?" she asked.

She hated talking to Bill on the telephone. It seemed an impersonal way to be talking to a husband, even if he wasn't really her husband anymore. Eighteen months after their divorce and she still couldn't refer to him as her *ex*-husband. While she welcomed the opportunity to avoid a face-to-face confrontation, she couldn't control the little leap her heart insisted on doing just hearing his voice.

Karen could hear Bill struggling to keep his worry and anger to manageable levels. She took in a deep breath before continuing. "That's hardly my fault, is it? You were the one who chose to leave, who divorced me and married that little size two idiot child."

"Karen, we've been there. I'm not sorry for my decision but I am sorry that you are still so hurt. Honey, you have to move on."

"Don't call me 'Honey'," she snapped. "What about our daughter? This is her home, too. The only home she's ever known. Forget about me, which you've obviously already done. Forget about me," she repeated, the icy lump in her throat distorting her words. "Are you going to throw your only child out on the street?"

"I'm not throwing anyone out on the street and you know it. If you would agree to sell the house we could look for something smaller for you and Alice, it would be more economical, and it would still be a wonderful home."

"So, you get in a jam and I'm supposed to turn my life upside down by moving. Is that it?" She wanted to finish by saying, *we're not married anymore, remember?* But, angry as she was, she couldn't make that statement. She couldn't call him *ex,* and she couldn't say the simple words, *we're not married anymore.*

He didn't answer. Maybe he had no answer.

"Oh, Bill, why do all these changes have to happen?" She had been standing, but now she shifted, found a seat, put a hand to her forehead and rubbed the beating pulse behind her temples. "What's so important that you're even suggesting this?"

"Karen, I have to talk to you. Go over figures. I have a plan, a plan that will be good for all of us. I'm coming over tonight to talk to you and go over these things." He made it a 'done deal' proposition, not open for discussion. The line went so quiet, Karen knew he had to be holding his breath.

When she didn't respond, he continued, "Karen? Karen? Did you hear me?"

"Yes."

"I'll be over around seven. Just to talk, Karen. No fighting, okay?"

"I guess."

After hanging up the telephone, Karen picked up the little ball of fluff lying in her lap and buried her face in the soft hair. "Oh, Missy, you always know when I'm sad or upset, don't you?" Her little poodle had jumped into her lap soon after Karen had sat down but she had been so intent on her conversation with Bill she had barely noticed the dog's arrival until now.

Karen Waterson put the little dog on the tiled floor and walked from the kitchen, through the lanai and outside. Missy followed and, at this unexpected outing, ran excitedly around the lawn. Karen shaded her eyes and looked over the hedge separating the Waterson property from the protected Savanna. Everything between their land and the river was protected and remained under the jurisdiction of the State of Florida.

She remembered Bill saying, "No one will ever build behind us, Karry." They put in a sturdy hedge of crown of thorns across the width of their lot. "It will keep our kids from going into the wilds out there." Our kids, she thought. They had wanted three or four but Alice was their only child, a beautiful little girl with

Bill's blond hair and blue eyes. Was the divorce because he had no son? No, she reasoned. He loved Alice and knew why there would be no more children. Not after the delivery of their one and only child. "Too dangerous," the doctor had said.

She shook her shoulders. "Don't keep digging up the past. It's gone." But despite her efforts, her mind went back to the day Bill told her their marriage was over and now, eighteen months after the divorce was final, the pain was still as fresh as it was on that late summer evening.

"I'm sorry, Karry," Bill said. He swayed from side to side as he always did when he had something difficult to talk about. Like the time he'd overdrawn their bank account or when he'd had an accident and demolished their car. She hadn't cared about the overdrawn account or the accident. He was all right, they were all right. That was what mattered.

"What is it?" She smiled, thinking he'd done something he thought serious and she would treat as silly. After all, accidents happen.

He looked away, staring through the window, and then slowly he looked at her. "I want a divorce."

It was such a simple statement yet Karen felt her knees turn to water. She reached behind her, her hand gripping the arm of the couch for support as she sank to the cushions. "What?" she stammered.

"I know it's a shock but... I..."

"Why?" she stuttered. "What have I done?"

"You haven't done anything."

"No," she said, forcing her quaking knees to allow her to rise. "No. This is a mistake. This is wrong. It isn't possible. I'm not hearing you right."

"Yes, you are," he whispered, closing his eyes and bowing his head. "It isn't anything you've done. I'm sorry."

"Sorry? You? Is there someone..." The word 'else' just couldn't be spoken and her heart and mind raced too fast to complete coherent sentences. It was too absurd, too far fetched. It was too painful.

He nodded and paced across the floor to the foyer then

turned, looking at her with the strangest expression she had ever seen on his face: sad, guilty, determined. He looked sick, as if he might become physically ill. He looked worse than when their six-year-old black lab, Corky, had been hit by a car and died at the edge of their driveway.

He shrugged his shoulders and spread his hands as he spoke, his words coming from a machine, like a recorder, not his own voice. "It's been going on for some time. I never thought I'd have to say this. Never thought I'd—"

"What?" Karen snapped. "Thought what? Never thought you could be so cruel, so dumb? Never thought you'd be dishonest? Never thought..." She began to walk toward him, her pace unsteady, her face pale, her hands twisted into a knot of fingers. Her voice, which had been raised before now lowered to a whisper. It was pure steel. "Who is she?"

2

Humble yourselves, therefore, under God's mighty hand, that He may lift you up in due time. Cast all your anxiety on Him because He cares for you.
1 Peter 5:6-8

Karen turned and went back into the house, calling Missy to follow her in. She made a salad for lunch and picked at it alone in her kitchen. She was almost relieved when the cell phone rang again. "Now who...?" she muttered, reaching for it and answering. "Hello?"

"Hi, Mom."

"Hi, honey. Is anything wrong? Are you okay?"

"Of course I'm okay. Why do you ask? I'm just..."

"Well, you took me by surprise, honey. You don't usually call me in the middle of the day, and with school closing in a couple of weeks I know you're busy. Are you all right?"

"I'm fine, Mom. I just called to tell you I'm coming home..."

"I know. In two weeks, right?"

"No." she paused, "I'm not waiting until the end of the term...I'm finished with school...at least for now...maybe forever."

"Alice, what on earth are you talking about? What do you mean 'finished with school'? Finished for this year? Surely, you don't mean forever?"

Alice didn't reply and the pause made Karen's stomach retract around the lettuce she'd eaten. "Alice, answer me."

"It might be forever... I'll talk to you when I get there... I'll see you in three hours... I'm okay. Don't worry; it's going to be all right..."

"But, Ali. This is so strange, so sudden..." Karen said, reverting to the pet name she and Bill had given her so many years ago. When Alice reached high school age she'd begged them to call her Alice, but it didn't really work. Everyone called her Ali.

"Mom, I'm going to hang up now so don't ask any more questions... Bye."

Karen hit the end button on the phone. Another call, more worry; what was happening to her world?

What if...she hated it when her thoughts turned to what she referred to as 'the what if' syndrome. But things today might have been so different if she'd seen the trouble in their marriage. Would it have made any difference if she'd been prepared? She knew in her heart nothing she could have done would have changed the outcome, at least when it came to Bill. As for Ali..., she sighed deeply. Who knew?

She replayed Ali's voice in her mind. Did she detect panic? Why was she coming home early? Why now? And not going back ever? She grimaced. Dear God, not another problem.

Karen watched from the wide front window. She stood back a little because she didn't want Ali to see her and think she was anxious about something, even though she was. Her heart fluttered painfully in her chest.

Ali pulled her car into the driveway but she didn't open the garage door and drive forward. Instead she opened the trunk and pulled a large duffle bag out, then reached for a smaller soft travel bag. There was something in the way Ali walked up the curved sidewalk to the front door that made Karen suck in a sudden breath as if she needed air.

When she heard the door open she walked toward the tiled foyer. A four foot floor to ceiling wall separated the entry area from the large living room so she didn't see Ali as she closed the door.

"Hi," Ali called.

Missy jumped from her cushion and ran to dance around Ali's feet, yipping her welcome. "Hi, Missy. Stop barking," Ali said, stooping to ruffle the thick curls on the little dogs head.

"Need any help with that?" Karen asked, nodding to the duffle bag and its companion.

"No, I'll get to that later." Ali stepped forward into Karen's arms and they hugged...longer than the usual back-home-from-school hug. Karen's heart took another flip in her chest as she felt her daughter snuggle her face into her neck. She leaned back, her arms still around her. "What's going on, honey? You sounded so unlike yourself on the phone earlier."

Ali wriggled out of her mother's arms and moved toward the living room. "Come in here, Mom. We have to talk."

Karen followed. "My, you do sound mysterious. Don't tell me you've gotten into trouble at school. I couldn't believe that."

"Not exactly." Ali sat on the long, over-stuffed sofa with the bright flowers on a stark white background. She patted the cushion next to her and Karen joined her. Missy settled herself at their feet.

"What does 'not exactly' mean?"

Ali drew in a deep breath and her lips formed a determined thin line.

Gosh, thought Karen, *she looks more and more like her father, especially when she's worried.* She waited for her daughter to speak.

"I have some news," Ali said.

"Trouble?"

"You could say that."

"Why don't you tell me instead of beating around the bush? You sound like your father when he's done something dumb."

"Dumb? I don't know if that's the right word exactly."

Karen waited, her patience definitely becoming strained. Her hands twisted in her lap. She watched as Ali stood and walked to the fireplace now filled with an arrangement of green ferns for the summer.

Stopping at the mantle, Ali studied a picture of herself when she was twelve and had won the junior tennis championship at the country club. Her graduation picture was in the white pearl-like frame on the opposite side of the mantle.

She turned around and faced her mother who was now sitting on the edge of the cushion. "I'm pregnant," she said.

The silence in the room deepened. The little mantle clock ticked softly but still sounded louder than normal.

"Pregnant!" Karen heard the shock in her voice and her eyes

immediately went to her daughter's middle. The tee shirt with her college logo seemed much larger than anything Ali usually wore. She frowned.

Ali nodded, obviously struggling to keep her tears contained.

"You're sure?"

Ali nodded. "I'm sure. The doctor said I was about eight weeks pregnant. That was back in—let me see. It must have been at the end of February."

"February! So that means— How far along are you?"

"More than three months."

Karen pushed herself back into the cushions as if that might lessen the anguish flooding her body, her face a mixture of shock and outrage. "Oh, my God, how did you let this happen? What the... Now, of all times... What were you thinking?"

"I guess you could say I wasn't thinking." Ali remained at the fireplace. Karen couldn't blame her. The cushion next to her mother probably didn't seem like a good place to be right now.

"The father..."

"It's Morgan, Mom. He's the only guy I've been with for two years. You know that."

Karen stood, moving toward her daughter with purpose. "And the wedding is... when?"

Ali put her hands over her face. "There isn't going to be a wedding," she said, her words muffled by her hands. "Morgan has left me."

"Left you?"

Ali nodded, head lowered, her fingers picking at a thread on her tee shirt.

"What happened?"

"I don't know. That's the whole problem, I don't know."

Karen remained frozen. Part of her wanted to rush to her daughter and gather her into her arms. But something made her stay where she was.

Slowly Ali dropped her hands to her side. "Say something," she pleaded.

"What do you want me to say? That this is the best news I've had in a long time? Well, it isn't. Ali, why didn't you tell me sooner?"

"Would it have made any difference?"

Karen shrugged. "It's your baby but what about...?"

"I knew you'd be upset but I hoped you'd understand. After all, having a baby is not something new, maybe just a little premature in our plans." A weak grin crossed her lips, her hands clenched behind her back.

"Don't try to be funny. This is serious and you don't even know how serious it might be. Didn't you think it would be a good thing to call me," Karen hesitated, adding, "or your father, before now?"

"I thought Morgan and I could handle this until after the school term had ended. We were making plans. He's graduating and there was that excitement. Now, I don't know what he's doing. He went away. He left me...." Her voice broke and tears rolled down her cheeks. "Oh, Mom...I knew you'd be mad when you heard. I'm sorry."

"I'm not mad, just shocked, and now of all times."

"You said 'now of all times' before."

Karen pursed her lips. *Now of all times*, she thought, remembering Bill's earlier phone call.

"I said, 'now of all times' because there are other problems. I'm not upset about you. Well, I am, but...I was upset before you came home. It's about your father."

"What about Daddy. Is he sick?" Ali inched forward, her hands quickly bunched together.

"No, just some financial things. He didn't tell me. He's coming over later to talk. It's nothing for you to worry about, honey." She paced. "Have you told your father?"

"No. I wanted to tell you first."

The pause was comfortable, mother and daughter together, yet their worry rested between them, just below the surface.

"Well, right now you have some pretty serious things to think about." Karen was searching for words. "I never knew you and Morgan were that serious. I liked him whenever he visited. It wasn't often but whenever you spoke of your relationship with him...well, it seemed kind of casual. You were always having fun together."

She stopped at the sound of her words. If things weren't so

serious this might be time for a laugh and God knows they needed a laugh. But the abject misery on her daughter's face melted her heart.

"Come here." Karen reached for her daughter, her own body absorbing the convulsive sobs.

"I'm sorry. Not sorry about the baby, Mom, just sorry you're so upset. Oh, Mom, I'm scared. I need you."

"We have each other, honey. It's an upsetting time but we'll face it together, okay?" She took her daughter's icy hands in hers. "Oh, Lord," she pleaded softly.

3

For He shall give his angels charge over thee,
to keep thee in all thy ways.
Psalms 91:11

Jack Coursky stretched, yawned and sat up. He looked out the cabin window at the lake, a stone's throw away. For years he'd fished, swam, even when the water still held its winter chill, and rowed until his arms ached, but nothing explained his presence here now, and nothing made sense. It seemed to be a timeless period. His mind was filled with a strange cold emptiness.

Who or what made me come here? He struggled to remember. *There was an accident but what happened? Have I been in a coma? Is that why I'm this disoriented? And who was that 'friend' I spoke to? I can't seem to remember anything. I remember the cabin and my dad...my foster dad, but that was long ago, or was it?*

He shook his head, uncertain of what he should do next. The cabin was familiar. Of course it was. He and his dad had come here for years, always just the two of them. None of those memories explained why he was here now. He took in his surroundings, taking comfort from their familiarity while simultaneously being saddened by the obvious signs of neglect. The rafters were covered with cobwebs, dust was an inch thick on the window sills; a musty smell embedded in everything. Despite the twinge of guilt he felt in not keeping up with the place, coming more often, he was glad he was here. But why was he here now?

Pulling on the jeans and shirt he'd worn last night, he went out onto the porch and leaned on the rickety railing. "I haven't even thought of this place for years." He frowned in concentration, trying to remember. *Where is Jennifer? Did she come with me?*

He had brought her to the cabin once before. The moment they'd stepped inside the cabin, he remembered, he'd known it had been a mistake. Jennifer was at home in five star hotels and luxurious surroundings. When she'd glanced around at the stark interior he knew, just by the look on her face, it was all wrong. Now he was here again, only this time he was certain he was alone. He didn't know where Jennifer was, but he was convinced she was not with him.

He sat down on the top step and looked across the lake. No one was in residence yet, it was too early in the season. In past years when he and his dad came up in the summer, they had friends all around the lake. Now the docks lay empty, the cabins unoccupied.

He sighed and walked to the water's edge. Bending, he picked up a flat rock and skipped it across the pond, watching the circles widen until they disappeared. He put his fingers in the cold water, then stood and squinted into the early morning light. Everything he saw and did sparked dim reminders of another time.

Climbing the steps, he pulled the screen door open and pushed his way into the cabin. One room served as kitchen, bedroom and sitting room. A small wall hid a bathroom with toilet, sink and wall space which took the place of a closet. Huge pegs held their clothes; his dad's favorite jacket, wrinkled and mildewed, still dangled there. The walls of the cabin were covered with dust-covered trophy fish and pictures of his dad and him holding fish or just hanging onto each other laughing while a neighbor snapped the camera. The one he loved best was the last one he'd taken of his dad—the one of him on the dock, etched against a sunset.

Something made him throw his clothes into the gym bag lying on the bed. "I guess it's time to move on…but where?" He glanced around the room then pulled the door closed.

His head ached as he walked along the lonely, rutted dirt road. He walked but didn't know where he was going.

"Good morning."

The voice came out of nowhere and Jack stopped in his

tracks and looked around. He saw a lone man standing next to the road. "My God, you scared me. Where the heck did you come from?"

"Oh, you'll get used to me," the man chuckled. "I'll be popping up from time to time. I'm your friend."

Jack plopped the bag down and a little puff of dust circled the bag and his feet. "My friend? Who are you? What's going on? I don't know you or why I'm here or..."

"My name is Samuel. I'm sort of an emissary, say a go-between for Heaven and here." Samuel raised his hand to prevent more questions. "I know. It does seem a bit strange."

"Samuel? Heaven? What the..."

"I'll explain. I'm here as your friend until you move on. Perhaps you'd better sit down on that log and I'll explain." He pointed to a huge downed tree along the lonely road.

Jack obediently settled himself on the log, peering at the man who stood just a few feet from him. He was short and dressed in a neat suit. *He looks like the kind of guy you'd find behind a desk in a bank, not some stranger popping out of nowhere,* Jack thought. The man had a bizarre kind of benevolence about him. Jack frowned. Nothing seemed right and yet he wasn't uncomfortable. In fact, he felt calm, as if all his troubles had just drifted off into the quiet forest around him and he and the stranger were the only men left on earth. "What the heck is going on?" he asked.

"Don't be troubled. Do you mind if I sit with you?"

Jack moved a few inches and watched as the man sat next to him.

"You see, there was an accident. Do you remember that?"

"No. Not exactly. I do remember something but it's all hazy."

"That's right. You were going home. You'd just taken Jennifer home. She was..."

"Crying. I remember. Is she okay?" Jack started to rise and the man put a calming hand on his arm.

"Jennifer is fine. She's upset, of course. It's been a shock, losing you."

"Losing me?" Jack said, jumping out of the little man's reach. "What do you mean losing me!"

"The accident. You didn't..." He sighed, a whisper of a sigh, and shrugged. "The accident was very serious, I'm afraid."

Jack sank back to the tree bench. "Serious. You mean like in..."

"Fatal? I'm afraid so."

Jack clutched his hands between his knees, his head bowed and shaking from side to side in disbelief. He stood and walked a few paces away, then turned. "You mean...?

"I'm afraid so," Samuel repeated. He remained seated, staring at Jack with a benign smile on his face. "Come, sit down. We'll talk."

Jack held his ground. "Wait a minute. You can't be right. I'm," he looked down at himself, ran his hands through his hair, patted his chest as if ascertaining there was really something there to pat. "No, there's some mistake. I'm just here at the cabin for a break. Jennifer and I had—well, words. We were arguing."

"I know."

"You know? How do you know? Were you there?" He watched the little man's head bob up and down.

"I know. You see, these things are all part of the big plan. Now we just have to work out your part and you'll be on your way."

"On my way where? I'm on my way all right. I'm heading back to Miami. I have a job waiting in the fall, I'm a history professor. I've just been made head of the department. We...um...I have plans to go to Italy for two weeks in August. Maybe things will work out with Jennifer. Although..."

Samuel shook his head again. "No. No, Jack, those are all things of the past. They are no more. Jack, things with you and Jennifer will not work out, you'll never return to Miami, at least not as you refer to when you speak of returning. You won't even be here much longer. But before you move on, there is something you're being asked to do. It is a great honor to be asked. It will be okay, I promise you."

"Why me?" Jack asked, his arms thrown out in frustration.

"You were asked because all throughout your life you were a helper; you overcame your own adversities as well as help others. Just think, Jack, of the hours you spent as a teacher, helping students. The hours you volunteered to mentor and tutor those who needed it. The time you gave your last dollar to that elderly couple with car trouble out on the highway."

"Who's asked me to do whatever the heck you're talking about?"

Samuel raised his bushy eyebrows making fuzzy arches over his eyes which were rolled upward. "The only one who could make this request," he said quietly.

"You mean...?"

Samuel nodded. "You have been chosen to be a herald."

Jack paced across the soft forest floor, his hands clasped behind him. He turned back to look at the little man on the fallen tree. "I've never been religious, Sam. Some of my foster parents took me to Sunday school. I once went on a retreat sponsored by a Christian Youth Group, but I wasn't a churchgoer. Maybe there's been a... a mistake."

"Oh, no, Jack. No mistake. Once this choice has been made it's made. No going back, no second thoughts. This will be okay, believe me."

"No, no way," Jack said, stalking away. He bent down to pick up his bag, his back to this annoying little person who had suddenly worked his way into his world. But as Jack tried to pick up the bag, it stayed firmly planted on the little patch of dirt road he'd left it on minutes ago. "I don't know what you're up to but I'm out of here. You're crazy. I'm here, look, I can pinch myself. I can see, hear, feel and touch things. I am not dead." He flinched as he uttered the last word, then turned around. "Whatever magic you've done to the bag to make it stay there doesn't matter. I don't need those things, anyhow. I'm walking out of here. Out to a road where I'll find help to get home."

The little man rose from the tree trunk bench, his hands extended. "I know it is difficult to take it all in. But, Jack, dear boy, you are dead to all you knew and to all who knew you. I can prove it. It will be painful, but if you insist." He paused, looking insignificant and yet compelling.

Jack took his hand from the bag and straightened up. "Prove it? How would you prove it?"

"Sit," Samuel said, patting the space next to him.

Although he didn't want to, Jack felt himself being unceremoniously propelled by an unseen force toward the little man and firmly planted next to him. "Who are you?" he asked.

"I'm Samuel and I'm your friend." He nodded his head with authority.

"Well, Sam, prove it," Jack said with all the sarcasm he could muster.

"It's Samuel," he corrected. "Just close your eyes." He slid his arm around Jack's shoulders, the move more directional than comforting. "What you will see is the accident and then I'll take you to Jennifer. We'll remove all the pain; it will be like looking at a movie for a little while."

Jack struggled to prevent his eyes from closing but was unable to do so. An eerie cold blanket covered him. Without movement he was transferred to another place and he watched as he saw his car speeding down the familiar narrow road he took between Jennifer's home in Coral Gables and his condo in North Miami Beach. Rain pummeled the car and roadway and the wet road glistened in the headlights as if it were wet marble instead of tar. He saw his car approach a narrow bridge he'd been over time and time again and then, with a silence and motion that held ballet-like movements, the car careened into space and became airborne. The wooden railing along the bridge splintered, the pieces flying like toothpicks into the darkness. There was a loud noise, quickly replaced with absolute quiet.

Without any sense of transition, Jack saw Jennifer. She was in her living room, sitting on the flowered sofa in front of the big windows looking out on the tiny walled garden behind her house. He wanted to reach out and touch her because she was crying, both hands hugging her face, her cheeks wet with tears. She was rocking back and forth.

Her best friend, Margie, knelt next to her. He couldn't hear Jennifer crying but he heard Margie say, "It will be okay, kiddo." He remembered hating it when Margie called everyone 'kiddo'.

Margie patted Jennifer's arm. "It was over anyhow, wasn't it?"

"I'm not crying because of that. We both knew it was over a

long time ago. It was just such a comfortable love." She pushed herself off the sofa and paced across the floor. "I did love him, for a very long time. But there was always something... something missing, I think for both of us. But I didn't want it to end like this." She buried her face in her hands again.

"Of course you didn't want it to end this way. We all know that," Margie said.

"Something was missing but I was comfortable with him. Now nothing's comfortable and I'm alone. I have no one," Jennifer sobbed. "He's gone, that's what I'm crying about. I won't hear his voice. We won't dance anymore. He was fun to be with, we laughed together. And, now he's gone and I had things I needed to tell him."

Jack felt the icy blanket lift from his shoulders and the scene before him vanished. With no noise, no movement, his view of Jennifer just disappeared. Once again the two men were alone in the thick woods; alone in silence, alone in time. Jack shuddered.

"I don't understand," he whispered.

"You will in time. Your place is here now, or wherever we're sent."

"Sent?" Jack questioned.

Samuel stood. "You'll find you're in a new place soon. There will be work for you to do but you won't know until the time is right. A situation concerning several people has been brought to my attention. You have been assigned to be involved. It will be clear soon and, as I said, I'll always be with you."

"How will I know what I'm supposed to do?"

"You have to be patient. You must have faith, Jack. Faith is what will lead you. And I'll be there. You won't see me often, but I'll be there. You won't always understand, but you must trust. Your purpose will become obvious. Now walk out to the highway and just let things happen."

Jack watched as his friend Samuel melted away and suddenly he was alone in the forest, standing on a rutted road, the fallen tree trunk gone. Had he dreamed this? He turned slowly, taking in all that was around him. He listened to the wind rustle the tops of the tall Slash Pines and the birds as they called from branch to branch. He was alone and yet he wasn't lonely. He picked up his bag, now easily lifted, and followed the rutted road to the highway.

The pavement under his feet was hot so Jack moved to the grassy strip that stretched along the road like a narrow blanket. He didn't mind the humid, scorching air as he trudged ahead, his eyes focused on just what was in front of him. He'd given up wondering what actually was ahead of him, just shook his head in disbelief. "I'm following a guy who disappears and I'm going somewhere I don't know and it all seems okay?" He paused and looked into the huge fields bordering the right side of the road. Hundreds of cattle huddled under small clumps of trees for as far as he could see.

"Need a ride?" Jack turned to see a teenager in a battered pick-up truck next to him. *I must be getting used to this nuttiness,* he thought. *I didn't even hear the truck or jump when the kid called.*

"Sure," he said, wondering if this was all part of Sam's plan. He stepped into the truck, pulling the door closed. The hinges crunched as if they were filled with sand.

"Gotta get those hinges oiled," the driver said. "Saw you walkin' and thought 'Not a day for walkin'. Name's Bobby," the young man said, stretching his hand toward Jack. "You have car trouble?"

"Jack," Jack said, gripping the work-hardened hand. "Car trouble? You could say that."

"Troubles come along in three's, don't they? Anyhow, that's what Granny used to say," Bobby said, "I can take you along for a piece. Goin' far as Gadara. Where ya'll headed?"

"Nowhere in particular. Gadara sounds as good as anywhere." Jack wondered if that sounded as crazy to the kid as it did to him.

Bobby put the truck in gear and ground his way back onto the road. "Nice little place. Kinda small but then it suits most of us that stay. No trouble either, not like the big cities. Dull sometimes, I guess."

"Sounds great."

"Gadara High School was the State champion basketball

team some three years ago," Bobby added with a measure of pride.

"That's nice," Jack said, not really caring about past local sports accomplishments. *Why am I headed to a town called Gadara and what the heck does it mean?* He sighed.

"Not much along this road. It runs from Fairfield to Gadara but this land alongside is cattle land." Bobby continued his informative monologue. "Houses are on the other side where State Road 56 runs. This is the back of the ranges. Other side of the road is just plain ol' Florida. We'll be comin' to citrus groves pretty soon."

"I saw the cattle," Jack said.

Bobby chuckled. "More cattle in Florida than folks. Where ya'll from?" He paused, then added, "Not that I'm bein' nosy. If'n you don't wanna say, that's okay, too."

Jack hesitated. "I'm from Miami."

"Right here is all I know," Bobby said. "Ain't fond of big cities. Went to Tampa once."

Jack leaned his head back and closed his eyes. He felt tired, no, drained. *"This whole thing is unbelievable,"* he muttered to himself.

"You say somethin'?" Bobby said, taking his eyes from the windshield for a second. Jack could only imagine Bobby wondering if his passenger was drunk or just weird. "Are you okay? Is somethin' wrong?"

"No, no, nothing. Just resting my eyes."

Jack must have drifted off because the next thing he knew, Bobby was saying, "We're comin' to Gadara. I can leave you off on the highway on the other side of town or wherever you want. If'n you're lookin' for a garage to get your car fixed, I'd recommend the station on the corner of State Road 56 and Riverview. Bowman's, it's called. Outta town about five miles. Good work and they don't run you up a bill. Ask anyone, they can tell you how to get there."

"Thanks. Don't bother going to the other side of town. Just drop me off anywhere and I'll figure out what I want to do. I really appreciate this help, Bobby."

"No, problem. I'm goin' across to the railroad station so I'll leave you off about a block from the circle. You can find most everything right around the circle. There's the Dilly Dally Café if'n you want to eat something."

Jack wasn't sure he heard the name of the café correctly. *Sounded like 'Dilly Dally', but that can't be right.*

Bobby pulled to the side of the road. "One block ahead is the circle. I'm gonna turn right here so," he stuck his hand out, "good luck, Jack."

Jack shook the strong hand and bent down to pick up his bag from between his feet. "Can I pay you for gas?"

"Heck no. I was comin' this way anyways. Folks 'round here think givin' a lift to a stranger is the right thing to do. No siree-Bob. Good luck, buddy."

Jack slid out of the truck and stepped up onto the sidewalk. He watched Bobby make his turn, his left arm out the open window and his hand above the cab roof as he waved goodbye. Jack waved and watched the old truck until it was out of sight, then turned toward the center of Gadara. He tried to think if his dad had ever mentioned Gadara. He was sure they'd never come this way.

"Funny name for a town," he muttered as he sauntered down the sidewalk, noticing the store fronts as he passed. A gun shop was next to a window full of colorful displays. *Scrapbooking* was blazoned across the door. The next building said *Salvation Army*. It looked deserted but when he passed the side alley he saw cars drawn up to the building.

At the circle he stopped. It was as picturesque as a post card. Giant live oaks and palms filled the center of the circle. He saw a sidewalk stretching across the middle of the park-like area and benches were scattered along the walkway. He stepped off the curb, crossed the street and dodged between the slow-moving traffic. Once inside the circle he discovered another paved path cutting across the one he stood on. He turned left and came out right in front of the Dilly Dally Café. "I'll be darned," he said, his mouth hanging open. "I think it must be time for lunch. Sam said to 'just let things happen'." He crossed the street and pulled the door open.

4

O send out your light and your truth; let them lead me.
Psalm 43:3

Bill Waterson strode up the pathway to the familiar front door. He'd made sure he appeared confident. He'd dressed carefully in a smart short-sleeved shirt, casual slacks and loafers. His blazer was ancient but still looked as if he'd picked it out last week. He'd given up wearing socks when Sonoma laughed at him. "You are so old-fashioned sometimes," his new wife had giggled.

He rang the bell and frowned. *I can't wait for Karen to move to another house. This is ridiculous; ringing the doorbell on a home I own and pay for. A new place for them will be best for everyone. I have to convince Karen....*

The door swung inward. He plastered a broad, congenial smile on his face. "Hi," he said and stepped forward as she backed away.

"Let's sit on the lanai," Karen said, turning away from him and going through the kitchen.

They didn't sit on the loveseat, choosing instead the wicker chairs. Karen wore a summery skirt which she smoothed over her knees, avoiding Bill's eyes.

"Karry, we can make this pleasant or...unpleasant. It's up to you. What I'm trying to do is to avoid any surprises, make sure each of us is cared for. I know you have your heart set on keeping this house but you know that's impractical, don't you?"

"No."

"Sure you do. Just you and Ali? It's too big and it holds too many memories."

"Memories aren't bad things. You've just forgotten them. I haven't."

"You could have the fanciest condo over on the new golf

course for half what this house costs. The taxes alone..." He stopped because he saw her grip tighten on the armrests. "I really want to do what's best, Karry."

"Perhaps you do, but it does seem unfair to me...and Ali. Our friends are all on this side of the town. Not out in that new area. I don't want to move."

"It's five minutes away."

"It's still not the same."

"This is not a time to be stubborn, Karry. If we don't make plans before the bottom falls out we may very well lose the house altogether." He stood and walked to the screened wall, looking at the garden he and Karen had landscaped together, he digging the beds, she planting the flowers.

Bill turned to look at his former wife. *She's lost weight.* "Will you at least listen?" he asked pulling an envelope from the inside pocket of his jacket.

"Wait, Bill," Karen said. "I have something to tell you first, before we get to whatever is on those papers."

"Oh?" He returned to his chair, laying the envelope on the table next to him.

This time Karen stood and paced across the floor. "Ali came home today."

"Early, isn't it? She must have finished quickly."

"No, she's thinking of not continuing at college."

"What! She has one more year. What's she thinking?"

"Things have changed."

Bill waited.

"She's pregnant."

Karen watched disbelief wash over his face.

"No."

"Yes."

He rose quickly and moved toward the double doors. "Where is she?"

"Don't look for her. She's gone to a friend's house. You remember Kristi, don't you? Ali will be back later."

"Wait. You're telling me she's pregnant and quitting school?"

Karen nodded. "She had to come home. She needs me...us."

"Is there a father in the picture?"

"Of course there's a father. You've met Morgan. He just isn't in the picture at the moment. Something terribly upsetting has changed his plans. Of course, that might change," Karen said, putting as much hope as she could into her words. "We don't know." Karen felt strength begin to percolate within her body.

"This is wrong. Why isn't he in the picture? For God's sake, Karry, can't we do something?"

"Ali needs us, Bill. She's doing okay. I was surprised at her calm acceptance after my initial shock. She's seeing a doctor as soon as we can make an appointment. I'll let you know whatever comes up when we do."

"I can't believe it, Karry. Our little girl..."

Karen watched as tears filled his eyes. She wanted to rush to his side, cradle his head against her shoulder but that wasn't to be. Not any more. "Why does nothing seem fair right now?" she cried, smothering her own tears.

Bill stood and moved to her side. "Karry, it'll be okay. We'll take care of our little girl." He took one of her hands in his and leaned forward.

"Don't." Karen jumped up from her chair. "Don't. That's another thing that isn't fair." She turned her back, swallowing with difficulty. The scene behind their house looked as if it were covered in water. She thumbed the tears away and turned back to him.

"Wasn't it the house you wanted to talk about, Bill? We can talk about this other matter later."

Bill shook his head, turned and picked up the envelope. "I've listed the expenses for both houses with a breakdown of potential increases." He smiled, "There never seem to be any potential decreases."

He offered her a piece of paper. She saw it was covered with carefully listed items and columns of figures, so like Bill. Karen didn't take it. "You're always so good at analyzing things. I don't want to read it, it means nothing to me. Just tell me the bad news."

"Oh, Karry, it isn't all bad news. Look. I've even looked at condos, picking out the nicest we can afford if we hit bottom."

"You said that before. What's changing to make you think

you won't be able to support both houses? You've been doing it for a year and a half."

Bill sat down. "Sit, Karry. I'll explain."

He told her the company he'd worked for over the past twenty years was having a hard time in the current economy. "They're laying off people and shutting down branches. Upper executives are being asked to retire early. It isn't a pretty picture and I just might have to move to a branch. They're talking about Omaha."

"Nebraska?" Karen's eyes widened and her mouth gaped at the news.

Bill nodded. "Instead of cutting us back at home they're giving us a *promotion,* moving us to another location, calling us managers of that district and cutting the salary and the benefits. It's already begun." He leaned back, his face a picture of insecurity. It was the first time in Karen's memory that Bill looked defeated.

"I guess if we have no choice we'll have to sell this house," she said, but the strength she felt didn't prevent her voice from cracking when she spoke.

"There's something else and I don't know how to tell you."

"Tell me what?"

He stood, turning slightly as if trying to find a clump of courage in the corner somewhere. "Sonoma is pregnant."

The silence was icy in spite of the warm evening. Karen rose and went to the door leading to the covered patio next to the lanai. She pulled the door open and walked outside.

Her heart pounded and she felt cold in spite of the warm evening. She didn't want to look at him. Her hand ran across the covered grill, then moved to the padded chairs and touched them as if needing to identify her surroundings. She sensed rather than heard Bill follow her outside.

Swinging around she confronted the man she'd called husband, the father of her child, the man she'd shared every inch of her life with. "You stupid, old fool." She steadied herself against the low railing. "Sonoma is pregnant. As if you didn't have enough troubles you do such a stupid, stupid thing. You came here looking for my sympathy. Poor Bill. He's got some financial problems so Karen should help him out. Karen should just chuck her house away so that Sonoma can have...what? A boy? Is that what you wanted? I wasn't enough for you? Alice isn't enough for you? So now you're going to start all over? Well, not with my blessings. I wondered why you left me. Why you fell for that little..." She was going to say slut but that, even in this moment, didn't seem fair.

"Was it the sex?" Karen shrank as she uttered those words. The thoughts may have crossed her mind but she'd never put them into words before. "What was it? Were you just tired of me? Was bed time not a fun time anymore? Did you need more?"

At the same time, they both heard a noise behind them and turned. Ali stood in the doorway, her face blank. She was leaning against the doorframe her arms folded across her belly.

My God, Karen thought, *she's bigger than I thought.* "How long have you been there?" she croaked.

"Long enough."

"We didn't mean for you to hear us arguing, honey," Bill said, inching toward his daughter. "We were talking about making some changes...some arrangements...I'm sorry..."

"It didn't sound to me like you were talking about changes or arrangements. Except maybe that you're about to be a father and a grandfather at the same time."

"Ali, I'm so sorry. Your mother and I never argued like this before. A quick shouting match maybe, months ago. This just happened..."

"Yeah, stuff happens doesn't it?" Ali's face remained unreadable, her position frozen.

Bill reached for her hand but she kept her arms folded. "Honey, there are other things we have to be worried about. I was just explaining to your mother that we might have to make changes."

"Like selling this house," Karen added. "I'm sorry you heard what you did, Ali. Your father is right. It is a first time and I'm so sorry you had to be here when it happened. We thought you wouldn't be home for ages." She felt so limp, she wobbled forward, trying to close the space between them which at the moment, seemed far more than this little distance.

"I came home early. Kristi had a date. She's engaged."

"We didn't hear you." Karen pushed past Bill and opened her arms. Ali unfolded her arms and slid them around her mother. She closed her eyes, ignoring Bill as if he wasn't there.

"It will be okay, honey," Karen whispered. "We'll be okay."

She turned to Bill. "Get out!" she said, pride and control in her voice. "You can go around the house on that brick path. Remember when we spent days lining up the bricks and pounding them into the sand? Sell this house? You bet you can sell this house. You have my blessing and the quicker the better. I'm sick of the memories. Everything in here was ours and now it's not ours. Do what you have to. I'm finished with everything. Now get out." She thrust her hand out, pointing. "Just go."

5

*"Courage does not always roar.
Sometimes it is the quiet voice at the end of the day saying,
'I will try again tomorrow.'"
Mary Anne Radmacher*

Later that night, after Alice was asleep, Karen walked through the house, the split design she and Bill had chosen so long ago was perfect. An east wing with the master suite the west wing with two bedrooms and a bath. As a little girl, Ali had chosen the smaller corner bedroom. Karen recalled it as the nursery it was at first, but Ali never outgrew the little room, changing it as she did through the years from frilly to the classic it was today.

The two wings branched off the living room which was spacious and bright. She sat on the couch facing a broad expanse of windows covered with sheer curtains and tastefully draped with a swag of cloth made up of bright Florida flowers. "It's just a house now," she whispered.

She leaned back against the cushions, eyes closed, hands folded in her lap. She thought about Ali and her spirits lifted just thinking about her. They were always close and now the closeness seemed to have increased. *Is it because we need each other more than ever?*

She shrugged her shoulders. *Well, my persistence about hanging onto the house is over and I truly won't be sorry to leave. Bill's right, for a change, and so are all my friends who said, "Make a new life. Get rid of the old stuff. You deserve it."*

"How come they were so smart and I was so dumb?" She chuckled softly as she walked down the short hall to her bedroom.

She lay in bed, her Bible in her hands, her back pressed against a pillow with Missy curled up on the soft blanket folded at the foot of Karen's bed. It was the same blanket that had been there the very first night Missy spent with Karen.

'You know, Missy?" she said. The little dog lifted her head, her wet black eyes blinking at her. "You know what he said? What colossal nerve he has? Crying to me about how tough he has it now. He's the one who destroyed our marriage. He chose that...that...woman. Now he's worried about how he can take care of two houses and a new baby. 'Business is bad, they're cutting back', he said.

"Well, he can sell this house. It doesn't mean anything to me. The past eighteen months I've proven I can take care of myself and Ali and anything else I need to do, even if I have to get a job." Her eyes rolled at that thought because it hadn't occurred to her before now.

She opened her Bible and turned to the page she'd marked last night. "Psalms," she said softly. "They always help."

6

In quietness and in confidence shall be your strength.
Isaiah 30:15

The next morning Karen and Alice sat in the lanai. Karen had raised all the telescoping vinyl window panels so there was a soft breeze coming through the screens. Two mugs of coffee and a plate of buttered toast rested on the coffee table. "Last night," Karen began. Missy lay at her side, hoping for a bite of the toast.

"Don't, Mom. It was a bad situation but I understand. I know things between you haven't been good. Not since Dad decided to...when he left.

"I know about lots of family problems. I haven't lived in a cocoon for the past twenty years, even if you broke your neck to protect me from these *bad* things that happen in life."

"I never wanted you to hear what we both said last night. Especially me. I'm embarrassed and ashamed."

"You don't have to be. I don't know how I'd have felt. Gee, look at how I feel about Morgan and we aren't married." Her voice broke. "But things will work out. No matter where we are, I know someday we'll be together." She laughed. "Look at me, giving you advice."

Karen laughed softly but her mind raced ahead. *If the house is sold and we move to a condo, will it be a good place to raise a child? For years I've pictured grandchildren playing on the patio, running through the grass at the back of this house. Now they're improbable dreams. What if Morgan doesn't come back? What if he does? Will they be a family then, marriage or not? I'm praying for so many things.* She stretched, easing the tightness all through her body, then ran her fingers through Missy's curls. She hadn't slept much last night.

"Have you thought about where you and the baby will live? I

mean if you don't want to come with me, if Morgan... Oh, honey, my thoughts are so mixed up. There are so many things I'm not sure of. But," she paused, "after last night I know we must sell the house. Whatever Bill's reasons are doesn't matter. Ali, this may sound selfish but the house doesn't matter to me any more. I'm glad. Can you see that?"

"I can, Mom. I understand and I want you to do what's best for you. All your life you've been trying to make everything perfect for me and Dad. Now it's your turn. Whatever you do is okay with me."

Karen closed her eyes and leaned back. She tried to relax against the cushion behind her but it felt hard and unyielding "You are a wonderful daughter, honey."

For several minutes they sat in silence, sipping their coffee, nibbling the toast. The air coming through the open windows felt good, and sounds of birds and insects wafted from the savanna. It was peaceful and Karen wondered what was going through her daughter's mind.

"Honey, after you see the doctor, you're going to have to make some plans."

"Plans?"

"Well, depending on what he says, you might want to consider getting a summer job. It would help take your mind off your problems."

"My problems? You mean Morgan, don't you?"

"Well, that and other things. The baby...what you are going to do."

"What about the baby?"

"This is difficult and I don't know if you've thought about it." She stopped and looked at her daughter. Dressed in summer pj's, her hair pulled into two ponytails, she looked like a little girl. *A little girl with a swollen tummy,* Karen thought. "I don't want you to be upset, but have you given any thought to having the baby and then giving it up for adoption? *Oh, dear God,* Karen shuddered. *I'm thinking about my grandchild as 'it' and I'd be devastated if Ali gave her baby away.* She watched her daughter's face but she already knew the answer and felt an immeasurable relief.

"I have, Mom, but I can't. The baby is part of me...and part of Morgan and I'm praying he'll...come back."

"Thank God. I don't know what possessed me to say that. Please forgive me. I can't believe I said it...or even thought of you giving your child away. It must be the anxiety or...oh, never mind. Tell me more about Morgan. When did you last see him?"

"The morning I left school. He was so angry, Mom. But, he might change his mind. About the baby, I mean. He could, couldn't he? I wish I knew what happened the last time he went home. The night before I left, he screamed at me. It was so not him. He changed so much it was scary. Then the next morning he just showed up to help me pack, it was like a ghost had appeared, he hardly talked even when I begged him to say something, to explain what happened, but he just helped me put the stuff in the car. There's a bunch more in the trunk and back seat I have to get..."

"I'll help..."

"We'll do that later, we have plenty of time. But, now you know why I'm not going back to school, right?

"But Morgan," she began again, and Karen could see Ali was fighting tears, "He kissed my forehead and closed the door. It was like he was seeing his sister off." She bit her lower lip. "When I drove off, he was just standing there in the middle of the road. He looked so lost. And I could hardly see I was crying so hard. About two blocks away I pulled over, I couldn't see to drive. It was so terrible."

Karen stood and knelt at her daughter's side, stroking her arm resting on the chair. "I can't even fathom what you're going through, honey. I'll try to do everything I can to ease your pain. I feel so helpless."

"There's nothing you can do," Alice said brushing her tears away.

"There is something. I can pray and that's what I'm doing, Ali. It might take both of us to have this baby but whatever you need, anything, you just let me know."

She watched Ali struggle to quell her misery. Returning to her chair, Karen waited. It was too soon to speak.

After several moments, Alice rose and walked to the back of

the room, looking through the screens; the scene behind the house was peaceful and the sight calmed her. Turning to her mother, she said, "I know how strong you are, Mom. I've watched you shoulder whatever came along both before and after the divorce. You may look like a cream puff but you're a steamroller when you need to be. Remember last time I was home you bragged to me about how you now reconciled your checkbook every month?"

The steel straps binding their emotions opened and they both doubled up in laughter. "I can, can't I?" Karen choked, standing to hug her daughter. It was just the moment they needed and they savored it together.

That afternoon, Ali drove Karen's car as they set out to do some shopping. She loved driving the sporty, pre-owned red Corvette, a gift Karen had given herself following the divorce; a car and Missy.

"I love this car," Ali said, pulling into the Mall.

"I do, too. I remember the day I got it. I just went from the courthouse to the agency and drove off with the snappiest red car they had. It felt so good at the time. Then I went to the pound and got Missy, just like that," she said, snapping her fingers. "And they were good choices."

"Yep." Ali cruised up and down the parking lot until she finally found a space not too far from the entrance.

"You know," Karen said, getting out from the passenger side, "I always think it's so funny. Everyone wants a parking space right up front but then they'll go home and run for five miles."

"Well, I don't feel like running five miles. Not lately, anyhow."

"How do you feel?"

"Today? I feel fine, but I can't believe how fat I'm getting."

"You're not getting fat, honey. You're pregnant."

Ali leaned into her mother. "Funny lady."

Inside they stood for a moment studying the layout of the stores. "I don't come here very often," Karen said. "I like to shop in the stores downtown if I can. And I like the stuff better there."

"I always liked this mall. More action. More choices. Here, lets go this way. We can look at several stores that might have what we're looking for. But first, let's hit the Mother-to-Be Shop." Alice took her mother's arm. "This is exciting, imagine me buying maternity clothes. Gosh, I can't believe I'm using words like pregnant and maternity."

"Well, you better get used to it. You just made an appointment for Friday morning with Dr. Perez. You'll get a whole new vocabulary there, I'll bet."

7

Be strong and courageous; do not be frightened nor dismayed, for the Lord your God is with you wherever you go.
Joshua 1:9

Jack glanced up at the tall trees on either side of the path. "Those must be the twin oaks," he murmured, taking the three wooden steps to the front door in one stride. A question about accommodations at the Dilly Dally Café had produced glowing reports of the cleanliness and value of Twin Oaks. In fact, not only did the waitress provide the information but several patrons turned around in their seats and assured him he could do no better in Gadara.

The porch ran the width of the house and was trimmed with white gingerbread; the porch posts and the railing were also a startling white. Wicker rockers were placed at even intervals all along the porch and a slight breeze moved several hanging baskets of flowers.

He pulled the screen door open and stepped inside, hearing a faint bell sound somewhere inside the home. Ahead of him was a highly polished desk. Open double doors on either side of the short hallway revealed a sitting room on the right and a pleasant dining area on the left. The furniture looked old, clean and comfortable.

A door at the back of the desk popped open and a tiny, bird-like woman hustled into the hall.

"You must be Mrs. Hamilton," he said, "The folks at the Café told me about this place."

"*Miss* Hamilton," the woman behind the desk corrected. "Folks call me Sarah Jane. This house has been in the family for over a hundred years. Kept it fixed up, of course. Granddaddy and Daddy were sure strict about that. I'm the last one left and I can't even imagine living anywhere but here at Twin Oaks. Once it was part of a big orange grove, all gone now. The groves in this part of Florida moved east or just closed up after those freezes we had a way back. My family was some of the first settlers in Gadara. But, oh, my, how I run on."

She fiddled with a neat notebook resting on the desk in front of her. "Just you?" she said, peering behind him as if he might be towing someone else along behind him.

"Just me."

"How long you mean to stay?" The little woman picked up a pen and opened the book.

"Uh, maybe a week."

Jack saw a puzzled frown flit across Miss Hamilton's brow. Apparently indefinites were not what Sarah Jane Hamilton was accustomed to dealing with.

"Not sure how long you're staying?" she queried, holding the pen in the air above the lined sheets in the book.

"Well, I'm just passing through. Thought the town looked...interesting. Let's say a week."

Miss Hamilton let her pen hover in the air for a few moments, then put a mark in the margin. "I'll put you down for a week and then if you need more time you can just let me know." She scribbled some information on the line next to the mark and asked Jack for his identification and how he was going to pay for the room. "Do you want to see the room first?" she asked.

"I think anything you have will be fine," Jack said. "I prefer to pay by cash, if that's okay." He slid several fifty dollar bills from his wallet. Jack grimaced. *Fifties? When was the last time I had fifties in my wallet?'*

"One week is..."

Jack watched Miss Hamilton do some quick arithmetic in her head, her eyes flashing as she totaled up the sum she thought might be acceptable. "Well, since one night is fifty-five dollars for one and that includes breakfast, I reckon one week would be ... five or seven days in your week?" she asked.

"Let's make it a seven day week." Inwardly Jack was chuckling at the inane situation. *I don't know where I am or what I'm doing and I'm negotiating with an old lady about room accommodations. Is this what you want, Sam?*

"Well then, seeing as you'll be here for seven days that would be... Oh," she said, her eyes getting bigger and bigger. "I couldn't charge you $350. Let's say...$175.00," she said cutting the figure in half. "Is that okay?"

Jack laughed softly at the woman's abject honesty and innocence. "Well, if it's okay with you, it's fine with me. I don't want you cheating yourself." *Oh, Sam, if only some of the inn keepers I've met around the world could hear her.*

He chuckled and Sarah Jane looked up, her forehead washboarded with puzzlement.

Suddenly a voice whispered in his ear, *Please stop thinking of me as Sam, Jack, it's Samuel, and don't be surprised at anything. Remind yourself, you're purpose will eventually be clear. Take it as it comes.*

Miss Hamilton rose to her full four foot ten and a half inches, "Something I said funny?"

"Oh, no. Not at all. No, not funny," Jack stammered as her hand reached across for the money in his hand.

Oh, don't worry, Jack. No one but you can see or hear me.

"It's the off season now," Sarah Jane continued. "I'm kinda glad that anyone is staying. And," she grinned, "company isn't bad. I love the summers although the truth be told you make your money in the winter in Florida. You familiar with Florida?" she said, coming around to the front of the desk and offering her hand to her new guest.

"I've vacationed on the coast for fishing but never traveled this far west. I'm looking forward to it." Somehow he didn't feel it was necessary to mention the cabin on the lake and certainly not to allude to any of the current situations, as if any of them made sense to him anyhow.

"Now today's just about perfect," Miss Hamilton said. "Not too hot, a nice little breeze. Heavenly, I think, don't you?"

"Heavenly," Jack echoed, smiling broadly.

"Some find it hot but I love it. It's the cold I complain about. Not that complaining does any good, you get what the Lord sends, I always say. Come on. I'll show you the rooms. There's four bedrooms and a loft. The loft's just for single guests. Oh, that'd be you, wouldn't it?" she giggled. "I'll show it to you and if it's not big enough," she glanced pointedly at Jack's lack of luggage, "I'll show you bigger rooms."

She continued her conversation as she skittered up the stairs like a kitten climbing a ladder. Jack followed behind.

He chose the loft which consisted of a single bed, night table with a deep drawer and a closet, triangular in shape due to the fact that a chimney ran up through the center of the house. The roof sloped and he had to duck when he looked into the closet. "This is fine, Miss Hamilton."

"You'll have to use the central bath just down the hall. I'll show you."

"Don't bother. I'll find it. Am I the only guest?"

"As of now. Of course, you never know," she said, letting her voice drop indicating there just might be a hoard of guests right around the corner. "Well then, I'll leave you. Have folks in the area?"

"No."

"Oh, silly me, of course you don't since you've never been in the area. That's what you said, didn't you?"

"That's right," Jack said, edging forward so that Sarah Jane Hamilton had to back out of the tiny room.

"Let me know if you need anything, directions or..."

Her voice was muted as the door between them closed.

Jack threw his bag in the corner and stretched out on the bed. The ceiling above him was made of slats of wood about four inches wide. It was painted white and looked restful. He glanced around the room. Two pictures were hung on the wall opposite the bed. One was of a flower-covered arbor the other of ducks along a stream. Jennifer would have hated this place, he thought,

He closed his eyes. "Maybe Sam knows what he's doing. This place is nice, the town seems interesting and I've suddenly got money in my wallet." If he was going to add to his thoughts it was too late because he closed his eyes and was asleep in minutes.

8

Be completely humble and gentle;
be patient, bearing with one another in love.
Ephesians 4:2

The Dilly Dally Café had been on the corner of Grant Street and the circle for as long as anyone could remember. Actually, it was the center of the social world in Gadara but didn't outwardly lay claim to that importance. To most folks, it was just the Dilly Dally Café, where you went when you wanted breakfast or lunch and to meet up with friends.

This morning Sarah Jane Hamilton slid into her regular booth next to Emily Jacobs. Seated across from them were Mildred Bench and Betty McCoy. The foursome was inseparable, meeting regularly at church for services twice a week and fellowship night, and playing cards at Sarah Jane's weekly. Sarah Jane and Betty McCoy were friends since first grade. The group met at Sarah Jane's because she couldn't leave her business to play cards elsewhere.

"What's new?" asked Mildred, wiping her silverware on a napkin.

"You know just wiping that spoon with a napkin isn't going to kill anything you might think is on it," Sarah Jane said.

"You didn't answer me," Mildred pouted.

"Not much new. I heard Alice Waterson came home from college early but I don't know why. Haven't seen her, have you?"

"No, maybe she just finished up early," Betty said. Betty was the one in the group who tried to play down the drama until all the facts were known. It wasn't an easy job.

"What will you gals have today?" the familiar red-headed waitress asked.

"Hi, Sandy. What's the special?" Emily asked.

"Soup of the day and half of any sandwich on the menu, only we don't have tuna. Soup is split pea."

"No, tuna?" Mildred moaned.

"You don't get tuna often anyhow," Sarah Jane said turning to Sandy, "I'll have the special with a ham and cheese on toast."

"That sounds good to me, Sandy," Emily said, handing her the plastic covered menu.

"Me, too," added Betty.

They waited while Mildred poured over the menu as if she'd never seen it before. Since the little group ate lunch at the restaurant at least twice a week, the others folded in their lips and shook their heads.

"I'll have the special with half a chicken salad sandwich," Mildred finally said.

"And four sweet teas, right?" They watched Sandy swish away, her red pony tail keeping time with her hips as she pushed her way through the doors to the kitchen.

"I heard that A.J. Handley missed the last meeting of the Historical Society and they think he might not be well. He never misses a meeting according to Denise," Betty said, ironing her paper napkin with the palm of her hand.

"Oh, that's too bad. He's a nice old gentleman. Real old school," Mildred said, sipping the tea Sandy had whisked to their table. "It's hard to believe he's the last of Gadara's founding family."

"Did anyone go out there to check on him? I worry about him being all alone out in that old house way out in the country. Why, he could fall over and no one would know!" Emily turned to Sarah Jane. "Did you hear anything?"

"No, but I'll ask Agnes when I get back. It's her day to be there." Sarah Jane didn't categorize Agnes as her daily help, they'd been friends for too many years for that ranking.

"Call us," Mildred and Betty chorused.

"I have a guest at Twin Oaks," Sarah Jane said casually.

"You do? Off season?" Betty said.

"Well, don't make it sound like I don't have any business until the snow birds come back. I'm a year-round business, you know."

"I didn't mean it that way. What's he like? Why is he here?"

"How do I know why he's here? He just checked in yesterday afternoon. In fact he said the folks here at the café recommended Twin Oaks to him." Sarah Jane could never hide her pride in her home and business.

"Well, what's he like?" asked Betty as Sandy slid four lunch specials onto the table. Mildred lifted the corner of her toast to make sure she'd gotten the chicken salad.

"He's young, maybe mid-forties." Anyone under sixty was still called 'young' by Sarah Jane. "Nice looking young man, has a neat beard. Said he's staying for a week. Only one small bag."

"You know how men are. Clothes don't matter much. A pair of jeans and a change of underwear and they're off on a two week holiday." Betty laughed, stirring the hot soup.

"I have a good feeling about him." Sarah Jane said with a nod.

Mildred sighed. "You never know."

"What's that supposed to mean?" Sarah Jane scowled.

The three women looked at Mildred. "Well, you know there are all kinds of evil people out there and they often look innocent."

"Evil," scoffed Sarah Jane but her mind was doing a quick inventory on her guest. After all, what did she know about him?

"I'm sure Sarah Jane is a good judge of character. Still..." Betty said.

"Now cut it out. Why would anyone who was evil come to Gadara? There's nothing going on here."

"No. That's exactly why they might. To hide out. And," she added, "he has a beard." Mildred's voice took on an ominous tone.

"Shucks," Sarah Jane began and then she saw her guest. "Why there he is now." She pointed to a man in jeans and a black tee shirt sitting on one of the stools at the counter.

All four women looked.

"He doesn't look dangerous, does he?" Betty whispered.

"Of course not, just the opposite."

"No."

They continued to stare. "Wonder where he went for dinner

yesterday," Mildred said quietly.

Sarah Jane turned back to her lunch and the others followed her. "Well, he doesn't have a car so it was probably Peg's. That's the only other place within walking distance from the house."

"He doesn't have a car?" Betty gasped.

"No, he said his broke down and he hitchhiked to Gadara. I guess he's making arrangements to get it fixed. I didn't ask." Sarah Jane was now quite annoyed at the turn of events at what was supposed to be a pleasant lunch before their afternoon card game.

"Who brought him here, do you know?" Mildred asked, finishing up her lunch and draining her glass of tea.

"No, I don't and I think we've talked about him enough. There are other things going on in the world you know. Like war and disease. Let's just drop the subject of my guest."

She snatched her check from beside her empty plate and stood. The others followed, even though Emily hadn't finished her sandwich. They walked to the end of the counter to pay their bills.

Just then Jack looked up, saw Sarah Jane, smiled and waved. "Hello, Miss Hamilton."

"Hello, Jack," she responded and walked out, shoulders high, a smug smirk on her face. Nevertheless, as they walked to Twin Oaks, she made a solemn vow to find out more about her guest. Had she been foolish? A man, alone in the house with her? She'd never had that concern before. It was mostly couples who stayed with her in the winter and most often return visitors at that. The occasional single man who visited was either a repeat guest year after year, or one vouched for by a regular.

During the afternoon card game she reneged twice and miss-dealt once.

9

We are not human beings going through a temporary spiritual experience; We are spiritual beings going through a temporary human experience.
Author Unknown

Karen and an obviously nervous Ali walked up the concrete pathway to a small modern-looking building in a medical complex just minutes from Gadara General Hospital. The concerns of a restless night had followed Karen into the kitchen that morning. As the two women drove to the medical building for Ali's appointment, Karen's insecure smile and mindless chatter hadn't been detected by Ali who had her own concerns.

"Mom, what if there are problems?" Ali asked.

"Now, what would make you say such a thing?"

"Well, you told me about my birth and all that stuff."

"Nonsense. What are the chances of that happening? About zero, I would think. Having a baby prematurely isn't a genetic problem. Anyhow, you can talk to the doctor if it's a concern."

A sign directed them to the office of Eduardo Perez, M.D., and they stepped into a cool, modern waiting room. Several women, obviously very pregnant, looked up as they entered, then went back to paging through magazines.

The receptionist behind a high counter smiled at them. "Ms. Waterson?" she inquired, pushing a clipboard through the window. "Just complete the forms on both sides. There are four of them, I'm afraid. Also, may I have your driver's license and insurance cards? I'll make copies and return them to you."

Karen nodded and slid the cards across the counter. "My daughter is on my husband's—" she grimaced, "her father's insurance."

For the next twenty minutes, Ali, with the help of her mother, completed endless questions about her health and possible family related health problems.

"Whew," Ali said when she turned the fourth page over and slipped it under the clip. "That's worse than college entry forms." Karen noted a slight flicker of a smile.

When the nurse opened the door and called Ali's name, she turned to her mother, her visage immediately changed to one of fear. Karen patted her hand. "Go on, honey. I'll be right here if you need me."

She watched her daughter cross the carpeted waiting room and disappear into the hallway. When the door closed behind her, Karen felt her heart skip a beat. *She's a grown up, not a child,* she warned herself, adding, *she'll do just fine.* She began paging through a magazine.

Later the door opened and the same nurse beckoned to Karen. "Mrs. Waterson, the doctor would like to see you."

Karen rose quickly, "Is anything wrong?"

"No, he just wants to see you. They're in the examining room, the last door on the right."

Karen hurried down the quiet hall and turned to enter the examining room.

"Ah, Mrs. Waterson," said a young man perched on a stool next to Alice who sat on the side of the examination table wearing a paper gown. His dark hair, tanned skin and flashing eyes were a stark contrast to his white jacket. "Well, Grandma," he smiled broadly. "I thought I'd go over what Alice and I talked about. Please, have a seat." He indicated a chair in the corner of the room.

"Alice hasn't been exactly truthful with us." His words hung in the air, tainted with wariness.

Karen looked at her daughter, then back to the doctor. "I don't understand," she said.

"Apparently Alice *hasn't* been to see a doctor as she said."

"Ali," Karen stuttered.

"I'm sorry, Mom. I got a book—"

"A book! Do you mean you haven't seen anyone about this pregnancy? How could you be so...so..."

"Irresponsible?" Ali filled in the gap. She looked down at her folded hands resting on the gown stretching across her distended stomach.

It was the first time Karen had actually seen, or noticed, the actual size of her daughter's tummy. "Oh, Ali. Why?"

"Morgan and I thought we'd keep this a secret until we had definite plans. Plans to marry, plans of where we were going to be. I followed the book, Mom, honestly." She paused and looked at the doctor. "I ate the right things. I didn't want to come home to Mom before we actually decided what to do," she said to the doctor. She paused and looked at her mother with tear filled eyes. "If Morgan hadn't..."

Karen looked at the doctor's eyes, which seemed to flicker between humor and concern. "What is her condition, Dr. Perez?" she asked.

"Alice is apparently in good health. Her pregnancy is definitely into the second trimester although I think she thought it was earlier. I'm ordering a sonogram immediately. My nurse will let you know when it's scheduled before you leave.

"Everything seems fine and since..." he hesitated, "since the father of the child is not around right now I thought you'd want to be aware of our planned care for your daughter."

"I do, and thank you. You said, 'everything seems fine'?"

He smiled again. "Alice has told me about your pregnancy and I think there is little likelihood of anything of that kind here, but we've made a note of it in her records." He stood and extended his hand. "I'll see Alice after I go over the results of the sonogram. You're welcome to accompany her if that's what she wishes." He patted Alice on the hand. "Sue will be in to help you get dressed."

"Oh, I can help her," Karen said, standing. She shook the doctor's offered hand and they watched him hurry away.

"I really don't understand you, Ali. How could you be so casual about this baby," she said, helping Alice down from the table. "Oh, I guess I understand given the circumstances, but really. What if there were problems? Waiting this long to get medical care is very foolish. You should have called me."

"I know. But I have a great book. It's all about pre-natal care and I've been real good about that. Even Morgan read the book and watched over me. That was before...Oh, Mom, I'm sorry. I know I should have told you before this. But I thought we had everything under control. Now, what am I going to do?"

"You're going to do whatever the doctor says," Karen said as Ali leaned forward and snuggled into her neck. Karen felt her daughter's hard abdomen press against her and realized that in the past few days Ali had always kept a distance between their bodies when they hugged.

Why hadn't I noticed that? she wondered. "It's going to be okay, baby," Karen brushed the tears from her daughter's eyes. "Dr. Perez is highly recommended and now you're under his care, we'll just take care of things as they come up. You'll always have me to help, you know that."

"I know," Alice said, buttoning the last button on her oversized shirt, "but how can Morgan...?"

Karen pulled her daughter into her arms again. She didn't say anything, what could she say? Her hand patted her daughter's back as if to soothe the cares away. *Can anything I do soothe the cares away? If only Morgan...*

Ali backed away, a smile suddenly lighting up the dreary face of a minute ago. 'Dr. Perez listened to my stomach for a long time and told me I'm going to have a healthy baby. Gee, Mom, this is so embarrassing."

"What's embarrassing?"

"Well, all the questions and touching and everything."

Karen smiled. "Just wait, honey. You'll get used to the questions," she said, and thought, *if she thinks this is embarrassing, just wait until the delivery.*

"He said I'm in good shape," she whispered to her mother as they left the office. "He says when they do the sonogram I can know if the baby is a boy or a girl.

"I told him about my entrance into the world and all those problems and he said he was glad I told him but he doubted that would happen. Still, he also said he'd watch for any problems. Like he wouldn't, anyhow," her laughter was a muted nervous giggle.

As they walked down the sidewalk, Ali suddenly tugged on her mother's arm pulling her to a halt. "I don't think I want to find out if the baby is a boy or girl yet."

"Well, that's up to you. The sonogram is scheduled for the day after tomorrow. You could change your mind. It might be nice to know ahead of time if you're giving me a grandson or a granddaughter."

"We'll see," Alice said, pulling the car door open, her brow furrowed again. "This envelope is full of stuff, like what's going to happen and when, but I think it's in the book I already have. I'll show it to you when we get home." Her face was a mixture of excitement, fear and bewilderment.

I think I'm going to have to get used to these sudden mood changes. Ali doesn't seem to know from one minute to the next if she's happy or sad, hopeful or gloomy and this morning was a perfect example. 'No. I don't want breakfast.' 'Will I have trouble with this pregnancy?' And now she's happy to have a folder full of diets and step-by-step instructions on how to have a baby. For a brief moment her mind slipped back to her disturbed night but she mentally closed that door with a slam.

Karen pulled out of the parking lot. "Want to go for lunch?"

"Great. I'm starved," Alice said, opening the folder and looking at pictures of babies prior to delivery. "This is just like in my book. Look at the pictures," she said, holding the book up for Karen to see. "Isn't Dr. Perez a hunk? Those flashing Latin eyes and dark hair. He's one good looking doctor."

Karen rolled her eyes. "Let's go to that new place out on the highway," she suggested. *At the Dilly Dally everyone will notice Ali's pregnancy and I think we just might want to wait and make an announcement to a few friends first.* She sighed. *I'm not ashamed...just...Oh, shoot, what do I care what people think.* "Want to go to the Dilly Dally?" she suggested.

"No, let's try the new place. I've never been there."

Karen smiled. "It's going to be okay, Ali" she said.

"Of course it is," Alice said, pulling a page of dietary suggestions from the folder. "I think I'll have a salad for lunch."

10

Wait on the Lord; be of good courage, and he shall strengthen thine heart; wait, I say, on the Lord.
Psalms 27:14

Morgan had been driving for a long time. He had taken strange paved roads and dusty country lanes that wound between huge citrus groves, and when the groves stopped, the endless acres of cattle country rolled past him. But not much of this really registered. He was running away and he had nowhere to go.

When he came upon the little village of Carter's Corners he slowed. Surely this place had been named correctly. It appeared to be just four corners, a filling station on one, the general store which had a Post Office sign in the window, a boarded up store of some past enterprise and The Corner's Pub on the other. A few dust and pollen covered cars and pick-up trucks were pulled up to a wooden fence that harkened from earlier days. Morgan's stomach grumbled as he inched across the intersection and pulled into the Pub's parking lot.

A few barstools were taken by men in baseball caps. They all turned to look at who had entered and when seeing it wasn't someone they knew, turned back to their beers. They wore black t-shirts with C and L Ranch emblems. Their jeans were well-worn and their feet were encased in leather boots. *Cowboys,* Morgan thought and slid onto the last stool. He glanced around the dim interior. Prints of hunting scenes adorned the walls, but nothing either outside or inside the bar gave credence to any thought this was a copy of an English Pub.

Morgan turned and noted the opposite wall held a line of booths, all empty except one where a woman and man occupied the same bench. They were too involved in each other to notice Morgan.

"What'll you have," the bartender said, plunking down a paper coaster in front of Morgan.

"Any food available?"

The bartender's shirt identified him as Cliff. He looked at the clock. "Kitchen closed a half hour ago. Let me see if Gloria's cleaned up yet. I know she's still back there."

He pushed his way through swinging doors reminiscent of a movie saloon. Morgan heard voices, his a low grumble, hers a high-pitched wail about over-time and a just cleaned kitchen.

Cliff reappeared, a sly smile on his face, "She says she can have a burger and fries in about ten minutes. That okay?"

"Fine."

"Drinking?"

"Beer," Morgan said, twisting the paper coaster.

"Tap, bottle, light or reg'lar?"

"Tap's okay," Morgan said.

One more beer and then Morgan switched to bourbon Manhattans, something he never drank. The clock ticked away the minutes but nothing eliminated the memories of the last time he'd been home. Home...

"I don't know what you're so upset about. We've told you all we know." His mother's mouth, normally small, now seemed old and puckered as she spoke, her words dripping with self-righteous bane. Puckered with evil, Morgan thought.

"You don't understand. You just don't understand," he said, his voice hoarse with emotion. He leaned forward, back away from the chair, hands gripped together and hanging between his knees.

"Son, we never thought you'd take the news like this." His father leaned back in the wing chair facing the empty fireplace. They were seated in the den, or as his mother like to refer to the room, 'our library'.

"Maybe not if I'd been six or seven when you told me, but at twenty three the news you were adopted, that your parents, or those whom you thought were parents, don't even know who your mother was; that doesn't strike you, either of you, as..." He couldn't find the words. He pushed himself upright and strode

away from the couple who'd raised him. That's how he thought of them now.

Turning he glared at them. "You don't know who my mother was. You don't know who my father was, if there was one in that distorted picture you've painted. You claim you don't know where I was born. You admitted the birth certificate you provided me for school was a fake. Everything is a fake. You're fakes. I'm a fake. I don't belong to anyone. My life is a...something worse than fake. No, that's not strong enough."

He ran his fingers through his hair. "You even had the gall to name me after a fictitious grandfather. You don't know who he was or where he is. Is he back in that never-never land you call my family history? Another lie?"

His mother sat upright in a straight-backed chair. She rarely, if ever, slumped into any piece of furniture appearing to be comfortable. Tall and thin, as her husband was, Eleanor Muldorn was proud of her slim figure and steady weight. Her face was almost wrinkle-free but her neck gave her age away. There the wrinkles fell in a soft cascade, disappearing into the top of her dress. "We did your mother a favor. She pleaded with us to take you. We had no children. Knew we never would. All we know is that her mother, your grandmother, worked for friends of ours. She was their maid." Mrs. Muldorn's voice was low and well-modulated, the heritage of expensive private girls' schools. "They, our friends, are both dead. I have no idea where your..." she hesitated and then continued, "your grandmother is. She left their employ shortly after we adopted you."

"Adopted? Are there records? No, you did it under the table. A nice sum of money for the woman who gave me life." He paced across the floor then turned suddenly. "Where did you get the fake birth certificate?"

The silence was so thick you could have stabbed a hole in it. Morgan saw his father's eyes narrow as he looked at his wife. "There is no need to give any more details, Eleanor. There is no way to check on anything. That's the way it was set up. Perhaps we should have told the boy earlier but the past cannot be altered." Winslow Muldorn squared his shoulders. He was Chairman of the Board of the Union Metropolis Bank no matter where he was. He turned to Morgan, who stood frozen in the middle of the floor. "We raised you with the best intentions. You've had the best we could give you. The best upbringing, the best schools, money..."

"All the essentials, right?" Morgan broke in. "Everything but love and affection. Everything but the truth."

"I still don't understand your wrath, Morgan. You've had the best, as your father said. We didn't think it necessary to explain our actions all those years ago. Frankly, I don't know why your father thought fit to do it now. I warned him," she said looking away. "I told him there was no need to do this."

"Why did you?" Morgan asked turning his attention to the man sitting in the leather chair. "Why now?"

His father took in a deep breath and then let it out slowly. He folded his hands over the vest covering his hard, lean stomach. "We were making plans for your future, if you must know. Changing things financially. There's the trust fund we set up right after you came to us."

"Came to you," Morgan whispered. "As if I was dropped from the sky and you said, 'Oh, look, a surprise package'. Why did you take me in? Poor, little, unwanted waif. Why?"

He watched his so-called parents exchange glances, then his father spoke. "We were very fond of the Johnsons. They were with us when we were in college. When their maid told them about her daughter's predicament, well the poor child needed the money to go away and make a new life. Things weren't as they are today, although that's something I wouldn't change." He shifted in his seat and Morgan watched him. "We had the money. We had wanted a child but doctors told us we never would. It just seemed like the best thing to do."

"The best thing to do. Just pick up this little nobody and pretend to be a family."

"That's harsh, Morgan," his father spat.

"No, it's the truth, isn't it?"

"No."

"Oh, yes it is. I remember feeling you didn't love me. I always wondered what I'd done. Was it that I was an inconvenience? When did you decide you'd made a mistake?"

His father bolted from the chair his eyes bristling. "See here, young man. You will not talk to us in that manner. We did our best. Perhaps we were too old to make that decision when we did, but we did our best," he repeated.

"Well, you don't have to worry about that trust fund now. I'm out of here. Tomorrow, I'll go back to school and I'll take what I must but I won't be back, so don't bother trying to contact me."

Morgan couldn't put that day out of his mind. The memory of him hauling his duffle bag with some of his clothes down the steps haunted him. He'd purposely left everything *they* had given him, but he had to have clothes. He slung the large, lumpy bag into the trunk of his car. Thank goodness, he'd purchased the car himself. He recalled the pride he'd felt when he saved his summer job money and surprised his parents when he drove home in his new car. Their comments? "If you'd wanted a car, Morgan, you should have let us know."

Callin' it a night?" the bartender asked.

"Not yet. Just stretching," he said, lifting his shoulders and spreading his arms.

"Need that every once in a while," the bartender added. "Closing time is one a.m. on Monday's." He purposefully looked at the clock on the wall at the end of the bar. The digital numbers indicated it was 12:24.

"You from the college?" he asked, pointing to the logo on Morgan's shirt.

"Yeah. I'm graduating in a week."

"So, this is an early celebration?" The bartender wiped imaginary spots on the shiny bar.

"No." His answer was firmer than he'd intended. "I mean, I'm not celebrating anything. I'm not even going to the graduation."

"Trouble?" When Cliff didn't get any answer he added, "Best to be with family when there's trouble. You sure you'll be able to drive home?"

"I'm okay," Morgan said, his words tinged with the bitterness of bile. "And as for family, that's a laugh. Family—the biggest joke in the world." He looked away, twisting his empty glass on the paper coaster.

Cliff sighed. His young customer was the only one at the long bar. He couldn't remember exactly when the young man came in because there was an early crowd but he remembered he'd started with a couple of beers and then switched to bourbon Manhattan's on the rocks. Seemed as if he'd nursed them for hours.

Morgan swiveled around to survey the room. The tavern was empty except for him and the bartender. The room looked larger than when he entered. It had a spooky aura as if it were suddenly incomplete and alien; the dim lights made small yellow circles, giving the room no depth or warmth.

Morgan turned back to the bar just as the bartender removed his empty glass. "Refill?" he asked, a strange sadness in his voice. He was hoping for a 'no' but sensed that wouldn't happen.

"Yeah, one more...for the road." Morgan meant it to sound humorous but it fell flat. Even his voice didn't seem to be his own. Not since...

He buried his face in his hands. *Where is Ali? Will I ever see her again?*

Morgan opened his eyes—blinked once and then shut them tightly, his mouth and forehead pinching together in pain. He groaned and tried to sit up but his stomach also tried to rise so he flopped back down on the bed. His hands explored the sheets and blanket. Without looking he knew it wasn't his motel room. They didn't have anything this soft. Again, he opened his eyes, this time in painful stages.

An eerie feeling of being lifted from anything familiar spread through the mantle of pain that gripped him. "Where am I?" he muttered. Once again he tried to sit up, this time taking it inch by inch, his elbows pressing down on the unknown bed, lifting him slowly upright. There was a window on his left, a bureau straight ahead of him, and when he gingerly moved his face to the right he saw a closed door. The pale blue walls, cream colored carpet and nice furniture assured Morgan he hadn't wandered into another room at his motel. No, this was someone's home, but whose?

Laboriously shifting his legs to the side of the narrow bed, he rested before trying to stand. The thunder pummeling his temples was something unknown to him. He'd had headaches but this was far beyond that kind of pain. Slowly he recalled last night, or as much as surfaced. The bar, a hamburger and fries, beers and then... He groaned. "Why did I order Manhattans?" He looked around the room. The bed was flanked by a small nightstand on one side and a chair on the other. His clothes were folded neatly on the chair, his shoes lined up beneath, awaiting their next use. Another thought drove through the pounding agony in his head. *Who undressed me?* He struggled, but as he pressed his mind to remember the cloudiness deepened. *The bartender? Who else was there? No one.*

He shuddered and tried to lift himself from the bed, regretting every sip of the liquor he'd ingested last night. *Never again.* Holding onto the windowsill, he crept to the foot of the bed, then grabbed the railing and inched himself to his clothes.

He was just buttoning his shirt when he heard a soft tap on the door. "Come in," he called softly, but the sound of his voice reverberated in his head many decibels above the volume he thought he'd used. He lowered himself to the side of the bed and watched the door open a crack and then be pushed fully open.

"Cliff," the man at the door said, pointing to himself. "You were at the Corner's Pub last night. Remember?"

"Barely," Morgan groaned.

"You tied one on. You okay?"

"I think a machine shop has opened up inside my head," he put his fingers tenderly on each temple.

"Yep, you'll have a headache, that's for sure. I brought you home after I closed up. You weren't very cooperative but we made it. Wife's got coffee on. I've got vanilla ice cream in the freezer. Best cure for a hangover. You ever used it?"

"I've never had a hangover before," Morgan whispered and even then the noise sounded much too loud. "I don't want to put you out or cause your wife any trouble. I better get going." He wobbled to his feet, reaching for the chair to steady himself.

"I don't think so," chuckled Cliff. "Come on through and I'll get you back on your feet. Need a hand?"

"I'll be okay."

The two men walked down a short hall and Morgan noticed flowered wallpaper along the walls. The kitchen was bright and cheerful. Too bright for Morgan, and he closed his eyes to narrow slits. Still the terrible light pierced each eyeball, causing tears to form. He brushed his hand over the offending tears before they could escape.

Cliff pointed to a chair. "You sit there. The sunlight will be behind you."

Morgan gratefully slipped into the chair and, elbows on the table, rested his pounding head in his hands. "I don't think I'd better have coffee," he mumbled.

"No. Best you get that stomach settled. I'll get the ice cream."

Ice cream, Morgan thought. *Great. We're having a party, only I won't be there.*

"Don't worry. I've seen worse than you. At least you can get upright." Cliff pulled a carton from the freezer and began to dip out a ball of vanilla ice cream. Dropping it into a small dish, he slid it in front of Morgan, then added a spoon. "Take little bits at first. Let them melt in your mouth. I'll get you more when you finish that."

"I'm not sure..."

"Eat it. I'm an expert on hangovers. This is a baby hangover compared to what I had. That was a long time ago, then I got clean and sensible. Don't drink anymore. Just give it to folks like you and once in a while—well, they just get too much to handle. Trust me, this is a great cure."

"Your wife?" Morgan mumbled, slowing letting a teaspoon of ice cream melt on his tongue.

"Gone to work. She works days, I work nights. Still we manage to get together enough. Someday she'll be able to quit and I might be able to get a day job. Here, I'll get you some aspirin now. You take it after the first scoop of ice cream is gone, then

I'll get you another. Works, believe me."

Morgan couldn't believe he hadn't thrown up the three dishes of ice cream he'd eaten. Now holding a cup of coffee, his hand trembling slightly, he lay back on a lounge chair on the patio behind Cliff's house. "I don't know how to thank you. And to apologize for the trouble I've caused," he began.

Cliff interrupted, "No need to apologize, these things happen. You needed a friend and I was there."

He made it seem so simple and ordinary Morgan wondered if this happened to him often. "Well I do apologize and I am grateful for the help."

"Take your time. These things have a way of kicking you in the butt just when you think you're over it. No need to rush behind the wheel of your car. Especially since it's still at the Pub."

Morgan cringed. He hadn't even thought of where his car was. "I'm so sorry I put you to this trouble, Cliff, and don't tell me it wasn't trouble. I'm ashamed of myself, but this isn't the first time this month I've done something absolutely awful." He grimaced and looked out across a fenced-in field. Cattle dotted the pasture right to the horizon. "Some of these cattle ranches are big, aren't they?" he murmured.

"That one's a few thousand acres. Belonged to Albert Carsleigh. He's dead, so now it belongs to his estate. Some folks over in England. Albert Carsleigh was from England and he settled here almost a hundred years ago. Ranch is called Carsleigh and London so the brand is C and L. He always wanted to be a rancher. Learned about it from movies so he came over here, worked a ranch for a while, became a citizen and bought up a whole lot of land and started out on his own. Rich, he was, but a nice guy. He was really old when I met him. Ranch goes on just as if he was there. The old foreman promised him he wouldn't change anything and when he couldn't work anymore he had his son, the present foreman, take over. Made him promise not to change anything either. Guess he listened. Good ranch. Has a great crew of cowhands. Some of them were in the Pub last night." Cliff sat back and folded his hands behind his head.

"I saw them," Morgan said. He was still rationing his words.

The terrible pain in his head had subsided but it was still there.

The silence was so pleasant that Morgan closed his eyes. But his serenity was suddenly broken when he sat up straight and said, "Oh, my God. I've been keeping you up when you have to go to work." He sprang to his feet, instantly regretting the sudden move. "I'll get out of your hair and on my way." He swayed, one hand thrust toward Cliff, who ignored it, the other holding on to the chair to steady himself.

"You stay right where you are. I don't go in tonight. Even bartenders get a night off. I slept all night. You just sit back down. Spend the rest of the day here. You want to call anyone to let them know you're okay? I should have thought of that earlier, you prob'ly have family worrying over you right now. Boy, I'm sorry." He stood and faced Morgan. They were the same height and their eyes met.

"I don't have anyone waiting for me," he said, slowly sinking back into the lounge chair.

"No one? No family, girl friend?

"No."

Cliff settled back into his chair and for several minutes the only sounds were those of insects and small animals in the brush at the end of the garden. A small tree housed several birds and they watched them intently as they fluttered in and out of the branches.

"Must have a nest in there," Cliff opined.

Still the silence enveloped them. The sun moved over the house and now the patio was shaded and the breeze made the temperature very comfortable.

"I know you must have some troubles, son. I don't want to pry, but if you want to let some of that out I'm here to listen."

Morgan fought back tears. *Must be the drinks*, he thought and took in a deep breath letting it slowly drift from his nose until he needed another.

"You're right, there are some things bothering me."

Again they watched the activities of the birds, studying them with intense interest. Morgan drained the last of the coffee from his mug. It was cold and the bitter taste seemed intensified or maybe it was just because it was cold when it should have been hot. He leaned forward to rest the mug on a small round table.

"You'll stay for dinner," Cliff said. It was more than an invitation, rather an already agreed upon decision.

"Oh, I couldn't. That would really be taking advantage of your kindness."

"I didn't really ask. I think you might be better off right here."

"Why do you think that?"

"Because you are still not over your indulgence of last night and because I have taken a liking to you. Stay. Millie will be delighted to have a guest for dinner."

"I'll bet," Morgan chuckled and the sound of his laughter, slight as it was, felt good.

"I mean it. We don't have much family down here. Most of them are up in the Carolinas. Get together a couple of times a year. Somewhere around the fourth of July we meet halfway and have a reunion. Then, for Christmas, as many as can go up to my brother Frank's place. It's the biggest house of the gang and way up in the mountains. Some of us hope for snow." He grinned. "Millie had one son. We lost Charlie in Viet Nam. She'll like you," he paused. "Stay another night. It won't hurt anything if there's no one looking for you."

Morgan was very quiet and he didn't look at Cliff. This outpouring of welcome and concern was something very foreign to him. He felt himself quiver as if a cold wind had suddenly brushed across the patio. Turning to Cliff, he said, "I would be honored to be with you for dinner but I'll have to leave after that."

"We'll see."

Cliff climbed out of the lounge chair and stretched. "Think I'll go in for a nap. Now you just do what you want. Want to eat? There's stuff in the refrigerator. Want to take a nap? Your bed is ready. While you were showering, I made your bed. I was hoping you'd stay over. Maybe we could play cards after dinner. Or whatever you want to do. Millie would be pleased to have you stay with us."

With that, he slid the double doors open and disappeared into the house. Morgan sat still. Never had he had anyone, especially a stranger, treat him with such friendship. He'd had plenty of friends through his school years. Their families had often included him for celebrations and picnics but this was different. This was 'take the run of the house, sleep with us, eat with us, we want you'. And for the first time in his life Morgan felt wanted. He'd stay for dinner. Overnight? Well, maybe.

He leaned his head back and closed his eyes.

11

Oh, Lord, righteousness belongeth unto thee,
but unto us confusion...
Daniel 9:7

Sarah Jane bumped her hip against the door leading to the fellowship hall of the Gadara Salvation Baptist Church on Longmeadow Road. The door was heavy and she pushed against the sturdy panels, her hands trying to control a plate of slippery deviled eggs, her usual weekly contribution to the potluck supper before Wednesday night services.

"Land's sakes, you look like you could use some help." Emily Jacobs reached for the plate of eggs sliding around under a film of plastic covering.

"Careful," Sarah said, relinquishing the plate and patting her hair into place. "Windy out there."

"Calling for some rain tonight, but those weathermen don't always get it right, do they? What do we know?"

"Probably more than those smarty-pants weathermen on the television with all their radar and that fancy stuff—huh, my knees are better forecasters. When my knees ache, it's going to rain and my knees are paining me something awful."

The hall was filled with people finding seats at the long tables that lined the center of the hall and there was a friendly buzz as folks called greetings to one another. Against one wall the buffet was set up and women were uncovering plates and stirring casseroles.

"Here, Sarah Jane," called Amelia, the pastor's wife. "We saved a place for your eggs. Everyone is looking forward to them."

Emily tagged along behind Sarah Jane and together they found places at a table where several ladies had settled. It was the same table they sat at every Wednesday night. "Room for two more?" Emily asked, sliding into a chair and patting the other one for Sarah Jane. "We were thinking it might rain later."

"That television guy said no rain this week," Mildred said, straightening her napkin-wrapped silverware. She was always nervous no matter how placid the setting was.

"What does he know? My knees are hurting something awful," Sarah Jane repeated, her face pulled into a plea for sympathy.

Mildred Bench leaned toward Sarah Jane and said in her usual stage whisper, "Well, what's with the young man you've got as a guest?" She emphasized the words *young man*.

"He's there. Doing fine," she said.

"Well, what's he here for? Got kin?"

"Now do you think if he had kin he'd be staying at my place? He's here..." Sarah Jane hesitated. It wasn't like her not to know all about anyone who was staying at Twin Oaks and she knew the women were waiting for the latest report. "Well, he says he's just visiting."

The women stared at Sarah Jane, waiting for more. When Sarah Jane began unwrapping her silverware and spreading her napkin, Mildred, who was directly across the table, sighed. "Well, is that all?"

"How do I know?" Sarah Jane asked. "Do I ask my guests questions? I'm the inn keeper, that's all. He comes and he goes. I hardly ever see him except for breakfast." Sarah Jane paused for a breath and to tease her listeners.

"You know," Mildred said, her face twisted with concern. "if you don't know what he's doing here, maybe there's something in the wind. Changes to Gadara or something,"

"Changes? What kind of changes?" Emily said, spreading her napkin on her lap. "Wish we got two napkins. Sometimes one of these thin ones isn't enough."

"Depends on what we get to eat. Sticky stuff, you're right. Otherwise, just be careful." Sarah Jane said, staring across the room as if looking for someone.

"Changes? If there are changes about, we should know about them don't you think?" Emily's voice was tinged with insecurity.

"Oh, Emily. If there were important changes the Daily Sun would be blasting the story on the front page. Lord knows, nothing new happens around here." Mildred looked at Sarah Jane. "If he was here about changes, you'd know, wouldn't you?"

"Why would I know? Do you think I have nothing better to do than to snoop around on my guests?"

"You know most of the stuff that goes on around the circle before anyone else."

"Mildred, you mind your own business. I don't know anything that everyone else doesn't know."

"Maybe A. J. Handley knows," she said, her eyes twinkled and her mouth pouted knowingly. Even though the rumor A. J. was sweet on Sarah Jane had fizzled out more than twenty years ago, every once in a while it drifted to the surface.

"That's enough."

"Well, anyhow, you know all changes aren't bad. Some changes are good, like the new mall out on the highway." Mildred was intent on having the last word.

"That new mall is an eyesore. Nowhere near as nice as the shops around the circle. You want something good, something classy, you shop at Myra's Gowns or Foster's Men's Wear, not those chains that have things you see coming and going. " Sarah Jane huffed. "Changes," she scoffed. "I like things just the way they are."

"Changes could mean a new highway, or school, or some factory on the outskirts of town," Mildred added.

"Factory?" the women chorused.

"If you're so all-fired interested, why don't you ask him?"

"You ladies ready to go to the buffet tables?" Pastor Finlayson inquired, leaning close to Sarah Jane's ear. "This table always goes first, you know."

As they circled the buffet table and chose their dinners, Sarah Jane silently hoped the subject of her new guest wouldn't come up again that night. "Don't be dim," she muttered to Edith. "We don't need to know what that man is up to. Besides, what kind of factory would be setting up in a sleepy little town like Gadara? I don't want to hear any rumors going around the Dilly Dally tomorrow."

But her mood was somber as she ate the tuna casserole, chicken wings and green beans with bits of ham. She'd saved room for dessert because the cakes and pies were home-made and nothing beat a good home-made pie. Still, when dessert was served she just pushed the berries and pieces of crust around the plate and left more than she ate.

She was pleased the discussion about her new young guest was not spoken of for the rest of the evening. She knew, however, the topic had been tucked away in the ladies' minds, sure to set the gossipy tongues in action the following morning.

Usually after the mid-week service and the singing, Sarah Jane's mood was one of benevolence. Especially if the choir sang *It Is Well With My Soul* as they did tonight. It was her all-time favorite hymn. But, walking home in the dark along the familiar sidewalk, her mood was solemn as if a cloud had perched on her shoulders and refused to budge. The night air felt damp and her knees hurt. "Drat that man," she muttered. "Why can't he be normal and just go about his business, whatever that might be, and move on?"

Sarah Jane stood on the sidewalk in front of the big old house that had been her home for more than seventy years. The front veranda light illuminated the sidewalk and the window reflected only the lamp on her desk that was still lit. She always left it on, even if she went out before dark. "He must be sleeping. That's if he's there," Sarah Jane muttered as she pushed the door open and stared into the dim interior. Her guests knew, as did everyone in Gadara, the front door to Twin Oaks was never locked. Her guests came and went as they wished and she didn't have to worry about being there to let them in. That's the way it was in Gadara. Not many folks locked their doors or took the keys from their cars.

Her eyes went to the stairs to the right. Sarah Jane's bedroom and bath were on the first floor tucked behind the parlor where the huge old pantry and the cook's quarters were when she was a child. She looked intently at the stairs. Should she? She began to climb the stairs, being careful to miss the one that squeaked. In the dim hallway, lit by a small nightlight on a narrow table, she paused and listened. "What do you think you'll hear?" she whispered to herself. She moved cautiously down the hall to the loft and pressed her ear against the ancient panels. Nothing. Dare she try the door? Her hand reached out tentatively and she was glad she'd seen the doors and the knobs in any room in her inn didn't squeak. WD-40 was wonderful stuff.

No, she thought. *I've never physically snooped before and I'm not about to start now. All that talk about him being a criminal or some rich run-away. Nonsense. Rich? Why he came in a pair of jeans and a tee shirt. He did pay with cash and he looked like he had plenty of money in that billfold of his. Speaks well. Okay, so he looks unhappy.* She turned away and crept down the stairs.

In a state of confusion, Sarah Jane undressed and pulled her soft cotton nightgown over her head. She turned back the covers and the sheet and fluffed the pillow on her beautifully carved bed but she didn't slide in between the sheets. Instead she settled into a comfortable chair. "I'll just listen for awhile."

But it wasn't long before she fell asleep. In the morning she was stiff from sitting up all night. A soft rain beat against her windows, her knees hurt and she knew just as much about her young guest as she had the night before.

***

At eight-thirty Jack drifted down the stairs and settled behind one of the small tables in the dining room. Sarah Jane brought him coffee. "Sleep well?" she asked.

"Just fine, thanks. I see it's raining. I was going to check out the high school. Maybe I'll go to the library for a while."

"I can give you a nice big umbrella," Sarah Jane offered. "You're still walking?"

"Yes. It's a new experience for me and I find I like walking. You're fortunate here in Gadara. Everything is within walking distance."

"Not everything," Sarah Jane grumbled.

In the kitchen she stirred the grits and pushed bread down in the toaster. Now her curiosity was fully aroused and she was going to have to get to the bottom of this mystery. The high school? It was so difficult to put a label on this mystery guest. He was so polite and considerate. He just couldn't be anything dangerous or evil. Mildred could be a doom and gloom character at times. Sarah Jane wished she'd never opened up a discussion about her nice guest.

She smiled as she placed the plate of food in front of Jack. "You sure are visiting all around. Heard you were at the Historical Society's museum. Not very big but it will be someday. They have tons of stuff stored away in a barn out on the Handley homestead," she said, her mouth drawn up in an artificial smile.

"I'm enjoying seeing what a little town like this has to offer," Jack said, returning the broad smile.

In the kitchen Sarah Jane slammed the kettle on the stovetop. Her back was stiff, her knees hurt and her pride was suffering an unexpected blow. Now, finding out her guest's purpose in Gadara was more important than ever. She jerked a tea towel from the rack as she heard the back door open. She knew it was Agnes. She growled an unenthusiastic, "Good morning."

"And a good morning to you," Agnes said, taking in the scowl distorting Sarah Jane's face.

12

...for truth has fallen in the streets
and equity cannot enter.
Isaiah 59.14

Sunlight bounced off the countertops in Cliff's bright kitchen. Morgan still sat with his back to the window but the light didn't bother him this morning as it had yesterday. Is it really only a day later? It seemed to Morgan he'd been here a week. What did bother him was he couldn't think of any way to thank the Crawfords for their hospitality. Last night at dinner with Millie and Cliff he felt as if he'd suddenly slipped into a segment of "Leave it to Beaver." He'd often watched the reruns of that program, marveling at the unbelievable family quality. Surely there were no real people like that. But the simple meal had become an adventure into another world. They laughed and told stories. They joked about everyday things that suddenly took on great value. And when he said he was going to bed, Millie kissed his cheek.

Morgan stood and looked through the glass double doors. Cliff was kicking the loose grass from his shoes before he crossed the patio and slipped out of his shoes.

"She's off," he said, pulling the doors closed behind him. "She sure enjoyed your company last night and this morning. Millie likes company. I told you," he said, sitting in the chair across the table from his guest. "Can you reach that coffee pot? I could use a refill if there is one."

Morgan poured coffee into Cliff's mug and then refilled his with the remaining coffee. "Got enough? We could make another pot," Cliff said, stirring three packs of artificial sweetener into the dark brew.

"This is fine. Look, Cliff, I've got to go. I just don't know how to repay you...and Millie... for...for everything," he said, spreading his arms to emphasize the vast amount of thanking he thought was due.

"Shoot. As I said before, you needed a friend and I was there. You'd have done the same."

Morgan thought about that. Would he have welcomed a stranger as Cliff had? Perhaps, if he'd had a home to welcome him to. His face fell, the smile that had grown to be a constant companion disappeared. His brow crinkled.

"Think about it, buddy. I could see you weren't a real drinker, nursing those drinks like you did. It was pretty obvious you were trying to drown something out." Cliff raised a hand, stemming any comment from the young man across from him. "I've seen it all before and I know you can't drown anything but yourself. Only makes it worse, really. I know I can't make you stay, but please take your time. Where are you going when you leave here? Who are you going to be with?"

Morgan stared into his mug of coffee. Where was he going? Who was he going to see? The loneliness of those thoughts made him suck in a deep breath and slowly release it. Nowhere and no one, that's where and who. He looked up at Cliff who was studying him.

"I don't know where I'm going…and there's no one…"

"Can't be no one, son. Maybe you should talk it out. I'm a good listener and I know when to keep my mouth shut."

The silence, only broken by the soft hum of the air conditioner, was deep. Morgan pushed his coffee mug away and, resting his arms on the table, folded his hands.

"I don't know where to begin."

"Begin with what happened to make you change because I can see this isn't the real you."

Morgan smothered a chuckle. The real me, he thought. I used to know who I was. He bit his lower lip and looked into Cliff's eyes. "It began last weekend. I came home from school. Brought some of my stuff home because I planned to clean out my dorm room. Graduation's in another week. Everything seemed so normal and then…"

Cliff waited. He sensed the inner struggle in the young man, his distress was so palpable.

"They...my parents..." Morgan rose and paced across the sparkling tile floor. His hands were fisted, his back rigid. He was surprised that once he started the words flowed without stop. A long sentence with no commas, no hesitations and finally a period. "I never knew I was adopted. Twenty three years and I didn't know. And now there's no way to find my birth mother. No way to fill in any gaps and there's nothing but gaps, is there? No knowledge of where I came from. No history, just a big long line of nothing behind me."

Cliff stood and came to stand next to Morgan. He slipped his arm across the trembling young man's shoulders. "Listen, son. What you experienced was a shock and I know it's going to take time to think things through. These things don't happen overnight and they aren't solved overnight. Let's sit outside. Somehow talking outside makes it easier. Like no one can overhear you because there isn't anyone around. Nothing but me and hundreds of cattle." He chuckled softly.

On the patio, Morgan leaned back. Somehow lounge chairs forced him to relax. The early morning breeze slipped across the yard making flowers bend slightly, turning their faces to the sun. "You're right, Cliff. Outside makes it easier to talk. But, I think I've told you just about everything. I don't know where to go. I've told you I have a job in Miami."

"Well, you're going to take that, aren't you? It'd be foolish to miss out on that."

"You're right. I've worked there for three summers and they gave me a wonderful offer but now I'm not sure about anything after this minute. I was going to work at the brokerage house and go to grad school. But now I won't be able to afford it and I'm sure not going to ask *them* for money."

"You got money to hold you over?"

Morgan nodded. He straightened his back. "Yeah, I have a bank account. It's mostly money *they* gave me over the years. Some of it is from my internship, of course, some of it comes from summer jobs I had back when I was in high school. I always had a job in the summer, lifeguard, washed cars at a dealer's. Once I worked for an old lady who advertised for help in the garden and around the house. Turned out she was just lonely and I was being paid to keep her company. Good money though, but I felt as if I was doing something wrong. She convinced me she really needed my help. She was a nice old lady. Kind of like the grandmother I never had, only I didn't realize it at the time." Morgan folded his lips together, shutting out any more comments. "Still some of the money is from *them*." He just couldn't push the words *my parents* out.

"Don't go cutting off your nose to spite your face, buddy. If you have enough to hold you over, use it. Use it wisely. You can go to Miami, find some place to live. Look for someone who wants to share an apartment. Work the summer and then see what happens. After all, you only have to take care of yourself and I just know by knowing you these past two days you can do that in a heartbeat." Cliff leaned forward and swung his legs over the side of the lounge. "See? I told you talking it out would help."

Morgan sighed loudly. "It's not just me."

Cliff frowned. "I thought you said..."

"That there was no one." Morgan nodded. "But I lied. And, I did such a dumb thing last week."

"You better finish off this story, son."

"There's Ali." When he said her name his heart scrunched up into a tiny ball in his chest and he gasped for air. His lungs were also squeezing the air out of him.

"Ali? Who's Ali?" Cliff asked softly.

"Alice," he said, a reverence coloring the single word. "She's my girlfriend. I guess you could even say fiancée, but we never used that word."

"She hurt you, too?"

"No." The word was brittle and sharp. "No, Ali never hurt anyone in her life. She's...she's special, and..."

"And?"

"And she's pregnant." Now Morgan bit his lip so hard it brought tears to his eyes. Or was it the thought of Ali and her baby? His baby.

"I think you'd better fill in the blanks, buddy. I'm assuming it's your child."

"Yes, it's my child but I told her I didn't want the baby, that

I didn't want to be a father. After all the trauma of that meeting with...with the people who raised me, I was so upset I felt I had to just wipe the slate clean. I didn't have any past so was I entitled to a future? I didn't want to be with anyone who had been there before. So, I just told Ali I couldn't be who she thought I was." He stood and paced across the concrete. "It was awful. She cried. As she drove away and I waved, she was crying." Morgan, his back to Cliff, cried softly.

"That changes things, doesn't it?"

Morgan turned, wiping his eyes on the backs of his hands. "What am I going to do?"

"Well the first thing I'd do if I was you would be to call Ali. I don't think you're the kind of guy who is going to turn his back on this part of your life. It has nothing to do with the other part. Am I right?"

"Yes," Morgan said softly, sinking back onto the lounge, his feet resting on the patio floor. "But after what I did how am I...?"

"You should call her."

"I'm not sure I'm ready for that."

"When are you going to be ready? When the child is grown up?"

The words stabbed into what was left of Morgan's heart. Just like *they* did? *My child would be the child, boy or girl, who would never know the father who wasn't there?*

Cliff turned his back on Morgan, studiously studying the fields behind his home. He glanced at the neat flower beds Millie kept, remembering her talking to the plants as if they were her children.

He swirled around. "Listen, young man. You might think you had it bad but you had a good home, money, college. Do you know how many kids are adopted into terrible situations? Poor homes, poverty, abuse? You had it made. I'm trying to be helpful but I think you've got it all wrong. You might not ever know who your mother was, who your kinfolk were. But there's always the chance that someday you'll find them. You might just want to consider if you're not over-reacting.

"Now that I've heard the whole story, there really is only one answer. Call your girl. Tell her you were wrong. Make plans that include her and your child because if you don't, you'll regret it for the rest of your life.

"And as far as those parents you had, just remember that no matter what, they took you in as an infant. Imagine the times they stayed up when you were sick. Think of the advantages you've had all because of them. Maybe not now, but some day in the future, son, you'll give all that a second look. There's more to being a parent than you think."

Morgan stood facing Cliff. For several moments, Cliff's icy eyes bored into his tear-filled ones. "That's something I'll have to think about—but right now I'm more worried about Ali than I am about them or their feelings—if they have any.

"How can I call Ali? What do I tell her? Do I tell her about last weekend? And this weekend? If I go to Miami, I can't take her. We couldn't afford it. Everything is changed. Everything is all mixed up. I'm mixed up."

"There are answers to your questions, son. The only thing you can do is take it step by step. Call her. Let her know what's going on."

Cliff stepped toward Morgan. He opened his arms, urging Morgan into his embrace. The two men stood quietly in the sunshine. One strong, the other praying for the strength he needed to face the future. A future of uncertainty. A future that didn't include the past. A future that must include Ali and their child.

13

Turn thee unto me, and have mercy upon me;
for I am desolate and afflicted.
Psalms 25:16

Morgan ended his call and pushed his phone into the carrier attached to his belt. He sighed with relief. He'd just left a message at Littman and Littman, telling the girl who answered the phone as 'Mr. Littman Jr.'s secretary' he would be in Miami on Monday. "I'll give him the message," she said, her voice a study in disinterest.

"That gives me almost five days to find a place to stay," he mused aloud. Yesterday, after he'd left Cliff's house feeling grateful, confused and chagrined, and he didn't know in which order he felt those things, he'd driven to Lake Wales, Florida. In looking at the map it seemed to be the half-way mark between Carter's Corners and Miami. On Cliff's advice, he'd decided the only smart thing to do was to keep the brokerage job intact. He'd chosen a tiny motel complex on Highway 27, avoiding the big, modern ones. "Too much action, noise and too many people," he'd rationalized to himself.

Now, nine o'clock the next morning, he spread the map out on the bed before checking out. He knew where he was going and was confused at this sudden urgency to look at the map again. His eyes wandered to the west coast. He found Gadara quickly. "That's where Ali is," he muttered and sat down on the unmade bed. *Would it be any use to go there? Would she even see me?* Two more unspoken and unanswered questions, he thought, quickly refolding the map. "Probably not after what I said last time I saw her," he muttered to himself, forcing the picture of Ali's tears to the back of his mind. He looked around the room, checking to see if he'd left anything, then closed the door. Tossing his bag on the back seat, he walked to the office to check out.

"I'm on my way," he said to the ultra-skinny young man with the acne-pocked face standing behind the desk. Morgan handed him the room key.

"Have a nice trip," the kid answered automatically.

But a short ride later Morgan suddenly pulled into a gas station, parking along the side of the building. He sat quietly for a moment and then pulled his cell phone from its pouch. He checked his saved numbers and then pushed the one for Ali's home in Gadara. Listening to the phone ring he was overcome with doubt and fear. *What if she answered? What if it was her mother? What if...*but he needn't have worried because he heard the answering machine ask for a message. He ended the call, put the car in gear and backed out of the parking space, hesitating before pulling out onto the highway again.

"Maybe it's better if I don't contact her until I know what I'm doing. But, will that be too late? Too late for what!" He rested his head on his arms on the steering wheel. "Maybe I should have left a message but what good would that have done? Damn, I'm so sick of unanswered questions!" He thumped his fist on the console next to him.

14

For we are strangers before thee, and sojourners, as were all our fathers...
1 Chronicles 29:15

For several days, Jack wandered the streets of Gadara, poking into the small museum and the library and loping over to the new high school complex to watch impromptu basketball and softball games. After all, he might just need to keep in shape although he wondered at that. It seemed as if he ate and slept only when there was nothing else for him to do. And that confused him the most, having things to do which often made no sense. Like finding the little park along the river and sitting for what seemed hours just watching people coming and going. A couple of lovers showed up at four-thirty each day. The usual collection of young mothers and small children using the playground and two men who spent hours fishing, but Jack hadn't seen anything caught. He noticed by the changes in their voices they argued most of the time.

Then there was a pretty woman who came and sat on a bench under a live oak and seemed to read, meditate or pray for a while and then leave.

"If I have a cause here, Sam, I sure wish you'd get to it," he'd lamented one afternoon.

Samuel, Jack. Will you never learn? And as for your assignment, well, there's trouble brewing in Gadara and it concerns that nice lady you noticed, but it's mostly her pregnant daughter who needs a helping hand. And then there is a kind old man who needs some companionship and encouragement. I think it's time you met the old gentleman.

***

A. J. Handley settled himself into the faded and slightly mildewed cushions of an old rocker on the front veranda. *Today folks might be calling it a front porch,* he thought, *but to me it'll always be the veranda.* He stretched his legs out and, with his toes, tapped the lowest railing along the front of the one-hundred year plus frame house he'd called home for over seventy years. The rocker slid into a soothing rhythm.

"A promise is a promise," he muttered, taking his glasses off and tucking them into his shirt pocket. He folded his freckled hands across the protruding stomach he'd become accustomed to. Still thin and lanky, his stomach had begun to swell with age. At least that's what A.J. thought since he'd not put many pounds on his old bones. With his eyes closed he drifted back in time, back to when he was a boy and his grandmother still lived with the family—back to the times they spent together right on this very veranda.

"You've a right to be proud, Andrew, proud to be a Handley," his grandma said sitting next to him as she shelled peas into a china bowl on her lap. "We was a big family once. Sickness and..." She grimaced and didn't say anything more and A.J., as he preferred to be addressed, looked into her wrinkled face.

She watched the curiosity form behind his blue eyes, eyes the color of a wind-swept sky. "Never you mind. Sickness and other troubles have whittled us down to a few but we're still Handleys. You're the youngest, but I declare you're the smartest. Your dear brother Jackson, dead in that awful war; well, we never found out what he'd amount to, did we? Promising boy, I always thought.

"That so-called cousin Alvin and his wife and their hellions, not true Handleys at all. Your Ma just having the two of you and your Aunt Felicity not having any children." She paused and stared across the white railing around the veranda. "Felicity," she murmured. "Never was strong and then after...well after she came home, she'd be not knowing whether she was coming or going. No, that's wrong, Felicity was a strong woman, even went

away to college, something not many young women did back then. Normal school they called it. But something happened...something happened. She came home and never went back to teaching. Looked poorly all her life after that.

"No, sir, you're the only hope we have after your daddy and brother passed. There was all those cousins but we never knew what happened to them. All traipsing off to the west after gold and other such nonsense. No, never kept track of them. Maybe there's someone out there, but not that I know of." Her voice held a certainty that couldn't be argued with. If grandma said it, it was so.

"You keep that in mind, Andrew. Marry a good girl from good stock. Have children, sons and daughters, so the family name will go on. Stay busy. Keep close to the Lord and preserve the history of our family and Gadara," she'd said. Her lips closed tightly after her words and her fingers flew even faster popping the shells and dropping the peas one after the other into the bowl. "You gotta make me that promise, Andrew." Her hands became idle and she reached out and touched him. "That mark...the Handley mark," she said pointing to the birthmark on his wrist. "You're a real Handley, you are, just like your father and grandfather. Why, we thought it had skipped a generation when your brother Jackson didn't have it. Lord a'mercy, your Mama searched that little body after he was born but no mark. Then you came along and we knew everything was going to be all right."

A.J. looked at the mark, a blurry star set in a spot that looked like a coffee stain. No bigger than a nickel, he somehow knew that to his grandma it was important. It had annoyed him when he first went to school and the children pointed it out, calling it a 'dirty spot'. Now it was just there. He smiled at his grandmother. Funny how some things were important to her that just didn't make sense, but then that was Grandma.

"You gotta take care of the homestead and the history that belongs to the Handley family." She stared at her grandson. "You promise?"

"I promise, Grandma."

A.J. shifted in the rocker. He spent several moments, remembering Jackson, nine years older than he and off to a war that sounded exciting. The uniform, the letters from overseas; he'd envied his brother and wished he was old enough to go to war, too. He didn't think of war as terrible until they got the telegram and his mother, Aunt Felicity and grandmother wept and wailed and he realized Jackson wouldn't be coming home, he wouldn't have a brother and the family had suffered a great loss.

Now, more than sixty years later, he sat on the veranda, the only living Handley left as far as he knew. Aunt Felicity? Why had he been thinking more and more lately about that elusive relative? His only memories were hazy. He remembered when she came to live with them, his mother and grandmother treated her as if she was not well. She always looked okay to him—a little distant and fuzzy about things but he, as a child, thought all older people were like that.

He opened his eyes and looked at the sky, a brilliant blue without a cloud in view. The breeze was slight but enough to rustle the shaggy brown palm fronds that hung down the sides of the tall trunk. "Have to get them bearded," he said to himself.

He'd tried to do what his grandmother wanted. He'd married Elizabeth Springer, daughter of a Baptist minister. They had high hopes of keeping the traditions of the family intact. *Elizabeth,* he thought and sighed. Prettiest girl in Sawgrass County. He smiled, remembering the excitement of bringing his bride back to the house. His mother and grandmother loved her, his father would have, too, if he hadn't gone and died when A.J. was fifteen. "You'll have fine children with this young woman," his mother had whispered in his ear. And they agreed. Oh, how they agreed. But the children didn't come and the years whittled away at the life they had dreamed of. His mother and grandmother died within a year of each other and the house seemed to grow older faster than before and surely was lonelier.

At first, Elizabeth wanted to move to a more modern house, one like the houses in the new addition to Gadara, but A.J. stuck to his promise and took care of the old house. For a while it was hard to keep the promise when money was so tight but then things got better. They always did.

He sighed and shifted in the rocker, bringing his feet back off the railing. One hand rubbed his chest as if trying to relocate an uncomfortable undershirt. A nagging heavy feeling seemed to fill his lungs. He shrugged it off and sat forward, his hands hanging limply between his knees. "Must be something I ate. Something in that can of soup."

The town boomed in the early 1900's. Folks from the north found the location ideal, just a few miles from the coast and spreading out along the river. Schools were built; a courthouse was raised when Gadara became the county seat of Sawgrass County. A.J. went to school and became a teacher. He loved the children he taught, making them, in his mind, the kids he'd never had. But retirement and burgeoning growth of the area pushed him aside and then he was really alone. Elizabeth died too young—only forty. No children. He often wondered if she resented him because they didn't have children or his refusal to move out of the old homestead, but he smiled to himself. No, she didn't resent him. She loved him right to the last breath she took. He was as sure of that as he was sure of anything.

He stood and walked along the length of the veranda, looking northward toward the orange groves that had sprung up after he'd sold the land. Now there was talk of the grove owners quitting the business and developing the land. He squinted into the distance, unable to picture rows of houses along newly paved roads where the sturdy green trees stood. He turned and looked east. In the distance, the sun glinted on the river flowing past the last of his property. He'd clung steadfastly to the acreage around the old homestead. It was a good half mile down to the river and he still had his old fishing dock and the little cove his grandfather had carved out of the river banks for a family area. The old picnic table and benches were gone but he'd toted an aluminum folding chair down there. He knew it was leaning up against the huge Pin Oak that shaded the area. Sometimes he'd take a book and walk to the river's edge. It was peaceful there and the river often lulled him to sleep, his chair tipped back against the trunk of the old oak.

Lost in memories he was surprised to see a stranger walking up the long, unpaved drive to his home.

"Hello," he called when the man got close enough. "Had car trouble?"

"No, I walked," the stranger said, gripping the offered hand. "Wow. It's sure is peaceful along this way."

"You walked from town? I'm sorry, but I don't think I know you."

"You don't. My name's Jack. I did have car trouble a while back and hitchhiked to Gadara. Got a ride from a nice young guy, Bobby something. I didn't ask his last name and now I wish I had. At the time though," he said, leaning against the railing, "I didn't know I was going to stay for a while." Jack grinned.

"Folks call me A.J. Andrew Joshua Handley is the official name, for signing checks and things for Social Security. Getting your car fixed?"

"Soon," Jack said, acknowledging no commitment.

"Well, where are my manners? Sit, Jack, sit," A.J. said, indicating one of the rockers. "I was just enjoying the afternoon." A.J. sat next to him. "I'd offer you sweet tea but I don't make it often anymore. Don't get visitors much. Staying long?"

"I'm not sure. I just thought I'd have a look around someplace I'd never been before. Staying at the Twin Oaks."

"Nice place. Clean. Convenient. Know Sarah Jane well."

The quiet was broken by the raucous call of Sand Hill Cranes as they walked out of a nearby grove.

"They always walk as if they're royalty," Jack commented, watching three tall lanky birds saunter across the open meadow.

"Been here longer than we have," A.J. said. "'Course, not many folks left that have been here longer than I have."

They rocked quietly as if they were old friends visiting on an early summer day. The breeze was slight and warm with the scent of earth and thick foliage.

"You planning on staying?" A.J. asked, forgetting he'd already asked that question.

"In Gadara? No, I'm just visiting."

"It's home to me. Has been for all my life. In fact, my family was the original founding family."

He turned to look at his guest who looked back with a smile on his face.

"Founding family. Gosh, that's great to be able to trace your family back so far. How far?"

"Well, if you're interested, I'll tell you. Not many young folks like to listen to this kind of thing."

"I'd love to hear your story. I'm a history professor at Miami U., so I'm always interested in history and especially Florida's history. I think a lot of it is undiscovered because of the sudden growth that hurried us past much of the earlier history."

"My great, great granddaddy came here in 1862; he and his wife and their eight kids." A.J. chuckled. "They had big families back then. Not like today." He drifted away, remembering tales he'd heard.

"Are there others here? Handleys, I mean?"

"As far as I know, I'm the last." His eyes glazed for a moment as he struggled with the niggling thoughts that had consumed too much of his thinking time lately. "At least, I think I'm the last.

"In the basement of this house you can see a part of the original foundation. Over the years, the family dwindled. Grandma, Mama, Daddy, my brother and I were the last ones to live in this house. Oh, I had an Aunt Felicity who lived with us for years, too. In fact, all of them died right here. Not my brother. He died in World War II. I'll be next," he chuckled.

"We had land back then, acres and acres of it. Sold it off piece by piece as the years went by. I sold all of that," he gestured toward the groves to the north of the house. "I kept twenty acres, the land this house stands on and the land down to the river. Have a little fishing spot down there."

"I'm a fisherman, I'd love to see it," Jack said, awed by the simple way this man encapsulated generations of history into such simple sentences.

"You're welcome to walk down. I'm afraid I can't make it. Well, I could make it down but the slope coming back is too much for these old legs," he said with a sad smile. "Lately I get out of breath easily."

"I'd love to see it. Would that be okay?"

"To walk down to the river? Sure, go ahead," AJ said, his voice wistful.

"Is it okay if I stop by on my way back?"

"Of course. I'll be here," A.J. chuckled.

He watched the young man skip a step as he left the veranda. A.J. stood and went to the railing. He watched Jack's long legs propel him down the slope. He sighed and returned to his rocker. "I remember racing my brother to the river and back. Didn't even puff back then." He shook his head.

Was this old house and bit of land all that was left of the Handley's? All that was left of him? He smiled as he remembered his promise to leave the Handley property to the Gadara Historical Society. For a museum, they claimed. Still, even when he knew better, he couldn't imagine the old homestead without a Handley. "But," he murmured to himself, "Grandma was right. A promise is a promise."

He leaned back and waited for Jack to return. Somehow he knew he would. He grinned to himself. *I promised the homestead to them but not yet. Kind of like cutting the roots off a healthy tree,* he thought.

As Jack walked down the long slope he could see the river ahead of him, the same river that rolled past the park he enjoyed so much.

Nice old gentleman, didn't I tell you?

"You were right. Very interesting but I don't see how he needs help. He seems to be happy right where his roots are. I can understand that."

But you don't see the whole picture yet. He's worried about his family line dying out. He's getting on in years and might need some help from time to time. And, Jack, remember the name Felicity. She has an important part in this drama.

"Well, I know when the time comes you'll be there to help out."

Of course, that's my job.

He came to a little cove and leaned against an ancient tree. An aluminum folding chair was propped nearby. Jack watched the water rushing past. "Pretty place. Reminds me of one Jennifer and I used to visit up state on the east coast. Only the river didn't rush like this, it just meandered.

"I miss her. We had our problems but I was convinced we'd eventually work them out...if we had the time. Now there is no time and I don't know how she feels, how she is. It hurts."

Ah, Jack, that's all in the past. Those memories will fade soon and so will the pain of separation and loss, for both of you. Believe me, Jack.

15

Let them be before the Lord continually, that He may cut off the memory of them from the earth.
Psalms 109:15

Ali sat on the rough bleachers at the side of the old ball field. When the new Gadara High School was built it came with fancy new baseball, football and soccer fields, with a large green expanse for track and field events. It was where the county tournaments were held. Sawgrass County had gone overboard with the extras at the new high school and the residents of Gadara, the County seat, had been dutifully grateful, contributing time and ideas to the completion of this magnificent school and sports facilities.

They had torn down all the old buildings, which over the years had grown like Topsy, a disjointed collection of small buildings, some of them connected with a covered walkway. But the old ball field and one small shack were kept. No one was quite sure why. Was it a reminder of how small they had started?

Ali felt the heat of the hot bench but the slight breeze off the river was enough to make it comfortable. Her mind wandered through her memories.

I loved the old school but the new one was so much better. All those computers, bright big classrooms and a really neat cafeteria. Coming to school was fun. It was fun from kindergarten on up. I wanted to finish school, to do well and then go on to a career. I thought I'd be a journalist.

I loved college, too. I remember what a big deal I felt when I got there. Scared to death but looking forward to reaching my goal. And then Morgan came into the picture.

Was it love at first sight? I don't know. I think our love grew out of something wonderful to something so special...there's no name for it. I miss him so much. Her eyes stung with unreleased tears and she stared down at the tips of her shoes.

Ali felt the bench move slightly and looked up to see a bearded man sitting on the opposite end of the long stretch of wood.

"Hi," he called.

"Hi," Ali replied.

"Nice day."

"Yep."

The man rose and walked toward her. Alice recoiled. She was alone. There was no one in sight and a strange man was approaching her.

"I'm new here," the man said. "Jack Coursky." He extended his hand.

"Alice," she said, reluctantly taking his hand in hers. His fingers felt soft and amazingly cool.

"I have this ever-present urge to be near schools. I'm a teacher, so I guess that's normal in a way."

Alice felt herself relax and wondered why. He was a stranger but he seemed harmless. Did she really want to think of him as 'harmless'?

"I went to this school," she said. "It's pretty new but I attended all four high school years in the new building. It's such a wonderful new school. Then I went to State."

"Are you still there?"

Ali turned away from the stranger and stared across the ancient field. "They used to play all their games on this old field," she said. "There were four high schools in the county and only two of them had fields, but one was almost unusable so we had a lot of games and practices to watch here. They took all the bleachers down but this one. I come here sometimes to remember and think."

"A good place to do that. I think visiting something familiar and special is a great place to think. Even though I don't know the history of this complex, it was one thing I wanted to see first when I came to Gadara."

Ali looked at the man sitting next to her. His profile was strong, nice nose, high cheek bones and eyes that seemed to look further than just the range before him. His beard was neat and suited him. She guessed his age to be around her mother's. "A teacher?" she asked.

"At Miami U. Actually a professor now, but sometimes that title makes me wonder where all the years went. Time moves so quickly that sometimes we miss things. Do you ever think like that?"

"Lots of times I don't know what to think." She sighed and shifted on the warm bench. "You asked me if I was still at college. The answer is no. But in a way I wish I was going back in September."

"You're not going back in September?"

She shook her head. "No," she said softly.

"May I ask why? If you don't want to talk about it, it's okay. I'm just a listener. I found that you can teach a whole lot more when you listen."

"That's about the wisest thing I've heard lately." Ali turned her eyes to his and a strange feeling of comfort enveloped her. "I'm going to have a baby in September."

"I see."

"You don't because it isn't...it isn't..." Her throat filled with a huge lump that wouldn't move and she fought tears she didn't want to share with a stranger. "I should be going," she said, standing.

"Don't go yet. You're upset, I can see. I hope I didn't say anything to upset you."

"It isn't you. It's just...I'm alone. Well, not really alone. I have my mom and dad and great friends. But..."

"But, your young man isn't here."

"He isn't here because he chooses not to be here." Ali's voice took on a rebellious tone.

"I'm sorry. Perhaps with a little time that will change. But, be thankful you have a family and friends. Never underestimate the value of family and friends." He paused, then laughed softly. "There I go again. Teaching. I'm sorry."

Ali smiled. She liked this man. "Thanks, Teach. Maybe I needed a lesson. Have a nice day." She waved and walked around the old bleacher, peeking through the woodwork as her new friend sat staring across the empty field. She wondered what he was thinking.

16

Oh, God of our salvation; who art the confidence of all the ends of the earth…
Psalms 65.5

"I'm going for the sonogram by myself," Alice said, rinsing her milky glass under the kitchen faucet.

"I could go with you. We can take my car to the medical center and then go shopping or to lunch afterwards." Karen didn't want to beg but she knew that was what she was doing. *Why the sudden burst of independence? For the past weeks she's been in my hip pocket twenty-four hours a day and now when I want to be with her for the sonogram she dismisses me!*

"Thanks, Mom, but I want to do this on my own. Everyone says a sonogram is a piece of cake. I'll be fine. I'll let you know how it went when I get home. Anyhow, I promised Marla I'd meet her and Kristi for lunch. I kind of want to tell Marla about the baby. You understand, don't you?"

"Sure."

"You sound upset. Are you disappointed?"

"Of course not. It'll be good for you to be with the girls again. Where's Jocelyn? Doesn't she usually join you?" The little group of friends who were never separated for more than a short time had survived after high school graduation, even with three of them going off to different colleges.

"She's over on the east coast visiting her grandmother." Ali brushed a kiss across her mother's cheek. "I'll be back early; Kristi has to go to work at five. She has the late shift this week." Ali's friend worked at a plush restaurant out on the river during the summer to earn college money. "We may go shopping, too."

Karen watched her daughter disappear through the door in the kitchen leading to the garage. "Have a good time," she called, settling back into one of the chairs at the small table in front of the double doors leading to the lanai. "I am disappointed," she grumbled to herself. "I wanted to be with her. What if she needs me?" *She said she'd be back early. Huh, early. Five o'clock isn't early.*

After putting the breakfast things into the dishwasher and making her bed, Karen wandered aimlessly around the empty house. *I could garden. There's laundry that needs doing. I have a book I've just started.* Her mind tumbled through activities that could take up the long space of time between now and when Alice came home but nothing seemed right.

Turning quickly, she grabbed her purse and library book and hurried into the garage and into her car. Pushing the button to lift the garage door, she backed out. "I'll go to the park. It's always so peaceful there and maybe I'll read for a while."

She felt some small measure of relief as she drove along the familiar roads and then parked in the parking area of Riverside Park. Strolling across the grass to her favorite bench, thankful it was empty, she felt her tension begin to ease. Her mind kept going back to her daughter, the test, and the long wait she faced before she could talk to her. "Don't be dim," she muttered to herself. "Even when Ali comes home she won't know any results. Still..." Karen just wanted to be able to talk to her daughter. *You're a fool, you know that? Neither one of you will know anything until you see Dr. Perez.* She was already including herself for the return to the doctor's office.

She sat on the bench watching some children throw Frisbees, their mothers watching from blankets stretched on the thick grass.

Opening her book, she was quickly into the thriller she'd picked up at the library a few days earlier.

"Mind if I sit here?"

Karen looked up, startled. A man, tall, thin and bearded stood next to her. Her eyes darted around the park and there were at least three empty benches within sight. She felt herself shrink with apprehension for a moment, then found herself unexpectedly saying, "Of course." She inched closer to her end of the bench.

"My name's Jack and I'm visiting Gadara. It's such a friendly little town." He extended his hand and Karen pushed her bookmark into the book and met his clasp, her fingers lightly gripped by the stranger. "I'm a history professor at Miami U.," he said, "and I find your local history very interesting."

Karen felt herself relax. "I'm Karen. Gadara is a lovely little town. I always feel fortunate to be part of it. In fact, I'm on the Board of the Historical Society. Have you seen the museum?"

"I have. I understand there are other artifacts and writings but they aren't available to the public now."

"Not until we get a new museum with some decent storage space and display areas. Perhaps I can help you. We do occasionally allow teachers or researchers to view the things that are jumbled in the back rooms of the museum and then there are boxes and boxes and some furniture and things like that out at Mr. Handley's home. We're planning on opening a new museum sometime in the future. Mr. Handley..."

"I've met him. Fascinating fellow. I'd love to take a look at those artifacts, both in your back rooms and at the Handley place, if possible." Jack felt as if he'd been transported back to his old life and glowed with pleasure.

Good going, young man. That's the trick, establish credibility. Much better than popping in an out of the local lives.

Jack smiled, recognizing Samuel's presence. *Like you do, old man? But I'm happy to receive a bit of encouragement.*

Jack felt Samuel's presence again disappear. He was getting better and better at feeling his guide materialize and then disappear, even if unseen.

"Do you come here often?" Jack asked, then tried to suppress the chuckle he felt straining in his throat, but he needn't have because Karen responded with laughter.

"That's a tired old line, isn't it?"

"I didn't mean it as it came out. I do that sometimes."

"We all do. And, yes, I come here quite often. It's so peaceful and when you're troubled or anxious it seems the perfect place to come and think things out." She glanced at him, as though regretting her openness with her new acquaintance.

"I know what you mean. I'm new here, but I did find this little oasis and I come here almost every day. It's a good thinking place."

"Are you visiting family?"

"No. Actually I don't have any family. My parents died young and I don't have siblings. I was..." he hesitated. He almost said, 'I was engaged' but that would be giving away too much information, too much of his past. "I just chose Gadara because I'd never been here before and since I'm at loose ends until school begins again, I thought it was a good choice."

"Well, welcome. We get winter visitors, you know, the folks who escape the winter weather up north. But most of them stay closer to the Gulf with the beaches and more activities. We tend to be kind of quiet in Gadara." Jack sensed her relaxing with her words.

"I'm staying at Twin Oaks," Jack said.

"Ah, Sarah Jane Hamilton. She's one of Gadara's treasures. Her family was one of the early settlers. Of course, you know Mr. Handley and he's a descendant of the original family."

"Yes, he's a treasure, too. I really enjoyed meeting him."

They sat in comfortable silence. Across the wide expanse of grass the children still played with their Frisbees and some other children had arrived and were on the playground equipment. Their voices, subdued by the distance, made pleasant inroads into the silence that Jack and Karen enjoyed.

"Has your family been in Gadara long?"

"My grandmother came here from Vero Beach. That's on the east coast. Oh," she laughed, "Of course, you'd know that coming from Miami. I lost my parents several years ago. Daddy died and mother just pined away. It was a shame because she was a lovely woman. I miss them every day." She paused, then added, "I have a daughter. She's just come home from college."

"Oh? What school?"

"Florida State." Karen hesitated to add any more information and was glad when Jack didn't ask any more questions. He stared ahead as if trying to find something hidden in the scene before them.

"That's the Onocoa River. It's fairly wide here and gets even wider where it empties into the Gulf. Not many miles up there," she indicated an inland direction, "the river starts in a little spring-fed lake but the spring is powerful and hasn't slowed down in years, centuries I suspect."

"There should be river boats on it," Jack said jokingly.

"At one time there was. You should be able to find something about that in the library or the museum store. They ran a sort of barge to the coast, taking produce and cattle from this area to the Gulf, but it wasn't much of an industry and most of the cattle were driven to Tampa for shipment." She smiled at him. "I feel as if I've donned the mantle of tour guide."

"I appreciate the tour," he said. "I'd love to be able to explore it more."

"There is a little marina to the west of this park. All private boats, but maybe you could hitch a ride when one of them is going out. I think there's a favorite fishing spot about three miles to the west of the library."

"I used to love to fish. There's something so peaceful about sitting in a small boat on a lake and not having anything to do but wait for a bite. And sometimes they don't bite," he laughed.

"My husband used to fish when we were first married but then as he got more involved in business...well, he doesn't fish anymore." Karen wondered why she would divulge such an inane piece of information to a perfect stranger. She moved an inch to the right.

"Sometimes we do let obligations get in the way of pleasures. It's a shame, but I guess we all do it at times. Is your husband in business locally?"

"He works for Magnus Incorporated but he'll be moving soon. Or at least I think he will. We're divorced."

Jack hung his head for a moment, then looked across the grassy lawn. "I'm sorry."

"It happens," Karen said with a shrug. "My daughter and I are adjusting."

"Still..."

"Oh, we're fine. It was a shock at first. He's remarried. There are more changes in my future, I think. We're selling the house. It's too big for just Ali and me and there are too many memories..." Her voice drifted off and she stiffened. Why was she talking about such private matters to this man?

"We don't always understand the mysteries that come into our life, but they are there for a reason."

Karen listened to his words and a deep sense of serenity engulfed her. "You're right. With God's help I have come to terms with these changes. I know we'll be fine."

Again, they sat in companionable silence. Karen looked at the man sitting next to her. He seemed so calm and unhurried. Maybe that wasn't the right word but there was something tranquil about his presence.

Jack stood. "Well, I guess I'll take a walk around the park and then go over to the high school complex. Quite a nice set-up there."

"It's fairly new. Sawgrass County consolidated all the school into one high school and combined several of the elementary schools, too."

"I like to run laps if no one's around," he said, backing away. "It was nice meeting you, Karen. Maybe we'll bump into each other again while I'm here."

Karen watched him as he loped away, his strong legs indicating that he did indeed, work out.

***

"Just relax," the technician in the pink top covered with multicolored balloons and smiling babies said. "This jelly will be cold. You can watch your baby in that screen up there." She pointed to a small screen over the foot of the examining table.

"Ooh, that is cold," Ali said.

"Umm."

Ali watched the shadows flicker across the small screen. "Is that the baby?" she whispered. The technician explained some of the images but it was totally confusing and she wished her mother was with her.

Ali heard a swishing sound. "Is that the baby making that noise?" If the technician responded, Ali didn't understand her so she kept her eyes glued to the squiggly patches of light and dark.

The test didn't seem to take very long and Ali was hoping for some kind of running commentary explaining what they were looking at, but after a short time the tech pulled the wand back and began cleaning Ali's abdomen.

"Is that all there is to it? she asked.

"Yep. The doctor will read the results and get in touch with you."

"But did everything look all right?"

"Um," she murmured, clipping papers together. "We don't make any reports here, your doctor does that. Your chart is marked that you don't want to know the sex of your baby so I didn't say anything. Have you changed your mind?"

"No," Alice said, wondering if maybe when she was filling out the forms, she shouldn't have said, 'don't tell me whether it's a boy or girl'. *Oh, why did I say that?*

The woman in the pink top left the room. Alice felt abandoned. She shrugged and finished dressing. When she checked out at the front desk she asked when she'd know the results, her face a picture of disappointment.

"Your doctor will call you. Let's see, oh, it's Doctor Perez. He's always good about doing his reports right away. You should hear from him in a day or two." The receptionist had an engaging smile and Ali smiled back even though right now she didn't feel like smiling. *I should have had Mom with me. I could have taken her home and then gone to meet the girls.* But by the time she crossed the parking lot and climbed into her car she'd convinced herself everything was fine and she just wasn't used to these procedures yet.

Ali and Kristi sat on a bench in a booth in the Gadara Diner on the highway. "Ooh, this is so exciting," Marla said as she slid onto the bench on the other side of the table. "Wait, stand up, Ali. I want to see your stomach."

"Really, Marla," Ali said, standing up and turning sideways. She pulled her oversized tee shirt tight to expose the extended belly she was now becoming proud of.

"Ooh, I'm so jealous," Marla said, grinning widely, her freckles bouncing across rounded cheeks.

"No you're not. You always exaggerate," practical Kristi said, pushing a plastic covered menu across the table. "We know what we want so when you're ready I'll give the waitress the high sign."

"I'm not exaggerating. You're engaged, Jocelyn is going to Europe for a month and Ali is pregnant. What about me? I'm just plain old Marla waiting for school to start again. What are you having?"

"Salads," the two girls chorused and they all dissolved in giggles.

Over three identical salads and three glasses of iced tea which were refilled several times, the girls caught up on all the important local news.

"Don't look now, but do you see that guy at the counter? He keeps staring at us."

"Where?" Marla said twisting in her seat to look over her shoulder.

"I said 'don't look now'," Kristi hissed.

"Well, then, why did you point him out to us," Marla countered and Ali giggled.

"Because he seems to be staring at us, that's why."

"You mean the guy with the beard?" Ali whispered.

"Yeah."

"He's harmless. I met him last week at the high school one day when I was just sitting on the bleachers. He's probably waiting for someone."

"What were you doing at the high school?"

"Reminiscing," Ali said.

"Whew," Marla said, wiping imaginary sweat from her brow. "I thought we might have a serial killer here or something."

"Geeze Louise, just because he's a stranger doesn't mean he's a serial killer," Kristi said, returning to her salad.

"Then why did you bring him up?"

"Well, I wish I hadn't now," Kristi huffed. "Just eat. Maybe we'll go shopping later."

For several moments their attention was returned to their lunch and then Kristi whispered, "He just left."

"Thanks for the update," Ali said, and the girls laughed.

"Changing the subject, you really aren't going back to college, Ali?" Marla asked.

""No. The baby is due in September."

"Maybe later? I mean, for college."

Ali shrugged. "I don't think so. Being a single parent doesn't seem to fit with college."

Ali turned to look out the window. Talking about being a single parent only reminded her of Morgan and his absence. She fought to hold back tears.

"Well, nothing's cut in stone," Kristi said.

"Can I ask about Morgan?" Marla whispered.

"Oh, for God's sakes, Marla," Kristi exploded. "You dummy." She looked at Ali and saw the tears she'd been trying to stem slide down her cheeks. "Now look what you've done."

"Oh, Ali, I'm sorry. I'm so dumb." Marla wailed. "Please don't cry. I'm so sorry."

"No. No, you're not dumb. I'm just...I don't know how to handle this yet. I'll get over it."

"No, you won't. I don't understand what's going on with that guy, but if anyone is dumb it's him. How can he just turn his back on you?" Now the subject had been opened up, Kristi let her anger flow. "It's his baby. He knows about it. By the way, I wish you'd found out whether this kid is a boy or girl. I hate to keep referring to it as *it."*

"I'm going to ask the doctor when he calls," Alice stuttered, choking back her emotions and scrubbing her eyes and cheeks with a napkin.

"When will that be?"

"The girl at the medical center said in a day or two. I can't wait." Alice sighed deeply, her voice charged with a smidgen of hope crowding out the melancholy. "I have to get over crying at the sound of Morgan's name. Anyhow, I'm convinced he will come to his senses and at least try to be a father. He was so excited when we found out I was pregnant. Even if he doesn't want to marry me..." Alice had to swallow the lump building in her throat. "He might want to know his son or daughter," she bit her lower lip and took a deep breath. "Oh, darn, you're going to have to bear with me."

The three girls held hands across the table and for a moment the high school loyalty they'd promised each other was back in force. "Let's go to the Mall," Kristi said, glancing at her watch. "We can shop for a couple of hours. What about maternity clothes, Ali?"

"Mom and I got some earlier this week."

"How come you didn't wear one today, then?" Marla was always the curious one of the group.

"Because I wasn't ready, but after the sonogram and lunch with you two, I am. What did I think I was hiding?" They laughed.

Their usual jovial mood was only slightly dampened and the threesome rallied. Soon they were in one car and giggling over what kind of shoes Kristi should wear as a bride. "Nothing with really high heels," Ali said. "You don't want to break an ankle on the way down the aisle."

"Maybe some nice white sneakers," Marla said and they all dissolved in laughter again.

Later that evening on the lanai, Ali and her mother were enjoying a cool fruit drink as the sun slipped out of sight over the river. "I love this time of day," Karen said.

"Me, too. It reminds me of when I was a little girl and you let me come out on the porch for half an hour before I had to go to bed. You and Daddy...Oh, I'm sorry," she whispered.

"Don't be, honey. You have wonderful memories of your childhood and your Daddy. Nothing will ever erase them and they're precious to you. Don't try and forget them or think you can't talk about them. I'm not that fragile. At least, not any more."

They sat in the quiet of the twilight for several minutes before Karen said, "So you felt good about your sonogram, didn't you? It must have been exciting. They didn't have them when I was pregnant with you, or at least I don't think they did. Certainly old Dr. Kincaide didn't suggest one."

"It was an experience. I really didn't know what I was looking at. I think not only didn't I understand what she was saying but I was so excited I wasn't listening."

"When you get the report it will make things clearer, I'm sure," Karen said, patting her daughter's hand.

"Still, I had this funny feeling she wasn't telling me something."

"She couldn't tell you anything, honey. The report has to be read by the doctor and then he'll talk to you."

"I know. But, there was something..."

Karen stood. "Worry wart. I'm going in. Do you want to stay out here?"

Ali sighed. "No, I'll come in, too. I picked up a book at the library on the way home. It's called *Nobody's Child.*

Karen put her arm around Ali's shoulder as they stepped into the house, the cool air welcoming them. "Don't try and read anything into the technician's actions, Ali. They are taught to be totally noncommittal."

"I guess you're right. I'm hitting the shower and then I think I'll read in bed. Is that okay with you?"

"Of course it is. You don't have to ask permission," Karen laughed and patted her daughter on the behind. "Good night, honey."

17

Why art thou cast down, O my soul?
And why are thou disquieted within me?
Hope in God for I shall yet praise him
who is in the health of my countenance.
Psalm 43:5

"You could give me some warning," Jack complained. He was sitting on a bench outside the courthouse in downtown Miami. "Whipping me from Gadara to Miami in a single breath. What the heck am I doing here? I thought I was through with all this," he said, spreading his arms to encompass Flagler Street and the crowds of people.

"Sometimes you're needed other places," Samuel said, leaning on the stop sign on the corner.

"What if Jennifer sees me? What if someone I know walks by? I'm supposed to be dead, you know."

"Who knows better than I? And you are dead, but don't worry, you won't be seen. Not here. Not yet, anyhow."

"You mean no one can see me? You can make me appear and disappear at will? Why now?"

"I needed to make you invisible here in Miami because, as you've suggested, there just might be people who would recognize you and, since you're dead, that might be quite awkward. See?"

"I don't know if I'm ever going to get used to this. But," Jack said softly, raising his hand in defense, "I know...you know what you're doing."

"Exactly. I have you here for a specific purpose. Soon you will meet a nice young man. He has ties to Gadara—to the daughter of the nice lady you meet occasionally in the park. Remember?"

"So now I'm meeting someone else. Why?

"Because we feel it is necessary. This young man has a big part in what you're involved in."

Jack huffed softly. "What I'm involved in? I haven't a clue."

"Stop complaining. You're the most stubborn herald I've ever had to deal with."

Jack jumped up then quickly returned to the bench, then stood realizing no one could see him anyway. "Herald!" he whispered. "What does that mean? I'd like to know why and who..."

"God, that's Who. And why? I wonder, but I'm not the one who chooses the messengers. You were chosen, so please try and go along with the plan. I'm not in charge. I'm just here to...facilitate things for you."

Jack sat on the bench and watched the five o'clock crowds rush along the sidewalks. The traffic noise and the rush of people reminded him of when he lived here. "Lived," he whispered then looked at the little man leaning against the signpost. "I'm sorry. I just don't understand. I apologize."

"Apology accepted. You know sometimes my hands are tied and I just follow directions. I was directed to put you here and in a few minutes you'll meet a nice young man who is part of this picture. He's...let's say remorseful, but just can't get up the courage to act."

"Okay," Jack murmured and watched as two very young women in tight skirts and stiletto heels glanced at him pityingly. *They think I'm talking to myself,* he grimaced. On the heels of that thought was the realization that he was visible to them. And Samuel was gone.

***

Ever since his Carter's Corner binge, Morgan limited himself to one occasional gin and tonic after work. It wasn't a nightly thing, so when his friend, Dave, suggested a drink before going home, he often joined him. Tonight was no different and yet it did seem different.

As if on cue, Dave turned to his companion and said, "You look different today. Problem?"

"No," Morgan answered quickly.

"Work related?"

"No. Nothing, thanks. Just things I have to think out."

"Sorry. Didn't mean to pry." Dave spun his almost empty glass on the shiny bar top. The crowd was noisy and they had been fortunate to get two barstools when a couple left just as they arrived. "Want to get a Cuban dinner? We could catch a movie afterward."

Morgan and Dave were the only two bachelors in the firm and often shared dinner, sometimes adding a movie if Dave was free. Morgan had been teased about his celibacy. At first there were rumors he might be gay but they were squashed when Dave's name was added to the equation and he made sure the truth was known. He had a live-in girlfriend.

Morgan drained his drink. "Not tonight, pal. I don't think I'd be good company."

Dave finished his drink and pushed the glass away, signaling the bartender they wanted their checks. "Okay. I'm going to grab a sandwich and take it home. The lady of the house is at a jewelry party tonight. There's that great Cuban sandwich shop right around the corner, sure you don't want one?"

"Thanks, but not tonight."

They both placed money on the checks in front of them and relinquished the barstools to those waiting behind them. "See you tomorrow morning," Morgan said, giving his friend's shoulder a firm grip.

They parted on the sidewalk in front of the bar, Morgan to catch a bus home and Dave to the parking garage where he kept the Porsche he was so proud of. Morgan chose the bus because it went right past his condo and he didn't want to pay the high parking garage fees. His savings accounts grew steadily every month and while he was proud of that, it was a hollow accomplishment.

As he walked along the sidewalk, he couldn't suppress the vision of Ali which had popped up all during the day. Her face had appeared unexpectedly while he was on the telephone and crept into his thoughts when he scanned the monitor for changing stock prices. He'd almost made a crucial error in one of his accounts but fortunately caught it himself. The glowing report of his last quarter's activity certainly didn't need any errors. He'd been told at the last review he was being considered for an upward move if he maintained the pace he'd established. "I can't get her out of my mind," he whispered as he waited at the bus stop. *If I can't find the courage to talk to her, maybe I could send a letter. Is that chickening out? Well, it might be better than total silence.* He watched his bus lumber to the curb. *I'll think about that tonight,* he thought cautiously then challenged, *will you?*

Climbing on the bus at the corner, he searched for a seat. Midway back there was one empty seat next to a bearded gentleman who was reading a magazine. He slid next to him; the man raised his eyes and greeted him with a smile.

"Evening," he said

Morgan responded, "Evening."

The bus ground away from the curb and after several stops, turned onto Biscayne Boulevard. Morgan enjoyed this ride home every night. The scenes between the towering hotels offered glimpses of the bay. Colorful crowds and bright umbrellas dotted outdoor cafés. He felt himself relax.

The man laid the travel magazine across his lap. The cover showed a rendition of the Coliseum, and Morgan asked, "Going on a trip?" He shocked himself because during all the many bus trips up and down Biscayne Boulevard he had rarely voluntarily entered into a conversation with his seat mate and never had instigated it.

"I had planned to go to Italy in August for two weeks, but now I'm not sure if I'll complete my work in Gadara in time."

The word 'Gadara' startled Morgan. "You know Gadara? You've been there recently?"

"For several weeks. Left yesterday. I'll return tomorrow or the next day. I'm doing some history research." Jack noted Morgan's sudden pallor and asked, "Are you okay? You look pale."

"Oh, I'm fine. I was surprised when you said Gadara. Not a lot of people down here even know it exists."

Jack smiled. "That's one of its finer points, I think. A well kept secret." He paused, studying the young man, noticing his hands were clasped tightly in his lap. "Do you know people in Gadara?"

"I do. My...uh...a friend from college lives there."

"Ah, well it's a lovely little town. Very quaint and with a lot of local history. That's what I'm interested in, as I said."

Morgan was quiet and Jack watched him out of the corner of his eye. He appeared to be in deep thought.

Jack cleared his throat. "I'm doing the research for a publication I might write about little known historical gems. I'm a history professor at the University."

"Miami?"

"Yes. I have a friend in Gadara whose daughter just returned from Florida State. Her mother's name is Karen. I met her in a park along the river."

Now Morgan's countenance changed from pasty white to splotchy red. "Karen?" he stuttered.

For heaven's sakes, Sam, give me a hand here. What the heck am I supposed to be saying?

You're doing fine. Samuel responded. *Keep him talking. Suggest dinner. Get off at the same stop he does.*

That's easier said than done. Jack scowled then cleared his throat. "I'm meeting a friend but he's not going to be free until eight o'clock." He glanced at his watch. It was five-thirty now. "Know of a nice restaurant where I could grab a bite to eat and kill some time?"

Morgan hesitated. He had an overwhelming urge to talk to this man but he didn't know why or what he would say. His mind churned almost as much as his stomach did and he regretted even the one drink he'd had. "I get off at 169th. There's a Seafood Shack about a block away. You could probably spend some time there. They usually don't hurry you out unless they're packed. It's early and you'd be gone before the late crowd moves in." Morgan was stunned at his willingness to give out this much information. He was often kidded about being close-mouthed unless there was a commission in it. "The food's good," he added.

"One-sixty-ninth street? That's amazing. Isn't there an office on that corner? That's where my friend, Bill, told me to meet him. Then at the last minute he called and said he'd be late. I'd already checked out of my hotel room. If our meeting isn't too long, I might head back to Gadara tonight if possible."

Nice, Jack. Now you're on the right track. Dinner is next.

I thought you were going to help me. So far I'm flying solo. Jack leaned back and closed his eyes. He found himself holding his breath in anticipation of more conversation.

Morgan thought a moment and then said, "Oh, a little real estate office. I almost forgot it. It looks like a house. In fact, I guess it was a private home at one time. It's dwarfed by all the condos up there." He grinned.

When the bus neared 169th Street, Morgan stood and pulled the signal for the bus to stop. Both he and Jack moved down the aisle to the front door which gushed open as soon as they arrived.

Stepping out onto the sidewalk, Morgan was overcome with a sense of urgency. He had to speak to this man; this man who had just come from Gadara and who knew Karen, Ali's mom. How could this be anything but a meant-to-be coincidence?

"Say, I have some time to kill, too. Would you mind if I had dinner with you? In fact..."

"Well, isn't that wonderful. It's not often that I get to spend some quality time with a young man who isn't one of my students and doesn't have ulterior motives. You don't have ulterior motives, do you?" He laughed.

"Oh, no, sir. No, indeed. I just have to kill some time because..." His mind raced. "Because, my girlfriend is working late." Morgan ended lamely.

Hey, Sam, he sounds as lame as I do. How're we doing?

Lame or not, you're getting the job done. Just let him talk. Girlfriend, indeed, but more on that later. Keep referring to Gadara, there's a link there. And, I think I'm prepared to clue you in when we return to Gadara. I think you're ready now.

"Well, it's about time," Jack mumbled, tucking the travel magazine under his arm.

"I'm sorry. Did you say something?" Morgan asked.

"No. I was just thinking loud I guess," he chuckled and followed Morgan's lead as they walked north along the sidewalk.

The scent of the sea was in the air and Morgan breathed deeply.

The interior of the Seafood Shack was dim but the waiter showed Morgan and Jack to a booth next to a window overlooking the bay. There were very few patrons but Morgan knew in an hour the place would be crowded and noisy. He savored the quiet.

Morgan raised the wooden blinds. "I never get tired of watching the waves come into the shore. It's kind of like knowing something is always going to be the same. Bigger waves sometimes maybe, but they'll always be there. You can count on them."

"Continuity in life is one of the best aspects. It's safe and comfortable."

"Yeah," Morgan said, picking up the huge menu, "like knowing who you are or what you're meant to do."

Jack smiled. "Sounds as if someone is a bit disconnected."

"You could say that. The Atlantic cod is good here."

"I saw it on the menu. I was thinking of shrimp tonight."

"That's good, too. In fact, the coconut shrimp or the Caribbean shrimp is out of this world. I forgot it until you mentioned it. I'm having the coconut shrimp." He closed the menu and put it aside.

The waiter took their orders, brought a basket of rolls and butter and placed a glass of beer in front of Morgan and a cup of coffee in front of Jack.

"Disconnected" Morgan said. "That about sums up my life right now."

"How so?"

"It's complicated."

"Well, I'm a good listener but I certainly don't want to pry." Jack stirred two packets of sugar into his coffee. "Sometimes talking to someone not involved is helpful."

Morgan sipped his beer and stared out the window.

"I left college at the end of May. I had plans to work here in Miami, which I'm doing, and then begin my graduate work. But, well, that's changed. I'm working here but I've put the graduate work on hold."

"Is there a reason for the delay? Again, I'm not prying, just listening."

"Yes, there's a reason. I messed up royally and now I don't know how to fix things."

The two men waited as their entrees were placed in front of them. "The coconut shrimp for you, sir." The waiter placed a large platter on Morgan's side of the table. "And for you, sir, the Caribbean shrimp. The plates are very hot," he cautioned. "Will there be anything else?"

"No, thanks," Morgan said, gingerly touching the edge of his plate. "Wow, that is hot."

After the waiter left, Jack continued. "I have no idea what 'messed up royally' means but I'm sure if you've made mistakes they can be corrected. What you need is some quiet time with a friend or family member who can help you."

"Family," Morgan said with disdain. "That's part of the problem. No, I don't think I'm going to be able to fix the family side of this mess. There's more though."

Jack separated a big shrimp from the rice and sauce. He carefully cut the tail away. "This is good. Thanks for suggesting it." He popped the hot shrimp into his mouth and savored the spicy sauce clinging to it. "Perhaps the other problem will solve itself with time. That often happens. Or, perhaps you could hurry a solution by contacting the other person involved. Just a suggestion. Unless communication is open between you it will be difficult to come to a conclusion."

Morgan sighed. "You're probably right, but I can't seem to find the courage to contact her...this other person."

"Think about it, Morgan."

For the remainder of the meal, Morgan and Jack talked about familiar places in Miami and fishing, something both were interested in. The subject of family or problems, was carefully avoided by both, but Jack was hoping Morgan would confide more in him.

***

"I think I messed that up," Jack sat on his favorite bench in Riverside Park. "We sat together for over an hour, I ate my shrimp and he pushed his around the plate. I didn't see any breakthrough, though. There is definitely something really serious on his mind but he didn't open up to me. Sometimes I felt as if he was going to tell me something but he'd clam up. There's some kind of secret he's keeping but he was reluctant to go there; it was a waste of time and nothing was accomplished. I didn't get any answers."

No, you did fine, Samuel reassured.

"But I didn't. I didn't find out anything. If there's a connection between Morgan and Gadara I didn't see it. He might have a college friend there."

Ah, and that may be enough for now. You noticed how he kept coming back to Gadara even though he admitted he'd only been there a few times? There's a connection, Jack, and you'll find it.

"And, by the way, my head is still reeling from the mental express we took from Gadara to Miami and back. How do you do that?"

It's a trade secret. Just know it's the next day and we're here. Now, I promised to fill you in. We don't often do it right at the start. There's so much to comprehend and sometimes too overwhelming for our heralds to understand.

"I can understand that. I still don't know what the heck is going on and we've been doing this...how long?"

Time is so unimportant, Jack. In earthly time, you've been dead for about three months, and since then you've been here in Gadara for about three weeks, give or take.

"Give or take what? And, by the way, am I visible or not?"

Jack, Jack, you've got to stop thinking as if you were alive and going about your normal business. That's all gone. You've moved on. But you haven't gotten to the final place yet. And, yes, right now you're visible but I'm not. The only time I make you invisible is if there's a chance someone from your past life might recognize you. We don't want to scare people, do we? I'm not visible to anyone but you. No one can see or hear me but you.

Jack shook his head. "It's difficult to evaluate this. I'm an analytical person. I want to know what's going on from one moment to the next. I want answers to questions, a chronological sense to things." He paused and stared across the sloping grassy area to the river's edge. The water moved from right to left, the surface ripple-free, and the scene was calm and serene. "You know what's the weirdest? If I'm in a situation where it's necessary to eat, I do, but if I'm not, I don't, and I don't care. I don't get hungry. I don't have bodily functions...I miss my life."

Whoa. We don't want to go there, do we? If I could only get you to accept without questioning. But, that will come. Believe me. Now, do you want to know more about your assignment?

Jack's attention was immediately focused on the little man who appeared perched on the back of the park bench. "Yes. That's what I want, what I've wanted from the beginning."

"Okay. Starting from the beginning, a little background. We all know who is in charge of everything earthly and heavenly. Big job, but He does it well. He has organized a system for all things, living and dead. When you suffered your tragic automobile accident, you left your earthly body. But," Samuel paused, raising one hand, "that wasn't all. God, in His infinite wisdom, chooses who will go where. I think you know the choices. He also decides who will be privileged to become one of his preferred helpers. These are referred to as heralds."

"I still don't understand why I was chosen." Jack said.

"Well you were, and I was sent to help you with your mission. I'm a facilitator."

"But if this is already decided, that I'm going to be an angel...Jeez, do you know how crazy that sounds? Why all the stuff about my mission—my assignment?"

"Not an angel, Jack. Angels are not and never were human, and humans are not and never will be angels. God created us with different purposes. You were simply selected for the special task of being a herald."

"Well, then, what's a herald, really?" Jack asked.

"Exactly what it says. God is preparing to bless these people and He is entrusting you to carry this message to them."

Jack spread his hands, humbled despite himself. "How?" he asked. "I don't feel as though I'm carrying anything. Or that I've ever been a blessing to anyone."

"You have been, Jack. A great blessing to a great many people. Remember when I said you were a teacher? And you taught many people many things. You were a good teacher. But that is a story for another day, and we have all of eternity.

"Being a herald and carrying a blessing is a mission, an assignment. You'll understand more as I give you the details, okay?"

"Okay," Jack mumbled. He was stupefied at what had just so casually been revealed to him. Had he mattered? Had he made a difference? God, or God's messenger in the way of Samuel, was telling him, "Yes." He had mattered. He had made a difference. He felt inexplicably like weeping.

Samuel was continuing. "The old gentleman you met out at his home just out of town is part of this. So is the pregnant young woman and the young man in Miami. Your friend Karen also plays a role. There is a tie between all of them that only God knows. Once that is understood and the pieces fall into place, you will have accomplished your mission and the blessing will be revealed."

Jack shook his head in disbelief at what he'd just heard. He folded his hands in his lap, leaned forward and studied the tips of his shoes. The quiet enfolded him like a well-worn quilt. His mind rambled through what he'd just heard, slipping back from time to time. He looked up to see if Samuel was still perched on the back of the bench. He was gone. Jack stood. "Now what?" he muttered.

Oh, I'm still here. I was giving you a chance to mull over what I'd said. Is it a bit clearer now?

"I don't' know if I'd use the word 'clear' but I guess some of the things are beginning to fall into place. But," Jack paused, searching for the right words. "When I was a kid I was raised in foster homes. Most of them nice, a couple of them...well, that happens."

I know. You did well for yourself, Jack. Getting the education you did, almost on your own. There was one fellow...

"Mr. Pryzski. He was the best foster dad I ever had. We used to go fishing together on that lake where..." Jack struggled for the right words, but could only think of, "where I woke up.

He was the one who told me, 'Everything is possible with a good education.' I never forgot that." He felt unexpected tears and blinked them back, not allowing them to escape. *Another bodily function no longer necessary.*

"Remember, I'm not sure I'm prepared for this job, Sam."

Oh, no, Jack. No mistake. Once this choice has been made it's made. No going back, no second thoughts. This will be okay, believe me.

Jack thought he heard a soft chuckle. "So there are no 'brownie points' necessary?"

Nope. And you're right, Jack. No more tears. Now, because you haven't the ability; soon because you will be so joy-filled that you won't need them. Kind of nice to know, don't you think?

But getting back to the subject. I know what you're going to say. You're wondering if there's a price to pay to get into Heaven, right? That you're kind of working your way up Jacob's ladder? Well there isn't an entry fee or a requirement that might keep you out. Christ paid your entry fee for you. You're on your way, this is just a slight delay.

"Does everyone who dies get chosen for an assignment?" Jack asked.

No, Samuel said.

"Is it because they already did enough and I. . . maybe I didn't?"

No, Samuel said.

Jack brightened, asked cautiously, "Is it because I. . . well, maybe I'm better . . . somehow?"

No, Samuel said again.

Perplexed, Jack asked impatiently, "Well, then why me?"

Maybe you're just willing, Samuel said. *It really isn't important who does it as long as it gets done, don't you agree?*

Jack sat up straighter on the bench. "Yes. Yes, I think I'm beginning to understand. It's not about me, it's about them. . ."

Samuel chuckled softly. *Spoken like a true herald,* he said.

Jack stood slowly. He pushed his hands into the pockets in his tan slacks and slowly paced away from the bench. Some children were in the playground area and he watched the rhythmic motions of the swings going back and forth. The pace of each swing was the same, the spacing different so that it looked like a metronome. The sound of the children's voices added a measure of reality to the scene. For just a moment Jack wondered what it would have been like to have children of his own.

He turned back to the bench but stayed where he was on the pathway. A slight breeze brushed strands of his hair across his forehead. Somewhere a grill was lit and food was being cooked. The scent was pleasant but stirred no memories. "You mean that it's up to me to get these three people together, to figure out their problems and solve them?"

No. You don't have to solve their problems, whatever they may be. You are just to try and give them faith that there is a solution, that if they rely on God, they will find it.

Jack spread his arms in frustration. "But how am I going to find a solution to problems I don't understand?"

That's the nice part of this job, Jack. You're not going to do the solution thing, just get them together and make them aware, with heavenly help of course, that there are alternatives. You'll see the problems as you get more involved.

"I don't know, Sam. It seems so complicated."

That's where the faith comes in, Jack. You're making it complicated. He'll help you with a push here and a whispered suggestion there. I'll always be here for you. This isn't a prerequisite to your getting to Heaven; it's just your faith and your willingness to help. Heaven knows you've done this before and didn't even know it. That young man, a student of yours who was at the end of his rope—no money, no support from his parents. You stepped in. The time you gave your last dollar to that elderly couple out on the highway with car trouble. You might not remember these things, you're not supposed to now, maybe later. But, there were so many times when you stepped in and helped. Now you just have one more opportunity and this one was chosen for you. Have faith, Jack. You've had faith so many times before.

Jack smiled. "You're something else, Sam. Okay, you've convinced me. Whatever comes along I'll just go with it. I hope I *can* help. This sounds so unusual, so impossible I'm just waiting to see it all happen.

That's my boy, Sam said.

"I don't know if I'll ever get used to this, Sam. See you later, maybe?"

An elderly man and woman, holding hands and strolling towards him, smiled. "Nice day," she said. As they continued along the path behind Jack, he heard the man whisper, "Was he talking to himself? He looks too young to be doing that."

Jack grinned and began walking on the path that led to the river's edge. Standing on a grassy knoll he reviewed what Samuel had told him. "Well, now I know who all is involved. Let's see...well, it doesn't take a rocket scientist to put the two young people together, I think even a dull history professor can do that. The stubborn young man and the pregnant young woman. But...," he scratched his head. "Where does the old man fit in?"

He trudged back up the path. *Maybe I'll discover something in the Historical Museum that might help, and if not, I'll enjoy nosing around in Gadara's past.*

18

God didn't promise days without pain,
laughter without sorrow, sun without rain,
but He did promise strength for the day,
comfort for the tears, and light for the way.
Author Unknown

"Ali? Ali?" Karen called when she heard the door in the kitchen open. She'd stood in the hallway looking directly into the kitchen waiting for Ali to return ever since she'd received the telephone call.

"I'm home, Mom" Ali said, pulling the door closed. "We had a great time at the Mall but, boy, am I tired. I feel as if I'm lugging a ton of books around under this shirt."

"You need to sit down and put your feet up. But listen, while you were out the doctor's office called. He wants you to have another sonogram tomorrow."

Ali threw her purse on the kitchen counter and leaned against it for support, the color draining from her face. "But I just had one three days ago. Is something wrong? Did he say anything else? Why would I need another? Oh, I just know something's wrong. Remember, I told you, the tech looked like she was hiding something or was confused or something. She wouldn't talk to me." Tears sprung to her eyes and she thumbed them away.

"It wasn't Dr. Perez, honey. A girl from the office called. It sounded like that smiley one at the front desk. Come on, sit in the living room and put your feet up. You do look tired."

"I am tired," Ali said, the dejection in her voice obvious. "But why would I need another sonogram so quickly? Do you think they found some problem? Oh, Mom, I'm scared." Ali sat in her father's recliner and poked the footrest forward.

"Now don't be negative, honey. Maybe the technician made a mistake. Maybe something wasn't clear or the test just wasn't what Dr. Perez wanted. There are a hundred reasons why you might need another test so soon." Karen said, hoping the confidence and calm she was trying to send was stronger than the fears shriveling her stomach into an uncomfortable lump just below her lungs.

"But, what if..."

"Don't do that, Ali. It's foolish to speculate. Tomorrow you'll have the test again. I'll go with you. Dr. Perez will read it and then you'll go in for a consultation to go over the results. Now just calm down, all this hysteria isn't good for you or the baby." *Or the grandmother, either,* Karen thought as she sat next to Ali. She struggled to appear as relaxed as she was trying to project. It wasn't an easy task.

Karen sipped a cup of coffee, deciding to forgo any toast this morning. She fondled the curls on Missy's head. "Sorry, doggie, no extras this morning, just the food in your dish. Go and eat that." The little dog tipped her head to one side. Usually there was something from the table for her. She shuffled her feet and then sat down next to Karen.

Ali had already thrown up the bowl of cereal she'd attempted to eat, something she hadn't done since the first month of her pregnancy. She sat in the living room, feet up, head back trying to calm herself. *The first month. Gosh that seems like so long ago and I have another three months to go.*

"You okay?" Karen asked from the hallway.

"Fine. Just waiting for the hands on that clock to speed up a little. The appointment is for nine-thirty, right?"

"Yes. Ali, believe me, it will be okay. I prayed last night about this and a beautiful, peaceful feeling came over me. I'm sure the good Lord is with us, honey."

"I prayed, too, but I'm so mixed up I'm afraid I didn't get any great calm like you did. Just the same unanswered questions. What's the problem and will the baby be okay? You know," she said, sitting upright. "I don't care if *I* have problems; I just want the baby to be okay. Is that crazy or what?"

Karen smiled. "Crazy? No, Ali, that's the first sign of motherhood. You're going to be okay and so is the baby. I just feel it and you know how mother's are?"

"Always right?" Ali laughed. "Okay, *Mrs. Mother-Knows-Best*, I'll just keep thinking good thoughts, although I don't know how easy that's going to be. But maybe by tomorrow we'll know why this second test is needed and what the results are." She moved forward. "Let's go. Maybe if we get there early they'll take me in right away."

Karen sat in the waiting room and twisted her hands, occasionally pacing across the floor. There were several other women in the room and they looked at her wonderingly but Karen ignored them. After all, it was her daughter in there, not theirs. Her heart leapt to her throat as the door opened and Ali came through.

"What...?" Karen asked.

"Let's talk outside," Ali said, pulling the door open.

They walked down the brick path to the parking lot and the car. Neither said anything until they were belted in. "Okay, tell me," Karen said, starting the car and turning the air-conditioning up.

"Well, this time there were two technicians, both mute. Apparently, to be a sonogram technician you have to take an oath of silence or give one word answers to questions," Ali began. "I tried to watch more carefully this time, Mom, but everything looked about the same as last time. A screen full of dark and light shapes, the same pulsing, swishing sound and not a word out of those two mummies. I asked if there was a problem and one of them mumbled, 'the doctor will talk to you about the report'."

"Dr. Perez is the only one who can solve this mystery, Ali, so please try not to get too upset. That won't help anything." Karen, equally worried, patted her daughter's hand resting on the console between them.

Ali let out a deep breath. "I know, Mom. It's just so scary not knowing what's going on. Let's go home. I don't feel as if I want to do anything but curl up in a chair and wait. I wish I could just go to sleep and wake up in Dr. Perez's office."

***

The following forty-eight hours were stressful, strained and uncomfortable for both women. The temperature in the house was too cool and then too warm. Alice was hungry and then couldn't eat. Karen forced encouragement she didn't feel which left an empty hole in several conversations. Tempers were strained but not out of control.

Ali repeated the same questions endlessly and her mother did her best to calm her, but it was difficult and at times tension strained at every fiber in both of them. Neither slept well and both jumped every time the telephone rang. Any phone conversation, whether it was with Karen's friends or Ali's, was hurried. They were, after all, waiting for an important telephone call.

When the phone rang at nine o'clock on the third day, both women paled and then Karen whispered, "You take it." Ali shook her head vigorously and Karen reached for the phone on the kitchen counter.

"Hello," she said cautiously. "Oh, yes...that's fine...yes...Alice will be there." She ended the call and turned to Ali. "That was Dr. Perez's office. You have a one o'clock appointment today."

Ali rose from her chair into her mother's waiting arms. "Great, now maybe we'll know something."

"A light at the end of the tunnel? We will know soon, Ali. At least this is a step in the right direction."

In the moment of relief, the two women did a slow dance around the kitchen, Missy nipping at their feet and barking to the obvious merriment taking place.

"It has to be good news, honey. It just has to be."

"Oh, Mom, I hope so. Let's see," she said, looking at the kitchen clock. "Three and a half hours. I'm going to take a long shower," she said and headed down the hall.

Karen stood in the kitchen alone with her little dog, shaking her head. "Mood swings," she sighed and stooped to pick up a very confused but elated Missy. "It's been a tough couple of days, hasn't it?" Karen murmured to the little dog. "Just wait, it might get better. Let's hope," she said, opening the French doors. "Come on, we need a walk around the garden."

It was the first time in two days Karen felt like going outside. Poor Missy had just been pushed out the open door and let in when she barked.

***

Ali and Karen were ushered into Dr. Perez's office instead of an examination room. When the young lady from the front desk left them, Alice turned to her mother. "Is this a good sign or a bad sign?"

"What do you mean?" Karen said, sitting in one of the chairs facing the desk and urging Ali to take the one next to her.

"Well, it's in his office. "

"That probably means you don't have to be examined and he's just going to talk to you."

"I'm so glad you're here, Mom. I'm so scared I probably won't hear what he says."

Karen slid her arm around her daughter's shoulders. "Remember those chickens."

"Chickens?" Ali stuttered.

"The ones you don't count before they're hatched."

Dr. Perez entered the office, closed the door and put a folder he was carrying in the center of the slightly cluttered desk.

"Hello. What a beautiful day. Only wish I could be out there fishing."

"It is a beautiful day, Dr. Perez," Karen answered. "I love this weather."

"Me, too," he said, opening the folder. "Well, I'm sure you're anxious to hear the report. Sorry if I caused you any worry, but there was something in the first one that seemed to need another look." He removed a sheet of paper, then turned and slid what looked like an x-ray into the view box next to his desk.

"Is there something wrong, doctor?" Alice stuttered.

"No. I'm sorry if this second sonogram made you worry unnecessarily. The news is good," he said and watched the tension in his two visitors visibly melt.

Karen took Alice's icy hand in hers. "Good news," she whispered.

"But there is something that needs to be discussed," he continued and picked up the paper. "In the first sonogram there was something that was unclear as to the baby's heartbeat."

"Oh," Ali gasped.

Holding up one hand in a stop-traffic-mode, Dr. Perez said, "That is not uncommon. Sometimes there is a second heartbeat which is really just an echo. I told you it was good news. Still, we had to recheck." He smiled from one to the other. "It seems the unusual noise was a second heartbeat. You, Alice, my dear, are having twins."

"Twins!" both Karen and Ali exploded. "But..."

"Is there a history of twins in your family?" he asked Karen.

"No. None that I know of."

Dr. Perez turned his attention to Ali who was staring at him in disbelief. "Are there twins in your...the babies' father's family?"

Ali continued to stare dumbfounded.

"Ali, do you know if Morgan has twins in his family?"

"No," she whispered. "I don't know." She put both hands over her eyes. "How would I know?"

Karen looked at the doctor's puzzled expression. "The babies' father is not in the picture right now. We are hoping that changes. But for now..."

"Oh, I understand. I'm sorry, I don't have Alice's complete file with me. I should have looked earlier. I'm sorry, Alice. Of course, having twins in the family is not always necessary for a mother to have twins." He waited for the young girl to compose herself.

"Well, see, I said it was good news. If you'd like to see the sonogram film I can show you the two babies. Do you want to do that?"

Karen and Alice looked at each other, complete awe etched on their faces. Karen squeezed Ali's hand. "It's up to you, Ali."

"I think I do, doctor."

Doctor Perez switched on a light and the film became visible. "Let me tell you a little about twins first, okay? There are various types of twins, identical, fraternal, monozygotic and mono-amniotic for instance. I know, those last two words are like a foreign language to you. In your case, Alice, you are going to have identical twins. They are unusual in that they are identical and there is one boy and one girl. That doesn't happen often in mono-amniotic twins."

He heard the two synchronized gasps and smiled.

"In monozygotic twins," he continued, "also identical, they share the same placenta but have separate amniotic sacs. In mono-amniotic twins, they too, share the same placenta but they also share the same sac. That's what identifies them as identical twins. Any questions so far?"

Both women shook their heads slowly from side to side.

"I don't expect you to remember the gibberish I just told you. Just remember that as far as we can see, they are both doing fine for the stage of their gestation period. Now would you like to see your children, Alice? You too, Grandma?"

"Oh, yes, please," they chorused.

"I can't believe it," Ali said, sliding into the passenger seat.

"Neither can I, but it probably explains why you appear to be farther along in your pregnancy. I thought you had just gained too much weight but I watched what you ate and you seem to stick pretty close to the diet."

"He said I might deliver early."

"A lot of twins come early but by then the doctor and the hospital are well aware of your condition and everything will go smoothly. Are you worried about that?"

"Mom, I'm worried about everything right now. This is such a shock. Here I was wondering how I'm going to take care of a baby and work and... And now there are two of them."

"You know I'll always be here to help you. But, I know you're thinking of Morgan, aren't you?"

When Alice didn't answer, Karen glanced at her daughter. "Are you okay? Have I upset you?"

"No, you haven't upset me and yes, I'm thinking of Morgan. I'm thinking what an ass he is," she stammered.

"He doesn't know about the twins," Karen said, already slipping into the easy referral to her two grandchildren.

"He knew there was a baby. What difference does it make if there is one, two or more for that matter? He's the father."

Karen slowed to make the turn into the driveway. She pushed the button and watched the garage door inch its way up. "Do you want to try and get in touch with him? Don't you have a telephone number for his parents or where he might be working? They should know where he is." She switched the engine off. Both women stared through the windshield. "What do you think, honey?"

"I think he's a jerk and he doesn't deserve to know about his children. I think I don't want to talk to him now or ever."

Karen heard the tears in Ali's voice and her hand reached for her daughter. "I want to say I know how you feel, but I don't." She pulled her purse from behind her seat. "Let's go in and have a cup of tea and talk about this, okay?"

"I'd love the tea. But, I don't know if I want to talk about what you want to talk about, no offense, Mom."

Karen smiled. Sometimes her little girl acted just like a little girl and sometimes there was an adult quality about her daughter that moved her beyond belief. This was one of those times.

19

...saith the Lord of hosts, if I will not open you the windows of heaven, and pour you out a blessing, that there shall not be room enough to receive it.
Malachi 3:10

Karen stood in the kitchen and made another pitcher of iced tea. She listened to the laughter coming from the lanai. For the first time in too long, Ali was entertaining her friends, Kristi and Marla.

"Jocelyn will just die when she finds out she's missing some of this excitement, Ali," Marla said, reaching for a cookie. Marla never had a weight problem, a trait which was envied by every girl in the senior class at Gadara Consolidated High School. The envy traveled into their college years.

"She won't die and she's not missing out on everything," Ali said. "I've got months to go and she'll be home in three weeks."

"I know, but the real fun is being in on the beginning." Marla was not one to be crushed easily.

"Silly, we weren't in on the beginning," Kristi, the ever realistic one, said.

"Ooh, you're being bad, Kris," Marla said.

"I think we came into the picture just at the right time. Now we can plan showers and help Ali. It's going to be a blast."

Ali leaned back in her lounge chair, proudly displaying her distended tummy. Now the news was out, she was even more eager to show off her twin pregnancy. "I can't believe it. Twins. I keep saying that to myself over and over again."

"You're feeling okay, aren't you?" Marla munched on another cookie.

"Physically I'm doing great. It's...it's..."

"It's Morgan." Kristi twirled the ice cubes in her glass with the straw. "I can't understand him and I can't understand you either, Ali. If it were me I'd have a private detective scouring the state looking for him. He has to be here in Florida somewhere. Didn't you say he was going to Miami to work for some big-shot financial company? Wherever he is, he's the father and at the very least you should get help from him. Money for these kids who are *his*."

"He doesn't even know you're having twins," Marla added.

"Look," Ali said, struggling to get out of the chair, "He knew I was pregnant. He was so excited at the thought of a son, not that he didn't want a daughter. He said so. But whatever happened to turn him away from me and his baby has to be something he can't handle right now. He may change but I'm not going after him. Poor little me. I'm having two of your kids instead of one. What would that make me?"

"Smarter?" Kristi said.

"No. Needier, and I can't do that. Not now, anyhow. Mom is being just great. Dad is open-mouthed stunned but okay with everything. I think being a grandfather was kind of a shock, especially since he's having a kid of his own."

"No." Kristi and Marla shouted. "Get out! You didn't tell us that."

Ali shunned the lounge chair and sat in one of the more comfortable wicker ones. "That's right. He told us Sonoma was pregnant the night my Mom and Dad had a fight over who knows what. Imagine having a child of your own and a grandchild—well grandchildren—the same year. It's obscene."

"Well, that's his problem. And one of the good things about all this is you're still on his insurance." Kristi could always find a sensible factor in any situation.

"I know, and I have so much to be thankful for. You guys, Mom, Dad and a great doctor. You should see him. He looks like Enrique Iglesias and he says the babies are fine. There's only one problem...how am I going to do this alone?"

"But you aren't alone, stupid. You just said you have us, your parents and a drop-dead doctor who's only the best in the county, maybe Florida." Kristi moved behind Ali's chair and gave her a sit-down hug. "You jerk. You'll never be alone. We can't replace the moron you love but we can be here for you."

Marla joined the group and wept. "You're so brave, Ali and we love you," she whimpered.

"Great, just great. Here we are celebrating the twins and I've got you in tears. Get outta here. Let's go look at baby clothes." Ali stood and opened one of the French doors. "Mom," she called. "We're going to the Mall."

Karen put down her knitting and rushed to the lanai just as the girls were leaving. "Wait, Ali. Remember you shouldn't be walking too much or over-tiring yourself."

Ali turned back and smiled at her mother. "I know. If I get tired I'll sit on the bench like the old guys do. It's just to get out for a little while. We'll be back in an hour, okay?"

She stepped outside and joined her friends. "Geez, I can just see her fussing over me for the next..." she paused... "the next however long this takes."

"You should be so lucky. And you are," Kristi said, pushing Marla along the path to the driveway. "I'm driving," she said with authority.

Karen looked at her watch. Two thirty-seven. She mentally calculated one hour. "Ha. I'll be lucky if I see her before five o'clock," she sighed.

20

In quietness and in confidence shall be your strength.
Isaiah 30:15

Morgan leaned back. He'd had a busy morning and his last appointment was standing in the reception area waiting for the elevator. The digital clock on the corner of his desk read 2:38 and he knew he wasn't tired because of the work he'd done. No, he knew it was because he hadn't had much sleep last night. Not last night nor the night before nor the night before that. He was exhausted.

He swiveled his chair around so his back was to the huge window separating each of the associate's offices from the lobby. With his eyes closed his mind went back to the same thing. Over and over again he'd wondered about the fellow he'd met on the bus.

Why did he say he had an appointment at that building on the corner? Consumed with curiosity, the next morning Morgan walked across the street and up the short drive to the building. A sign on the door read 'Atlantic View Realtors' but a large red and white banner stretched across the window announced the building was for sale or rent. *He said his name was Jack, but never gave a last name. Why lie about a reason to be on that bus? Why that bus? And why did I feel as if I had to have dinner with him? As if it was important to be there with him at that time? Why did he keep saying 'Gadara'?*

A tap on the window startled him and he swung around. "Getting forty winks?" Dave asked, leaning on the open door.

"Wish I could. What's up?" Morgan pulled himself back to the present.

"You know you looked like the dog dragged you in this morning. What's wrong, buddy?"

"Not sleeping very well lately, I guess."

"So, then, what's up?"

"Nothing really," Morgan shrugged his shoulders. "I checked my calendar and I don't have any more appointments this afternoon. Think I could ask for a few hours off? Maybe that might help."

"It's so slow it's depressing. I don't think they'll miss you for a few hours. Why don't you knock off? I'll get Marie at the front desk to send any of your clients to me if they should wander in. It's Friday, get a head start on the weekend. I'll see you Monday," Dave said and gave his friend a smile and a two finger salute.

Morgan stood in front of the large window in his condo's living room. It had been advertised as a 'bay view' apartment but the only way you could see the bay was if you stood on your tip toes, face pressed against the glass and squinted between two two-story buildings across the street. His balcony was off the bedroom and overlooked the tennis courts behind the building. Still, it was a luxurious home compared to the dingy walk-up he'd shared for six-weeks with a drug-driven musician when he first moved to Miami as an intern. Three years ago, he mused.

He sighed and threw himself on the couch. Not accustomed to having extra time to himself confused him. He could go to the gym but he didn't feel like it. The thought of time on the beach didn't interest him either. "I'd be better off at work," he mumbled to himself. "At least I wouldn't be thinking about..." He bit his lower lip. *Ali, that's who's consuming my thoughts.* He glanced at the phone resting on the arm of the chair where he'd put it when he came home half an hour ago.

Reaching for the phone he pulled up the menu. His finger hit the phonebook. Ali's home number was five. His finger hovered over the five and then he pushed eight. He breathed deeply as he heard the phone ring in Carter's Corner.

"Hello," Cliff said.

"Hi, it's Morgan. Did I wake you?"

"Heck, no. I was just putting the groceries away. Millie left a list for me. She'll be home early today. Something about shutting down the office for some extra cleaning or something. How are you, kid?"

"I'm doing okay."

"Work okay?"

"Yep. Steady, especially in these times. Most of the people want to know if their investments are safe. I got a good review last month."

"Great. I knew you'd be okay once you got your feet on the ground."

There was a pause and the line between them crackled. "You still there?" Cliff asked.

"Oh, yeah. I was just thinking."

"Thinkin' about what? Have you been in touch with your girl yet?"

Morgan recognized the stern tone and remembered his last time with Cliff. It was funny how they'd known each other for just two days and yet a totally unexpected bond had formed between them, something completely out of the usual run of things, a closeness that was foreign to Morgan and yet welcome. He swallowed with difficulty.

"No. I haven't called Ali. Not yet."

"You waitin' for somethin' special to happen. Like the child being born and you not there?"

"It's not like that, Cliff. I want to call her. I just don't know what to say. I've left it too long. Now I'm afraid she won't want to hear from me."

"And how will you know all that? How will you know she don't want to hear from you or that she ain't waitin' to hear from you?"

"I don't. I try to think how I'd feel. Would I want to hear from someone who turned their back on me?"

"Well, that's a good sign. At least you're seein' what you did. Turned your back and ran. Left her on her own."

"It's the chance of another rejection, Cliff," Morgan said, finally putting his fears into words. "I always felt rejected by my...parents. Now as I look back I think that's why I was always wary about friendships. I guess I was kind of cold to offers by school friends. I know I was known as a 'loner'. But," he stopped and took in a deep breath. "When I met Ali it was different. I wasn't afraid to..."

Cliff waited. After several moments, he prompted, "You wasn't afraid of what?"

"I wasn't afraid to love her."

Neither man spoke and the silence deepened, stretching across miles and yet touching them as if they were in the same room.

"You thought she loved you, and you loved her, didn't you?"

"Oh, yes. I thought it was real. At last I felt as if I belonged."

"And then you found out about your adoption and that single thing wiped out all the love you had for her?"

"Not wiped it out. But it made me feel as if maybe it wasn't as sure as I thought. That maybe she was just going along for the fun. We did have fun together, we were always laughing about something."

"Do you still feel that way?"

"Honestly, Cliff, I don't know how I feel. All I know is that I miss her, and I feel guilty. God, guilty as hell!" he exploded.

"She might still love you as much as you thought. You know what? I think you need to talk to someone a whole lot smarter than me. Have you thought about goin' to one of those...whatever they're called?"

"A shrink?"

"Yeah, that's it. Might help."

"It might. Maybe I'll look into it. I have a friend at work, Dave, he might know of someone. I wouldn't have to tell Dave what the problem was."

"There you go. Get some help, son. And while you're at it, call Ali. She just might be needin' you as much as you need her."

"She has her family. Her mom and dad and her friends."

"But what she needs is you."

"How do I know that?"

"Well, son. You ain't never gonna know if you don't call or at least get help." He paused, "You know you could write her a letter if you're leery about callin' her. I'm not good at writin' things down but you must be, goin' to college and all."

Once again a line stretched between the two men, an invisible cord tying them together in a wonderful yet scary way.

Morgan shivered. "I'll call her, Cliff. And maybe Monday I'll look into getting some help."

"Good." Now Cliff's voice was the old cheerful, helpful voice he'd heard the morning after his binge at Carter's Corner.

"I'll never forget what you did for me, Cliff."

"Ah...you'd have done it if I'd needed help."

"Now I can say 'yes' to that, but back then... I don't know."

"Heard from your parents?"

"No. They don't know where I am. Well, they must know where I'm working—if they cared."

"That ain't right either and you know it."

"I'm not sure about that, Cliff. After last time...it's hard to even think about it."

"Listen, son, like I told you before. They took care of you, they gave you everything you needed and they loved you the best they could. Not everyone loves the same way, you know."

"I guess."

"Listen, why don't you come up for a visit? Me and Millie would love to have you. Come up for a weekend. Just let us know so we're sure to be here, not that we go anywhere much. But call first, anyhow. Okay?"

"I'd love to come. I'll call you soon."

"And call that little gal, son."

"I'll call her, Cliff. Good to talk to you. Call me soon, okay? I miss you."

Morgan ended his call and slumped into the chair. A smile tweaked the corners of his mouth as he recalled his time with this friend whom he knew for such a short time and who had become a mainstay in his life. He wondered how many times they'd talked on the telephone since that first meeting. But the smile dissolved and his lips formed a grim, hard line.

His fingers fiddled with the phone for several minutes. The quiet was comforting and yet eerie. Traffic noises were not like the early evening bustle on Biscayne Boulevard one block away. He held the phone up and pressed five. He straightened and sat stiffly as he listened to the phone ring in Gadara. He promised himself after four rings he was going to hang up. But after the third ring he heard Ali's mother's voice.

"Hello?"

Morgan's hand held the phone in a death grip.

"Hello?" Karen repeated.

"Um...aah...is Ali there?"

"No, she's out with friends. Who's calling? Can I have her return the call when she comes home?"

Morgan frowned. Did he want to leave his name? Why not? Why? His mind roiled. "Um...no. Thank you, but no. I'll call again."

Morgan hung up before Karen could speak. He tossed the phone on the couch as if he needed to disengage himself from the instrument that had joined him to a far off place he didn't want to think about. *Why didn't I leave a message? I wanted to hear Ali's voice but maybe her mother's was better. Still, I could have left a message.*

Standing quickly, he went to the kitchen and took a bottle of Scotch from a cabinet next to the refrigerator. He hadn't had a drink alone since...since that time before he met Cliff but he needed one now. Carefully, he poured the dark liquid into a juice glass. *What message would I have left?*

He dropped two ice cubes into the liquid and walked into his bedroom. Pulling the sliders aside he stepped out onto the balcony. Voices from the tennis courts blended with the traffic on the side streets. He sank into one of the chairs pulled up to the umbrella table. The balcony was small and sparsely furnished with a table with furled umbrella, four chairs and a folded aluminum lounge leaning against the wall. The umbrella and chairs were dotted with mildew. One potted plant, left by the former occupant, was slowly dying and Morgan had no interest in extending its life. He sipped his drink slowly, staring into the late afternoon sky devoid of clouds. He closed his eyes and saw Ali on the inside of their lids, her cheeks wet with tears, her hair falling forward as she pushed a box into the back of her car. He saw her driving away and his heart crumbled in his chest. How could he? *How could I just leave her? How could I not call her? Did she think of me?* He pushed his glass away and leaned forward, resting his head on his arms folded on the plastic table.

He knew what he should do but how could he make himself do it? "What a damned idiot you are," he mumbled.

He sighed and the sleep he'd missed suddenly engulf him, shutting out the worry, the fear and the loneliness he hadn't recognized had become such a controlling factor in his life. It was dark when he awoke.

***

In Gadara, Karen paced across the kitchen floor, stopping to straighten the tea towels on the counter, touching the baking dish ready to go into the oven for their dinner. She watched the second hand on the wall clock jerk its way on another trip around the face. *Where can Ali be? She said an hour. It's three hours now. I'll shake her when she gets here, putting me through all this worry.*

She heard the front door open. "Hi, Mom, I'm home. Sorry I didn't call. We went to the Mall and then decided to see a movie instead of shop."

Ali hurried to give her mother a hug. "Sorry. We had such a good time though. The movie was funny and I guess we all needed a laugh, at least I did." She pulled her mother to her chest, the baby bulge separating them.

"I could just shake you."

"You'd better not. I don't think shaking is a good thing right now. Should I go to bed without dinner?" Ali leaned back still enfolded in the hug, her smile begging for forgiveness.

"Oh, Ali. If you only knew how worried I was. But I'm glad you're home safe and had a good time. Did Kristi just drop you off at the door?"

"Yep. She said she didn't want to 'face your wrath', her words not mine."

Karen pushed Ali away with a laugh. "Let's not do this again, okay?"

"Okay. What's for dinner?" Ali turned to go down the hallway to her room. "Any calls?" she shouted over her shoulder.

Karen stopped in her tracks. Her worry had made her forget

about the phone call earlier. Had it been Morgan? Should she tell Ali? She pushed the baking dish into the oven.

"We're having soupy chicken and rice," she called, referring to the chicken and soup casserole, always a favorite with her daughter. She paused and added. "And someone called you but didn't leave a message."

Ali returned to the kitchen, her face flushed, her breathing irregular. She leaned against the wall, "Who?" she whispered.

"I don't know, honey. It was a man. He didn't leave a message, just said he'd call later."

"Was it Morgan?"

Karen twisted her hands in front of her. "I don't know. I'm not sure I'd recognize his voice. I didn't speak to him often. Not on the telephone."

"He said he'd call later?"

"I think that's what he said. Maybe he said he'd call again."

"Oh, Mom, it might have been Morgan. Why didn't you ask?" Ali's face was blotched with uncertainty. "Who could it be if it wasn't Morgan?"

Karen shrugged helplessly. "He hung up before I could ask."

Ali slid into the nearest chair. "What if it was Morgan? Maybe he's changed his mind. Maybe..." She bowed her head and rested them on folded arms. Her voice muffled, "Why did I have to go to that stupid movie?" She looked up at her mother. "What time did he call?"

Karen winced. She hadn't thought to look at her watch and then she was so concerned about Ali she'd almost forgotten the call until Ali asked. Feeling inadequate and helpless, she stuttered, "I don't know, honey. I didn't make a note of the time."

Dinner that night was very quiet; Ali pushed her food around the plate, eating little. Karen urged her to eat more, reminding her she was now eating for three. It brought no humor to the table.

The rest of the evening Karen knitted and Ali held a book on her lap unable to focus on the words, her phone within reach. There were no other telephone calls.

Later that night Karen's prayers included a fervent plea for some help in mending the broken fence between her pregnant daughter and the father of their children.

She leaned back against the pillows. It had taken her months to reach across the bed and tuck Bill's pillow behind hers but she admitted it made reading in bed easier. Her Bible still lay open across her lap and she randomly turned the pages stopping at Isaiah. She ran her finger down the page and when it stopped she smiled. *In quietness and in confidence shall be your strength. 30:15.*

"Right," she said softly and, at the foot of the bed, Missy lifted her head and peered at Karen, her ears perked, her moist eyes blinking quickly. "We'll be okay, Missy, because we can be quiet when we're confident. It's when everything is upside down that we get rattled. No, I feel confident. I think the call was from Morgan, and that means he's thinking about Ali."

She slid her Bible onto the nightstand, turned the light off and settled down under the sheet and light cover. "Thank you, Lord," she whispered.

21

*My soul waiteth for the Lord more than they
that watch for the morning.
Psalms 130:6*

The oppressive July heat kept Karen and Alice inside most of the time. Even the lanai with the air conditioner going full blast was too hot to enjoy unless it was very early morning or late evening.

Karen enjoyed the time with her daughter even though she had become almost unresponsive unless Karen instigated conversation. Ali jumped at every phone call, carrying her cell phone with her everywhere, even resting it on the counter in the bathroom when she showered. But there were no more telephone calls. Karen also recognized the reddened eyes when Ali had been crying alone in her room. It made her heart ache.

Ali's friends visited her often and Karen was so pleased when she heard laughter coming from the bedroom.

This afternoon she put her knitting aside and walked down the hallway to Ali's room. The door was ajar but she still knocked.

"Come on in, Mom. This isn't a secret society meeting," Ali called. Karen smiled. Did she detect a bit of humor?

"I thought you gals might like iced raspberry tea and some cookies. I baked yesterday and made the tea a few minutes ago."

"Oh, yes, please," Marla said. She and Kristi were sitting on chairs, their unshod feet stretched across to Ali's bed. Ali was propped up with extra pillows and had a pillow under her knees. It seems this position was the most comfortable right now.

"How about you, Kristi?"

"Can I have fake sugar?"

"Sure. I didn't add any sugar when I made the tea, just in case," Karen winked. "How about you, honey?"

"I'd love it. Peanut butter or chocolate chip cookies?"

"Both. Everyone want fake sugar?"

"Yes, please," Marla and Ali said in unison.

Later that day, after her friends had left, Ali came and sat with her mother in the living room. "Still knitting?" she said, sliding into the recliner.

"Still knitting. I'm making light blankets because even though the twins will be born in September, it's cool wherever you go and we keep the house cool."

Ali laughed. "If they were going to be born in the Sahara Desert you'd be knitting blankets. And, wooly things to wear, too."

"Oh, I've got lots of patterns for knitted suits and sweaters and caps for winter time. You know how cool it gets in December and January, even here."

"Cool is relative, Mom. It gets a bit cooler here, in Maine and Minnesota it gets real cool...like cold."

The click, click of Karen's needles was a comforting sound and both women were quiet for several minutes.

"You know, Ali, we're going to have to make some plans. Those people who came to look at the house last week were very interested. The agent called earlier this morning and said they'd like another look. That might mean a sale is imminent."

Ali stared out the window. "It will be strange to live in another house," she said.

"I know, but I think it will be for the best. Why don't we go and look at those condos your father suggested. We can at least look."

"When?"

"Whenever you feel up to it."

Ali glanced at the clock on the mantle. "Why not go now?"

Karen put her knitting in her lap and stared at Ali. "You mean that?"

"Sure," Ali said, pushing herself out of the chair with some effort. "Why not?"

"Well, I was afraid you might resist."

"By resist, you mean fight and cry and cause a scene? No, Mom, I'm beginning to think, too. Just because I want that fairy tale to come true I don't think it will. Morgan might have moved on and so should I. I have you and Daddy and my friends. You've been super, Mom. I'm so sorry if I've seemed unappreciative. I know you're worried about me and other things. Why should I make it more difficult for you? Kristi said it was time I wasn't a baby, there wasn't room in this body for any more babies." She laughed softly. "No, let's go and look. We don't have to make a decision right away but it might be fun to see what's available."

"Which one did you like best?" Ali asked as they drove home.

"I'm not sure. How about you?"

"You're not going to trick me like that. I'll be happy wherever you are and they all looked comfortable. I think the area is a lot nicer than I thought. There's a lot of room between the units and the landscaping is nice. I can just see me pushing the stroller along those shaded sidewalks."

Karen laughed out loud. "You are changing, and for the better. Well, you asked so I think the third one was the nicest. It had a really nice view from the deck and the rooms were fairly big. We're going to have to have three bedrooms and the first two offered three bedrooms but one was more like a little den. With twins you're going to have two of everything you know."

"I do know and that's scary. This is going to be expensive, Mom, and I'm not going to be able to contribute much for a couple of years."

Karen looked at her daughter who was staring out the side window. "Honey, your father and I know that and we are both willing and able to take care of those expenses. We don't want you worrying about money. Even though he's bemoaning his financial state, as he calls it, we'll be okay."

"Last week when I saw him he said he definitely is being transferred. He just doesn't know where. He thinks it might be Omaha. What if he gets transferred before the babies are born?"

"Then we'll call him and tell him he's a Grandpa."

"He already knows that. I mean will he be able to be here?"

Karen grimaced. She was still uncomfortable talking about Bill and yet knew he'd always be Ali's father. She sighed. "If he can't be here in person he'll be here in spirit, honey, and I'm sure he'll fly home when he can. Why don't we just put those thoughts on hold? After all, he hasn't been transferred yet. Who knows what will happen."

But, as they turned onto their street they saw Bill's car in the driveway. "Oh, boy, speak of the devil," Ali said. "Dad's waiting for us."

22

So that we ourselves glory in you in the churches of God for your patience and faith in all your persecutions and tribulations that ye endure.
2 Thessalonians 1:4

A.J. Handley knew something was wrong; he just didn't want to admit it. The constant band of steel wrapping his chest tightened every once in a while and wasn't natural. *No use worrying about it*, he thought, *who'd really care?* He dropped down onto his favorite rocking chair on the veranda and stared into the past.

Once the house rang with voices, his mother's and grandmother's were the ones he remembered the most. Maybe because as a child he spent so much time with them. His father was off early in the morning and home late in the evening. A.J. remembered him cleaning up in the shed, running water into the old zinc laundry tub before coming into the kitchen, scrubbing the dust from the fields or groves off his muscular arms.

A.J. recalled envying those arms that always seemed to be strong enough to do whatever job was called for. "You study, son. I've done the field work for you and your brother," his dad had said. "Studyin' is a whole lot better than chippin' away at those never ending dang weeds. They'd be chokin' the groves to death if me and the hands didn't chop at them regular. Them books is what'll take you away from the field work, not that it's somethin' I regret. No, your granddad taught me well and he worked even harder than I do. One thing, son, you come from strong stock. It's a right shame there ain't more of us left but you never forget where you come from."

Memories of his granddad were dim, only vestiges of stories told by others. He'd died before A.J. was born. *It was Grandma and Mama who had the most influence on me. And Aunt Felicity. She was really the one who took the time to encourage me, who wanted me to become a teacher.* A.J. shook his head and watched a flock of starlings suddenly take off and circle the trees on the other side of the road. He sighed loudly. Why was he constantly thinking of his aunt when she was such a shadow in the family history? Going off to school when women didn't do that often, he remembered. Then coming home without warning, the huddled conversations between his mother, grandmother and aunt. Aunt Felicity rarely left the house after that, crocheting or reading hour after hour. "Don't ever underestimate the value of books, A.J.," she'd said over and over again. The happiest he remembered his aunt being was when he graduated from college and took a teaching post right here in Gadara. "You're smart, A.J., not to go off to some strange place. Stay near home, it's safer."

"Why did she think Gadara was safe and other places weren't?" he mumbled, watching a car go by much too fast. The dust on the roadway curled after the car like a comet's tail.

The air was thick with humidity this early in the morning and A.J. tried to take in a deep breath but his lungs just wouldn't expand. Struggling out of the rocker, A.J. stood, resting a moment to catch his breath. Maybe he needed a change of scene. Maybe a trip into town to have lunch at the Dilly Dally would lighten his mood. *More like brunch, but someone will be there to talk to.* He looked at his watch and then shuffled into the house. *Got to check to see if the coffee pot is unplugged.* He laughed softly.

"Unplugged. Used to have to make sure it was off the burner," he said, his words sounding hollow in the kitchen, once such a hub of activity. He looked around the room as if he needed to take inventory. It was so bare now, the counters were empty, gone were the things women needed like bowls, pitchers and canisters. Even the curtains had disappeared years ago. The freezer held microwave dinners and there was milk, eggs, a piece of cheese that needed to be eaten soon and some questionable leftovers in the refrigerator. He stood for a minute and a picture of the old ice-house came into his mind.

"Daydreaming of those times won't bring them back," he said, pulling the front door closed behind him. He couldn't remember the last time he'd locked the door. "Not that I want those old times. No one to share them with except maybe Sarah Jane." He started his car and backed slowly out the unpaved driveway.

***

Jack leaned back against the bench. It was his favorite place to be when he wasn't anywhere in particular and this morning, after breakfast with Sarah Jane, who'd taken to sharing her breakfast with her only guest, he'd tried to make plans for the rest of the day. It wasn't to be, though, and he reminded himself what he did wasn't governed by him any longer. It was a strange feeling.

He remembered draining his coffee and standing. "Going out?" Sarah Jane asked.

"For a while," he'd answered.

"Have a nice day." Summer wasn't the time for guests and Sarah Jane had come to enjoy Jack's company. The rumor and speculation about his stay at Twin Oaks had died down somewhat. No one could figure him out but no one objected to his stay. He was just an enigma and they finally accepted that. She watched him stroll down the sidewalk toward the library.

They often talked about history and times gone by, she from memory and he from his studies. History of any kind had always fascinated him and it was nice to have someone to share this love with. Jennifer hadn't been interested in history; she was always too caught up in today. He grimaced at the thought of Jennifer but then those thoughts flitted away.

He'd wandered around the circle, dropped into the library, but nothing seemed the right place to be so he came to the park. He'd almost become accustomed to the spaces of time that disappeared periodically. He was alone as far as he could see. "Too hot for mothers and kids this morning," he said, his voice drifting off into the muggy air.

"Aren't you glad the heat doesn't bother you anymore?"

Samuel appeared next to Jack.

"I still wish you'd clear your throat or something when you just pop up next to me. Where have you been?"

"Watching you."

"That must be a boring assignment. I meant to ask you, are you coaching another dead guy while you're with me?"

"Heavens, no. You are my only charge at the moment."

"You know, I think I've worked out part of the problems here. That pregnant girl and the stubborn young man in Miami are connected, aren't they? I just can't figure out how the old guy is in the picture."

"Patience and faith, remember? You'll know when you need to."

Jack sighed. He wondered if he was visible or not, but then with no one around what did it matter? "So what's on the menu for today?" he asked.

"You might want to check out the café and this park later on."

"Nothing specific, huh? Okay, if that's what you suggest. Always glad to get some input." But as he said those words, Samuel was again gone. Jack thought he caught just a hint of giggle fading in the air.

***

Karen stood with her hands on her hips staring into the huge pantry. It served not only as a pantry but as a catch all for everything without a specific home. "It will take a week to sort this all out," she mumbled.

It was still early and Ali hadn't gotten up yet. Karen enjoyed the quiet times early in the morning, she always had. Already she and Missy had walked around the garden, her shoes and the little dogs feet wet with dew. She'd put fresh food and water in Missy's dishes and then had a cup of coffee. On a page of tablet paper always kept in a kitchen drawer, Karen made a list of things to be done before they moved.

She paused. The thought of moving, of picking out what to take and what to leave or sell had settled slowly onto her shoulders. When Bill had dropped his double edged sword on her, she'd felt numb with disbelief. Not that she hadn't anticipated either move, but not both at once and not both so urgent. There was a contract on the house. And Bill's transfer had been handed to him yesterday afternoon. He and Sonoma were moving to Omaha. They'd already arranged for a moving company to pack up their furniture and belongings. Arrangements had been made through the company for Bill's transfer and for a small home in a suburb of Omaha. For them it all seemed so simple, but for Karen it seemed an impossible burden.

Her list was as disorganized as her mind. "Measure things at the new condo, call a moving company, purchase furniture and whatever else was needed for the twins, (do this now or after we move?), schedule a garage sale? Call the minister, see if Shirley and Martin will help... Karen knew they would. Lifelong friends, Shirley and Martin Owens had been part of Karen and Bill's social life; they'd only drifted apart because, after her divorce, Karen wasn't as social as she was when Bill was in the picture. She put her pen down and refilled her coffee cup. Staring out the window over the sink, Karen was lost in thought.

"What are you doing up so early?" Ali stood in the kitchen, her feet bare, her shorty pajamas failing to cover her bare tummy. Karen realized she hadn't even heard her come in.

"I've been up for hours, and you need bigger pjs," Karen said. "What would you like for breakfast?"

"That junky weed tea and some cereal, I guess." Ali sat in one of the chairs around a small table.

"Junky weed tea? You, of course, mean the lovely herb tea Kristi gave you. It's mentioned in the book you got from Dr. Perez."

"It's awful. All I can say about that stuff is it's hot." Ali made a face.

"She meant well. After you discussed your diet with your friends they're just trying to help you get adjusted to it. Remember, they even had this 'junky weed tea' with you the other afternoon?"

"Martyrs," Ali mumbled, getting a package of cereal from the cupboard. "Why is the door to the pantry open?"

"I was trying to figure out what to keep and what to get rid of, but first I have to find out just what's in there. It's been years since it was really sorted out."

"I'll help you after breakfast."

"No, you won't. You can't be lifting and hauling things."

"Well, I've got to help somehow if we're to be out of here in time for the new owners to move in. They probably won't want you puttering around in their pantry."

"Well, you won't help with sorting and packing." Karen put the kettle on.

"Kristi and Marla will help; they said so when I called them. Jocelyn might be home soon. She'd help too if she were here."

Karen sat across the table from her daughter. She smiled at the disheveled hair and the one shoulder strap slipping down Ali's arm as she poured milk over her cereal. "I'm sure your friends will help you, honey. I'll be relieved if they can just help you with your room. There's a houseful of stuff in there. I'm afraid we might not be able to take everything but I've had an idea. Why don't we get one of those storage units and put anything you'd like to hold on to in there."

"We can put your stuff in there, too, Mom. That's a great idea. Is it on your list?" Ali asked, pulling Karen's list closer to her.

"No," Karen said, retrieving the notebook. "But it's going on there right now. And I won't need any storage space. I'll just take what I can use for our new home. Oh, Ali," she said, fighting tears. "This is such a mess. I'm such a mess. Why did everything have to happen at once?"

Ali rose and went to her mother, leaned down and hugged her. "We knew this was coming, Mom. That's why we went to look at condos. Isn't it a good thing we did? Now we at least know where we'll be going. I'm sure that guy in the sales office yesterday was in seventh heaven to have a purchasing customer in these times so you probably got a good deal. Dad said so last night. And," she added, "you said it would be best for both of us."

She leaned down and kissed her mother's cheek. "I'm not sure what I'll need. Stuff for the babies, but my stuff...? When you don't know what's ahead, it's kind of hard to plan. A box full of stuffed animals doesn't seem like much to worry over."

For over a week Karen had watched Ali go from deep depression over the mystery phone call to excitement about her babies. "What if he never calls again? Should I try and find him to tell him about the twins?" she'd mused aloud. Then with her girlfriends it was, "I can't wait to decorate the nursery. You should see their room, plenty of space for cribs and all that stuff. Maybe we can go to the Mall to pick out some baby clothes, Oh, God, I don't even know what I need."

Kristi and Marla had spoken to Karen secretly about having a baby shower. "We should wait for Jocelyn to get home. I think she said she'd be home next week. Oh, Mrs. Waterson, this is going to be so neat. Can we have it here? Your house is bigger." Of course all that was before the sudden sale, move and general upset came on the scene.

Karen looked at her list and then added 'call about a storage unit; talk to girls about the shower— later?' She flipped the tablet closed and tucked it into her pocket.

"What did you write?" Ali asked.

"A reminder to call about the storage unit," Karen said, standing. "I'm going to look up some telephone numbers. Moaning about how upsetting everything is isn't going to help. I don't know why I let myself get into these negative moods. It's not like me. In fact I feel very much in control this morning. Here's your tea. Drink it while it's still warm, it's better that way."

"Nothing would make this stuff better," Ali grumbled, hoping her mother would leave the room quickly so she could pour it down the sink.

That afternoon Ali called Kristi and Marla. Karen overheard her say, "I'm going to take a nap so let's not get together this afternoon, okay?...no, nothing's wrong I'm just tired...I'll call you later. Maybe we can go to a movie tonight...Okay. Yes, I'm okay."

Karen, pretending she hadn't heard the call, poked her head into Ali's room. "I'm going to the library and then I'll probably sit in the park for a while. You and the girls will be okay here while

I'm gone. Don't get overtired, honey."

She was turning to leave when Ali said, "I just called them. They're not coming over."

"Oh," Karen said, feigning ignorance. "Why not?"

"No reason. I think I'll take a nap."

Karen re-entered the room. "You feel all right?"

"Sure, just a bit tired. I didn't sleep real good last night. And watching you mess around with all that stuff in the pantry made me tired," she joked.

"Well, if you're sure you don't need me, I'll go. I won't be too long and you have my cell phone number if you need me." She leaned down and kissed Ali's cheek. "Put the television on, that always makes me sleepy."

23

And we know that all things work together for good to them that love God, to them who are the called according to his purposes.
Romans 8:28

"He's still with you?" Mildred asked, dealing the cards.

"Yes, he's still here and one of the nicest guests I've ever had. No trouble at all. I just put clean sheets on the bed once a week. I cleared that with him right away. No need to change sheets every day and I swear sometimes it doesn't look as if he's slept a night in that bed. I check the towels and they never really look used but I change them anyway. He's the neatest man I've ever had stay here and always so polite. Eats anything I fix for breakfast and then goes about his business. He's a good guest," Sarah Jane said with a nod of her head.

"Are you going to bid or pass?" Emily asked, drumming her fingers on the card table set up in the parlor of Twin Oaks for their weekly pinochle game.

"Sixteen," Sarah Jane said.

"You got it," Mildred said with a sigh of relief.

"Hearts are trump," Sarah Jane said, putting her meld on the card table.

"I just don't understand why he's here and what his business is," Mildred continued with a frown. She placed her ace of hearts on Sarah Jane's ace of spades and scooped up the trick.

"I see him all around town. Seems to me he never changes clothes, always those tan slacks and striped tee shirt. Does he do laundry?"

Mildred played the king of diamonds. "I've only ever seen him in jeans and a black tee shirt."

"That's my trick, hearts are trump," Sarah Jane said with authority, pulling the four cards to her side of the table. "I don't know if he does laundry. Do I keep a calendar of events for him? He's here and he's no trouble."

"Still, I thought it was a week or two. It's been over a month now. Must be almost two months." Mildred puzzled over which card to play while Betty drummed her fingers again.

"Well, I wish he'd go because then maybe we could get a hand done before dark settles in." Betty tossed the queen of hearts on the last trick and triumphantly called, "That's going to set you."

As tradition would have it after the last hand had been played and the four dollars doled out to the winner, Sarah Jane brought the refreshments in on a large tray.

"Iced lemonade and pumpkin cheese swirls. Got the recipe from a *Kraft* magazine I saw in Doctor Phillips' office. They're good, I tasted one after they cooled a bit.

"I'll just try one," Emily said, always diet conscious and yet never losing any weight anyone could see.

"Umm, they are good," Betty said, licking her lips.

The sound of the front screen door closing made the foursome look to the hallway.

"Oh, Jack. Come on in and have some lemonade and cookies. All home made," Sarah Jane said standing.

"Thanks, Sarah Jane, but I don't want to disturb your card game."

"Game's all over, winner has been paid, and we're just relaxing. Cookies are good, but then everything Sarah Jane bakes is good. Come on in and join us," said Betty.

Jack stood in the hallway, uncertain as to what to do. "Thanks, I'll have a cookie and then be on my way." He sat in the wing chair facing the card table which was still set up in the middle of the room. "This is a lovely room," he said, taking a cookie offered by Sarah Jane. "I never realized how nice it is in here. I just walk past every day and don't pay attention."

"A lot of the furniture and the pictures came from my grandma's house. My grandma on my mama's side," she added. "A lot of the things in this house, though, belonged to my daddy's mother. It's my daddy's family home, really."

"It's peaceful," Jack said, struggling for conversation. "This is really good," he added, popping another of the pumpkin cheese swirls in his mouth and rising. "Thanks for inviting me in."

"Oh, don't go yet. You just got here. Have some lemonade. Have another cookie," Emily said.

"Yes, please stay. The ladies would love the company," Sarah Jane said, her eyes flashing at Mildred.

"Thanks, but I have some reading to do," Jack said, moving toward the hallway. "Book's upstairs," he added and fled around the corner and out of sight.

The women listened to his footsteps as he climbed the stairs. The one next to the top squeaked and Sarah Jane let out a soft sigh. "He doesn't seem to like crowds," she said.

"Four old women around a card table isn't a crowd," Mildred said, taking another cookie. "I wish he'd stayed. We could have asked him about what he's doing here. Maybe get a clue as to who he really is. I, for one, don't even think his name is Jack whatever he said."

"I suppose that's just why he left, Mildred. He doesn't like questions. Why don't you just drop it? He's a nice man who isn't hurting anyone."

"Yet, but we don't know enough about him to judge, do we?" Mildred said, getting in the final word.

24

Blessed is he whose transgression is forgiven,
whose sin is covered.
Psalms 32.1

In Gettersburo, Florida, at the home of Winslow and Eleanor Muldorn, Morgan's parents stared at each other and the box which rested on the table between them. Seated in the library at a small table where Eleanor did jig-saw puzzles, they were overcome with indecision.

"I wish I'd never found it. I'd forgotten all about it," Eleanor said, a definite tremor in her voice. "In fact, I didn't remember ever seeing it before until I found it."

"That's not the problem. Do we give it to him or not?"

"What would be gained by giving it to him?"

"Perhaps some peace of mind for the boy."

Again they remained silent, giving in to their thoughts.

Boy, Eleanor thought. *I never could call him son. I always introduced him as 'our boy'. I hated Mother's Day when he'd bring home those hand-drawn cards. Happy Mother's Day. It was all a lie. A mistake from the first week. I loved him as a person...but not as a son. I wasn't a mother. I never wanted to be one. Oh, I thought I did but that was short-lived. No, it was all a sham and I'm just as guilty as Winslow, but there is no forgiveness.* She stood and walked to the French doors leading out to the flagstone terrace at the side of the huge home. *Perhaps forgiveness is the wrong word. There is no justice in being sorry. No peace.*

She turned back to her husband, "Send it to him," she said.

He stretched his neck and looked at the ceiling as if to find a response. There was none. Winslow took the box in his hands. It was wooden, with a small handle on the top and a lock and key at one side. He replaced the box on the table, stood and went to his wife.

"I know you are upset at finding the box. I truly didn't remember receiving it when they brought Morgan to the house. His mother must have put it in that large cardboard box with some clothing for the babe. You didn't want the clothing so everything was put in the attic. It's strange we never looked into it until this morning. Why did you go up there?"

"I thought I might have saved some old clothing, turn of the century things belonging to my mother and aunts. The local little theater is looking for things like that. Oh, Winslow," she said, tears unexpectedly filling her eyes. "Did we do such a terrible thing?"

Her husband of some forty years pulled her slim body to his. "We tried to do our best, Elly," a name he hadn't called her in ages. "Our first thoughts were good, it was when we realized the responsibility, a strange responsibility we weren't ready or equipped for, became a reality... Morgan had the best nannies, the best schools, the best of everything, and you and I tried to make his childhood and life as...," he searched for the elusive word that would complete his sentence. "...as pleasant and comfortable as we could. We were wrong to keep the truth from him. Now perhaps there is something in this wooden box to help him. I'll send it off tomorrow."

Eleanor pulled away. It was strange but somehow comforting being held by her husband. Hugging and kissing had ceased so many years ago it made her knees weak just to think of it. "Where will you send it? We don't know where he is."

"I'll send it to him in care of the firm in Miami where he worked for three summers. I know he had an offer of a job following graduation. I expect he is there. If not, they will return it and we will have done our best."

He picked up the box and left the library to go to his small den which served as his retreat from things annoying and which also held his neat and highly polished desk, a relic from his own father. As he walked down the hallway he remembered his father, a distant lonely widower who walked as if his trousers were starched. *Dear God, have I become my father? Was I that kind of father to Morgan?* He sighed, entered the room and sat at his desk.

***

In Gadara, Karen left the library with two books in her cloth carry bag. She turned and walked up the sidewalk along Riverview Drive. The park was just two blocks away and even though the temperature must have been in the high 80s, she enjoyed the walk. Huge banyan trees shaded the sidewalk. At the park she took the first path and hoped her favorite bench was unoccupied.

As she wound her way along the narrow path through the slim young pines and came to the open grassy slope to the river, she was pleased to see *her* bench was empty and she hurried to it and sat down.

Putting her purse and bag next to her, she opened one of the books. She read the back cover and then the acknowledgements first. She smiled. Ali always made fun of her beginning her books with this unbreakable routine. But, she contended, looking to see who the author gave credit to was part of the story. It was who he or she had relied on for help and assistance and she felt it gave another insight into the enjoyment of reading what the author had written.

She was unaware of anyone standing close to her until he cleared his throat and stepped from the trees to the pathway.

"Oh, you startled me," Karen said, recognizing the nice man who was staying at Twin Oaks.

"Sorry I didn't mean to. I've been wandering among the trees. Shady back there," Jack said, moving closer to the bench. He looked at her purse and bag and she reached to move them closer to her.

"Sit, please. I shouldn't have taken up the whole bench. There's plenty of room."

She shifted a trifle nearer the edge of the bench. "Hot, isn't it?"

"I don't seem to mind the heat."

"Neither do I, really. I don't garden in August in the middle of the day. Maybe early in the morning. I used to be an early riser, but lately I've been sleeping later." Karen wondered why her sleeping habits seemed to be so easy to share with this stranger.

He settled on the bench and stretched his arms high above his head. "I've been reading more about Gadara and its history. Very interesting. I saw you in the library, by the way."

Karen shut her book on her finger. *Was he telling me he was watching me? Was he watching me?* She looked cautiously at her visitor. His profile was pleasant, his beard neatly trimmed. He was staring at the river in the distance. Behind her, birds called in the shade. Voices from the play area were dimmed by distance and yet they were alone. *Am I being foolish? What do I know about him? He told me he was a history professor at Miami U. He's interested in history. Oh, you fool. What are you worried about? He's a nice young man and certainly not interested in you.*

Karen looked at her watch, she didn't want to leave Ali alone for long, but then again she could call if she needed her. She felt the knot at the base of her neck soften.

"Yes, I was in the library. I didn't see you, though."

"I was in the reference department."

"Oh, yes, looking up more Gadara history."

"There's quite a bit, but I understand there's more in the hands of the Historical Society. I just don't know who to contact. I suppose Sarah Jane could tell me," he said, a small chuckle accompanying his words.

"I'm sure she could. And A.J Handley surely could help you. Are you working on a study?"

"Not really. Just killing time."

Karen, her book still closed, stared at the flowing river waters. She remembered her grandmother telling her that sitting by moving water helped remove all worries. She laughed softly. "Are you waiting for something...or someone?"

Jack turned to look at her, a puzzled frown wrinkling his brow. "Waiting for someone or something? No, why did you ask?"

"You said you were killing time."

He nodded and smiled. "Of course. No, not really. I have no place to go right now and when I arrived at Gadara I loved it so I just wanted to stay as long as possible. I won't be here forever, of course."

Karen smiled. "Of course not, you'll be going back to school next month anyhow, won't you." It was a given not a question. She sighed. "My daughter would have been a senior this year but she's not going back. Not now, anyhow."

"Why isn't she going back? Or maybe I shouldn't be so nosy," Jack said, wondering if he needed help here. He looked around, but Samuel was nowhere to be seen.

"She's pregnant," Karen said simply.

Jack thought for a moment and then said, "Your daughter is Alice?"

"Yes. How did you know?"

"I met her one day when we were both at the high school."

"I didn't know she went there. Why...?"

"Oh, I expect when we want to think things through, difficult things, we go back to somewhere safe. A place with good memories."

Karen stared straight ahead. What was it about this man that evoked such a feeling of calm? Briefly, she wondered what he and Ali had discussed, if anything. She turned to him with a smile. "I'm glad you met my daughter. She's a wonderful young woman and she has some tough times ahead of her, I suspect."

"Ah, but she'll have you."

"Yes. And our prayers. I truly believe God will see us through anything we need to handle."

The quiet was so comforting. It seemed to Karen as if she and Jack were enclosed in a serene sphere, untouched by the world for just a moment. "Do you believe in God, Jack? Is that a rude question?"

Jack pondered for only a moment and then said, "I do believe in God. Maybe I haven't always but I think the notion, the realization He exists has been hidden by our modern need to think we can fix everything by ourselves."

"Yes," Karen agreed. "We get busy and then all of a sudden we're middle-aged, divorced, have an ex-husband starting a family with another woman and have a daughter with no husband having twins. And by the way, we're told we have to move, too." She gave a little laugh.

"Twins?" Jack asked. "She didn't mention twins when I spoke with her."

Karen looked at her companion on the bench, trying to decide if she should be annoyed that her daughter had confided in him, a complete stranger.

He must have read the newly guarded expression on her face, for he said, "I apologize if I've been rude. I didn't mean to imply I'm anything but what I am, a history professor. I only listened to Alice because she seemed to need to talk. I'm happy I discovered Gadara, but I don't want to intrude on your or Alice's life"

Karen stood suddenly and gathered her bag and purse, pushing the virtually unopened book into the bag. "No apology is necessary. I'm sure almost everyone in Gadara knows Ali is pregnant...and her young man has chosen to leave the scene for now. We're sure he'll come to his senses. By the way, I'm not sure if everyone knows she's having twins yet. She's being very careful but I think I should go home now. She's alone for the afternoon."

She held out her hand to shake his, unsure of why she suddenly felt the need to perform this formality. "Have a nice day," she said, gripping his cool hand. She briefly wondered why his hand should be so cool but dismissed the thought as inconsequential.

"I'll walk you to the street. I'm going myself." Jack fell into step with Karen on the narrow path, their elbows touching sometimes as they strode along.

"You don't have to do this, you know," Karen said.

"I know. I was going anyhow. I sure hope you aren't hurt by our conversation."

Karen slowed and Jack kept pace with her. "I'm not hurt one bit. We're thrilled that Ali is pregnant and with the news about the twins. Maybe I should apologize for over-reacting."

Jack laughed aloud. "I think that's enough apologizing for one day, don't you?"

Karen laughed in response. He was a pleasant person.

They walked to the library parking lot, Karen turning in, Jack remaining on the sidewalk. Once inside her car, Karen pulled out of the parking lot and turned left. She waved to Jack as he stood on the crosswalk.

He watched her car until it was out of sight. "Nice lady," he said to himself.

Very nice, Samuel said. *She's got a lot on her mind, some of which you're going to ease.*

"Now you show up, you little pain-in-the-neck. Where were you when I needed you? I was flopping around like a fish out of water back there."

You did okay. Patience and faith, Samuel said, sliding into obscurity again.

Jack walked up the street to Twin Oaks. *Now what?* he thought. *I've got to either think of something to do or disappear. Sam, are you still here? Can you make me invisible until bed time? Then all I have to do tomorrow morning is invent a place where I had dinner tonight for Sarah Jane.*

If anyone was walking on the other side of the street they apparently didn't notice the young man with a beard suddenly disappear from the opposite sidewalk.

***

Winslow Muldorn licked the envelope and placed it in the mailing carton on top of the wooden box inside. He knew the box contained several letters and a small, tattered blue ribbon inscribed First Place, Sawgrass Festival. He had not read the letters and only noted that the jewelry, which rattled against the side of the box when it was tipped, appeared to be of little value.

He stood for several minutes staring out the window overlooking the terrace. Convinced this was the proper thing to do, he turned and sealed the carton. Tomorrow he would take it to the post office. He glanced at the label addressed to *Morgan Muldorn, c/o Littman & Littman* one last time.

His letter to Morgan ran through his head and he recalled

the words he'd penned to his son.

> *Dear Morgan, Your mother and I found this little box in the attic when she was looking for some clothing to donate to the local theatre group. We have not examined the contents but thought they might be of value to you. Apparently the box was inadvertently stored in the attic around the time...*

Here Winslow paused, recalling his search for the correct word. Did he say 'we acquired you' or 'you came to us' or 'we adopted you'? He puzzled for quite a long time before choosing.

> *...we adopted you. We trust you are doing well in your chosen career and wish you much success in all your endeavors.*

Winslow had another pause when he searched for the proper signature. Finally he chose:

> *Fondly, Father.*

***

In Carter's Corners, Cliff and Millie were sitting in the screened room. "Too buggy tonight to sit outside," Cliff said, turning the glass of iced tea in his hands.

"They been stirrin' up the fields behind us, that's why there's so many bugs out there. That's why we have this room, Cliffie."

The sound of the night animals and insects hummed against the silence of the evening. Comfortable in their companionable stillness, Cliff and his wife sat side by side in matching chairs.

"You know," Cliff said, "I been thinkin' about Morgan."

"You think about him all the time. Did you call him today?"

"No, but I been thinkin' about him ever since that last call. He still can't find the courage to call that poor girl."

"You don't know 'that poor girl' isn't doin' just fine without him."

"You don't mean that, Millie. She's pregnant with his child. It's his duty to call her."

"You're right, but you can't do anything about it, honey. We just have to keep prayin' he'll make the right decision. It's kinda outta our hands."

"Just the same, I think I'll call him tomorrow."

She reached across the small space and took his hand. It was wet and cold from holding the glass. "Need more tea?"

"No, thanks. All I ever need is you, Millie. I thank God three times a day for you."

"Three times?" she laughed.

"Every time I eat and before I go to sleep. See, that's four times."

Their hands remained entwined until it was time to go in for the night.

***

In Miami, Morgan sat out on his balcony. The night breeze kept the temperature down and the bugs away, not that there were many because of the pest control procedures to keep Miami bug-free. The city fathers didn't want the tourists annoyed by insects as they walked the beaches, spent their money at the restaurants and cafés and kept the economy going. Full time residents were thankful for both the pest control and the tourists.

Earlier in the evening, Morgan had eaten his dinner at the table and now as night settled in, he propped his feet up on another chair. A can of beer and his cell phone rested within arm's reach.

He closed his eyes but even that didn't erase thoughts of Ali. All day he'd been plagued with guilt. The last words of his telephone conversation with Cliff still rang in his ears. "Call that little gal, son."

Twice today when he was alone in his office, he pulled his cell phone from his belt and stared at the numbers. And twice he'd pushed it back unused.

He squinted at his watch. It was just after ten o'clock. She wouldn't be in bed this early would she? But would she even be home? *Maybe she had a date*? He frowned. *Did pregnant girls date? What made me think of that? I'm not dating.* "That's because you're a nerd. A guilt-ridden nerd," he told himself.

He leaned back. The shrink he'd visited this past week had told him he was dealing with denial; denial about his parents, denial about his responsibilities to Ali and denial about his ability to overcome these short-comings. "But," she'd said, "I can help you. I think a series of twice a week visits for six weeks will do a lot to get your mind where it should be."

Yeah, right, twice a week for six weeks at $90 an hour just to tell me I'm a loser who needs to do the right thing. And I even know what the right thing is and I don't do it.

His hand went to his cell phone but then pulled back with the can of beer instead. Ten o'clock was too late to call Cliff. That's who he needed to talk to, but they might already be in bed, or else he'd be at the bar and Morgan didn't want to disturb Millie. He grimaced. *If I could have chosen a mother, I'd have chosen Millie, and...*, he added to his thoughts, *I'd have chosen Cliff for a father.*

He knew Cliff was usually off Mondays but some nights he filled in for the other bartenders. Tomorrow. He'd call Cliff tomorrow.

25

Oh how great is thy goodness which thou hast laid up for them that fear thee...
Psalms 31:19

"Ali," Karen called. She ladled the chicken noodle soup which had been simmering on the stovetop for an hour into two bowls on the table. It was one of Ali's favorites and Karen enjoyed cooking when it wasn't for one. One dinner, one small bowl of soup, or one anything for that matter was just too lonely. She smiled and placed the napkins and spoons on the place mats, reflecting that she really enjoyed having Ali home with her.

Karen looked at her watch. Almost seven and they were just now eating, but she was later than usual coming home from the library and park because she'd stopped at the bakery to pick up some cookies. Cooking was one thing, but baking in the middle of summer was another. It was just too hot.

Karen filled Missy's dish with her dinner. "Come on, Missy. You won't get any table scraps tonight. You don't like soup, do you?" She fondled the little dog's ears and watched as she sniffed at the food and then looked up to see if this was really all there was. "That's it. Eat it. Now where is that naughty child?"

"Ali," she called again, this time a bit louder. "Soup's on. Come and get it." She listened for her daughter and when she didn't hear any movement, walked down the hall to her room.

"Dinner's ready, honey. Your favorite—chicken noodle soup—home made." She peeked into Ali's room to see her daughter lying on her side, her head buried into a pillow.

"Don't you feel well?" she asked, creeping close to the bed.

"I'm okay. I just don't feel like eating."

Karen sat on the side of the bed. "What's wrong?"

"Nothing," Ali said, her tone defensive and short.

Karen waited a few moments, her hand stroking Ali's arm. "Can't be nothing if you don't want dinner, especially when it's your favorite soup."

Ali pushed herself up, leaned back on the pillows against the headboard. "I'm sorry, Mom. I didn't mean to snap at you. It's just..." Ali sighed. "I guess being alone all afternoon gave me too much time to think."

"I'm sorry, honey. I shouldn't have left you alone so long. I—"

"Oh, Mom, don't go there. Don't get all guilty because you left me for four hours. I'm not a baby. It wasn't because you went out that I'm in such a bad mood."

"Well, then, what? Did you get a call?"

"A call? Ha! You mean from Morgan. Don't be silly. That last call probably wasn't him, either. I'm ready to write him off, Mom." She spoke firmly but her face told another story. Her expression was one of dismal despair. "If he doesn't care, then I don't either." She choked back tears, her hands viciously twisting the edge of the bedspread.

Karen felt helpless. What empty encouragement could she give Ali? Why hadn't Morgan contacted her? He knew where she was. *Oh, if I only knew where he was I'd...well, maybe that's an empty threat. But, still, he could show some interest in the woman he'd loved enough to make a baby with...two babies.*

The bedside clock, a miniature of a ceramic mantle clock, ticked loudly. Both women avoided eye contact for several minutes and then when their eyes did meet, Karen moved forward and Ali leaned into her outstretched arms. "I'm sorry, honey," Karen whispered. "I wish I could help."

"Me, too, but there's nothing anyone can do. I thought all afternoon about Morgan and how excited he was about our baby. Now he doesn't know there are two. He doesn't care about them...or me," she sobbed softly.

"You don't know that, Ali. He may be going through torturous times, too."

The women stayed locked in a crooked embrace, uncomfortable for both of them but neither wanted to move. Finally, Ali slid back onto her pillows, wiping her eyes and cheeks with the corner of her tee shirt. "Torturous times! Well, the heck with him. I don't care if he ever calls," she said, swinging her legs awkwardly over the side of the bed. "Let's have supper. He can go straight to...the devil." She stood and headed for the hallway, a confused mother following closely behind.

"Do you think you might feel better if you contacted Morgan? Called him or wrote to him?"

"No." Alice's answer was more than abrupt, it was a signal the conversation was over.

Dinner was quiet at first but then Alice perked up. "Marla called and said she and Kristi were going to Jocelyn's house tonight. They were going to come over here, too, but I was in such a snotty mood I told then not to. Maybe tomorrow afternoon. Boy, was I a pain. I didn't even like myself this afternoon. I'm sorry, Mom."

"Don't apologize, Ali. In your condition, that's to be expected."

"Condition, baloney," Ali said, smiling. "There's no excuse for being rude and I was rude...rude to you and my friends. I am sorry, Mom. Forgive me?"

Karen got up and removed the soup bowls. "Of course," Karen said, giving her daughter a hug. "I stopped by Kagle's Bakery and bought you some of those cookies you like."

"You like them, too. You just buy them for *me* so you have an excuse to eat them."

"You're right. Sometimes you can be a brat. Let's take the cookies and some iced tea through to the living room. Even with the air on, the lanai is too warm until the sun goes down and by that time I'm ready for bed."

Settled into their chairs in the living room, Karen asked, "Want to watch television?"

"There's probably nothing good on. Mostly re-runs now, anyhow. I have a book I'm reading, I could go and get it," Ali said pushing on the arms of the chair and wriggling forward.

"I'll get it for you."

"No, never mind. I've changed my mind. I'd rather talk, if it's okay with you." She looked meaningfully at the basket of knitting next to her mother's chair.

"Talking is fine with me. What do you want to talk about?"

Ali took in a deep breath. "Well, in addition to being all sorry for myself this afternoon, I did think of some things we need to talk about. For instance, moving to the condo. Do you know when this is going to happen?"

"I spoke to the real estate agent for this house today and she said the new owners are anxious to get in by the end of the month."

"This month?"

Karen nodded. "Our condo is all settled. We can move in any time. I also spoke to the moving company and they're ready to come and pack and move our things. Your father and I agreed trying to pack all this stuff by ourselves is too much and you certainly can't do any lifting, pushing or packing. For once we agreed on something. He's even going to pay half the moving costs. I've kind of got an idea as to what we'll be taking. I was going to talk to you about that today. Funny you should bring it up tonight."

"Well, all I really want from this house is my bedroom stuff. What are you bringing?"

"I made a list," Karen said, reaching into the magazine rack at the side of her chair.

She read a list which sounded very long to Ali who nodded and smiled as her mother numbered the items she wanted to take to their new home.

"Wow. That sounds like a lot of stuff."

"You can't imagine what's in this house that's not on that list, Ali. I've lived in this house for twenty four years and..." She stopped short and Ali looked up at her mother's distressed face.

"What's wrong, Mom?"

Karen pulled herself upright and inhaled deeply. "Nothing, honey. I just realized this December would have been our twenty-fifth wedding anniversary.

"I'm sorry, Mom."

"What do you have to be sorry for, Ali. It's not your fault."

"It's not yours either."

"No, but that's old news," Karen said, going back to her list.

She took in a deep, steadying breath. "Then I have the items we'll need to purchase before or shortly after the move. Two cribs, a large chest or two small ones. I think I measured correctly and either will fit in the twin's bedroom. Then we'll need a twin-sized stroller and a changing table and..."

"Whoa," Alice said, sitting forward. "That's a lot of stuff. I think Marla and Kristi are planning a shower for me. They couldn't keep a secret if it killed them. But those big items, Mom, they're going to be a lot of money."

She folded her lips and stared out the front window. The two bottle-brush trees stood listlessly on the front lawn, the stifling absence of any evening breeze leaving their branches limp. "I have some money in my bank account, money that you and Daddy gave me for expenses at college and a little of what I earned last summer working for the Historical Society. It probably won't cover all those costs but it might help."

"Oh, no, honey, that won't be..."

"Don't, Mom. Please let me contribute what I can. I'm a helpless burden right now but someday I'll pay you back. I promise." Alice wiped the corners of her eyes.

Karen moved to her daughter's side, sliding one arm around her shoulders. "You'll never be a helpless burden, Ali. That's what parents are for. I was planning on talking to your father before he left. I'm sure he'll want to contribute in some way to his grandchildren's new home. I'll call him tomorrow."

For the next hour they talked about the changes in their lives, each careful not to bring up sentimental memories from the past. At nine-thirty, Alice announced she was going to take a shower and go to bed and read.

"I think I'll be right behind you, Ali. I'm tired for some reason."

Alice laughed. "Maybe it was all those boxes you hauled to the Salvation Army this afternoon before you went to the library."

"Maybe it was, but I was happy we could get that much out of the closets and garage. I think I'll just call them or Habitat when we leave here to remove any leftovers."

It was a struggle for Alice to get out of her chair and when she stood, she put her hands on her lower back. "My back aches today."

"You sure you feel okay?" Karen asked, a worry line forming above her eyes.

"I'm fine, Mom, and I'm sorry for being such a brat earlier. You know, I'm not mad at Morgan, just disappointed. I thought he was better than that." She said the words with sad conviction and a small measure of assurance, but as Karen watched her walk down the hall she wondered if this was just some bravado to alleviate her worries.

"Leftovers," Ali laughed heading to her bedroom. "Like we cooked too much food."

"Like maybe we kept too many memories," Karen whispered to herself.

The following morning Karen was up early sorting through things in her bedroom, deciding what she needed to keep and what she could part with. Several items traveled from one stack to the other before a final decision was made.

Looking at the clock, she sat on the side of the bed and dialed her ex-husband's office number. She rarely, if ever, called him at his home, not wanting to chance having to speak with Sonoma. He answered after the first ring.

"Hello."

"Hello, Bill. Do you have a minute?"

"I have a minute, Kar, but I also have a meeting about to start. What's up? Ali okay?"

"Yes. In fact, I'm calling about Ali. There are several things we're...she's going to need for the babies when they come home. Cribs, chests of drawers, a changing table, a stroller..."

"I've thought about that. Get a figure on what it's going to take and we'll see what we can do. Listen, Kar, I have to go. I've got to finish up here. I'm leaving next week."

"Next week!" Karen exclaimed. "I didn't know it was going to be that quick."

"Neither did I, but apparently things have changed. I'm going to Omaha next week. Sonoma is not coming until the beginning of September." Bill didn't add anything more. He knew the less he spoke of his new wife the better and he never, ever mentioned her pregnancy.

"Okay, I'll get some prices. If you can help, I'll take care of the rest. I know you have a lot of expenses right now, moving and..." She wasn't going to mention Sonoma's pregnancy either. "Right now, Ali is feeling confused as to what to do about Morgan and she's a lot more worried than she lets on."

"I know. I plan to see her this week. I'll call first, though."

"Okay."

"Sorry, I have to rush, Kar."

"I understand. I'll be in touch."

When Karen hung up, her hand lingered on the phone. Just talking to Bill was still painful but not nearly as painful as it was a few months ago. "I guess I have other things on my mind now. Alice...two babies...a new house..."

"Are you talking to yourself?"

Karen turned to see Alice standing in the doorway. "Sleepy head. Did you have a good night's sleep?"

"Not really. I'm so big and fat now I roll over like I'm chasing an oversized beach ball."

"You're not fat, I told you. You're pregnant." Karen stood and gave her daughter a half hug. "Get dressed and I'll have breakfast with you. I was talking to your dad and we're going to work out the furniture and things for our grandchildren. No arguments, no fights."

"Well, that's good, but I am fat. I just caught sight of myself in the mirror in my room. Mom, I look like a hard boiled egg on stilts. And, you *were* talking to yourself."

Karen laughed. "Just mumbling about all my blessings," she said, pushing Ali toward her room again. "I'll meet you in the kitchen in ten minutes. An omelet?"

"Sounds good. A small one, please," Alice said, shuffling along in her slippers.

26

Why art thou cast down, O my soul?
And why art thou disquieted within me?
Hope in God; for I shall yet praise him
who is the health of my countenance and my God.
Psalms 43:5

A.J. pushed his coffee cup back and massaged his chest. The nagging and annoying tightness that had been pestering him for some time seemed stronger this morning. He rose, swayed and grasped the edge of the table.

Shuffling through to thc front room, he picked the telephone receiver from its upright cradle and dialed Dr. Phillips. Dr. Phillips had taken over old Dr. Van Doren's practice and A.J. still slipped and called it Dr. Van Doren's office from time to time.

"Good Morning, Dr. Phillips' office," a cheery voice answered the phone. "How may I help you?"

"This is A.J. Handley. I'd like to see Dr. Phillips."

"Let me see," she said and A.J. heard fingers tapping on a keyboard.

"No one keeps paper records," he mumbled softly to himself. "I remember when you heard pages flipping when you waited for an appointment."

"The first opening is next Tuesday at two thirty."

"I may not live that long," he responded, rubbing harder at his chest as if that might help.

There was a studied silence for several moments and then the cheery voice, not so cheery now, asked, "May I ask who's calling. Is this an emergency?"

"It's A.J. Handley. I'm seventy-seven and my chest hurts."

"Oh, Mr. Handley. I didn't recognize your voice. You're in pain? Perhaps you should call 911."

"No, I shouldn't call 911. I just want to see Doc Phillips." A.J. not only felt crotchety he sounded it and he grimaced to himself.

"Well," she said, tapping on her keyboard. "We can squeeze you in at ten-thirty this morning. Are you sure you can make it in to the office, Mr. Handley? I'm Velma Stephens' daughter and I remember my grandma, Phyllis Mellcamp, talking about you. She was one of your students. Maybe you should get someone to drive you into town."

"I remember Phyllis. No, I'll be okay. See you at ten-thirty. Thanks," he said, hanging up before the young woman could reminisce or offer any more advice. He had to shower and change and there was no time for idle chatter. He moved slowly to the bathroom which was where the old summer kitchen used to be. "Nothing's the same anymore," he muttered.

Forty-five minutes later he picked up the car keys from the hall table. He'd go early and maybe they'd take him in before ten-thirty.

As A.J. closed the front door behind him he saw that new young man loping up his driveway. Raising his hand in a greeting, he called, "You're out early. I see you're doing your walking again."

"Yes, and since I was out this way I thought I'd stop by and see you. But I see you're going out."

"To the doctor's office."

"Well, I wouldn't want to hold you up."

"You wouldn't. In fact, I'm early. I just thought if I went early they'd take me early but I know they don't do that. Come on up on the porch and we can talk." Even though A.J. Handley was known as a very friendly fellow, he was a little confused by his enthusiasm about this young man and the fact that in spite of his eagerness to get this doctor thing over, he invited his visitor to stay awhile.

The two men settled into rockers. A.J. drew in a deep breath.

"You feeling okay?" Jack asked.

"Pretty good for an old codger, but sometimes..."

"Sometimes you don't." It was a statement not a question.

Jack noticed his friend's pale face, the slight glow of moisture on his forehead and upper lip and the tremble in his hands.

"It's so nice out here," he said. "Peaceful and quiet. But, maybe a bit isolated for you now, Mr. Handley."

"Call me A.J. All my friends do."

"Thank you. It's a compliment to be listed as one of your friends."

"I like you. You don't come stirring things up or making waves. So many of my friends are harping at me to get some help. Have someone live in with me. Can you imagine that? Me with a baby-sitter? In my own house? Nonsense," he snorted.

Jack stared across the road at the grove. Small green oranges could be seen hiding in the protective foliage. "They mean well, A.J. Having a little help isn't all that bad. Why, if you picked the right person you'd have someone to play cribbage with right here in your home."

"How'd you know I played cribbage?"

"You look like a cribbage player."

The men laughed and A.J. felt a small tweak in his heart, not a warning kind of tweak but a warm, good feeling. "I might consider it if it were someone like you, Jack."

"Well, there must be others, old friends or someone recommended by a friend. I'm not going to be here long." There was a note of sadness in his voice.

"I know. You're going back to the big city. Must be interesting. I wouldn't like it, I know."

"Teaching was all I ever wanted to do."

"I was a teacher, too, you know." A.J. leaned back and set the rocker to slowly move back and forth. "I did it because it was the only thing I wanted to do and, I guess, because my Aunt Felicity urged me to. I loved kids. Never had any," he sighed.

"I wanted kids too."

"Didn't have any?"

"No. Never married."

"Regret it? I mean not getting married?"

"Yes, I do, and I think I didn't realize it until this minute."

The impact of that revelation touched both men, each thinking of children they never had, A.J. remembering Elizabeth, and Jack weighing his lost chances with Jennifer.

With a push against the arms of his rocker, A.J. rose. "Guess I'd better be going. It was good to talk to you, Jack. You're easy to talk to."

Jack stood and offered his hand to the old gentleman. "I'm glad I stopped by."

A.J. walked to the steps. "I'm going to Gadara. You finished walking or would you like a ride?"

"I...I'd love a ride. Guess I've walked enough for today, or for right now, anyway."

Jack offered A.J. his arm and they walked to the graveled driveway. He matched his pace to that of the older man.

Dr. Phillips didn't look old enough to be a college graduate, never mind a practicing physician. A.J. sat on the examining table while the doctor moved his stethoscope around his chest.

"Lean forward, Mr. Handley," he said. "Take in deep, slow breaths for me." He moved the stethoscope to A.J.'s back. "Okay," he said, pulling the shirt down, "you can sit in the chair now." The doctor patiently held the old man's arm as he cautiously descended to the floor.

"Those examination tables seem to grow taller each year," A.J. said as he settled himself into one of the chairs against the wall. He peered into the young doctor's face looking for hints as to what he might say. The doctor, perched on a round stool on wheels, gave no hint as to what he was about to say.

"Mr. Handley," he said, glancing at the chart which was on a low table next to him. "You're seventy-seven years old, so there is naturally some weakness indicated in your heart. I'd like to have a cardiogram taken so we can see just what's going on."

"You mean a test... at the hospital?" A.J., as did so many seniors, had a fear of hospitals. In his earlier days, going to the hospital for anything was serious, serious business. His face contorted with anxiety.

"No, no," Dr. Phillips said with an encouraging smile. "We do the test right here. I'll have my nurse come in and prepare you. She'll do the test, which is very simple and doesn't take any time at all. We'll have the results right here in the office. If I see anything, I might want to order an echo cardiogram but we'll talk about that later."

"Those other tests would be at the hospital?"

Dr. Phillips stood and ran his hand across A.J.'s shoulder. "It would only be in the out-patient, radiology department. Let's just see what the cardiogram shows." He glanced down at his chart again. "These meds up-to-date?"

"As far as I know."

"Well, a vitamin, an aspirin and one blood-pressure pill a day is amazing for a man of your age. I do see, however, that you haven't been in our office for over a year and you haven't had any blood work done. You really should let us schedule six-month check-ups. I'll order a routine blood work-up. You can get it done at the lab on Walnut Street. Do you live alone, Mr. Handley?" he asked.

"Yes, I live alone." A.J. didn't add that he also drove and took care of himself very well, thank you.

Dr. Phillips smiled and opened the door. "I'll send Carolyn in. She'll do the test and then I'll be back."

If the doctor hadn't come in when he did, A.J. would have left. Sitting alone in a small room, hearing voices and movement on the other side of the door for twenty minutes was as long as his patience could be stretched.

"Sorry to keep you waiting. We're exceptionally busy for July," Dr. Phillips said, straddling the stool and looking at the papers in his hand. "Well, A.J., I think you've earned a trip to the radiology department. I'd like to have an echo cardiogram done, just to be sure.

"To be sure of what?" A.J. asked, his temper checked by worry.

"To be sure of what measures need to be taken. Your cardiogram shows some slight thickening of the arteries.

"By measures, does that mean surgery?"

"No. But that's why we need more information before we can decide on the best course of action."

A.J. squirmed on the armed chair he sat in. "I don't like

'course of action' words either. What does that mean?"

Dr. Phillips stood, moved to A.J.'s side and slid into the chair next to his patient. "I say course of action, meaning medications, or simple techniques, not necessarily surgery. However, to be completely truthful, and I know you want me to be truthful, there is always the possibility of the need for more invasive measures." His fingers touched the back of A.J.'s hand resting on his knees.

"You know, doctor, I'm an educated man. Oh, not like you and not like the average college graduate of these times, but I know the meaning of words and I think you're playing hop-scotch with your words."

Dr. Phillips laughed aloud. "Oh, my. Well, I'll admit I was talking 'keep the patient happy 101' and you caught me. I don't think you will need surgery but to cover my butt I said the things needed to be said. Personally, and don't hold me to this, I think surgery might be avoided. What I think you need is some help. I know where you live, Mr. Handley, and I know you live alone. You need to be somewhere where there's a little help."

"You mean nursing home?"

"No, not at all. Perhaps an assisted living facility like the one just built out on Riverview would be just the thing. You should check it out. You get what help you need and want and perhaps a little companionship thrown in as an extra. But," he said, standing, "we'll cross that bridge when we come to it. Think about it, Mr. Handley. My gal at the front desk will schedule the tests at the hospital." He turned to go, opening the door but before he stepped into the hallway he faced A.J. again. "And don't think of these tests as being 'at the hospital', they're just in a side building the hospital built for just this sort of thing. It keeps the hospital open and ready for people who really need it." He left the door ajar as he disappeared.

A.J. sat still for a moment. "I like him," he said as he struggled out of the chair. "But assisted living? I'm not sure about that."

He shuffled down the hallway to see Phyllis Mellcamp's granddaughter. "A lot of nonsense about nothing," he said, unconvincingly, tapping his chest as if to dare it to hurt again.

27

...ye ought rather to forgive him, and comfort him, lest perhaps such a one should be swallowed up with overmuch sorrow."
2 Cor. 2:7

In the foyer, Bill pulled Ali to his chest. No matter how pregnant she looked, she was still his little girl and he buried his nose in her hair.

"Hey, you cut your hair. And you're using a new shampoo or my nose has lost its memory."

"Your nose is right on target. Do you like my haircut?" Ali slid her arm around her father's waist. "It's easier to take care of. That long hair was becoming a burden and my back wasn't up to all the washing and combing.

"Come on in. Mom's in her room. She'll be out in a minute. Are you really leaving Gadara the end of this week?"

Bill perched on the edge of one sofa cushion fondling Missy's curly head. "Yes, I have a Saturday afternoon flight out of Tampa. You glad to see me, Missy?" The little dog had shown her usual excitement to anyone who visited the Waterson house, dancing around Bill's feet as he'd walked into the living room.

He smiled as he watched Ali ease herself into his old recliner. He'd resented leaving it when Karen had objected saying, "It's part of the living room furniture. You can buy another one." Now he was glad it was here for Ali to enjoy.

"How are you feeling, honey?"

"I'm doing okay. My back hurts almost constantly now, but I guess that's all this weight in one great lump in front of me." Ali caressed the swollen tummy holding her two children. "You know, sometimes I just can't believe that there are two real, little people in there."

Bill laughed. "I can't either, honey. You're my baby and it's hard to believe that my baby is having babies."

They sat quietly for several moments, then Ali asked, "I can't believe you're leaving the end of this week."

"Saturday. That's why I had to come over tonight. Tomorrow there are things I have to wind up and the next day...well, there are things at home..."

"I know. How is Sonoma?" It was difficult for Ali to mention his new wife's pregnancy yet she was curious.

"She's doing fine. She'll follow me in September. The condo hasn't sold yet, but there are some people interested. I guess we'll have to drop the price again. We've already done that twice."

Ali saw her father's distress and was about to change the subject when her mother entered the room.

Bill rose to his feet. "Hello, Karen," he said.

"Hi, Bill. So formal?" She reached for his hand. "You look well."

"So do you. As for me, I don't know. I'm torn in thirty directions, mentally out to Omaha and back here, you, Ali, the babies, work..." His words and worried frown endorsed his state of confusion.

"Well, let's see if we can get some of this settled tonight. You said you'd pay for half of the things we'll need for the twins."

"Yes, do you have a figure?"

"Ali and I looked at baby furniture at Wesley's out on the highway. We found two chests that will fit in their room at the condo, and two cribs and a changing table that will fit at the bottom of one of the cribs. It might be a squeeze but we'll manage. A twin stroller was more expensive than we'd thought, but the total comes to around $1,800.00.

Bill reached into his back pocket and extracted his checkbook. "Wow. Well, it's money well spent. I'll write you a check." Both women averted their eyes while he scribbled out a check. He handed it to Karen but his eyes went to Ali. "I wish I could be here when these babies come into the world, Ali." She heard the regret in his voice.

"I know you can't, Daddy. We'll let you know what's happening. Do you have an address in Omaha?"

"I do and I have it here," he said, handing Karen one of his business cards with the new address written on the back. "I'll be using my cell phone so you can always reach me." He stood and went over to his daughter. Leaning down he touched his lips to her forehead. "We're...I'm praying that everything goes well, honey. Quick and safe."

He returned to his place on the sofa and looked at Karen who had remained standing. "I hope you'll both be happy in the condo," he said. "I know it's going to be a little difficult to leave this old place. But, it will be better for both of you to be in your new home." He looked to Karen for support.

"I think we've both adjusted to this change and I know I'm looking forward to the move. Something I never thought I'd say." Karen laughed softly.

"Do you have everything taken care of for the move? Send me the amount for half the moving costs. I'm getting a 'change of status' bonus, whatever that means. I can't understand how they figure things. Paying us to leave and putting me in Omaha at a reduced salary and then giving me a bonus for leaving. Anyhow, I'm just glad I can help out. Who knows what's in the future, but you shouldn't have any money worries, Karen."

For a moment the former husband and wife locked eyes. What each of them saw was a mystery to the other and time stood still. When they looked away things seemed different but the difference was intangible.

Bill stood, looked at Karen, then turned to his daughter. "Stay there, Ali." He waved and smiled. "I love you, honey." Turning to his ex-wife, he said, "I'll let myself out, Karen." Still he remained where he was, and for a moment the awkward silence deepened.

Karen walked to his side. "Nonsense. I'll see you to the door. Thanks for coming, Bill." She tucked her arm into his and they walked to the foyer.

They didn't see Alice's mouth open in amazement and she didn't see her mother ever-so-briefly kiss her father's cheek. She did hear her say, "Have a safe trip, Bill. Best wishes for you and

Sonoma in Omaha."

When Karen returned she found Ali crying softly. "What's wrong, Ali?" She knelt next to the recliner.

"Nothing. It's just..."

"Just?"

"You still love him, don't you? After what he did to you, you still love him."

Karen leaned her head on Ali. "I'll love him as your father, Ali. I'll love him for all the good years we had. It's just a different kind of love."

"Maybe that's why I still love Morgan. I don't like him but I still love him. I was really mad at myself for hating him and now I know I don't hate him but he's wrong. It's almost evil what he did. He's not only hurting me but the twins. I can't see forgiving him either. I thought I understood this love thing when I fell in love with Morgan. It seemed so right, so perfect and then... Mom, are these thoughts awful?"

Karen rose and sat in her chair opposite Alice. "No, honey. Not awful. I've come to know that there are many kinds of love and that every one is appropriate for the time and place. What Morgan did to you is inexcusable but then doesn't it say in the Bible that we must forgive? That was part of my nightly reading last night."

Ali looked away. For several moments there was no sound in the room except Missy's toenails clicking on the tiles.

"I'm confused, Mom. If I forgive Morgan, it's as though he gets away with all this." She slumped down in her chair.

"We'll have to pray for understanding. I marked the passage to ask Pastor Finlayson at Bible Study on Sunday evening. Maybe he'll have an answer we can understand."

Ali struggled out of the chair and when she stood she held her stomach with one hand and her back with the other. "I don't know, Mom. You'll have to ask him for a magic answer. Right now I'd...I'd punch Morgan if he were within arm's reach. I'm going to bed."

She hesitated, then blew her mother a kiss.

Later, lying in bed her mind churned through her thoughts. Why had Morgan turned away from her at such a time when she was sure both of them loved and wanted the baby? Why, when she knew deep in her heart he had loved her? What had changed? Would he ever change his mind? And, after much tossing about, she asked herself, "Do I want him to change his mind just because I'm pregnant?"

Her pillow was wet with tears before she finally fell asleep.

28

He shall call upon me, and I will answer him:
I will be with him in trouble;
I will deliver him and honor him.
Psalms 91:15

A.J. sat in the only padded chair in the parlor. He still referred to the front room as the parlor even though he knew the term was about as outdated as he was. His eyes traveled around the room, touching on each piece of furniture, the old brocade sofa with the antimacassars covering each arm and back. Aunt Felicity had crocheted them. He remembered her sitting in the maple rocker next to the front window, her fingers flying as stitch after stitch fell into place.

The chair he sat in had the same crocheted protectors. "Antimacassars," he mumbled. "Bet that's another word that's been put out to pasture."

He ran his hands over the pieces, feeling the stitches drawn into circles and flowers. The workmanship had escaped him until this moment. How many years had these treasures been right in front of his eyes?

The rocker still sat angled in front of the window and A.J. could visualize his Aunt Felicity sitting there, the afternoon sun providing the light necessary for her to stitch or read. "She used to fiddle with that old wooden box, too. I think she stored her precious stuff in that old thing and she'd carry it to and from her room like it held the Hope Diamond. I don't remember her ever showing anyone what was in it and I can't remember what became of it after she died. Hmm..." He screwed his face in deep thought. "Wonder whatever happened to that little old box. I don't recall seeing it when Mama was clearing out stuff."

His eyes went back to the curtains. He remembered replacing them. "It must have been ten years ago. They must be ready to be retired, too."

His grandmother's china cabinet was filled with the treasures his mother and grandmother felt suitable for saving on the glass shelves. That would go to the Historical Society along with any other pieces of furniture they chose to keep. A.J. closed his eyes. "Assisted Living, he called it. Dr. Phillips thinks I can't manage on my own."

He rose and walked to the little desk in the corner. It was where he'd once prepared his school lessons and marked papers. The drawers were filled with things, probably unimportant things that had found a home there until someone threw them out. His fingers ran over the carved back of the chair which matched the carving on the backboard of the desk. "This will go, too," he said softly. He turned and rescanned the room. Each old dusty piece had a history and as he looked at them he realized he couldn't even keep this room clean. The curtains were a dim cream color when they should have been white. The tabletops were dusty. He drew a circle in the dust on the desk.

Walking from the parlor through the dining room with its share of old, precious but dusty furniture, A.J. entered the kitchen. Barren of all the trinkets his mother and grandmother had filled the shelves with, it stood a naked souvenir of the past.

A.J. Handley walked down the hall and picked up the telephone. He stood with the phone in his hand, puzzled. Who would he call to see about the dreaded Assisted Living facility? Sarah Jane? He dismissed that thought. What if he went to see it and then chose not to go? The news he'd even thought of leaving his home would be all over Gadara in twenty minutes. He replaced the phone, pushed the screen door open and sat in his favorite rocker. Thinking was a lot easier outside with the breeze and the smells of the grove and grasses in the air. He listened to birds calling. Rocking quietly for several minutes with his eyes closed, he came to a conclusion. Rising, he felt for his car keys in his pocket. Taking them out, he walked down the three steps to the gravel driveway. He'd go to Gadara and look at this Assisted Living thing. Out along Riverview, Dr. Phillips had said. Okay, he'd check it out for himself. He could still do that.

Defiantly he backed out of the drive and turned toward Gadara. How many years had he done this? Ever since he was fifteen, but back then he drove a lot faster and raised a lot more dust.

A.J. was on a mission.

29

Multitudes, multitudes in the valley of decision;
for the day of the Lord is near
in the valley of decision.
Joel 3:14

"You've got a package, Mr. Muldorn." The receptionist said, placing a box and some envelopes next to the in-box on Morgan's desk. "Is it your birthday?"

"No. It's probably some junk mail with samples of stuff. Thanks, Marie."

Morgan watched the pretty girl who answered the phone and greeted clients swish along the open hallway to the next office. *I don't know why she doesn't break an ankle on those shoes. The heels must be five inches tall.* He smiled. She always was pleasant and took all kinds of guff from clients and workers alike. Morgan liked Marie and if things were different...well that was out of the question.

He reached for the package and when he saw the return address, his morning coffee and Danish churned in his stomach. A box from his...father? Had he forgotten something important when he left a couple of months earlier?

His fingers played with the tape at the ends of the oblong carton. It was neatly sealed and for a brief moment he could picture his father smoothing any unwanted wrinkles in the tape before deeming it fit to mail.

He imagined his father's den and desk and remembered he hadn't been allowed in that room until he was in his teens. It was a sacred place to be occupied by his father and his chosen guests and no one else, except the cleaning lady who came twice a week. Mrs. Andersen's face suddenly appeared to Morgan and he smiled, recalling the cookies wrapped in a paper napkin she'd secretly slipped to him.

Morgan held the package in front of him. He reread the mailing label. There was no mistake, it was from his father and addressed to him.

"Hey, what's up? Someone send you a thank you gift for all your excellent advice and work?" Dave stood in front of Morgan's desk.

"Hey, yourself. No. Just something I ordered. Don't know why I had it sent here." He slid the box from the desktop to a drawer and pushed it closed. "What up with you?" Morgan asked, trying to dismiss the stress just looking at the package had caused him.

"Thought if you weren't busy tonight you could join Patty and me. We're going to some kind of festival at her church. Outdoors. She said food and games, that kind of thing."

"Sounds like it could be fun. Unfortunately I have an appointment tonight so I can't make it."

"Appointment or date?" Dave said, grinning.

"Appointment, Dave. Don't get your hopes up. I'm not ready to date, okay?"

"Sure I just thought you might enjoy a night out with scintillating friends."

Morgan laughed. "Thanks, Oh, Great Scintillating Friend, but I'll have to take a rain check. It does sound like fun and any other night I might have said yes."

"That would be a surprise. You've turned down everything I've suggested to get you out into the social world."

"I just might be ready for the social world soon. We'll see," Morgan said, pulling a file in front of him. "Have fun and tell Patty I'm sorry about not making the festival...next time I'll say yes."

Dave studied his friend for a moment and then shrugged and left.

On the bus home that night, Morgan stared out the window, his fingers gripping the small box in his lap.

Once inside his condo, he went into his bedroom, casually tossing the package on the bed. After he'd removed and hung up his suit and changed into Khaki shorts and a white tee shirt, he retrieved a bottle of soda from the refrigerator and the box from his bedroom and sat in the living room. He took a long swallow of soda and stared at the sealed carton on the coffee table in front of him.

"You'll never know what's inside unless you open it," he scolded himself, holding the cold soda in both hands.

After several minutes, he placed his soda next to the dubious gift, wiped his wet hands on his shirt and picked up the box. Prying the tape off, he pulled at the cardboard. Carefully looking inside, he saw a white envelope with his name hand-printed on it. Picking it up, he turned it over, but there was nothing on the other side. For a moment he held it in his hand, his brow furrowed. This is so strange, he hadn't thought of hearing from them, especially in a letter with something sent to him. Baffled, he slid his thumbnail along the seal. A single sheet of paper was folded in three, the appearance professional and almost official looking, but when Morgan unfolded the paper he saw a handwritten letter and recognized his father's elegant penmanship.

Slowly reading each word he refolded the letter and reached inside the carton for the box. A small key was in the lock. He stared at it, unsure of whether he wanted to see what was inside. "...the contents might be of value to you" the letter read. *Was this a trick? Would whatever was inside the box bring me more of the same kind of hurt I'm struggling so hard to get over?*

Morgan picked up the letter and read it again then let the letter flutter to his lap and with both hands massaged the painful knot at the base of his neck, his eyes closed as if not seeing the box and the letter would help erase this sudden overwhelming feeling of anguish.

He put his father's letter back on the coffee table and picked up the box. He turned the key in the tiny lock, his fingers poised on the lid. *All day you've wanted to know what could be in here and now you'll know.* He pulled the lid up and saw several small envelopes and folded pieces of paper. There was some jewelry, a gold bracelet with a heart dangling from the thin chain and a locket, dulled with age. When he popped it open a man and a woman stared back at him. From the little glimpse of their appearance and attire, the photos appeared to be very old.

A small, blue ribbon rested on the top of the pile. Reverently, he picked the ribbon up and studied it. "First place, Sawgrass Festival" he read. *Who won first place?* he wondered. *For what?*

He gently lay the ribbon aside and picked up the pile of what appeared to be letters. With shaking fingers, he began to sort them, some in envelopes and others seemed to be folded pieces of paper with messages on them. The envelopes had no addresses on them and had apparently been hand-delivered or left in mailboxes. There was no indication they had been actually mailed. *That's strange. Letters that were apparently delivered but not mailed.*

He put the three envelopes aside and began to unfold the other papers making a neat stack. He chose one of the envelopes first. The letter was written on quality writing paper, lilac in color and feminine. He held it to his nose but any perfume or scent had long disappeared if it had ever existed. His eyes blinked rapidly when he saw the date written on the top of the first paper he opened.

September 8, 1932

Dear Mother,

It is over. I will never again feel whole but there is nothing else for me. Everything is taken care of but part of me will always remain in Chesterton. Since you have so kindly said I can come home, I will arrive on Friday. There is a train which will bring me to Gadara Station at 4:45 in the evening. Thank you for your love, understanding and forgiveness. It is immeasurable given the circumstances. I trust God will also forgive me.

The letter was signed, *Felicity.* Morgan blinked rapidly. Was this someone from his past? From Gadara? Was this a cruel quirk or was there some truth to his father's remarks that these papers would be of interest to him? Who was Felicity and what had she done that she needed forgiveness? His hands trembled as he tenderly placed the letter next to the box. He moved his soda bottle further away.

The next folded piece of paper was almost illegible, apparently written with pencil on cheap paper. It was discolored and the creases were ragged. There was no apparent date but Morgan squinted and held the paper closer to the lamp. There was something scribbled—numbers that might be 9~~~2.

Child, you have done what you could. Your father will never know.

The next line was indistinguishable because the fold distorted the words. Then he read,

Only God knows all ~~~~~~~~ but you must ~~~~~~~~ and never ~~~~~~~~ I love you.

There was no signature. The handwriting was one of someone uneducated, and using a pencil indicated something but Morgan couldn't think what at the moment. He leaned back. This wasn't much help. The date was obscure and there were no identifications as to who wrote the note or who received it. He had planned to put the papers in date order to see if a picture could be drawn.

Surprisingly his excitement mounted. *What if these people, whoever they were, were related to me? Could this be the path to finding my true parents?*

He carefully laid this paper on top of the other. Now he eagerly took the second envelope and opened it. He began his analysis, the paper appeared to be of good quality, plain white and written in ink in what appeared to be the same hand as the first one.

There was no date and no greeting

This is so difficult to write. I know I've been forbidden to contact you and I know I promised not to, but after a full year my heart is bleeding with remorse. Not that I have any

remorse I chose you, but because I had to make the choice in the first place. I want to know how she is. I'm not questioning your care. I want to picture her, and know what she likes. Does she laugh a lot? If you could just return this letter with any information, her name, her likes and dislikes, anything at all I would be so grateful. I've enclosed a stamp so that you can return this letter with your response without any cost to you. I pray you are well and every night I ask God's forgiveness for me and blessings for you and yours.

It was signed with a single initial—'F'.

Morgan turned the letter over looking for a response from the recipient. There was nothing. Then he looked into the envelope. Had he missed the reply? Was it on one of the other pieces of paper? Apparently the sender had received their own letter back but without the hoped for responses. There didn't seem to be a reply. Who was 'F' and who was this letter directed to? Was the sender the Felicity from the first letter he'd read? Who was the 'she' referred to? There seemed to be no answers in the letters but they raised so many questions.

With a measure of sadness he replaced the letter in the envelope and placed it on the others. He tentatively reached for the next envelope but instead, took the folded papers, opened them and pressed them flat with the palm of his hand. His stomach rumbled to remind him he hadn't eaten since lunch and darkness was now pressing against his windowpanes. Still, he straightened the letters, putting the two envelopes to the side. He pushed the bottle to the edge of the table. Dinner would have to wait; he was on a quest now. The letters and notes had become a challenge, a puzzle that had to be solved.

He took another small note, turning it carefully. Again there was no date so how was he going to put these in proper order? Didn't these writers realize how important dates and places were? The paper and ink seemed the same quality as some of the other notes but that didn't tell him anything other than they didn't write on the back of envelopes or grocery bags.

Hello, dear friend,

I know I promised to write sooner but things got a bit hectic. After you left they hired another teacher but, oh my, what a harridan she was. The poor children were in tears every day. I am happy to report she did not last long and another lovely young woman has taken your place, not that anyone could really take your place. We all miss you and hope you can find the time to write to us. Please don't feel any of your friends here are judging you. True friends don't do that. I miss you terribly. Please write when you can.

Your friend, Frieda

Morgan frowned. This seemed to be going nowhere. Who was Frieda and who was the dear friend she was writing to? Now he had two people with the initial 'F', Frieda and Felicity. *The mystery gets deeper and the answers more obscure.* Morgan put the note on the top of his growing pile of letters he'd read and looked at the unread stack. There were only four more wrinkled papers in the unread stack and one envelope left unopened.

He chose the largest and less wrinkled of the loose papers. Studying it for a moment he concluded it appeared to have been torn from a book or pad of paper, the left edge ragged and uneven. After scanning it he frowned. "It looks as if it were torn from a diary or journal of some kind. Small like a woman's, not as if it were part of business records.

He read:

December 1936

It has been four years. I can find no peace, and as time goes by it doesn't change, the chasm deepens and I go further and further into it. Mama says it will pass, that time heals, and I believe she is well-meaning, but the pain goes on. I pray and pray but there are no answers and there never will be. To commit one sin after the other would be more than wrong, it would be evil and so I go on but noth-

ing will change. I see the pain in Mama's face and I know that Papa, while he will never know, feels something is wrong. He calls me a recluse now because I don't go out except to church and when I'm there, I feel as if even that is evil in a way. Is a precious life something evil? I can't and won't believe that. I am the evil one. Will I ever be forgiven? That is to be reckoned at the end, but to wish for the end is another sin. I have no hope.

In a postscript, by a different pen but the same hand, Morgan read:

I must destroy this page in my journal, it is too dangerous. What if Mama or Papa should read it even after my death, which I pray for daily.

Morgan read the words and felt a chill come over him. Goosebumps appeared on his arms as he held the paper in his trembling fingers. The writer had transmitted her pain and fear in well-chosen words. She didn't destroy the page. Whoever this is kept the lone page in her box of memories. *By the writing, she must be educated. But what could have caused this kind of grief?*

He leaned back against the couch cushions. Was this the writer of one of the letters? Perhaps both of them? He leaned forward, placing the page carefully on top of the pile he had read. With his arms hanging limply between his knees he considered what he had read this evening. Straightening, he rose and walked to the window. Darkness, punctuated with the lights of the huge condos along the bay seemed to add to some of the mystery contained in the wooden box his father had sent him. Why had he sent it? Why now? Did it really have anything to do with his past? He returned to the coffee table and picked up his father's letter, rereading it carefully as if it were a contract between them and he must be sure to find the loopholes, if there were any.

The box was found in the attic but he didn't say where. Was it with other things belonging to his past? Was this really important to him or was it just another game?

He paced the floor, gripping the letter in one hand, the other combing his hair with fingers still holding a tremor, a shadow of the emotion captured on that single sheet of paper torn from a diary paced with him. Who did the diary belong to? Did he need to know?

He sat in a chair facing the couch and coffee table. His soda stood in a puddle of bottle sweat, the papers stacked next to the open wooden box. "I need a system. I need to make a list of what is known and perhaps where it might lead." Morgan stood and went to a small desk in the corner of his bedroom. Opening the top drawer he pulled out a steno pad where he jotted things down when he was working on his computer. "I'll write down what I have discovered, what things may lead to an answer to this confounding puzzle and then transfer the info to the computer. Right now I don't have a thing I could pursue in research on the internet. Maybe later." He pushed the drawer closed and returned to the living room.

"First, though, I'd better read the rest, one more envelope and one more sheet of paper."

He picked up the half-empty bottle and took it into the kitchen. Grabbing a paper towel he blotted up the water on the coffee table and threw the towel on the floor to retrieve later. He laid the pad next to the things already read.

This wrinkled page was more obscure than the others. It appeared to be a list of dates. Scribbled in an uneven column, Morgan read:

September 3, 1932
September 6, 1932
September 3, 1936
April 20, 1954 (have I lost her forever?)

Morgan glanced at the last single sheet of paper and decided to take the last envelope. He withdrew the letter, noting it was the longest letter of them all. The paper was cheap, the writing almost illegible at times with several words inked out like untidy blots scattered across the page. He read:

April 20, 1954

Dear Miss,

I have long wanted to write you but Mr. Donnigan would not allow it. I kept your address from the other letter hid away and hope you are still in Gadara.

If you remember, Mr. Donnigan was the one that wanted total secrecy and I thought maybe he would ease his rules but he didn't. He was a strong man, a good husband, and a good father to Susan. That's what we named her. She was a lovely child and I often thought of how much you would have loved to know about her but it was not possible. I wanted to answer your letter long ago but it would have caused to many problems. Susan was a happy child. You asked if she laughed a lot, she did. But the teen years were difficult. She was headstrong and there was battle after battle between her and her father. When she left, it almost killed him and I think that is what brought on his early death. He died six months ago, Lord rest his soul. I am sad to report I don't know where Susan is. She left a year ago with a young man we didn't even know. One night she just said she was going away with Frankie and that was that. I suspected she was pregnant and told her it didn't make any difference, but she went anyhow. I pray every day to our Holy Father she will contact me. There is so much evil in the world and I fear she has made a contract with the Devil. I know this will be sad news for you but if I ever hear from her I will write to you. I don't know the man's last name.

God bless you for giving us our daughter.

Yours truly, Theresa.

Morgan picked up the envelope again, studying it. "It hasn't been mailed," he muttered. "Whoever received it put it in a clean envelope and kept it in the box. That's why none of the envelopes have addresses or cancellation marks. Whoever kept them didn't want any identification on them so no one could trace them if they fell into the wrong hands. Well, one thing's clear, I think. There's a child involved."

The last piece of paper was hand-written and again seemed as if it had been torn from a journal. The hand-writing was shaky as if the writer was old or infirm. It didn't seem to match any that Morgan had read earlier in the evening. The words were simple and to the point. He read:

There's another child. Theresa sent me a note today which I foolishly destroyed. I'll never see Mary Ann but then I didn't ever see Susan. My daughter and granddaughter, lost in a world where I never existed. There is no longer any hope. What a fool I was to believe there ever would be.

Somehow the pain seems less. Maybe it's because even hurt comes to an end if you wait it out.

He stood and threw the letter and the last note on the coffee table. "That makes the job even more difficult," he said, stamping into the kitchen. He looked at the clock on the stove. "Eleven-thirty," he grumbled, opening the refrigerator door. "And I haven't had dinner. I have to go to work tomorrow, so I can't do anything with that mess in the living room tonight. I don't know which way to go first, anyhow. Should I call my father and see if he has any more information to give me? Why did he think this would be something of value to me?" His confusion was palpable, his determination strong. As his words drifted into the quiet of the kitchen, never had his apartment seemed lonelier.

Pulling a plate of last night's pizza from the refrigerator, he sat at the small table and ate it cold, sipping a beer. "There's got to be an answer to the riddle of all the names and mismatched messages," he said, his mouth full of pizza crust, tomato sauce and cheese, "but it'll have to wait until tomorrow night."

His mind raced, peppered with the words he'd read tonight but it was a painful jumble and later, when he turned the light off and went to bed, his emotions were a hodgepodge of wonder and anger. *Why me? What can this mean?* But an underlying feeling convinced him this was important in some way and he *had* to solve the mystery. He tossed and turned for an hour before surrendering to sleep. In the morning, he felt as if he'd never slept and he was in a bad mood the moment he stepped out his door. What he really wanted to do was stay home and begin to sort out the enigma that may or may not even have anything to do with him.

He tried to concentrate on the newspaper as he rode down Biscayne Boulevard but the news seemed insignificant and his mind churned with his own mystery. *Who? What? Why? Where? and When?* He mentally added *How?* to that list, remembering his professors' instructions that in studying any problem, all of those questions should be answered.

"Well maybe the 'where' is Gadara. It seems that word creeps up too often lately," he whispered to himself and immediately thought of Ali in her mother's house in Gadara.

30

For you have been my help,
and in the shadow of your wings
I sing for joy.
Psalm 63:7

In Carter's Corners, Cliff ended his phone call and turned to his wife. "Great news. Morgan is comin' this weekend. I finally convinced him he should take a break from the big city and come on up here where he can think."

Millie, who was loading the dishwasher, looked at her husband's joyful face. "It is good news, Cliff. You know," she said shutting the dishwasher door and pushing the start button, "I think you love that boy like a son. You do, don't you?"

"Well, maybe. He just seemed to come along and need someone and I was there. Things like this don't happen unless they're meant to be, Mil. I always thought of Charlie as my son. He was only seven when we got married. It isn't like Morgan is takin' his place or anything."

Millie put her arm around Cliff's waist. "Things like this have God's hand on them. I wasn't sayin' he was replacin' Charlie. I'm happy the two of you like each other as much as you do. How'd you coax him up here?"

"Well, I didn't really have to. Seems he's got somethin' he wants to show us and talk about. He was pretty excited. In fact, he seemed almost happy. Anyhow, we'll know what it's all about tomorrow. He said he'd get here around noon."

"Great. I'll get his room ready."

"It is ready."

"It may need dustin'."

"If it needs dustin' it ain't in this house," he said, giving his wife a tender pat on her behind. "Dust knows better than to collect around here," he laughed, watching Millie take a dust cloth from the pantry closet and head down the hallway to the room they now considered Morgan's.

"I'll find some," she called.

***

In Miami, Morgan couldn't wait for the day to end. A bundle of nerves, he had accidentally hung up on a client, ran Dave out of his office so he could secretly review the information he'd tried to put in some order, and he'd lost a file Marie later found for him. The project of making some sense and finding use of the information found in the box his father had sent him had taken on monumental importance. Not that he didn't question the futility of this endeavor but once begun, he had to finish.

His fingers rested on the steno pad. For the past two evenings he'd pored over every letter and scrap of paper. He'd even tried to make photocopies of the faces in the locket but gave up and put the piece of jewelry back. He'd decided to take the whole thing, jewelry, ribbon, letters and papers with him when he visited Cliff and Millie this weekend. Although he admitted his list was certainly incomplete, as there were still too many unanswered questions, he was eager to get to Carter's Corners. He sat at his desk and watched the digital numbers on the computer screen count off the remaining time he had to spend in the office. His desk was cleared of papers; his files were closed and locked pursuant to office rules. He tucked the steno pad with his project information into his thin briefcase and turned his computer off.

As he left the office, he checked to make sure the lights were off and then pulled the door closed behind him. In fourteen hours he would begin his journey to Carter's Corners. Filled with the usual excitement of revisiting his friends there, this trip seemed to have added importance. *Maybe, just maybe, they can help me find the key to open whatever door this stuff represents.*

When he arrived at the elevator he found Dave waiting for him.

"Hi," Dave said, pressing the down button. "Great plans for the weekend?" He had meant the remark to be his usual prodding to get his friend to commit to some social fun, a project he had taken on and failed at up until now. He was startled by Morgan's answer.

"Yep. I'm leaving early tomorrow to go up-state to visit some friends."

"Whoa. That's a surprise. Well, buddy, I hope you have a great time. Gals and all that good stuff involved?"

"No, just really good friends. I'm looking forward to the visit."

Dave looked at Morgan and recognized a spark he hadn't seen since the summers they'd shared as interns. As the elevator doors opened at the ground floor he patted his friend on the back. "Whatever. Have a great time. See you Monday. I'll want all the details," he said, pushing through the huge front door and turning right toward the parking garage.

"Have fun, yourself," Morgan shouted, hurrying to his bus stop.

After dinner at Cliff and Millie's, Morgan pulled out the outline that he had spent his evenings working on.

1. 9/8/32 – Felicity has family in Gadara. She is coming home from somewhere. (?)She is sorry for something she has done. What (?) Is the box hers (?) Who are the people in the locket(?) Family (?) Asks for forgiveness (?) Mentions God- religious (?)

2. No date: Since the letter is so poor only conclusion is that it must be from someone's mother or relative. What is hidden from the father (?) Also mentions God. Is there a theme here(?) Are these people religious (?)

3. No date: Who is writing this letter (?) It is signed "F" but in another letter there is a woman named Frieda. It could be either, although since the letter seems to be written by the person who wrote the first one then it would be

Felicity's letter. The letter is confusing. Why has the writer been forbidden to contact the recipient (?) Who is 'she' -- a child (?) Again God is mentioned. A trend (?)

4. No date: Letter to whom (?) from a friend. Letter mentions someone has taken recipient's place. Where (?) Why (?) Signed Frieda. No last name, no location mentioned. Two names that begin with F.

5. 12/36 - A page from a diary – probably a woman's. Is it Felicity's (?) She mentions her mother and father. She again relates pain and sorrow for something she has done. (What?) Postscript states she has torn the page from her journal so her parents won't see it. Hints at suicide? Seems to be filled with hopelessness.

6. A list of dates: They don't seem to mean anything. The time between the date 9/3/32, just before Felicity comes home to Gadara, and the next entry 9/6/32 is three days. What is the significance of the first date? The time between that date and the next one is 4 years, the time between that date and the final date, 4/20/54 is 18 years. The final date (4/20/54) indicates that the writer is fearful she has lost (her) forever. Who (?) Why (?)

7. 4/20/54 - Same date as the final entry on the list of dates. This letter is poorly written but contains a lot of information. Her husband wouldn't allow the writer to contact the recipient. He's dead so wife writes. (Why?) What secrecy does Mr. Donnigan insist upon? Mentions a child named Susan. Susan has apparently run away from home with a man. Suspects pregnancy (?) What does this mean to recipient (?) Who is recipient (?) At least here we have a name of the sender, Theresa Donnigan. Of course, it's been 53 years since that letter was written. I have Googled Theresa Donnigan and there are hundreds but I don't have a location to pin down a particular one to begin a search. What significance did the mention of her daughter Susan have to the re-

cipient (Felicity?). Who is Mary Ann?

General Questions:

1, Who kept all this information in the box? Has it always been in the possession of one person? Is that person Felicity and who is she? What is the connection between Felicity, Frieda, Theresa Donnigan and her daughter Susan.

2. How did my parents come to have this box and for how many years?

I will have to contact my father for this information.

"See?" Morgan said more than an hour later. "There must be a thread that joins all this stuff together. But, without dates, locations and names it looks impossible." Morgan leaned back. "Some of the information intertwines and others just seem like loose ends."

"Well, now, I think you're right, thinkin' the key figure is Felicity," Millie said, going over her copy of Morgan's list which now contained penciled in questions or comments.

"And, strange as it sounds, I think Gadara is where this all began. And Gadara is close to your heart, son. That's where Alice is." Cliff put emphasis on the word 'Alice' and looked at Morgan.

"But I can't see any connection to Ali...or to me," Morgan said.

"You never know. You don't know her family background, do you? Maybe after you contact her you could ask a few questions. Who knows, maybe you have the same great-granddaddy or somethin'. But for sure you should get in touch with your..." he paused, he had almost said 'daddy'. "...your father; either by phone or letter...phone would be best...to see if you can find out if he knows where the box came from." Cliff leaned back and stretched.

Morgan sighed. Contacting his father had been a dark cloud hovering over his head ever since he'd received the package. "I guess you're right. If I knew where it came from, maybe I could contact that person." He paused, then said, "I've been thinking... if the box is filled with stuff that had been left when they...when someone took me as an infant to them, then maybe that person would know who my mother was."

It was the first time Morgan had courage enough to put thought to words and he stared over the heads of Cliff and Millie, not able to make eye contact with them. It was late last night when he had allowed himself to even think of the possibility the contents of the box might belong to his family in some way and maybe even to his mother.

For several moments, no one spoke, then Mille said, "I think that's a possibility, Morgan, and after all, isn't that who you want to find?"

Morgan sighed. "You make it sound so simple and all this looks so confusing."

They were sitting around the kitchen table after dinner. The sky filled with the colors of a beautiful sunset seeped through the window over the sink. Outside the sounds of night insects began their chorus.

Cliff rose and came to sit in an empty chair next to Morgan. "Sometimes in life, son, we're the ones who make things tough. This box and these things belonged to someone. They ended up with your parents. There has to be a tie to some folks in the past and they might be your folks. God works in wondrous ways, son."

"You know," Millie said, "you guys are lookin' at all this like a couple of men."

Cliff and Morgan looked at her, then at each other. "That's what we are, Mil," Cliff said, a puzzled look drawing his brow into a crevice above his eyebrow.

"What do you mean?" Morgan asked.

"Well, look at the list Morgan drew up. To me, as a woman," she looked from one to the other to confirm their attention, "it's obvious this Felicity had a baby with no husband in sight. To her, back then, that was a big sin, today nobody'd even notice. She told her mama but not her papa, probably scared to death of what he'd want to do. You'd be pretty upset if it was a daughter of yours, wouldn't you, Cliff?

"Anyhow, the rest of that stuff just shows she never had any way to see her baby and then after that there were other children. Not hers, of course. The lady who adopted Felicity's baby contacted her long after the kid was grown and gone, her husband being dead and all. Felicity never got to see her baby and then with the child run off with someone, well, that's the end of the story."

The silence in the kitchen deepened with every second. Then Morgan said, "You mean this is all a dead end? There's no use in going on?"

"No, not at all. Don't be silly, there's things you can do, like Cliff said, call your daddy, see where the box came from."

Millie pushed herself back from the table. "I think it's time for a cup of tea and a piece of chocolate cake we didn't have room for after dinner." She filled the tea kettle and began to set out plates and mugs.

"Can I help?" Morgan said.

"Just sit. I'll get it."

"You should know better'n that, son. Millie's kitchen is Millie's kitchen and she'll do the doin' if she's home."

They laughed and Morgan relaxed. *Funny how this home is so much a home. It's something I think I wanted all my life and didn't even know it.*

"I'll call my father tomorrow. He's always home on Sunday." Morgan was surprised at the ease with which he was able to say that simple sentence without his usual anxiety kicking in for once.

"And your girl, son. Either call her or write to her. I was never one for writin' but it might be the way you can break the ice. Think about it," Cliff said accepting a plate with a huge slice of chocolate cake. "This is enough for four truck drivers, Mil."

"Oh, go on. You can eat that and more. Here, Morgan," she said, handing him a plate with a similar portion.

"I'm not going to complain about the size, Millie, but it is pretty big. Let's see who leaves any on their plate," he laughed.

The young man who had shouldered a heavy burden of anger and anguish felt like a different person from the one who lived in Miami under a cloud of depression. "I might try and get Alice, too." But as he made that promise his chest tightened. Was he ready to speak to Alice? Would she speak to him? Would a letter be easier for him?

31

They shall perish, but thou shalt endure;
yea, all of them shall wax old like a garment;
as a vesture shalt thou change them,
and they shall be changed.
Psalms 102:26

Karen marveled at how quickly things seemed to be falling into place. Yesterday a truck came from the Salvation Army and picked up all the things she had ticketed as not going to her new home. She leaned on the sink and stared out across the back garden she and Bill had taken such pride in. Soon nothing would be the same and she was torn between the loss of the old things and the excitement of a new beginning. She smiled. "Look forward, not back," she reminded herself.

After the big truck with the red shield on the side pulled into the driveway, she'd gripped her cold hands together for the first hour, trying not to mourn the loss of the items that had been part of her life for so many years, like the little desk which had fit perfectly into the corner of the kitchen and had been her mother's. She watched Ali's face as a box full of her toys was pushed into the back of the truck but she could read no emotions. Ali seemed calm as Mr. Bunny and Tony the Turtle were borne away. When Karen asked her if this bothered her, she'd said, "No, Mom. I've kept a few of my best dolls for my little girl. The rest will go to kids who might not have many toys. They're all in such good condition, the Salvation Army lady said she was happy to get toys and games she could pass along to needy kids."

Karen glanced at her watch; the kitchen clock had been

packed. The first team of packers had arrived two days ago and after she'd directed them as to which cabinets and closets could be packed first; it seemed as if a very short time passed before the job was done. Now very little remained until the final move, which was only three days from now.

Blinking rapidly to quell threatening tears, she turned and looked around the kitchen. All the knick-knacks were gone. Her steps sounded hollow as she walked through to the living room. Was that because the pictures were no longer on the walls? Surely, with so much of the furniture left there shouldn't be such an un-lived in sound to her footsteps, should there?

The only actual packing left to be done was their personal things and Karen planned to do as much of this as she could, making sure Ali didn't try to help. Four large cardboard wardrobes had been provided by the moving company. Already Karen had emptied her closet and now she turned to go toward Ali's room. As soon as Ali was awake she'd start emptying her closets, too.

She was startled to see Ali leaning against the open doorway to her bedroom. "Good Morning, honey. What..." but Karen stopped. Tears covered Ali's cheeks and one hand cupped her swollen stomach. "What's wrong?" Karen stuttered, reaching to pull her daughter to her chest.

"Oh, Mom. I just got out of the shower and...and...there's blood." She clutched her robe closed over her naked body.

"Blood. Oh, honey," she said, turning her daughter gently back into her room. "You get into bed and I'll call Dr. Perez. Do you need anything? Is it a lot of blood or just spots?"

"It didn't look like a lot but I was scared when I saw it. Mom, the babies...I can't..." As her mother settled her gently on the bed and arranged the pillows behind her head Ali began to cry in earnest. "What's happening?"

"I'm not sure, honey, but I'm calling the doctor. Don't cry, Ali, that won't help anything. We'll get help." Karen pulled the sheet up over Ali's distended body." You lie there, pull your knees up and stay flat on your back. Do you need more pillows? Here let me put one underneath your knees. I hope this is the right thing to do. Oh, honey..."

"Call the doctor, Mom," Ali sobbed, adjusting the sheet over her raised knees.

Karen rushed to the kitchen to get her phone lying on the counter, remembering as she hurried that Ali's phone must be right there on the nightstand. In their panic, neither of them thought of that.

Dialing the doctor's office she silently prayed this wasn't the beginning of a terrible day. "Dear God," she prayed, "don't let anything happen to those babies." She added, "Or my baby, either."

After she'd spoken to the receptionist, then been put on hold which seemed to last hours, she spoke to Dr. Perez's nurse.

"We can squeeze Alice in around 10:00. The doctor wants to examine her. Come to the window and we'll take her right back."

Karen ended the call and rushed back to Ali's room. "They said he wants to see you and they can squeeze you in at ten o'clock. That's less than an hour from now. He says you're to stay off your feet until we leave. I'll help you dress."

Ali struggled to sit up and Karen put one hand on her shoulder. "You stay put, we'll get you dressed right where you are." She glanced around the room. Ali had already thrown clothes over a chair, obviously planning to wear them after her shower.

"Get those things, Mom," she said pointing to the clothes. "Oh, darn, my hair is still wet. I didn't get to blow dry it or fix it."

"I think wet, un-fixed hair is the last thing you need to worry about now, honey. Lie still, please," she said as Ali tried to push herself up on her elbows. "You're making me nervous."

Karen grabbed the top and slacks from the chair and threw them on the end of the bed.

If it wasn't a serious situation, the struggle to get clothes on Ali's still damp body without her standing or sitting up was funny, but the job was finally complete. Ali lay on her bed and Karen paced around the room, opening and closing drawers and moving things on the top of the bureau as if they needed to be rearranged. She kept glancing at Ali who lay still with her eyes closed.

"You're fussing, Mom. Please stop, you're making me nervous. Is it time to go yet?" She opened her eyes and saw the distress on her mother's face. "Sit here," she said, patting a narrow space next to her.

Karen sat, her hand automatically reaching for Ali's.

"Is this natural?" Ali asked, struggling unsuccessfully to keep the quiver from her voice.

"I'm not sure, Ali. We'll know more when you see the doctor." She glanced at her watch. "I think sometimes when a woman is expecting twins this might happen because of the extra weight and stretching, but I'm just guessing, honey. It won't be long. The girl at the front desk said they were getting you in right away."

"Not right away. An hour later," Ali moaned.

"Bed rest for three weeks," Ali said, leaning back as her mother drove into the driveway. "And we're moving in three days. How are we going to do that, Mom?"

"He said partial bed rest, which means lots of rest and lying down. Don't worry, we'll do just fine. You weren't going to do any packing or moving anyhow."

"I could have helped a little."

"Well, worrying certainly won't help anything. I think Dr. Perez was pleased with you. He said this is not unusual when you're carrying twins. See, I was right." She glanced at her daughter's pale face as they watched the garage door travel upward. "It'll be okay, honey. We'll take care of whatever has to be done."

"You mean you'll take care of whatever has to be done. I'm just a big lump of inconvenience."

"Stop that silly moaning. Get to bed and stay there. I'll get someone to move the small television we were going to take for the deck at the condo into your bedroom for the time being. We'll only be here for another three days."

Ali struggled out of the car and began to climb the three steps to the kitchen. "Right, another job for you to take care of, supplying me with entertainment."

"Ali," Karen said, shutting the door behind them. "Stop the pity party. I'm sick of hearing you complain. These small things have to be done and it's all part of my big job, if you want to call it that, to take care of you. That's my labor of love right now, to take care of you because I love you." She pulled Alice to her for a brief hug. "Now get into bed. I think you'd be more comfortable in pjs don't you?"

"Okay," Ali said, creeping down the hallway. She moved as if she were carrying a plate of eggs.

"And, remember," Karen called. "They said to lie on your left side and move your legs and feet occasionally. I'll bring you a pitcher of water and some juice. Plenty of fluids, remember?"

Later that afternoon, a much stressed Kristi and Marla arrived breathlessly at the Waterson's front door. "Ali called us, Mrs. Waterson. Is she okay? We were so scared we came as soon as we could," Kristi said softly as she and Marla moved into the living room. "Gosh it looks bare in here already."

"Can we help?" Marla asked, her brow still wrinkled with worry.

"You can help Ali by visiting her. She's going to be kind of confined to her room for a while, here and when we get to the condo. Company for her would be a big help."

"Oh, we will, Mrs. Waterson. We can come over every day, can't we?" Marla whispered, looking to Kristi for endorsement.

"Of course we'll visit every day. Can we do anything to help you? With the move I mean?"

Karen put an arm around each of the girls. They'd been like additional daughters over the years. "You're such good friends to Ali. Go on in and cheer her up," she said, pushing the girls toward the hallway leading to Alice's bedroom. "And," she whispered, "you don't have to whisper."

Kristi and Marla looked at Karen then burst into laughter. "Thanks, Mrs. W.," Marla said as she started down the hall.

"Mrs. W.?" Kristi asked, giving her friend a gentle shove. "Mrs. W.?"

"Well... Hey Ali, here we are to the rescue; ta-dah," Marla called, disappearing into Ali's bedroom.

Karen collapsed into her chair. She'd rescued her knitting basket from the packer's and it sat on the floor where it had for more years than Karen cared to remember. But she didn't reach for the knitting needles as she usually would; instead, she closed her eyes and listened to the laughter and chatter coming from her daughter's room. "Just what she needed," she murmured. "And, just what I needed, too." Later, she'd make tea and take cookies in to the girls but right now she needed to do nothing.

"Absolutely nothing," she thought, taking in a deep, stress-free breath.

32

The Lord will give strength unto his people;
the Lord will bless his people with peace.
Psalms 29:11

Morgan threw his cell phone on his bed and reached for the slider to the balcony. Even though it was six o'clock, stepping outside he felt the heat of the day press on him like a wooly blanket. The western sun broiled its way toward sunset. His hands gripped the top rail of the wrought iron railing and he gazed across the empty tennis courts. He reeled in shock.

After coming back to Miami following his weekend visit with Cliff and Millie, he'd felt a strange melancholy. Yet, maybe things would work out. Was it the letters that encouraged him? Was it Cliff and Millie's positive thinking?

Whatever it was, the day dragged on because he had finally decided what to do. He was going to call Ali. "Don't worry if she's all put out," Millie had said when he left late last night. "Just tell her the truth." She leaned into the car and kissed Morgan's cheek. "You call us after you've talked to your gal, you hear? It'll be okay, we're prayin' for you."

The Monday work day seemed endless and the bus ride home after work felt as if many more miles had been added to the route. At his stop, he'd rushed across the wide boulevard, scaled the stairs two at a time and fumbled with the door key when he got home. Without changing clothes, he'd thrown himself on the couch and dialed the familiar number. He had to contact Ali.

His fingers trembled as he pressed her number in his phonebook. But there was no answer. No request to leave a message. Nothing. Had she gotten another phone, another plan? Then when he tried her mother's land line he'd received a recorded message advising the telephone number was no longer a working number.

Where are they? Where could they go? As far as I remember her family had lived in the same town for generations.

Later that night, lying on his back on his unmade bed, Morgan, hands behind his head, stared at the ceiling. He glanced at his watch. Eleven-thirty. He just couldn't get to sleep. Where were Ali and her mother? Memories of the weekend haunted him, too. Good memories of the time he'd spent with Cliff and Millie, but he kept hearing the words Cliff had said: "And your girl, son. Either call her or write to her."

He squirmed to the edge of the bed and rose. "I can write," he said aloud. "I'll write her a letter."

Morgan sat at his desk, his laptop open. He created a new document and stared at the blank screen in front of him. "How do I start?" he asked, his fingers poised over the keyboard.

Two hours later Morgan held the finished product in his hands. He hadn't eaten dinner but he hadn't noticed. Mixed emotions coursed through his mind, pride because he'd finished the task, fear he might not mail it, and terror at the thought this might actually be the tool for Ali to reject him.

He walked into the living room, the letter, a check and envelope in his hand. He'd already put a stamp on the envelope, an indication of his sincerity. He'd signed the check. Still, he hesitated to sign and slide the letter into the envelope.

He sat on the sofa, leaned forward and placed the letter on the coffee table. He signed the letter, *I love you ~ Morgan,* quickly folded the paper around the check, pushed them into the envelope and ran his tongue along the glued edge. Pressing the envelope flat, he picked it up, grabbed his keys from the hall table and dashed through the door. Running down the stairs, he reached the sidewalk outside the building. He raced to the corner where a Post Office mail box stood, opened the flap and tossed the letter inside. For several minutes he stood frozen, one hand still on the flap, the other still poised where he had released the envelope. "It's done," he whispered and slowly walked back to his condo. "It's done," he repeated as he trudged up the stairs.

In his apartment he didn't want to go back to bed. He knew sleep would elude him. Instead he went out onto the balcony and threw himself in a chair next to the table. The night sounds were muted now at this hour. It was after midnight and while the restaurants and bars of South Beach would be going strong, up here it was quiet.

The words of his letter haunted him. Did he do the right thing? Would Ali forgive him and give him another chance?

I left her. I left her alone and facing the rest of her pregnancy without me. I'm a... Morgan momentarily searched for the right word but all that came to mind were inadequate to describe his self-loathing. *That child is mine and I want to...*

Awkwardly, he pushed himself from the chair, off balance he staggered to the railing again. *What if she didn't want the baby? What if she...?* "She couldn't! She wouldn't," he added without conviction.

Morgan paced across the small concrete floor. Why hadn't he thought of this before? "Because you are a selfish, rotten person, that's why. Because if you had any sense at all, you would have called her right away instead of wallowing in your... your fixation about yourself. So you were adopted. So your parents, or that couple who raised you, weren't a fairy tale sequel to The Brady Bunch. You punished her for your stupid disappointment."

His hands hurt from the painful wringing he gave them as he strode back and forth on the balcony; the space had suddenly become a prison cell. Quickly moving to the slider he flung it open, rushed inside and closed it with a bang. Leaning against the glass he sobbed. "You are a fool!" He flung himself across the bed. Sleep eluded him for hours and when he did sleep it was accompanied by strange dreams where nothing and no one made sense.

In the morning, when his alarm clock bellowed its wake up buzz, Morgan raised his head and then flopped back into his pillow. "I can't go in to work. I just can't. I'm wasted."

An hour later, stepping from the shower he felt a little better. He opened his phone and called the office.

"Are you ill?" Marie inquired when he begged off today.

"I think I have a bug," he lied. "I'm all sweaty and shaky."

"Well, you haven't missed a day all summer so take care, Morgan, and I'll tell Mr. Littman, Jr. you won't be in."

"Thanks, Marie. I'll be there tomorrow."

Morgan flipped the phone closed with a deep feeling of guilt. He didn't like lying.

He put coffee and water into his two-cup coffee pot and made himself a peanut butter and jelly sandwich. After his breakfast, he took the second cup of coffee into the living room. He flipped the television on but the cheerful morning newswoman annoyed him so he shut it off.

"I need to talk to Cliff," he said. He looked at his watch. Now nine-thirty, he knew Millie would be off to work. Cliff might be up or was he still sleeping?

With a deep sigh he pressed his saved phone numbers and selected Cliff and Millie's. He hesitated a moment then pushed number 8.

After three rings, Cliff answered. "Hello?"

"Hello, Cliff, it's Morgan. Did I wake you?"

"No, I was readin' the mornin' paper. What's up? Did you call your gal?"

There was a long pause and then Morgan said. "I wrote her a letter and mailed it last night."

"Well, good for you. You did the right thing."

"I don't know, Cliff. What if she doesn't want me? What if she can't forgive me? Maybe I should have waited and called."

"Now, son, don't go gettin' all up tight about this letter. It was the right thing to do. Now give her some time to think about it. Did you say in your letter you'd call her?"

"Yes."

"Well then, just wait and see. No sense worryin' over what might happen. You know that, don't you?"

Morgan nodded.

"You there?"

"Yes, I understand. And, you're right. I'll just have to wait. I did say I'd call her. I'll try later. Maybe in a couple days. Give her time to get the letter."

"That's the spirit. Now you just kick back and enjoy the day. You near the beach?"

"Yes, it's right across the street."

"Well, go there and watch the waves. I remember you tellin' me how you liked to do that. Just don't get sunburned, they might not believe your sick story." He laughed and Morgan could picture the wrinkles above his cheeks deepen. "Now don't spend the whole day worryin'."

Morgan felt drained; drained of any ambition to do anything. Maybe he'd go to the beach later in the day, but now all he wanted to do was go back to bed. Maybe he was really sick. Emotionally sick.

He locked the front door and walked into his bedroom. But instead of throwing himself on the bed as he'd wanted to do his eyes traveled to the computer. Maybe he should re-read the letter.

"What the heck good would that do?" he asked himself. "It's gone now. If you want to change anything it's too late."

But he sat in the chair at the desk and turned his lap top on, searching for the letter he'd written. Suddenly his heart crunched in his chest. He'd saved it hadn't he? It had been so late.

The blue screen blinked and then the document appeared. Slowly he read the words that had poured from his heart last night.

Sweetheart,

I don't know what to say…I'm so ashamed at how I've behaved and I'm about to ask you to forgive me and I don't even know how to begin. I've tried to call you several times. Truthfully, I have, but I never got beyond listening to a couple of rings and then, like the coward I am, I hung up. Never have words been so elusive because there are no words I can use to let you know what I'm feeling.

There's only one message that's important—I love you with

all my heart and I'm so sorry I went away. I almost said 'left you' but I haven't left you. Ali, you are in my heart every moment of every day. How can I say that? Because it's the truth.

Something happened when I visited my parents that last time. Something that messed up my mind beyond description. I know it's a situation I have to work out and I WILL work it out. It has nothing to do with you or our baby. Just writing the words 'our baby' makes me shiver. I hope you are doing well

I think you understood long ago that there was little love in my life growing up. I lacked for nothing except the one thing I longed for. Love. I guess that's why when we fell in love it was so special. You were the first and only person in the world who made life meaningful. I don't want to lose that! Remember my special name for you? Ali Baba, because you were the magician who brought me to life.

And now for the big question. Ali, will you wait for me? Will you give me another chance? I'm not sure if I can hope for a response from you right away but will you think about it? I need you, my Ali Baba. I'm just so afraid of being hurt again and I'm ashamed to admit that, but here I have admitted it. I'm sending you a check to help out with the costs because I know there are costs. It seems like a cold thing to do. I'm working at Littman & Littman and my home address is on the envelope. You have my cell number.

I'm begging your forgiveness, Ali. I'm begging you to be patient because I'm making headway. I will call you, I promise.

I love you.

Morgan closed out the document file and shut the laptop down. He turned and threw himself on the bed, face down, burying his face in the rumpled pillow. He lay still but the muffled sobs permeated the silent room. When he finally fell asleep, his tears had drenched the pillow beneath his head.

33

Wait on the Lord: be of good courage,
and He shall strengthen thine heart:
wait, I say, on the Lord.
Psalms 27:14

"It's back to Miami for you, my man." Samuel leaned against the bureau in Jack's loft at Twin Oaks.

"What's up?" Jack asked sitting on the side of the very unused bed.

"Things are coming to a head and you have to persuade Morgan to telephone Alice. You know, Karen's daughter. You see, Morgan is the father of Alice's babies..."

"I knew it!"

"Well, yes, and he just has to get his act together. He has to contact her, not just words on paper or phone calls he hangs up on before talking to anyone or even leaving a message. You've got to convince him of this."

"Swell. What do I do, wrestle him to the ground and pummel him for being such a fool?"

You'll know what to do, Samuel said, drifting back into his other existence.

"Wait, you'll be there too, won't you? Jack listened. "You will, won't you?"

Jack sighed. "He'll be there, the little pain-in-the-neck."

***

Morgan hurried to his bus stop. He was late getting out of the office by five minutes and that might just be the difference between making or missing his bus.

"Hello. Morgan, isn't it?"

He stopped short. The bearded man from the bus last week stood next to him. "Um...ah...what are you doing here?"

"Well, not the friendliest greeting I've had. I was needed back in Miami and I finished my business just minutes ago further down on Flagler and I remembered you took this bus home. I'm at loose ends for the evening, and I remembered our nice dinner together the last time we met, so I thought if I saw you I'd at least say hello."

"Well, you sure surprised me. I'm sorry about the greeting. It is nice to see you again."

"I'm free for dinner, are you?"

"Well, this is unexpected, but," Morgan said, watching his bus pull away from the stop ahead, "I guess I am. This is so off-the-wall. Forgive me if I was rude."

"Not rude, surprised and you acted accordingly. I'm tired and I won't be leaving Miami to go back to Gadara until late tonight, so a quiet little out-of-the-way place would suit me fine. Have you ever heard of Stowaway's? It's a nice kind of bohemian bar with an outdoor eating patio several blocks south. It's usually not crowded until after nine, they draw more of a late night crowd. Should we hail a taxi or walk?"

"I know Stowaway's. Haven't been there in a long time. I'd prefer to walk, if you don't mind. I try to walk everywhere to get some exercise after being cooped up in an office all day. Is walking okay with you?"

"Actually, I was hoping you'd say that," Jack said, watching the crowd pass and hoping no one he knew saw him. "Let's duck down this side street and then you can lead the way." *Maybe if someone does see me Sam will strike them blind for a moment until I get out of here. I should be nervous and I'm not. Sam, are you here? Samuel?*

Jack and Morgan sat at a marble topped wrought iron table. Two matching chairs with colorful cushions kept the chairs from being uncomfortable. The outdoor patio was enclosed with lattice panels, allowing the ever-present breeze to waft through. Colorful ornamental parrots in cages were hung from the edge of the corrugated tin roof, and baskets of greenery were distributed between the cages.

"I can't believe I forgot about Stowaway's," Morgan said, sipping his tall glass of beer. "How did you know about this place?"

"It's a well-kept secret." Jack was hoping none of his old professor friends would show up early. When he was with them, they never arrived before nine o'clock. Nevertheless, he had chosen the chair with his back to the rest of the room.

A pretty girl in incredibly short shorts and a midriff-showing top placed a basket in front of Morgan. "Nachos with jalapeño cheese for you," she said and placed a second basket in front of Jack. "And, refried beans and guacamole with a side of rice for you. Anything else? Want your beers topped up?"

They declined and the waitress swished her way back to the kitchen.

"Pretty girl," Jack said, tasting the refried beans.

"And well-dressed," Morgan laughed.

"Yes, and then they wonder why men come on to them."

"Maybe that's the point," Morgan said with a smirk.

"You're so right."

The two men enjoyed their meals, exchanging small talk about weather, politics, and the latest Miami scandal.

"Finished?" the waitress asked removing the basket and wicker-enclosed plate. "Another beer?"

Morgan looked at Jack. "Do you have time?"

"I have all the time in the world. My ride isn't going to pick me up until eleven."

"You seem to travel late," Morgan remarked with a grin.

"I go when it's convenient for my friend. I'm kind of a night owl so it doesn't bother me."

"I've become a night owl lately. Thanks," Morgan added to the girl when she placed two more huge glasses of beer on the table. "Wow, these are huge. Maybe I shouldn't have had a second."

"You don't have to finish it," Jack said. He watched Morgan who, while seeming to enjoy his dinner, too often had a far away look in his eyes. "You said last time we met you were dealing with some problems. Fixed them yet?"

"I don't know if they're fixable." Morgan's right hand grasped the cold glass.

"Is that a birthmark?" Jack asked, pointing to the brown, ragged circle on Morgan's wrist.

"Yes. I've had it since birth. It never bothered me. Most people don't even notice it, and if they do they probably think I need a wash," he joked. "You don't miss a thing."

"I thought it might be an old tattoo. I've seen a similar one recently." He pulled Morgan's hand closer to him. *Yes, it's exactly like the one on A.J.'s hand. Could it be...more than a coincidence?* Jack's mind reeled as he released Morgan's hand back to him.

"You asked about my troubles. I don't know why I feel compelled to share my woes with you. I don't even know you."

"I'm a good listener. I remember telling someone recently you can teach a whole lot more when you listen. I'm very willing to listen if you need to talk. Sometimes talking to someone who is in no way involved helps clarify things a bit. Not that I'm a miracle worker or anything, but my students often came to me for advice." He paused and looked into Morgan's eyes. "If I've overstepped my bounds, I apologize."

"No. No. It's just so strange, but I think I want to talk to you."

For several moments the hushed conversation between several couples at the small tables seemed to diminish. ""You see, I've done something stupid, something hurtful to someone I love and I don't know how to make it up to her."

"What do you think would help make things right?"

Morgan pushed against the orange cushion behind his back. He closed his eyes for a moment and immediately saw Ali's tear stained face. "Maybe I've waited too long. I hurt the one I love more than anything in the world. I let a selfish tantrum become more important than her or the baby we'd made."

Jack sat quietly watching Morgan's agony envelop him.

Morgan turned his head away but not before Jack saw the glimmer of tears in his eyes.

"We all do stupid things. I let someone go," Jack said, thinking of Jennifer. He grimaced and then realized he could say that now without the pain he'd felt before. *That's what Sam was talking about. The pain is being erased. If only I could help erase Morgan's pain.* "Have you tried to tell her what your feelings are?"

"I wrote a letter. I tried to call her several times but I always hang up before anyone answers, or I don't leave a message. Now apparently there's a problem with the phones up there. I'm afraid to hear her voice and yet that's what I want. I'm afraid to be hurt anymore."

"She hurt you?"

"God, no. She's the most wonderful girl in the world. She's... kind...good...and I know she loved me. We were going to get married. We hadn't set a date and then when we knew about the baby...I was so excited." Morgan could no longer stem his grief and tears seeped from the corners of his eyes.

Jack pulled a clean, ironed handkerchief from the pocket inside his jacket and pushed it across the table. "Never be afraid to show emotions, Morgan. That's what makes the human race different from the animal kingdom. God knew what he was doing when he gave us tears. Tears are not just for women, although for years that's what I thought." He waited for Morgan to gather himself and when he heard him sigh, he continued. "Let's hope whatever you did is reversible. Perhaps you have to do something more than write or hang up on your girlfriend. Maybe it's more important to first take care of whatever made you change, whatever caused the, what did you call it, the selfish tantrum."

Morgan studied the nearest parrot cage. He wadded up the handkerchief and stuffed it into his pocket. "What made me change was stupid, it was overblown by my egocentric need to be part of something I'll never be a part of."

Jack waited for a few moments, then asked, "Who hurt you?"

"The people who raised me."

Jack watched as more people came into the eatery. He was running out of time. He couldn't risk being seen by any of his old colleagues. *Why did I recommend this restaurant instead of somewhere else? Sam, where are you? I need help.*

I'm right here. You're doing great. Don't worry.

Jack turned his eyes back to Morgan who was staring vacantly into space. "You mean your parents?"

"They weren't really my parents. Just people who raised me."

"I was a foster child all my life. I had some really nice foster parents. Some had problems but I also had a good case worker. That's why I became a teacher. I loved kids," Jack said.

Morgan looked at his newfound friend with interest. "You had foster parents?"

Jack nodded.

"But these weren't foster parents. They adopted me."

"Well, I don't understand... wasn't that better?"

"Not really. I think I was so upset because I didn't find out until this May. At the age of twenty-three I found out I didn't have any family. Not real family. And here I was going to have a child of my own and who did I look to? Who was I? I suddenly realized the reason I'd felt guilty all my life was because my so-called parents didn't really love me. All along I thought it was because I wasn't doing what they wanted. I thought it was my fault there was no affection. I have no chain of family. I have no roots. I was like a tumble weed that had landed in a place where it really wasn't wanted."

Morgan's eyes had fire in them now as he released all the tension and hurt that had built up in him. Jack saw the revelation.

"You were hurt and so you had to hurt someone else?"

Morgan bowed his head, eyes closed. "I didn't think of it that way. I lashed out at them, the people who raised me. I felt so abandoned, and after talking to them I knew they never really wanted me. I was a favor to a friend of a friend, for God's sake. They didn't even know who my mother was and I realized I probably would never know either."

"So you left Alice and her baby to face what? A life without a husband and father? Is that what you thought would fix your problem? Abandon them like you were abandoned?"

"No, no, no. I don't know what I thought I was doing." He looked up into Jack's eyes. He saw comfort, understanding and something else. Love? He was a stranger. "I made such a mess of things, didn't I? And for what reason?"

"Morgan, we don't always know the right path. It takes time and thought and love to discover where we should be. I think you know where you should be, don't you?"

Morgan nodded, unable to look his friend in the eye. He stood and reached for the check the waitress had put on the table when she delivered the last beers. "I've taken up so much of your time. I don't know how to thank you, Jack. Why couldn't I open my eyes months ago? Have I left it too late?"

Jack stood and took the bill from Morgan's finger. "I'll get this. Have you left it too late? I don't know. But I do know that doing nothing will fix nothing. It's up to you." He guided Morgan to the outside door. The noise from the bar was increasing and Jack knew it was time to leave.

As they walked along the sidewalk, uneven because the Banyan tree's roots had lifted the slabs of concrete, neither man spoke. Night had fallen while they were at Stowaway's. The sound of palms rattling their fronds in the breeze from Biscayne Bay was familiar and comforting.

"I don't know how to thank you, Jack," Morgan said, breaking their silence.

"You don't have to. I told you, I just listen."

"I think you did a lot more than that. You made me see what I have to do. You made me realize what a fool I've been. I just pray Ali will forgive me, that we have a future. And," he stopped walking and turned to look at this benefactor who had come from nowhere. "I will never forget what you've done no matter how it comes out." He reached for Jack's hand, not for a handshake but a two-handed grip of gratitude. "I've never known anyone like you and I probably will never meet anyone like you ever again. Somehow I know this is special. I don't know where you came from or when I'll see you again, but thanks, friend. Thank you from the bottom of my heart."

Jack squeezed Morgan's hands and then in a quick motion, pulled the young man to his chest for just a moment before he released him and pulled away. "I never had any children, Morgan, no son of my own, but I've had hundreds of students. If I had ever had a son, though, I would have wanted him to be just like you."

He walked a few steps, turned and looked at Morgan standing in the shadows a few feet away. "I'm going. If I turn here I can meet my friend. Good bye, Morgan. I hope you and Alice and your children have a happy life together."

Morgan watched as Jack quickly turned the corner and disappeared into the shadows of the canopy overhead. "Wait," he called, hurrying to the corner. "I don't know how to get in touch with you." He stared down the deserted street. Calypso music came from one of the homes but there was no sign of Jack. Puzzled, Morgan walked a few feet along the sidewalk. "Jack," he called but there was no answer.

In a daze, he walked back to Flagler Street and went to his bus stop. He sat on a bench to wait. *Was it real? I feel as if I've just awakened from a dream,* he thought.

34

Behold, I will send my messenger,
and he shall prepare the way before me...
Malachi 3:1

A.J. hesitated. He had just wanted to see the building, just drive by so he could say he went, but something compelled him to park the car and go into the main building. The tall pillars in front of the double doors with the gleaming brass hardware were impressive. Stepping into the attractive reception area was like walking into a five-star hotel. Comfortable groupings of furniture, colorful artwork on the walls and a huge grand piano in one corner expressed an ambiance of elegance.

Boy, he thought. *This looks like money. I think I'm in the wrong place.* He turned to leave but a woman with softly curling white hair greeted him. "Good morning. Welcome to Sylvan Hall. Are you here to visit someone?"

"No. No, I just wondered what the place looked like. Very nice," he said, edging toward the entrance, hoping to make a hasty retreat.

"Oh, perhaps you'd like a tour. Are you considering assisted living?" The woman's voice was touched with a soft drawl. Aunt Felicity suddenly came to A.J.'s mind.

"No, I just wanted to see what this..." he hesitated, captivated by her pleasant smile. "Well, I was advised by my doctor to consider this but I don't think I'm ready yet. I don't want to hold you up. You must be busy." He took a step back. Why in the world was he blurting out private things to this woman?

"We're so proud of our community we just love showing off. Why not just take a quick look around since you're here? It will only take a few minutes." She extended her hand. "Jacqueline Souders," she said.

He barely touched her hand before pulling away quickly. "A.J. Handley," he croaked and cleared his throat nervously. He hadn't felt this insecure in decades. *What the heck's wrong with me, acting like a high school kid on his first date.*

"Would you like a brief tour, Mr. Handley?"

"Ah…well," he mumbled looking at his watch as if he had something important on his agenda. "Well, maybe a quick look, Mrs. Souders."

Her face lit with a bright smile. "Oh, you'll enjoy this. As I said, we're proud of our home. Let's start here. This room is the lobby which somehow has acquired the title 'Great Room' but it's also used for group meetings, such as the book club, and once a week we have a small tea for those who enjoy that little nicety. We also have several sing-alongs scheduled, singing is optional, listening is a treat," she smiled.

She took his elbow and guided him toward a wide hallway. "Along here you can see some smaller meeting rooms where the residents play cards or just meet to chat." Each room opened off the corridor with wide doors and he could see soft furniture around the perimeter with card tables and chairs in the center.

"We also have a television room where residents can watch movies and sporting events but most units have their own television sets. It's kind of nice to be with others, though, when you're enjoying an old movie or rooting for your favorite team. We have satellite television throughout the entire complex."

She moved slowly along the hall, greeting residents when they looked up from whatever they were doing. There were three women sitting in a corner talking and doing needlework and he quickly envisioned Aunt Felicity's flashing fingers. At a hallway junction, Jacqueline turned right. "Along here we have some of our units. These are mainly single units for one resident. If the door is open you are welcome to look inside. If the door is closed that means the resident doesn't want visitors at this time. It's kind of an unwritten rule of the house," she laughed. "As you can see, several doors are open. Oh, there is Mr. Wills, Hello, Frank. How are you today?"

They stopped in front of an open door and A.J. saw an elderly man in a recliner in front of his wide screen television. From what he could see, the room was furnished nicely and everything looked spotless. "Hey, Jackie. Doin' just fine. Waiting for lunch and then pinochle like always." He looked at A.J. "If you're thinking of joinin' us, you couldn't do better. Good food, good folks." His smile was broad and genuine.

"Thanks," A.J. mumbled, embarrassed at the obvious welcome extended.

Moving down the hallway, Mrs. Souders continued, "You'll notice the rooms are all furnished nicely. We furnish them unless the residents wish to bring along their own furniture or perhaps just a favorite piece or two. It's entirely up to the residents. We do the cleaning. There is laundry service and we have a resident nurse on staff twenty-four hours a day for whatever medical assistance is needed. Nurses Janet and Melody oversee medications, check blood pressures or help out in any instance where they can. Of course, we keep records of the preferred doctors so the residents' health care continues as before coming to Sylvan Hall."

They continued on the tour, A.J. not noticing it was far more than a brief look as he had expected. They viewed the exercise room, complete with a licensed trainer, other activity rooms and two beautiful dining rooms, the largest competing nicely with any upscale restaurant in the area.

Ending the tour at the lobby where he'd entered, A.J. was overwhelmed at the facilities and the friendly atmosphere. Along the way, he'd been invited by residents, one single gentleman and a couple who clung to each other as if they were teenagers, to join in on some card games in the afternoon.

"Why don't you stay for lunch, Mr. Handley? We'd love to have you as our guest." Jackie asked.

"Oh, I couldn't..."

"Do you have something you must attend to? You'd be comfortable here, Mr. Handley. I just know you'd fit in. Already you've been invited to several card groups. We'd love to have you stay for lunch. Would you like that?"

A.J. hesitated. What did he have to do for the rest of the day? Nothing. Sit on the veranda, watch cars go by, listen to the birds. He'd planned to go to the Dilly Dally for lunch. Surely he'd meet someone he knew there. Still, he hesitated. "You know, Mrs. Souders, I think I will stay for lunch," he said, shocking himself. Why had he suddenly agreed to something so foreign to him, he couldn't imagine where the words had come from. *Lunch? In this fancy place?*

Jacqueline pointed to a comfortable chair facing the piano. "Mr. Santino will be here in a few minutes," she said, glancing at her watch. "He plays music for about an hour during the lunch periods. In the meantime, I'll get you some literature on Sylvan Hall. I'll come by and take you down to the dining room at eleven forty-five. I'll be back in a moment. There are some magazines there, too, you might enjoy." Her smile was so engaging, A.J. couldn't help but return it.

"I hadn't planned..." he began.

"I know," she said, face still beaming." I'm so glad you decided to join us for lunch, Mr. Handley, and it's Jackie. Around here the staff is always on a first name basis. We think it's friendlier and it's easier to remember first names and then there's no need for titles." She patted A.J.'s shoulder.

As he sat alone in the great room a woman came in the front doors, looked at him and said, "Hello. Am I in time for lunch?" But she didn't wait for a response and hurried through the room.

Not long after that a tall, thin man with salt and pepper hair and beard came in, went to the piano and adjusted the bench before he sat down. "Good afternoon," he said and A.J. detected a slight accent.

"Good afternoon," A.J. said.

"Here for a little music?" the pianist asked, running his fingers lightly across the keys. Even the little practice sounded good and A.J. remembered the old upright piano in the homestead's parlor. *It disappeared after Aunt Felicity died. Had it been hers? I can't remember if I ever heard her play it. In fact, I don't remember anyone playing it. Why hadn't I asked questions when there was family who could have answered them?*

"I'm waiting for Mrs. Sounders," A.J. said, his voice modulated to suit the quiet of the room.

"Oh, Jackie. Here she comes now."

"Mr. Handley. Here's a copy of our brochure and a copy of the facilities available here."

"Is there a price list too?"

"We don't have a price list," she said, her voice lowered because the pianist began playing something classical. "If you decide to think about coming to Sylvan Hall, we'll discuss your needs." She added, "Let me take you back to the dining room and introduce you to the gentlemen you'll be dining with."

A.J. pushed himself off the deep cushion and rose, but he lost his balance and grasped for the arm of the chair.

"Are you alright, Mr. Handley?" Jackie asked, her concern evident.

"I'm okay. Sometimes I get a bit wobbly."

"We'll stand here a minute until you're steady."

"No, I'm okay."

They started off, arm in arm like old buddies. He tucked the brochure into his back pocket and watched residents coming out of rooms, singles and couples, cheerfully calling to each other. Aromas of food drifted to meet them and he thought of his empty kitchen and the silence that usually accompanied him at his meals.

Maybe, he thought. *Maybe.*

Before A.J. pulled out of the parking space and turned to leave, he paused a moment, staring at the columned front of Sylvan Hall. The memories of his tour, Jackie, and the lunch he had just shared with five other single men were fresh in his mind. He recalled the friendly banter, talk of a movie tonight and a game of gin in the afternoon. The lunch had been good, a cut above the Dilly Dally although he'd never badmouth that decades-old testament to the down-to-earth values of Gadara. But his lunch was well prepared and the choice of a cold or hot lunch was no tough decision for him to make. He had noticed the menu listed a cold and hot meal for lunch and another for dinner. That way the residents could control their food choices.

He remembered thinking *I can eat a cold dinner at home.* The hot meal consisted of thin slices of beef with clear gravy and mashed sweet potatoes reminding him of his grandma's. The mixed vegetables could have been cooked a bit longer and the dessert, fresh fruit with a dab of something, not whipped cream, but something, was just right.

He sighed. It was all so different. Would he fit in? He glanced at his reflection in the rearview mirror. "Since when did you ever worry about fitting in?" he said with a tight-lipped grin. He put the car in gear and drove out the circular drive leaving Sylvan Halls.

Turning right on Riverview he headed home but was surprised to see his friend Jack loping along the sidewalk. He slowed the car. "Hey, you sure get around on those legs of yours. Want a ride?" He was thinking Jack would turn him down and keep on running and was surprised when he stopped and walked over to the car.

Bending down to speak through the open window, Jack smiled. "I do get around on these legs of mine. I've been running for about half an hour and ready to quit, only I have to get home."

"Well, if you want a ride, hop in."

"Will I be taking you out of your way?"

"Nope," A.J. said, leaning across the seat to open the door.

Jack slid onto the bench seat in A.J's ten-year-old Buick. "Thanks. Sometimes I extend myself a bit. I ran farther than I had intended."

"Never a good idea to over-extend yourself," A.J. laughed. "Especially if you're over seventy."

"I'll remember that." Jack said with a grin. "What have you been up to? Had lunch at the Dilly Dally?"

A.J. pulled away from the curb, going slowly along the tree shaded street. "Nope. You'll never guess where I've been. I just had a fancy lunch at Sylvan Hall."

"The assisted living place? Tell me about it."

A.J. hesitated. "Well," he began. "I don't know what possessed me to go in that place. I was just driving by to get an idea of what it looked like. It looks like someone relocated Tara in Gadara."

"The columns are impressive. I've never been inside, though, so you have one up on me."

"Well, let me tell you, that place is like a really high class fancy hotel, only all the guests are old folks. The lobby is like a movie scene. This nice lady, Jackie, she said to call her; I'm not sure about that much familiarity but I guess it's what goes these days. Anyhow, she met me as I was on my way out. I was just going to look. Everyone called her Jackie. She's the manager. She took me on a tour. Nice place, I'll give it that. Then she invited me to lunch, set me up in the smaller dining room with five other old guys and we had a real nice lunch."

Jack looked at his companion. A.J.'s face was more relaxed than he'd ever seen the old gentleman. "Nice, huh?"

A.J. nodded. "You could say nice."

"Thinking of going there?"

"Oh, now, I'm not saying that. Not saying that at all. Why, that's a big decision and big decisions take time, take a lot of thinking."

"But, you liked it, didn't you?"

"Yes, but..."

"I know, there are always 'buts', aren't there? But," he said, chuckling, "sometimes the right thing comes along and you just don't want to miss it by malingering. I know. I've missed out on something very special because I thought there was time. Then time ran out."

A.J. slowed to make the turn onto Market Street. Twin Oaks was two blocks ahead. "What did you miss out on that a little more time and thought might not have changed things?"

"I missed out on the lady I should have married and didn't."

A.J. pulled to the curb across the street from Twin Oaks. He turned and looked at his companion. "Couldn't you just make the decision now?"

Jack shook his head from side to side slowly. "No. It's too late."

"She married someone else?"

Jack was startled by A.J.'s comment. "No," he said. "It's just too late."

"I'm sorry," A.J. said.

"I am, too," Jack said. "But you have time. You'll think about it, right?" He pushed the passenger door open and stepped out.

Closing the door he went around the front of the car and stopped at the driver's window. "Think about it. Thanks for the ride. I'll see you again soon."

A.J. watched Jack walk up the path to Twin Oaks. "Thanks, son," he called. "I'll think about it." He'd never seen Jack move so slowly or felt so protective about this strange young man who had wandered into his life. "I never called any man 'son' before, either," he muttered as he drove home.

35

Sing unto him a new song;
play skillfully with a loud noise.
Psalms 33:3

"What a day!"

Karen with Shirley and Martin Owens sat on the deck of the new condo. The sun was setting and the evening had a mixed glow of past and promise, the sky mottled with streaks of pink and gold. Missy curled up on Karen's lap. "This is all new to you, too, isn't it Missy? Did you have fun being with Ali and the girls?" She ruffled the curls on top of Missy's head. The little dog put her head on her paws.

"I think she's pooped out. She'll sleep tonight like she'd done all the work," laughed Martin.

"It's over," Shirley said, a glass of tea in one hand, the other drooping limply over the arm of her chair.

"You both worked so hard, how can I ever thank you?"

"When we move you can help us," Martin said, stretched out on a lounge chair.

"Like that's going to happen. I'm set for life, thank you very much," Shirley said with a laugh.

Karen sighed. "I thought I was too, once." She scanned the crowded patio. "I'm going to have to get rid of some of this patio furniture. The old lanai was much larger than this deck. I didn't realize how much larger."

"Give it away," murmured Shirley.

"To whom?"

"Us," Martin said.

"You'd want this stuff?"

"It's good stuff. I'm thinking of adding a covered patio like you had. If I ever get it done, our screen room stuff would go out there and this nicer furniture would go inside."

"You can have it, with thanks. I'd love to see someone use it, especially you." Karen put her glass of tea on a table which was temporarily scrunched between two large cartons. "Boxes, boxes everywhere," she sighed.

"Maybe having the new porch furniture will spark him to get going on this idea he's had for...how long, Martie?" Shirley said.

"Don't ask and don't be sarcastic. Remember, 'honey gets you more than vinegar'," Martin said, sitting up and swinging his legs over the side of the lounge. "If I stay there much longer, I'll be asleep. I guess we'd better be getting home, Shirl."

"Don't worry about the boxes," Shirley said to Karen. "You can open them up as needed. Those packers did a fantastic job, everything is so clearly marked and the things you're going to need most, like kitchen things, are just sitting in the kitchen waiting to find a home," Shirley twisted in her chair to look through the sliding glass doors. "The other boxes you can do bit at a time."

"You know Karen, Shirl," Martin said. "She'll have this all away by the end of the week. It'll look like the cover of House Beautiful before you know it."

They laughed. Tired as they all were, they were enjoying this end-of-the-day break together.

"I can't believe you thought to bring a picnic lunch for everyone, iced tea and treats for the girls and that huge cooler with more food and drinks. You are so considerate." Karen looked at her long-time friends.

"That's what friends are for."

Karen stood and gathered the empty glasses. "I'll wash these and get them to you."

"Don't bother. They're plastic. Just toss them."

"They're pretty though," Karen hesitated.

"Toss them or keep them," Martin said, rising. "Come on, Shirl, let's go."

"I'm going to say goodbye to Ali and her girlfriends. I can't believe they're still here. You said they picked Ali up at eight? They sure are good friends."

"Like us," Karen said, giving her a hug.

Martin leaned down and brushed a brief kiss across Karen's cheek. "Let us know if you need more help."

Karen and Martin stood in the small foyer waiting for Shirley to return. When she did she had a wide grin on her face.

"What's so funny?" Martin asked.

"You should hear them. They're taking turns reading *The Merchant of Venice.*"

"And that's funny?"

"Not when I read it in high school English Lit class. Maybe it's what they're reading *into* it that's funny. 'Night, Kar. Call me tomorrow," Shirley hugged Karen and took Martin's hand. "Let's go, honey."

Karen watched them pull out of the parking space and then closed the door. The door felt strange, not as heavy as the one in her house. *You have to stop comparing. The house is history. This is the future.*

"Hey, girls. Time to go home," she called, walking down the short hall to Ali's bedroom. "Oh, how nice you have this room already."

"It's still kind of junky, Mrs. W., but we'll be back tomorrow to help. That is, if it's okay." Kristi and Marla stood at the end of Ali's bed. Ali was propped up on pillows and despite a multitude of boxes gracing the room it almost looked homey. The girls had opened the smaller boxes and had all Ali's knick-knacks spread across the bureau. They had also taken all the clothing from the two cardboard wardrobes and hung them in her closet.

"They are very good babysitters," Ali laughed. "Now I know who I can call when I need babysitters for the twins."

They laughed and Marla said, "Ali will have to give us directions for the rest of the cartons when we come back tomorrow."

"You're welcome to come tomorrow and visit, but please don't think you have to do any more. You've helped me and Ali immeasurably." Karen felt tears press the corners of her eyes. *It's because I'm tired that I'm so emotional.* "But, dear girls, it's really time you went home. You must be exhausted."

"We're fine, Mrs. W. Really," Kristi said as she and Marla gave Karen a joint hug. "You're tired, too. We'll see you tomorrow."

"Not too early. Maybe we'll sleep late."

"We'll call first," Marla called over her shoulder as she followed Kristi down the hall.

"I'll see them out," Karen whispered to Ali, who lay back against her pillows looking wan and tired. "I'll be right back."

At the new front door, Karen took Kristi's and Marla's hands in hers. "I really appreciate all you've done today. You helped so much getting Ali here and settled. This was a terrible time to be moving with Ali confined to bed most of the time, but you made it possible. As for tomorrow, I think she might need a lot of rest and quiet so why don't you come in the afternoon for a visit? What isn't opened and put away in her room can wait. Let's see how she feels, okay?" She pulled the girls to her. "You're just like two extra daughters, you know that?"

"And you're like an extra Mom, Mrs. W." Marla said, mumbling into Karen's shoulder.

Karen watched their car pull away, closed the door and hurried back to Ali.

"How are you feeling, honey?" she asked.

"Tired. Like I did all the work Kristi and Marla did today. They were so good, weren't they?"

"They were. Now, I think you should just slide down into bed and go to sleep."

"I'm still dressed."

"I'll help you," Karen said, pulling a clean pair of pjs from the bureau drawer that Kristi and Marla had seen to. "Here, slip these on and I'll get you something to drink. What do you want, milk, water or juice?"

"Could I have iced tea?" Ali asked.

"No," Karen said. "I'll bring you juice. Shirley left a whole cooler with things to eat and drink. We could live for a week on that," she laughed.

Karen returned with the juice and sat on the side of Ali's bed. Ali looked so pale and she complained of increased back pain. "You're not going to get up at all tomorrow," she said patting her daughter's hand.

"Not even for potty breaks?"

"Well, I guess those, but gingerly and with care. We don't

want those twins popping out before their time."

She pulled a light cover up over Ali's shoulders. "Sleep well, honey. I've put a little bell on your bedside table. If you need me during the night just ring and I'll be here, okay?"

"Okay," Ali said, her eyes fluttering closed, her voice tinged with sleep. "Love you."

"I love you, too, sweetheart."

Although Karen was tired beyond description, she didn't go to bed. Instead she went back to the patio and, leaving the slider open a crack so she could hear if Ali needed her, she leaned back in the lounge chair Martin had occupied a short time ago.

She listened to the night noises of small animals and insects in the brush between the manicured lawn behind her builing and the golf course that wandered through this new community. *Even the bugs sound different,* she thought, remembering the lanai and her garden. "Don't do that," she scolded herself.

She was enjoying relaxing for the first time today when she was startled by the sound of her cell phone ringing. Glancing at her watch before picking it up, she saw that it was nine-thirty. Not late really, but who could be calling her tonight? Her friends knew she was moving today. Bill also knew and wouldn't be calling from Omaha, surely not tonight unless it was an emergency. These thoughts raced through her mind as she answered the phone with a shaky, "Hello?"

"Mrs. Waterson?" a man inquired.

"Yes, who is this?"

There was a short pause and Karen thought about hanging up when she heard, "It's Morgan, Mrs. Waterson."

Stunned into silence for an instant, Karen swallowed with difficulty. "Morgan?"

"Yes. I'm calling Ali, Mrs. Waterson."

"Ali is in bed and asleep, Morgan. How did you get my cell phone number?"

"I found it on an old email from Ali I had printed out. I don't know why I kept it. It was in a pocket in my briefcase. I was looking for something else and there it was. I've been trying to call, Mrs. Waterson, but there was a message your telephone number had been disconnected at the request of the listing party." Morgan's voice trailed off as though he wondered why he thought this detailed description of where he'd found Ali's mother's cell phone number was necessary.

"We've just moved. Today, Morgan. The new number is not working yet." She, too, wondered why she bothered to explain. *Did he deserve answers when he provided none?*

When the connection crackled, Karen was afraid she was going to lose the call. "Morgan, are you still there?"

"I'm here. Is Ali okay? Could I speak to her?"

Karen stiffened her spine and put her legs over the side of the chair. "No, you can't speak to her, Morgan. She's asleep. It's been a very difficult day. Morgan, I think you have some explaining to do. Not to me, to Ali, but not tonight either." As she continued, her confusion gradually changed to courage, "I'm not sure she wants to speak with you. You've done a terrible thing, abandoning her."

"I know." His response was a whisper.

"If you know, why haven't you contacted her? It's been months. Where are you?"

"I'm in Miami. I have a job here..."

Again an uneasy pause joined the tired, anxious mother in Gadara and the frightened and remorseful young man in Miami. "I've been stupid, Mrs. Waterson. Stupid beyond belief. I let an upsetting personal crisis cloud my vision. I ran away from that turmoil and without thinking, I turned away from Ali. But I love her, Mrs. Waterson. I've never stopped loving her." His voice cracked and he waited for a response.

Sitting on her new deck, surrounded by chaos, worried about her daughter and grandchildren, Karen felt tears slip down her cheeks.

"I can't speak for Alice, Morgan. You'll have to make your peace, if there is any, with her not me. I know how hurt she's been and I don't know what made you change. It's not up to me; you'll have to do whatever you think is best. I can't answer for Ali."

"Can I call her?"

"You can. I don't know what kind of reception you'll get. In the morning I'll tell her you called." She heard him draw in a deep breath, then sigh.

"Thank you, Mrs. Waterson. Should I use this number?"

Karen thought a moment. "Did you try Ali's cell phone?"

"I did. It apparently isn't working. Has she changed phones?"

"She probably hasn't charged it. The last few days have been hectic." Karen thought of the move, the sudden need to see the doctor, Ali's partial bed rest order. These things just piled up in her brain and she felt nauseous. "You can use this number but don't call too early. She's very tired."

"But she's okay?" Morgan felt sweat trickle down his spine.

Karen hesitated. She couldn't tell Morgan anything. She couldn't mention the twins or Ali's pregnancy problems. She couldn't tell him of the sadness he had bestowed on her daughter, the pain she'd seen and felt during these past three months. That was up to Ali. "She's okay," Karen whispered into the phone.

Morgan tried to swallow the huge lump in his throat. "Did she get my letter?"

"Letter? No, I don't think so. When did you mail it?"

"A couple of days ago."

"We've changed our mailing address, Morgan. But it should be forwarded."

There was a pause. When Morgan again spoke, she could hear the distress in his voice, "I'm sorry she didn't get it...I wanted her to have it before I called..." He sighed before finishing softly, "Thank you, Mrs. Waterson. I'll call tomorrow afternoon, if that's okay."

"I'll tell her. All I want is what's best for her, Morgan, keep that in mind. Goodbye," she said softly.

"Good night, Mrs. Waterson."

In Gadara Karen slipped the phone into the pocket of her jeans. She pushed the slider open and went into her new home. *So many changes, so many decisions and so much depending on that irresponsible boy in Miami,* she thought. *A letter? Did he really send a letter?*

***

In Miami, Morgan pushed his phone into the back pocket of his jeans shorts and went out onto the balcony. The dark, empty night and the muted sounds seemed comfortable. He opened the rickety lounge chair and stretched out, his hands behind his head. *I should call Cliff,* he thought but didn't move. He was confused by his emotions, a strange combination of frustration and accomplishment, anxiety and a strange peace. Maybe it was because he'd finally taken the challenge, he'd called and Ali would know it tomorrow. Yet as he laid there alone, he envisioned Ali when they sprawled on the grass on campus, when they shared a pizza and beer in Stoney's Bar and Grill, when she melted into his arms. Would he be speaking to her tomorrow? What would she say? He knew what he'd say. He closed his eyes, not sleeping but trying to sneak away from reality. "Tomorrow's another day...Ali Baba. I love you."

***

Karen peeked into Ali's room. Dodging some small boxes she stood next to her daughter's bed and watched Ali sleeping quietly. She wondered if she would make this room a duplicate of the one she'd grown up in. Shrugging her shoulders, she went to her own room. It was big and the queen-sized bed looked smaller than...*Don't go there. No comparisons, remember?* she warned herself.

Pulling her clothes off and throwing them on a chair she took a nightgown from the drawer, stepped into the bathroom and turned on the water in the shower. As she stood under the pulsing spray she prayed and cried, soaping the grime of today from her body, but nothing washed the worry away.

Later, propped up on pillows in bed, she took her Bible from the drawer in the night stand. But before she opened it she leaned back, closed her eyes and prayed silently. When she sat forward she saw Missy looking at her from her little soft bed. "You're watching over me, too, aren't you? Well, I'll be okay. All I need to remember is that I'm not in charge, God is, and He's seen us through a lot of things. He'll see us through this too."

She opened her Bible and randomly flipped the pages, stopping at Isaiah 41. Her finger ran down the page to 41:13. Missy put her head on her paws and blinked as she listened to Karen read. "For I the Lord thy God will hold thy right hand, saying unto thee, Fear not; I will help thee."

"There," she murmured to Missy. "See, I don't need to worry." She closed the Bible and slipped it into the open drawer. Turning off the light she pulled the covers up.

"Good night, Missy. Tomorrow's another day."

36

Courage does not always roar.
Sometimes it is the quiet voice
at the end of the day saying,
'I will try again tomorrow.'
Mary Anne Radmacher

"I do declare," sighed Emily as she pulled in her trick at the card table. "There's changes all around Gadara lately."

Sarah Jane, Emily, Mildred and Betty were sitting at the card table in Sarah Jane's parlor for their weekly pinochle game.

"You mean Karen and Alice Waterson moving over to those big condos along that fancy golf course? I told the City Commissioners when they first decided to put that new section in, 'It will ruin Gadara,' I said."

Sarah Jane was always at City Council meetings making sure changes didn't effect what she thought of as a perfect ambience for the town that had grown to a nice little city during her lifetime. No, she didn't welcome excessive growth. Gadara was not crowded and unmanageable as some of the towns. She'd seen them grow and grow until you couldn't recognize the comfortable friendly place of their beginning. She didn't want that for Gadara and it was growing too fast already.

"They're really nice condos. Did you ever go through the models?" Betty placed her card on the table with a smug grin. "That's trump," she said.

"No, and I'm not interested. All that fancy stuff that won't last a decade much less a century," Sarah Jane huffed.

"Well, with Bill Waterson gone to Nebraska, if you can imagine that, Karen had to move. I heard Bill was having financial difficulties."

"And he brought them on himself, running after that flighty

Sonoma Jacobs. She must be twenty years younger than Bill, and now pregnant. I heard Karen wasn't at all sad to leave the house anyway," Betty said. "Someone, I can't remember who, said the old house was full of old memories."

"Well, it would be. They must have been there twenty years. Sometimes family memories hurt when the family gets broken up like theirs did. I never liked him as much as Karen. She's a sweet girl," Emily said.

"I thought Karen took it real well."

"She didn't. Look at how skinny she's gotten." Sarah Jane sighed. "And now with her daughter home and pregnant and not a husband in sight…"

Mildred shuffled the cards. "Is it my deal?"

"Yes, but the real news is A.J. Handley moving into that assisted living place," Betty said.

"No!" Sarah Jane shouted. "He wouldn't leave that old house of his."

"You mean you hadn't heard? Yes, he's going to move into Sylvan Lakes. I guess the historical society is jumping for joy. They've wanted that old house for ages." Mildred smirked. It wasn't often that anyone had a piece of news before Sarah Jane knew.

Sarah Jane put her cards on the table, the colorful backs fanned out in a perfect arc. "I can't believe he'd leave that old homestead," she whispered. "Are you sure?"

"Yes, my cousin, Amy, works there and she saw him a couple of weeks ago checking out the place. Next thing you know his name is on the 'Welcome new Residents' sign in the big game room." Mildred was enjoying her one-upmanship. "I don't think he's actually moved in yet but he's on the list."

"Don't take it so hard, Sarah Jane. He's old and alone. Why, he could just keel over and no one would know for days, living out there alone like he is."

"The mailman would know." Emily said. "Sam Hitchings would see A.J. hadn't taken in his newspaper or the mail. He's one nice mailman, Sam is. He looks out for his customers. Is that the right word for postal clients? Anyhow, a man can't do for himself like a woman can. He should be where he can get some help, as old as he is."

"He's not that old." Sarah Jane picked her cards up.

"How old is he?" Betty asked.

"Three years older than I am. He was ahead of me in school."

"And," Emily asked innocently, "How old is that?"

"Never-you-mind. Play." Sarah Jane said, slapping a card in the center of the table.

Emily patted the back of Sarah Jane's hand. "Look on the bright side. A.J. will be living right here in town. Closer to you. You could visit."

"I told you, there would be changes in Gadara right after that man in your house arrived," Mildred said.

"He's not 'that man in my house'," Sarah Jane said, sweeping the trick toward her. "He's a very nice young man who minds his own business, more so than some around here. He decided to spend the summer in Gadara before going back to work this fall. He'll be leaving soon, I guess."

The three women looked at each other, amazed at the sadness they detected in Sarah Jane's voice.

Inside, Sarah Jane's stomach was churning. A.J. moving into assisted living? She couldn't get over that fact or that she was the last to know. Maybe she'd call him this evening before going to church. She sighed. He never came to mid-week services or the dinner anymore. He used to. She sighed again and picked up her new hand but her enthusiasm for the game and the company was gone. Sarah Jane couldn't wait for the afternoon to be over. *And then there's tea and cakes. Mildred's sponge cake. My favorite, and now it's all spoiled. How could he, and not even talk to me? As if I had any influence on him, but...*

***

In Miami Morgan hopped off the bus at the corner of Flagler and 8th. He always got off several blocks from the office building so that he could trot along the sidewalk, counting this as his morning exercise.

He was early and most of the nine to five people weren't

crowding the sidewalks yet. His mind was amazingly clear. He knew what he was going to do. This afternoon he would call Ali. He knew what he was going to say because he'd been rehearsing since five o'clock this morning. With so little sleep last night, he was amazed at his vigor. "It's knowing I'll soon be talking to Ali," he murmured, pushing the elevator button.

He smiled at the people who joined him on the way up to his office, joked with Marie in the break room as he poured his coffee and paused in front of Dave's office on the way to his own. "Good morning," he said with a smile.

"Hey, man. What's up?" Dave said leaning back in his chair. "You look chipper."

"I'm feeling on top of the world," Morgan said. He gave him a thumb's up and disappeared into his adjoining office.

"Wait a minute. I haven't seen that boyish grin in months. What happened?" Dave asked following Morgan. He placed his coffee on Morgan's desk and slumped into one of the client chairs across from him.

"I feel as if a thousand pounds has been lifted from my shoulders."

"I don't know what's been bothering you, and I don't need to," Dave said, raising his hand. "But I'm glad for you. You've been glum ever since you came in May. Problems solved?"

"Well, maybe not completely solved but I'd say hopefully on the way to a solution."

Morgan sipped his coffee and Dave gazed out the glass panel separating the small offices from the lobby. He pushed himself up from the chair. "Well, I'm glad. You look almost like the old intern. Hope everything works out."

"I'm feeling optimistic," Morgan called as his friend left the office.

He looked at his watch and checked to see if it agreed with the time on the computer. He'd mentally scheduled his call to Ali for two o'clock. *Not lunchtime, but soon enough after lunch. It's going to be okay, I just feel it.*

He reached for the phone on his desk, then changed his mind and pulled out his cell phone. He dialed Cliff's number in Carter's Corners, knowing it was early in the day to contact him but he just couldn't wait.

When Cliff answered, his voice was clouded with sleep. "Hello."

"Cliff, it's Morgan. Did I wake you? I did, didn't I?"

"Yep. Guess Millie's gone already. I didn't even hear her go. What's up?" Cliff asked.

"I'm sorry I woke you, but I just couldn't wait to tell you. I called Ali last night. Well, I called her mother's cell phone because that's the only number I could find that worked. They just moved, so they'll have a new number and Mrs. Waterson said Ali probably hadn't charged her phone because of the move." Morgan knew he was babbling but the words just spewed from his mouth.

"Did you talk to Ali?"

"No, I called after nine-thirty but she was already in bed and asleep. They moved, as I said, and I guess she was tired out. But, I talked a little to Mrs. Waterson and then I told her I'd call Ali this afternoon."

"That's good, son. How did her mother sound?"

"Well, I guess she was surprised to hear from me. She was kind of...I don't know, hurt or angry for Ali's sake. But she did say I should call today. Not early because they might be sleeping in late. Because of the move." *Babbling again,* he thought. "I'm sorry, I'm jabbering away like a magpie," he said slowly. "But I'm so excited. I've been rehearsing what I'm going to say all morning."

"Now slow down, son. You know how *you* feel, and that's great, but take it slowly. Find out how *she* feels. You know, she's been wonderin' what the heck happened to you. I'm sure she's been hurt by what you did. I'm happy you're gonna call but don't be upset if she ain't all that keen on hearin' from you right now. Do you get me? I'm not bustin' your balloon, but you might have to move slow for a while."

"I know, Cliff. I'm excited but scared to death. I want to tell her how sorry I am. I want to explain why this happened and that I know now I over-reacted. The hurt is still there, Cliff, but the thought of hearing Ali's voice is so...I don't have the words. I can't wait and I know you're right. She probably is mad and hurt and all that stuff. I'm going to have to be patient, but it's a start," he said.

Cliff heard the hope in his young friend's voice and smiled. "I'm proud of you, son. Let me know what happens, and don't be surprised if you don't get a brass band welcome at first," he cautioned.

"I won't, and I'll let you know tonight. Are you working tonight?"

"Yep. But call me at the pub. If I can't talk, I'll call you when I can, how's that?"

"Okay. And, Cliff, thanks for everything. You've been such a good friend. More than a friend." Morgan paused. "You know, if I could have chosen a father it would have been you."

He waited for a response, holding his breath. Had he said something wrong? Was Cliff upset with him? That was the last thing in the world he wanted.

"Cliff?" he said tentatively. "Are you still there?"

"I'm here, son; and I'm swept away by what you just said. Son, if I could'a picked out a boy, I'd'a picked you. I never had any children and Millie's boy was my son, too, but we lost him. I'm right proud you said what you did."

Morgan had difficulty swallowing the huge lump of cotton in his throat. "Thanks, Cliff. You're the greatest. Give my love to Millie. I'll call you tonight."

In the tiny office in Miami, the one with no outside window, the room glowed for Morgan as if brightened by sunshine. He leaned back in his chair, hands behind his head and smiled. Was his life going to change? He knew Cliff had made a wondrous impact on him right from the first time they met. And then there was Jack who kept bringing up Gadara and making him think of Ali more than ever. He shrugged and pulled the keyboard toward him. It was time for him to get to work. He'd take his lunch break at two. Morgan knew just what his plans were. The little park three blocks away would be where he'd call Ali. Sitting in the sunshine on a bench facing the reflecting pool would be perfect...a perfect place to start over. Not the office, not his condo, but a bright place outside with the sun and breeze. He just knew this day was going to be the first day of his renewed life. He didn't know what lay ahead in the coming days, but he was ready for whatever it was. Ali and he and the baby would be together and life would begin all over again for him.

37

That which hath been is now;
and that which is to be hath already been;
and God requireth that which is past.
Ecclesiastes 3:15

Jack stood in the barn and looked around in amazement. A slight smell of stale air and dust filled the air, but all in all it was the cleanest barn he had ever seen. Not that he'd seen many, but he remembered a school trip to a farm in south Dade County as a child and remembered the disorder and rank smell.

Stacks of boxes of various sizes rested on a wooden platform along one wall keeping them off the concrete floor. At the rear of the barn on another platform were pieces of furniture draped in sheets, like neat ghosts arranged between more large boxes.

"Who knows what's in these boxes?" he asked a member of the Gadara Historical Society.

"A.J., and he's given us a list of not only what's in the boxes, which are all marked with numbers, as you know since we've been arranging them this morning, but a list of what's in each box. He's also listed the furniture and the dates applicable to them. Then in the side shed, which is really another smaller barn, the farm equipment and miscellaneous things are stored."

"And the house?"

"We're going to leave that as is for now because it will eventually be the museum."

"I'd love a tour of the house, if that's okay?"

"Sure. Clara is in there now taking inventory. Just yell hello so you don't startle her, she's as jumpy as a mouse."

Inside the old home, Jack and Clara walked through the rooms. The parlor, dining room, kitchen and A.J.'s bedroom were sparsely furnished but seemed to hold an aura of better times. Upstairs, the rooms showed signs of neglect and abandonment. Bed frames were folded against the walls of three rooms and the bare floors sounded hollow as they walked across them. Their footsteps were muffled because they walked softly, as if heavy treading would be irreverent. "If only these rooms could talk," Jack whispered.

"I'm sure A.J. has many stories he can tell."

"I wish he'd write them down or tell someone else so that they could be preserved. What a memoir he must be keeping inside his mind and heart."

Clare smiled. "Spoken like a true history teacher."

"I guess it never leaves you."

"Passions rarely do."

"Thanks for the tour. I'm going back out to the barns. I had no idea A.J. was so organized. You are getting a real treasure here."

"Yes, but it will take months, maybe years to sort it all out. My hope is that we get the house refurbished and set up as a museum first and then think about building some kind of additional building or buildings on the property to show the other things. The old farm equipment, which A.J. admits no knowledge of, were his father's and grandfather's and perhaps even older. They should have a separate building, but that will have to wait, I'm afraid."

"Well, I'll get back to the barn to see if I can be of any more help there. I'll be seeing A.J. this afternoon. Again, thanks for the tour." Jack reached for Clara's hand.

She smiled as she watched the tall, young man lope across the grassy area between the house and the barn. *Strange*, she thought. *His hand is always so cool no matter how hot it is or how hard he's worked. He rearranged twenty or more boxes, putting them in numerical order this morning and he's cool as a cucumber. A strange but very nice young man.*

***

It was after nine when Karen tiptoed into Ali's room. She

opened the blinds, letting the sun into the room, savoring for a moment the solitude and warmth. She'd let her daughter sleep longer than usual but the fact Morgan had called last night was constantly pricking at her and she was anxious to share the news, but also fearful of Ali's reaction.

"Honey," she murmured, stroking Ali's arm. "Sleepyhead, it's after nine o'clock. Time to wake up."

Ali squirmed and stretched, blinking in the morning light streaming through her window. "I was almost awake. What time is it?"

"After nine."

"You should have gotten me up earlier. Have you been unpacking?"

"A little. I'm starting in the kitchen and don't know exactly where things should go yet. It'll take time to get settled. I'm in no hurry."

"Let me take a shower first, okay? Then I'll help."

"You'll do no such thing. Take your shower and then come and have breakfast. I made room on the deck last night with Shirley and Martin's help. It's not neat, but we can at least sit out there and eat. Since it faces west we can enjoy the shade in the mornings."

She patted Ali's shoulder. "Need help with the shower?"

"No, Mom. I can do that. The doctor said partial bed rest, which doesn't mean I'm an invalid. But thanks. I'll be out in a few minutes."

She started to push herself away from the pillows and Karen reached for her hands. "Here, let me help you up and remember to use the shower chair."

Ali laughed. "I will be an invalid if I'd let you have your way. Go away," she joked.

Later seated on the deck, Karen twisted her hands under the tablecloth.

Ali leaned back in her chair. "Thanks, Mom. That was a great breakfast. I guess Kristi and Marla will be over later to help me set up my room. I wish I could help you more. It looks as if there's a thousand boxes to open."

"They'll be over later this afternoon. I told them you might sleep late and you did. And don't worry about all those boxes. They're all marked and it will be easy to unpack. Shirley said she'd come over if I need help, but I don't think I do. There's no rush. We're not entertaining," Karen smiled. "I have something to tell you, though, honey."

"What?" Ali looked puzzled.

Karen drew in a deep breath. "Last night, after you were asleep and after Shirley and Martin left, I had a phone call."

"From Dad? Is he okay?" Ali leaned forward, anxiety wrinkling her forehead.

"It wasn't your dad," Karen said, her voice faltering. "It was Morgan."

Ali's jaw dropped and her mouth gaped open. "No. When? What did he say?" she stuttered. "Oh, for God's sake, Mom, why didn't you wake me?"

"It was late. I knew you were asleep. It was a tiring day..."

"But it was Morgan, Mom! You know I've been waiting—"

"I do know, but I thought it was best I not wake you. He talked to me."

Ali leaned back again, her face drawn and pale. "What did he say?"

Karen reached for Ali's hand. "He said he'd been stupid. He said he'd let a personal crisis cloud his vision, that he'd run away from that and not you. He said he was sorry." Morgan's words ran through her mind. "He said he loved you and that he never stopped loving you."

Ali closed her eyes but Karen saw tears leak from the corners. She squeezed Ali's hand. "Are you okay?"

"I'm okay. What else did he say?"

"He asked if he could call you today."

Ali's eyes popped open. "What did you say?"

"I told him he could call you this afternoon. He's going to call me on my cell phone because our other line is not up yet and your phone apparently isn't working."

"I haven't charged it in days. Too much else to think about," she replied, wiping tears from her cheeks. "How did he sound?"

Karen thought a moment. How had Morgan sounded last

night? She'd remembered the words but how he sounded seemed vague. "I don't really remember. He spoke quietly." She paused recalling the words but not the tone. "I think he sounded sorry," she finally said.

Ali appeared to be studying the golf course, watching a foursome approach the hole directly behind their building.

The quiet morning seemed to close in on them. The temperature was rising and the breeze had just begun to move the leaves on the trees.

"Do you want him to call, Ali?"

A bird called, breaking the deep silence. "I...um...I guess so."

Karen stood and moved to the back of Ali's chair. She gently massaged her daughter's shoulders, feeling the tightness there. "I think you should talk to him, honey. Not that I'm trying to interfere. But not talking will leave so many things unanswered. Maybe if you two talk you can work something out. Anything would be better than nothing. You have to think of the babies, too."

Ali looked around quickly. "Did you tell him there were two babies? Did you tell him about my pregnancy? Did you tell him...?"

Karen interrupted. "I didn't tell him anything, honey. I remember telling him he'd done a terrible thing and he said he knew."

"He said he knew," Ali said, her voice a whisper.

Karen reached for the breakfast dishes. "Why don't you go and rest? I'll clean up here and then start on the kitchen boxes and, no, you aren't going to help. I think you'd better call Kristi and cancel this afternoon's visit though. You won't want them here when you talk to Morgan, will you?"

"If he even calls," Ali said, pushing herself away from the table and standing. "If it were a little cooler, I'd stay out here. It's really a pretty view, isn't it?"

Karen smiled at Ali's attempt to return to normal. She knew there must be a thousand feelings pummeling her daughter's heart.

She put the dishes down and pulled Ali to her chest. "It's a beautiful view and you are a beautiful daughter, Ali. Just remember that all things are possible if we rely on God's help. He'll help you, honey; just don't close the door completely when you talk to Morgan. Now go get some rest. I'll be in to make your bed in a minute. Sit in the chair for a few minutes, okay?" She picked up the dishes and entered the house, Ali following behind.

"I think I'll sit in the living room for a few minutes. I'm sick of always being in my bedroom."

"You haven't spent much time in this one," Karen laughed. "Go ahead. You'll like your new bedroom better when it's not so junky, as Marla said."

Karen went into the kitchen and put the dishes in the dishwasher. She looked around. "Junky," she whispered. "Cluttered and junky, but it will get better, just like the clutter in Ali's heart will. Oh, Lord, she needs help. Please be with her today."

The hours ticked by slowly. Karen kept busy unpacking and Ali looked with disinterest at television shows. No one mentioned the time, Morgan or telephones. Karen was in her room sorting out clothes in the cardboard wardrobes when she overheard Ali calling Kristi. She only heard Ali's side of the conversation.

"Don't come over this afternoon, okay?—No, I'm all right, honestly. I have something else to do—Oh, don't be so nosey—I'm not being mean. It's just...well if you have to know, Morgan called last night. Geeze, don't scream like that, you'll break my eardrum—No, I didn't talk to him. Mom didn't want to wake me—I know, but she didn't. She talked to him—I don't know what she said, exactly. But anyhow, he's going to call me today—He told Mom around two, that's if he calls at all—Who knows?—Yes, I'll call you later but don't expect a miraculous change in anything. It's been three months—Kristi, I said I'd call. Not the minute I hang up, even if he calls—but I promise—Bye."

Lunch was a brief interlude in the monotony of the day for Ali. Half a sandwich and a glass of milk, courtesy of Shirley's cooler which remained in the kitchen supplying food and drink for them until Karen could get to the store. Right now, Karen didn't want to leave Ali. She tried not to hover but was never more than a shout away.

Ali went back to bed and willed herself not to look at the

clock, but her eyes constantly watched the minutes and hours slowly tick by or zeroed in on her mother's cell phone which rested silently on her night stand.

One mid-morning call from Shirley panicked both of them. "You answer it," Ali whispered.

"No, it might be for you."

"It's too early, answer it," Ali begged.

After that a funereal quiet settled into the new condo, broken only by the sound of rustling paper as Karen unpacked another box.

At ten minutes after two the phone rang. Ali pushed herself higher on the pillows behind her back. Her hand trembled as she picked up the phone and answered it.

"Hello," she said softly. She looked up and Karen stood in her doorway. Ali waved and Karen moved away. She couldn't allow herself to stay within hearing distance and hurried to the living room, cautiously sitting in her favorite chair which suddenly seemed unusually uncomfortable. She could hear the murmur of Ali's voice but not discern any words. Time stood still as she waited.

In Miami, in the picturesque park Morgan had chosen to make his phone call, the temperature suddenly rose and he dabbed at perspiration on his forehead and neck with his handkerchief.

"Ali? It's Morgan."

"I know. Mom said you would call."

"Ali, I don't know where to begin. I love you, sweetheart. I've never stopped loving you." He waited.

"Where are you?" she asked.

He detected the coolness in her voice. "I'm in Miami. A few blocks from the office. I went back to Littman and Littman right after...right after I left school. I had to be somewhere quiet, somewhere pleasant when I called you. I'm in a little park; there's a reflecting pond and I'm sitting on a bench under a banyan tree." *Why do I have to describe the setting?*

He waited. "Are you there?"

"I'm here."

"Are you okay?"

"Yes."

"Ali, I'm so sorry. I can only beg you to understand and to forgive me. I was so upset."

"I know you were upset but I don't know what upset you. You sent me home, Morgan. You left me alone, not knowing where you were or if I'd ever hear from you again." Her voice sounded thick.

"I'm so sorry, sweetheart. I did a terrible thing. I don't know how I'll make that up to you, but I swear, Ali, I'll never stop trying." He paused, then added, "I wrote to you."

"Well, I never got the letter."

"Your mother said she changed your mailing address and the letter will probably arrive soon."

"Maybe," she said without any conviction.

"I'm sorry for what happened. I'll do anything to fix things." He waited, and when there was no response, he said, "I was confused and hurt, Ali. So hurt." Why was the silence so ominous, the seconds stretching endlessly?

"What happened?" she whispered.

"When I went home that last time I found out some things I didn't know about my life, Ali. I found out why my parents never loved me and getting this information was just too much. I know now I over-reacted but at the time I was so hurt. I was so sure there was no way I could be a father...or a husband... or even be loved by anyone." His voice broke.

"I knew you would be a good husband and father. I loved you. I don't understand what changed you so much."

Morgan noted Ali said 'I loved you' in the past tense. He got up from the bench and paced along the winding brick path, the phone to his ear. "I was dumb. I see that now. What happened to me in the past has nothing to do with us. Nothing to do with our future. Our family," he said, struggling through the words *our future* and *our family.*

There was no response from Ali. The silence stretched out.

"Ali? Are you okay?"

"No, I'm not okay and I don't know if I can forgive you," she said, her voice strengthening. "What you did was terrible. No concern for me. No concern for..." she hesitated, as though she were going to say something and then caught herself before saying it. Instead, she ended, "I don't know what I feel, Morgan. This is too hard to handle right now."

"Can I come and see you, Ali Baba?"

"No," she said quickly, and then added, "not now."

Morgan drew in a deep breath. "Can I call you again?"

Ali hesitated, then whispered, "If you want to."

"I want to, sweetheart. I love you and I always will." He waited, desperately wanting to hear her say she loved him but the silence deepened between Gadara and Miami. "I'll call you tomorrow, is that okay?"

"Give me a few days, Morgan. I have a lot to think about right now."

"Okay." He hesitated. "Is the baby okay?"

"Yes, okay. The baby is okay. I have to go now, Morgan. Goodbye."

Her voice was garbled when she answered. With tears? Morgan wondered.

"Bye, Ali Baba," he murmured, holding onto the phone long after he heard her break the connection.

When Karen heard the brief silence after Ali hung up and then the sobs that emanated from her room, she rushed down the hall.

Cradling her daughter in her arms, they rocked back and forth, the age-old action of a mother comforting her child, whether a baby or a grown woman, there was no difference. The need to cling together universal. Her fingers stroked the back of Ali's neck. Words were unnecessary. They rocked. Ali's sobs eventually softened but the pain racking her body remained and became part of Karen too. Time stood still.

***

In Miami, Morgan sat on the bench, covering his face with his hands so that people going by couldn't see his tears. The sun scalded the back of his neck but he couldn't move. Had he lost her? He pulled his handkerchief from his pocket and mopped his face, hoping it looked like he was wiping perspiration and not tears. He stood and swayed a moment, grabbing the back of the bench for support.

"You okay?" an elderly man asked, stopping in front of Morgan.

"Yeah, just got a bit too much sun, I guess. I'll go where it's cool. Thanks," Morgan said, hurrying away.

"Take care," the man shouted at his retreating back.

Morgan was due back in the office in twenty minutes but he needed a cool drink in a dark place first.

38

Blessed be the ties that bind...
the fellowship of kindred minds
is like to that above...
Words from a hymn by John Fawcett

Jack walked through the spacious entry room at Sylvan Hall and stopped at the piano. A small, pretty woman approached him.

"May I help you?" she said.

"I'm here to visit with A.J. Handley. Could you tell me where he is?"

"I'll take you to his room. He's just down this hallway. I'm so happy to see you," she said extending her hand. "I'm Jackie."

Jack laughed. "Well, I'm Jack."

They laughed together, the sound tranquil in the huge room. "Well, at least I'm not Jill. That would be even funnier. I'm so happy to see A.J. has a visitor. Although he's only been here a week, no one has come to see him and we like our residents to maintain contact with their friends and family outside our facility."

"A.J. doesn't have any family."

"I know, that's what he's told us, but he must have friends. Perhaps they don't know he's moved in yet."

They walked down the hallway to room 117. The door was open and Jack saw A.J. sitting in a comfortable chair in front of the television.

Jackie smiled at him and eased him toward the door. "Just go in," she whispered and turned away.

Jack tentatively stepped into the room. Not sure if A.J. was napping, he said, "A.J. are you awake?"

He saw A.J. pull himself upright. "Yes, yes, I am. Who is it?"

he asked, twisting in his chair. "Oh, Jack, come in, come in. How nice to see you. Pull up that chair," he said pointing to a smaller, padded arm chair. "I'm so glad you came to visit."

"I was out at your old place. Lots going on there. Sorting and moving and such."

"I expect that. Gave the whole kit and caboodle to them to do as they please. Seems they have some grand plans. Well, I promised it to them but I didn't think they'd get it until I died. Not dead, yet," he laughed. "But they sure were happy."

"I don't see why not. It was a lovely gesture and I'm sure they will always remember your generosity."

"Well, I'm the last Handley. Who else would I give it to?" A.J. leaned back a little, his hand pressing the off button on the television remote even though he'd had the sound turned down. "Don't need that. Not as I have you to talk with."

"Do you like it here?" Jack asked, sitting next to him.

"Oh, yes. Great food and look at this nice room. All brand new. You know, I never had new furniture in my life. Even when Elizabeth and I got married and moved in with Mama and Grandma, we had family stuff. This is all brand new," he said, spreading his arms.

"It's very nice, and you deserve it, A.J. Making friends here?"

"Gosh, it's hard not to. Everyone is always doing something. The only quiet time we get is in the afternoon when most of these folks take naps or read. Sometimes there's a gang of them in the television room watching a movie. I'm not much on movies but I've seen a couple and they were pretty good."

Jack smiled. "It seems this was the right move then."

A.J. leaned forward. "You know, Jack, I think it was you who suggested I really consider it. Thank you, son. I don't think I'd ever had a notion to give this a try. I flat out disagreed with Doc Phillips," he laughed.

"I didn't do anything, A.J."

"You know, there's a couple of sodas in that little fridge there. Get them and we'll toast..." A.J. paused, uncertain of what he wanted to toast.

"Your new home and your new beginning here at Sylvan Hall, how's that?" Jack said, bending down and taking the two sodas from the refrigerator under a shelf that held a microwave.

He popped both cans open, handed one to A.J. "Here's to your new home and a great life here at Sylvan Hall," he said, touching the soda can to A.J.'s.

"And to you, Jack. I'm sure glad you walked up to my place that day. Seems like I've known you for a long time and it was only at the beginning of summer, wasn't it?"

Jack stared at the back of A.J.'s hand holding the soda can. "That birthmark you have. I'm sure I've seen one just like it not long ago," he mused.

"Couldn't have. It's a Handley feature. Goes back decades, maybe centuries. Every generation a male child has this mark. I never had any children...sons," he said, his voice touched with sadness, "so I guess it stops with me."

Jack shrugged. "I could be mistaken," he said.

They chatted over their sodas, talking about pinochle games and great food until the cans were empty.

"Guess I'll be going. You're probably either ready for a nap or off to another game of cards. You said you sometimes play dominos, my foster dad loved to play dominos. I remember watching him and some of his friends play out on the picnic table in our back yard. Funny, I hadn't thought of that in a long time."

He stood, took A.J.'s soda can and put them in the waste basket next to the refrigerator. "You've got a real nice place here, A.J. Enjoy it."

Jack shook A.J.'s hand and smiled at the old man.

"I'll walk you to the door," A.J. said struggling forward in the big recliner.

"No, you sit there. I'll find my way out."

He began to walk toward the open door when A.J. called out," Wait. Thank you."

"Nothing to thank me for."

"You'll come back for another visit?"

"I'll try. I'll have to be leaving Gadara soon."

"I know. To go back and teach. I know how it feels at the end of summer. You want to get ready for the next group of kids, start new lesson plans. I remember..." he said, his voice drifting off.

"See you," Jack said and walked into the hall.

Well look who it is, Samuel said.

"Where have you been, is the question. I haven't seen you in...well, we don't deal in time anymore, do we? But, you've been gone and I've missed you. I thought you were supposed to be guiding me."

You didn't need me. I've been watching and you're doing fine on your own. It won't be long and we'll both be out of here.

"You mean it? I don't know, Sam. I'm getting used to this place and the people."

Told you not to do that. This is only temporary. Now with a little nudge from you, Morgan is in contact with Ali. A.J. is in the assisted living place, the Gadara Historical Society is delighted with A.J.'s old house and property and Alice and Karen are in their new home.

"So what do you need me for now? If everything is in place, couldn't I just fly away," Jack said, flapping his arms as if they were wings.

Not quite yet, Jack. Just a few little strings left to tie up.

"What strings? Why don't you just point me in the right direction and we can get it all over with. If I'm not going to be staying here we might as well get going."

Ah, Jack, you are still an impatient one at times. No, there are things that have to fall into place before we're done. You'll know when it's over.

"Wait," Jack called, but it was too late. Sam was gone. He trudged up the walkway to Twin Oaks. He may as well sit on the back porch with Sarah Jane as wander the streets with no purpose. Try as he might he couldn't think of any loose ends. He sighed as he let the screen door slam behind him and walked through the house to the kitchen.

"You out on the porch, Sarah Jane?" he called.

"Yes, come on out. I have an extra glass. There's tea in the pitcher. I thought you might be by."

Jack opened the screen door and saw Sarah Jane sitting in her favorite rocker. "You know, these look like the rockers A.J.

had on his porch," he said, sliding into the rocker next to hers.

He noticed her hands tremble as she poured his tea and he looked into her face. She looked pale and drawn; her eyes didn't have the spark they usually had.

Taking a sip of the tea, he continued to study her over the rim of his glass. When he placed the glass on the little table between them he asked, "You seem distressed, Sarah Jane. What's wrong?"

It was a simple question and he was totally unprepared for the sudden gush of tears and sobs that emanated from Sarah Jane. Her body shook.

"Gosh, Sarah Jane, I didn't mean to upset you. Can I help?" He felt totally helpless and looked around to see if his buddy Sam was anywhere around. Naturally, he wasn't. Jack stood and took one of her hands in his. "Sarah Jane, what's wrong? This isn't like you."

She shook her head from side to side, mopping her face with the corner of her apron. "No, it isn't and I'm sorry. I don't know what came over me."

"Was it something I said?" Jack asked, struggling to remember what he had said. He went over the past few minutes. He'd remarked the rockers were like A.J.'s and then she burst into tears. Was that it?

"Can I get you anything?" he asked as she dried her eyes and blew her nose in a handkerchief she pulled from her apron pocket.

"No, Jack, and I apologize for that outburst. Don't know what came over me. It's not like me to go all soppy for no reason. Please, just forget it, Jack."

"I will, Sarah Jane, but perhaps if you talked about what's bothering you it would help. Was it my mentioning A.J.'s rocking chairs?" He watched her eyes flood again and her bottom lip trembled. "It was, wasn't it?"

She nodded, unable to speak; her handkerchief balled up in one hand and pressed to her lips, her eyes closed as if to shut out the grief.

"I just saw A.J. He's happy in Sylvan Halls. Have you visited him?"

Again Sarah Jane just shook her head from side to side.

"I don't know what to say. I sure didn't mean to upset you," he repeated.

"It's not you, Jack," she mumbled through the hankie.

"Well, what is it? Maybe I can help."

"I'm being silly. I just heard he was in that place," she said, her voice taking on some strength. "I don't know why it affected me like this. It's no skin off my nose if he wants to go giving up his home and land and go into...*that place* and not tell me. After all, I have no strings on him."

Strings? Is that what Sam meant? "He's happy there. He's making friends. Out at his home he was alone. His doctor suggested it to him and when he told me I agreed."

"See? He told you. I've known him since first grade."

Jack began patting her hand. "I'm sorry you're upset, but really, he's happy there and he would love company. He's adjusting nicely but there's always room for an old friend. Why don't you go and visit him?"

Sarah Jane leaned back in her chair and opened her eyes. "I will, Jack. I was just being silly. A silly old woman with her nose out of joint, that's what I am."

They sat quietly for several minutes. The garden was fading in the last of the hot summer heat. A few birds flitted from tree to tree. "You know," she said, "I once thought I loved A.J. Back many years and some time after Elizabeth died. She was A.J.'s wife, a lovely woman, and just right for him. I was too set in my ways. Too settled here at Twin Oaks. It's hard to make changes sometimes and," she paused, "and sometimes changes are good. I'm glad A.J. is happy there."

She stood. "I'm going to make dinner. Just homemade soup and some leftover cornbread. Want to join me?"

Jack had never had that offer before. He smiled. "I'd be honored."

39

For the wrath of God is revealed from heaven against all ungodliness and unrighteousness of men, who hold the truth in unrighteousness;
Romans 1:18

Ali belabored over whether to even talk to Morgan, if and when he called again. She sat on the deck, now set up with furniture in place, bamboo shades installed and a small fountain that gurgled in the corner thanks to a gift from Uncle Martin and Aunt Shirley, as she called her mother's friends. She was stretched out on a lounge chair, remnants of breakfast on a small table next to her.

It was two days after Morgan's phone call. His letter had arrived yesterday. She'd taken it into her bedroom to read, closing the door behind her.

Karen had waited, anxious to learn what the letter contained but careful not to look as if she cared. When Ali opened her door, she came into the living room and handed the opened letter to her mother. "He sent me a check for one thousand dollars."

"You want me to read the letter?"

"Yes. Please."

Karen slowly read the letter and then re-read it. She looked up to see Ali sitting in her father's recliner, staring out the window. "What do you think?"

"I think...I think it's a start. But what was the problem?"

"He doesn't say. He says he loves you, that he's sorry," Karen said, listening to her words and finding them inadequate. "I don't know how to advise you. Yesterday when you spoke to him were you convinced of his remorse?"

Ali sucked a deep breath, her lungs tight. "I think so and

then I wonder. I don't know what to think."

For the rest of the day no mention was made of the letter or Morgan. Kristi and Marla came over but the conversations in Ali's bedroom were quiet, void of the usual laughter, and the girls left after an hour, Ali telling them she was tired and wanted to take a nap.

Now this morning she made no reference to Morgan or the letter until breakfast was finished.

"I don't know what to do, Mom. Do I forgive him unconditionally? Do I insist on...I don't know...what could I insist on? That this doesn't happen again? Is that a possibility or a shadow that might hang over us forever?"

"Have you made any decisions?"

"You mean to take his next call, if he calls? I don't know."

"I haven't asked before, but does his letter make any difference? I'm not counting the check. I hope it was a good faith offer of some support for you during your pregnancy."

"His letter was...brief, but perhaps sincere. I'm not sure yet. He still hasn't told me what exactly happened at his home that upset him so much."

"You can always ask him."

"I think you want me to talk to him again, don't you?"

"I don't see anything to be gained not talking to him at this point. Remember the decisions you make now will affect you and your children for many years."

"But, Mom, even if he's sorry and he means it, what's to prevent this from happening again? If we were a family and he got hurt or upset about something and over-reacted, his words by the way, would he disappear again?"

"You don't get a lifetime guarantee, Ali. I thought I had one with your dad. I've forgiven him but it took time. You have to follow your heart. You have to make the decisions. As I said, I don't see how not talking to him will help. You still have the final word. You have his letter and the check. I'm not saying just because he sent you money it should influence your decision."

Ali sighed and stretched her arms over her head. She yawned a fake yawn. "I think I'll take a nap."

"It's ten thirty. Are you tired? Didn't you sleep well last

night?" Karen edged forward in her chair her eyes searching Ali's face, which was pale but not as drawn as the day of the infamous call.

"I slept as well as I usually do with this humongous lump I'm carrying around. And I'm still not used to sleeping on my side. I'm a belly sleeper."

Karen laughed. "You'd roll off the bed if you slept on your belly. It would be like trying to balance on a beach ball."

Ali laughed. "Thanks. I feel like a beach ball."

"Let me help you out of that chair," Karen said, extending her hands to Ali and pulling her upright.

"Oof. Will I ever be comfortable again?"

"You will, I can guarantee that. And just think what you'll have when your beach ball belly isn't there anymore? You'll have my two grandchildren. Oh, Ali," she said, pulling her daughter to her, "you don't know how excited I am about these babies. I can't wait for them to be here, tuck them into bed, push the stroller along the sidewalks."

"I'm going to have a chance to put them to bed and push them in the stroller once in a while, aren't I? The baby furniture will be delivered next week, won't it? I'm excited too, Mom. It's just..."

"It's just Morgan, isn't it?"

Ali leaned her head on her mother's shoulder. "You know, Mom, even though I could strangle Morgan for putting me in this position, and I don't mean pregnant, I mean what he did, I still love him."

Karen held her daughter close. "Think carefully, honey. I know you're young and these are difficult times, but think carefully because so much depends on it."

"You make it sound dreary, having babies, being on my own. But, Mom, I don't want to be on my own and I don't want to be a burden to you."

"I've told you before. You will never be a burden. You couldn't live long enough to be a burden to me. I'm very proud of you, honey."

"Proud of what? That I messed up?"

"That you didn't take the easy route. That you're facing what you're facing with grace and faith. If anyone messed up it was Morgan and now he's trying to make amends. I know," she said, preventing Ali from speaking, "I know what you are facing isn't easy but I will...and your dad will also...do everything to make your life as easy as possible. And it won't be forever. You'll make your way, Ali, because you are smart and responsible."

Ali pulled away and looked into her mother's face. "You have such faith in me. I don't know if I deserve that kind of faith."

"Faith is unquestioning belief and that's what I have in you, Ali, and that's what I have in God. We aren't alone." Karen reminded her.

At ten minutes after two that afternoon, Ali's cell phone rang. She was propped up against extra pillows reading a book Karen had brought back from the library.

Karen was in her own room when she heard Ali say, "Hello?" She slipped into the hallway and peeked into Ali's room. Their eyes met and Karen blew her daughter a kiss and then retreated. She closed the door to her bedroom. Listening wasn't an option. Ali would tell her what she wanted her to know. Nevertheless, sorting clothing and rearranging things in the closet and bureau were not the most challenging jobs and her thoughts were with her daughter across the hall.

"It's Morgan, Ali. Can you talk?"

"Yes, It's okay," she said, shifting into a more comfortable position, if there was one. The twins were doing a dance, feet and arms bumping the inside of her belly.

"How are you, sweetheart?"

"Do you really care?"

"Of course, I care. I keep telling myself what an idiot I've been missing out on our baby's..." he stumbled and Ali could hear him struggling for words.

"Our babies gestation? Development?" she asked. "Whether things were going as they should? You have missed out, Morgan. More than you can ever know." Ali didn't like her tone but she had to be defensive. If he was going to waltz into her life again she somehow had to make him pay a little.

"I'm sorry. I'm really so very sorry. But I've said that, haven't I? I want to be part of your life and our baby's life. I know I've missed a lot and you have every right to be angry. But, sweetheart, I do love you. I love the baby. I want to make things right and I don't know how to do that unless you let me know what I should do. Can you forgive me, just a little? Can you let me in again? I keep thinking of the first couple of months when we knew about the baby. I was happier then than I've ever been. Your love made me happy."

"Maybe I need to know what made you change, Morgan. What was so all-fired important you just changed overnight; changed from who I knew to someone I didn't know from Adam? Someone who just ran away." Ali gripped the phone too tightly, her fingers becoming numb. She flexed her hand, catching the phone between her cheek and shoulder. "I think you owe me that much, at least."

"You're right. Well, I'll tell you what happened but you have to wait until I've told the whole story, okay?

"Okay. But..." she sighed. "Go ahead."

"I went home that last weekend to take my things from the dorm and pick up what I needed to take to Miami. My parents were in the den. They looked like they'd just received bad news but it was I who was going to receive...news. At that time I thought it was bad, so bad I didn't know how to take it. But, in retrospect, it's answered a lot of questions.

"Ali, I told you I never felt wanted, loved or even needed. At first, when I was a little kid, I thought I'd done something to make them turn away from me. The housekeeper used to read to me, play with me, give me cookies and things like that."

"But," Ali interrupted, "even if they didn't love you like other parents, you had a good home. You had it a lot better than lots of kids." Her brow furrowed. "What was so bad about that?"

"You're right and that's what Cliff said, too. He and Millie..."

"Cliff and Millie? I never heard you mention them before. Who are they?"

"They're the people who saved my life but I'll tell you about that later. Honey, when I went home that weekend they called me into the den. I thought I was going to get a lecture on how disappointed they were in me. It wouldn't have been the first time, but that's not what happened. That, I could have taken. Instead they told me I was adopted twenty-three years ago. Wait, that's not all so bad if they'd told me when I was five or even ten. But why did they wait until I was graduating from college? They explained and the explanation was unbelievable to me. I know now I over-reacted, I said that before. What they also told me was they had no idea who my mother was, whether there was a father in the picture. They made up my name and told me I was named after my grandfather. A grandfather who was never really my grandfather."

Morgan paused, as if to catch his breath and Ali heard the pain in his voice as he croaked some of the words out and had to clear his throat. She waited.

"You see, I was rejected from birth by a mother who didn't want me and my so-called parents just bought me. They thought they wanted a baby and could afford one so they purchased me. They admitted to me it wasn't long before they changed their mind. So, I was rejected by them too.

"My birth certificate is fake, I'm fake, even my name is fake. I couldn't understand how I could be a husband and father when I didn't even know who I was. And they told me I'd never know because the crooked lawyer who handled the fake birth certificate and, I guess, the transfer of me to them like a sack of groceries, was dead. I'd always felt rejected but this was the worst rejection of all. I just lost it, Ali. It wasn't anything you did. It wasn't fair to you. I was reacting to years of rejection I hadn't even acknowledged until that weekend."

Morgan sounded as though he were fighting tears. Ali's slid down her cheeks.

Finally, Morgan said, "Are you still there?"

"Yes," Ali whispered.

"I'm sorry."

"I didn't know."

"I didn't have the courage to tell you. It was Cliff who helped me."

"And who is Cliff?"

"He's a friend. A new friend but someone who...I'll tell you next time I call. Right now all I want to talk about is us."

He waited. Would there be a next time? Would Ali reject him because of his one time weakness? Would there be an 'us'?

"I had to find a way to be truthful. Truthful to you and to myself. I don't need sympathy to get me back on track. What I need is to keep working to overcome that earlier rejection. What I need is you, Ali." He paused, then summoning all his courage, said, "I'm praying you'll let me be the husband and father I want desperately to be." He waited.

"Morgan, this is so hard. I've missed you. I was so hurt when you just shoved things in my car and stood there watching me drive away. I waited to hear from you. There's been so much...so much I needed to share with you."

"I know, baby. I know and I'll make it up to you, I swear."

"I'm trying to understand. What happened to you at your home is hard to digest. I guess I can't relate because I have such a good family. I can't imagine being rejected as you were."

"It's the past, Ali Baba. It's the future we have to work on." Morgan held his breath, waiting for her to say the magic words, *I forgive you.* He waited. "I love you Ali, more than anything in the world." He prayed for her response.

"I loved you, Morgan."

"Can you still love me?"

She hesitated, then, her voice just above a whisper, "I do love you."

His heart pounded. "We'll be okay, honey. All we have to be is truthful, share everything and love each other."

He listened to silence for much too long before he heard her say, "There are things I need to tell you."

Morgan's heart sank. What did she have to tell him? Had she found someone else? Was there trouble with the baby? He'd heard of such things. *Oh, dear God, no.* He gritted his teeth and asked, "What? What do you need to tell me?"

Taking in a stuttering breath, Ali spoke softly. "It's about our baby."

"What!" Morgan gasped.

"Well, it's not just a baby, Morgan, there are two. We're having twins."

Morgan exploded up from the bench where he'd been sitting. "Twins!" he yelled. "Twins. Two babies." He paced across the grass of the park, the phone to one ear the other hand holding the top of his head as if it might fly off. "Oh, my God. Ali, are you okay? I don't know what to ask, what to say."

"You might say you're happy," she whispered into the phone.

"I'm happy. I'm so happy I'm in a trance. Are you okay? Oh, my God. Twins," he repeated.

40

On his days shall the righteous flourish;
and abundance of peace so long
as the moon endureth.
Psalms 72:7

The three hour trip from Miami to Gadara never seemed so long. Unable to sleep after talking to Ali a second time on Friday and arranging a visit for Sunday at noon at her new home, this morning Morgan was showered by five-thirty.

He glanced at the plastic bag resting on the passenger seat. Last night, time after time he'd opened and then re-wrapped the boxes containing the two teddy bears he'd purchased. Were they appropriate? Would Ali accept them?

Morgan frowned as he drove north. The other small package in the plastic bag—was that going to be a problem? He recalled the time he labored over his purchase in the jewelry store on Flagler Street and finally chose, with the help of a pretty young clerk, a platinum ring with four diamonds, hoping the stones would represent Ali, the two children and himself, the family he longed for. *Two children, two babies,* he thought and felt a dual tug at his heart. He'd wished he could have chosen larger diamonds but the young lady with the big smile assured him these were lovely and quite appropriate. "You can get a larger diamond for her twenty-fifth anniversary," she said with a broad smile.

Now as the scenery flashed past his windows he wondered, was he rushing things or was he too late? The mantra of her words, "I do love you" followed him through every waking hour. Surely this meeting would be what he hoped. She'd invited him, or at least agreed to meet. She was the one who chose Sunday, wasn't she? He slowed down, pulling to the side of the road. He was not too far from Gadara now and he was two hours early. Should he continue and find somewhere to wait and kill time? A restaurant maybe? A park? He pulled off the highway to think. His GPS showed another twenty-seven miles.

Re-entering the roadway, he made up his mind. He would follow Ali's directions to see where their new home was, then go back into town and find a place to wait. "What's so difficult about that? College grad, you should be able to work that out." He smiled and turned the radio on, finding a station with country western music. After a short while he was singing along with Randy Travis.

Leaving the highway and following a sign indicating the way to 'Historic Downtown Gadara', Morgan soon found himself approaching a circle. As he drove slowly he was impressed with the neat buildings and businesses along the way, the little park in the center of the circle and the peaceful, relaxed atmosphere. *When I visited Ali at her mother's home I don't remember seeing this,* he thought, *but that was a while ago.* "Must have come into town another way. Ali knew some short cuts, I guess," he murmured, following the instructions to the golf course and the subdivision now housing Ali and her mother.

The gates to Windom Lakes announced 'A Golfing and Tennis Community'. Morgan slowed down and observed the golf course along both sides of Country Club Drive. He drove under an overpass allowing golf carts to cross the incoming road safely. "Nice," he mumbled watching golfers along the fairways. Coming to an intersection, he turned left and found himself driving through a community of town houses. He slowed, looking for number 1192 Winding Way. When he passed the house he was overcome with a mixture of feelings. Was she really in there? Did they see him scouting out the place? If they noticed the car would they think him foolish? He increased his speed, turned at the next intersection and wound his way back to the entrance.

"You are a jerk," he scolded himself. "Why would they notice a car driving slowly? There are thousands more Chevy Cavaliers just like this one even if Ali saw you." He retraced his route, coming to the circle again. He went around twice before he decided to drop into the Dilly Dally Café. Parking on a side street, he strode purposefully toward the entrance. "Dilly Dally Café," he muttered to himself. "What a silly name."

The restaurant was packed and a young woman with flaming red hair pulled into a pony tail, greeted him. "Good mornin', I'm Sandy. Just one?" she said, looking behind him.

"One, please," Morgan said.

"We don't have any booths open right now. You could wait outside on a bench and I'll come get you when one is free or you could go to the counter," she said, looking over her shoulder. "There's one stool left."

"I'll take the counter. Thanks," Morgan said. There were ten red leatherette covered stools, nine of which were occupied by men in jeans and cowboy boots.

Locals, Morgan thought as he swung his leg over the stool. *I must stand out as a stranger, but then I guess everyone in here is local so I would be the only outsider.* He picked up the plastic covered menu before him.

"Coffee?" the young man asked as he slid a paper placemat in front of Morgan.

"Yes, please."

"Regular or decaf?"

"Regular, thanks."

"Ready to order?"

"Do you have any pie, or pastries?"

"All our pies and pastries are homemade. We have apple pie, crumb cake, strawberry cheese cake and a few donuts left." The young man filled the cup. "Cream and sugar are on the counter. I'll be back in a minute."

Morgan looked at the menu. He really didn't want to eat anything. Maybe this wasn't a good idea but he couldn't leave now. His stomach churned. *But,* he thought, I *didn't have anything yet so maybe eating would be a good idea.*

When the young man came back, Morgan ordered apple pie.

"Nothing else?"

"No, thanks."

He was reading the placards along the wall, all covered with homey sayings when he heard a voice calling his name. "Morgan. Morgan. What a surprise to see you here."

Morgan turned to see Jack standing behind him. "What the devil? Where did you come from?"

"Just what I was thinking. I thought you were in Miami?"

"And I hadn't a clue as to where you were. What a coincidence. Good to see you." Morgan stuck his hand out and Jack gripped it firmly. He liked Jack and while he didn't know exactly what made him think of him as a friend, he was glad to see him.

"I have a booth. Come join me," Jack said, pointing to a small booth along the wall directly behind Morgan's stool.

"I've ordered," he said.

"No problem. Kenny," Jack called, "this gentleman is joining me."

The young man behind the counter smiled and nodded and Morgan sat across from Jack. "This is so surprising. You just turn up at the darnedest times."

"I do, don't I?" Jack said, smiling. "What are you doing in Gadara?"

Morgan looked away for a moment. "I'm here to visit my girl. Something I should have done months ago. Now I'm praying it's not too late."

"If it's meant to be, Morgan, it isn't too late."

"I don't know. I've been such a fool."

Jack drank from his coffee mug. "If you recognize your mistakes and do something about them, then you are no longer a fool. It's only if you keep doing whatever you think was foolish that you remain a fool."

"Well, I'm trying. But how do I know what I'm doing is going to fix the problems?"

"You trust, Morgan. You trust."

Morgan sighed as a waitress put a plate with a huge slice of apple pie in front of him. He picked up his fork and then replaced it, looking into Jack's eyes. "What if I fail?"

Jack smiled. "You won't fail, Morgan. Just do what you think is best. Best for you and your girl."

"There's more to consider."

"Oh?"

"Ali, that's my girl. Ali is pregnant...with twins." Morgan bit his lip looking at his companion, waiting for the judgment he expected.

Instead, Jack smiled. "What great news! Are you happy about this?"

Morgan blew out a huge, stifled breath. "I'm so happy I don't know what to do with myself. But I'm scared, Jack. Scared I've waited too long, scared she won't want me in her life or the lives of our...our children."

Jack reached across the small table. He patted the back of Morgan's hand. "It will be okay. Believe me." Jack felt a little poke from Samuel who was unseen. "If you are sincere," he continued, "if you have faith, it just has to work out. When are you seeing her?"

"At noon," Morgan said, looking at his watch. His excursion around Windham Lakes and the time in the diner had taken longer than he thought. "Oh, gosh. I have to go," he said pushing his plate away.

"You haven't eaten anything."

"I don't have time, it's eleven-thirty and I have to be there at noon."

"It doesn't take that long to get there, does it? Eat a little," Jack urged.

Morgan looked at him. Why did he always seem to calm things down? He shook his head and cut a piece of the pie. "I have about fifteen minutes," he said, tasting the sticky sweetness of the apple filling.

"You'll do fine, Morgan. Eat half and then I'll walk you to your car."

Later, driving back to Windham Lakes, Morgan wondered how Jack would know he'd have plenty of time? *And he seemed to know right where my car was parked.* Strange, but he couldn't worry about that now. Eleven-ninety-two Winding Way was just up ahead. He pulled to the curb and felt for the plastic bag. Holding his breath, he got out of the car and walked up the curved brick path to the double doors, the bag dangling from one hand suddenly took on an unexpected weight.

Sun glinted on the brass hardware. His stomach contracted around half a piece of homemade apple pie. Ali was inside.

***

Karen sat on the end of Ali's bed. For ten minutes they had watched the green digital numbers on the clock slip away. Now there were five minutes until twelve o'clock.

"We talked about this last night, Ali, but I want to make sure this is what you want to do."

"If he comes," Ali said softly. She was bolstered by several pillows with the coverlet pulled up to her chest. Lying on her side, one frilly little pillow propped against her stomach as if it could hide or distort the large swelling under the covers.

"You still want me to talk to him before he comes back here?"

"Yes, please, Mom. I don't want to scare him to death the first time he sees me."

"He won't be scared."

"Shocked, then."

Karen sighed. The confusion and apprehension etched on Ali's face was painful.

"I don't think it will matter, but if that's what you want, I'll meet him and talk to him. I just don't want you upset."

Ali looked at the clock. 11:56. "He might not come..." Her words were interrupted by the doorbell. She looked to her mother. "Is my hair a mess?"

"It's beautiful."

"Too much makeup?"

"Perfect."

"Oh, Mom..."

"You look beautiful, Ali."

"Answer the door, please." She closed her eyes and snuggled further into her pillows.

Karen brushed Ali's hair back. "It'll be okay, honey," she said before leaving the room.

She reached for the doorknob on the heavy front door, her fingers icy. Coaxing a smile to her lips she began to pull the door open. Karen had met Morgan on several occasions, some at college and some when Ali brought him home for a visit. Her mind flew back to one time when he had stayed overnight, sleeping on the pull-out in the den. Was that when...? "Oh, don't be dumb," she warned herself.

The door swung wide and she greeted him. "Morgan. Good to see you. I hope your trip up here was comfortable." Karen felt as if she had become a robot, echoing pre-planned phrases. She stepped back.

"Hello, Mrs. Waterson." Morgan said, remaining where he stood.

They stared at each other. Karen remembered Morgan's good looks but she didn't remember him as being so tall. Morgan recalled thinking Ali looked more like her father than her mother.

"Oh, come in, Morgan, come in." She reached for his arm, tugging him into the foyer. "We'll go out on the deck." Dropping his arm and without looking back she strode to the sliding glass doors leading to the patio. The bamboo shades had been lowered to keep the direct sun out and a large fan in the corner made the room almost comfortable.

"Sit there, Morgan. I have some iced tea or would you prefer a soft drink?" Karen still felt as if she were playing a role and an uncomfortable one at that.

Morgan eased into the chair Karen had indicated, still clutching his plastic bag. "Tea is fine, Mrs. Waterson. Is Ali..." He didn't know how to finish the sentence. Was she there? Was she hiding because she didn't want to see him? Had she changed her mind? His heart flip flopped in his chest. "Is she all right?" he asked,

"She is, Morgan. But I wanted to speak with you before you two get together. You see, there are things you don't know, things have happened during her pregnancy. Ali is uncomfortable seeing you until you are aware of them."

"Developments? Is she okay. Are the babies okay? Gosh, Mrs. Waterson, I'm confused. I don't know what..."

"I know you must be. Have some tea, Morgan, and we'll talk just a little before I take you back to see Ali." Karen poured two glasses of tea, handing one to Morgan. "You see," she continued, "because of her pregnancy and the twins and the weight of the two babies, Ali was having...problems." She really didn't want to go into the bleeding, that seemed like such a personal thing. She sighed. "So the doctor has ordered her to partial bed rest which really means she spends the greater part of every day and night in bed."

Morgan balanced his tea on the table and stood. "Why didn't she tell me?"

Karen looked at him. His face was tortured with concern. "I think she thought you didn't care, Morgan. Wait," she said, when she saw he was going to make a quick denial. "After all, she hadn't heard from you in months. She'd gone through the pregnancy thinking you would never contact her again, or maybe I should say scared you wouldn't."

Morgan melted into his chair. "I'm so sorry, Mrs. Waterson. I know I've done a terrible thing. I want to make it up to her, I really do, but I don't know how. I love her, Mrs. Waterson. I feel so...crummy. I want to fix things. I want us to be together forever and maybe I've lost my chance and won't..." He prattled, his embarrassment flushing his face a strange color.

Karen recognized his distress. "Ali is afraid you will be shocked at her appearance. She is...well, let's say large. Carrying twins is difficult and for a first pregnancy, it is..."

"She's afraid of how I'll act because she's..." he searched for a kinder word, couldn't fine one and finished..."big?"

Karen smiled and nodded. "She's a girl, Morgan. Her appearance is important and especially when it's being seen by the man she loves."

Morgan stood and took one of Karen's hands. "She'll just have to learn the man who loves her doesn't care how she looks, Mrs. Waterson. Especially now. I'll bet she's just as beautiful as ever."

"I think you're ready to go back. Last door on the left. She's waiting."

Karen watched the young man hurry through the living room to the hallway and disappear in a rush. She leaned back in her chair and closed her eyes. Had she said the right things? Was it her place to use the words 'man she loves'? She reached for her tea. She'd find out soon enough.

41

***As unknown, and yet well known; as dying,
and behold we live; as chastened and not killed;
as sorrowful, yet always rejoicing;
as poor, yet making many rich;
as having nothing
and yet possessing all things.
2 Corinthians 6:9-10***

The door to Ali's bedroom was slightly ajar. With an icy hand, Morgan pushed it open. Ali lay against several pink pillows, her blonde hair framing her face, a flowered coverlet covering her. A lacy pillow leaned against her body. Their eyes met, neither able to look away as Morgan walked slowly toward her.

"You're beautiful, Ali."

"Mom told you to say that."

"No. No, you're even more beautiful." He edged next to her bed, unsure of whether to kneel down beside the bed or sit next to her on the bed. There didn't seem to be a chair in the room. The plastic bag dangled from the fingers of his left hand.

Ali patted the bed. "Sit," she said, her voice a breathless croak, her eyes uncontrollably filling with tears. He inched onto the bed. "I'm so sorry, Ali. Sorry for everything, every hurt, every..." He leaned forward, wanting with all his heart to kiss her, to pull her to him, but he was afraid. Instead, he whispered, "I love you, Ali. I always have and I always will."

Ali lifted one arm as if inviting him closer and he bent forward. He felt her hand on his arm. "Ali," he whispered and then felt the stinging blow as her fist punched his chest.

"You left me, you rat," she cried, wild sobs accompanying her words. "You left me," she repeated, her body convulsed with the agony of the moment, her hand repeating the blows, weaker and weaker as time moved forward. Her other hand clutched his arm, her fingers digging into his flesh. "You left me," she said, his body muffling her voice.

He slid both arms around her and pulled her to his chest, the plastic bag slipping to the floor beside the bed. "Don't cry, Ali. Please, don't cry. I'll never leave you or hurt you again. Never. Never!"

They rocked back and forth together, he leaning forward, Ali engulfed in his embrace, her heart-wrenching sobs piercing the quiet of the room. For several minutes the only sounds in the room were her sobs and his murmurs of love.

"You left me," she hiccupped, her body stiff with tension.

"Never again, sweetheart. Never again. I promise." They remained entwined, the warmth of their bodies stirring memories of a past love.

He felt her relax and loosened his grip but continued to hold her. Gently, he kissed the salty tears from her cheeks. She lay in his arms, her eyes closed, her breath coming in soft gulps.

"Are you okay?" he whispered, afraid to move.

Ali didn't answer but nodded her head slightly. She kept her eyes closed.

Morgan waited, watching Ali, feeling her body in his arms.

"Are you okay?" he whispered again and felt her lay back against the pillows.

"Uh huh," she stuttered, mini-sobs still choking her.

"It can't be good for you to cry that hard, sweetheart." Tentatively he pulled one arm from behind her, feeling her relax slightly. He slid his hand behind her neck, her hair silky against his skin. More memories flooded his heart. "Let me push this pillow behind your neck," he whispered.

Her eyes fluttered open. "Why, Morgan? Why did you leave me? Leave us?" she said, her hand caressing her stomach.

"I told you, I let something I thought was monumental cloud my vision. Finding out about a lifetime of deceit is a shock and I let it take over my reason. It was as though the whole world got jerked out from beneath me. I had to figure out what was still real. It took me time to realize that you were still real. I was selfish and stupid but I promise I'll never think like that again.

I've learned my lesson. The hard way," he concluded sheepishly. "I'll never let anything ever come between us again. Between us, or..." he tentatively moved his hand across the covers to where her stomach was. Their fingers touched. "...or between me and our kids."

Ali sighed, her eyes probing his. "How can I believe that, Morgan? It was so important for you to be with me these last few months. To help me and support me during this pregnancy and you weren't here. I needed you and you weren't here. I felt so alone," she said, her voice breaking.

His eyes closed, Morgan bit his lower lip. Painful regret surged through his heart. "I can only promise, Ali-Baba, with all my heart, I'll make this up to you. I'll be the best father. We'll learn how to be good parents together. You can teach me." He raised his head, his eyes fixed on hers. "I know you needed me and I realize how much I needed you, too. I thought somehow if I retreated from everything hurting me I could erase what my family had done to me and I just made everything worse for everyone. How could I be a good husband or father with no background, no family of my own? I felt my lack of any family, my non-existent past was too overpowering and would ruin my future and anyone else's it touched."

He felt her fingers grasp his. She pulled his hand onto her stomach, pushing the silly pillow aside. "Our babies are moving," she whispered and then watched as amazement widened his eyes and made his jaw drop.

"Oh, my God. I feel them. Ali, I feel them moving."

For several minutes they remained joined, the young man, the young mother and the babies they had created. It was a first bonding for them all.

Ali withdrew her hand and Morgan followed. He sat straighter. "I meant it when I made those promises. I meant it when I said I've always loved you and always will love you."

"I want to believe you."

"You can believe me, sweetheart. I promise."

Ali studied his face. Her mind sped back to when she met him, tall and good looking, his dark hair curled over his ears, his brown eyes flashing with excitement. It was so right then, something she'd never experienced before. *Love at first sight?* She'd thought. *Could it be?* And, as they grew to know each other, the bond grew stronger. She remembered the times they'd made love and the things they'd promised each other. Could she trust him again? She closed her eyes and prayed, asking God for guidance. When she opened her eyes she saw the young man she'd fallen in love with. "I love you, too, Morgan," she whispered. She reached for a tissue on the nightstand and dabbed at her face.

"That's all I prayed for all the way from Miami to Gadara, honey. I prayed I'd hear you say those words. I promise I'll make you happy."

"Forever after?" she said, trying hard to quell the smile threatening her lips.

"Forever after," he said solemnly.

"That's a long time."

"I only have enough love to last you forever, sweetheart."

She looked at him intently. He looked anxious. She balled up the tissue and tossed it on the nightstand. "I feel all sticky."

"Let me get you a washcloth. Where...?"

"That door. It's my bathroom," she said pointing.

Morgan hurried back with a damp washcloth and Ali washed her face. "Can I get you anything else?"

"A drink of water, please. Would you go and ask Mom for water for me and whatever you'd like to drink? I'm sorry, but I can't get up right now. I'm limited on how much movement I can do in a day."

He looked puzzled. "Go," she said with a hint of the first genuine smile of the day. "I'll explain when you come back."

When he returned, clutching two glasses in his hands, he found Ali sitting up more. "There's a white chair in the room across the hall. My friends, Kristi and Marla, put it over there when they were here yesterday. They're always 'helping' me," she said.

When Morgan returned to the room with the chair he was uncertain as to where to put it.

"Put it next to the bed so we can talk. What was Mom doing?"

"She's reading. Out on the patio," he said, pushing the chair close to the bed and sitting down.

"I promised I'd tell you about my pregnancy. Well, I'm fine and the babies are fine. It's just that twins are heavier than one baby so there was some trouble a few weeks ago. I began bleeding."

Morgan jerked forward. "Bleeding. Are you...are the babies..."

"I'm fine and they are doing really well but the doctor ordered partial bed rest. That means for most of the day and night I have to be lying down, feet up. I can get up to go to the bathroom. Usually Mom or one of my friends takes me. It will only be for a little while. I just report to him every week that nothing has changed."

Morgan reached for her hand, shaking his head from side to side. "And I wasn't here to help you."

"Let's be practical, Morgan. You couldn't have been here anyhow. Your job in Miami is important. More important now than ever."

"But I could have been in touch, talking to you every day, seeing you on weekends."

Ali looked serious. "You could have but if there's one thing my mother has taught me it's not to rely on the 'could haves and would haves' in this world. She's been such a help to me. My dad, who just moved to Omaha, has been good, too. And I have friends, wonderful friends who've helped. But," she said, gripping his hand. "You were the one I wanted, the one I needed to talk to, to share all this with."

Morgan saw tears glint in her eyes again and leaned forward and kissed her gently. He felt her respond and the kiss lingered, growing with intensity. "I've wanted to do that from the minute I got here," he said.

He moved the chair closer to the bed. One leg caught on something and when Morgan looked to see what it was he saw the plastic bag. Reaching for it, he guiltily picked it up.

"What's that," Ali asked.

"It's something I brought with me."

Ali waited, watching his face. She blinked, a small smile

creeping across her lips. "Well?"

Morgan fumbled with the two bigger boxes. "I hope this is all right, Ali. I brought something for the babies. Gee, I still can't get used to the idea there are two babies."

"Well, you just felt them having a game of handball in there," she joked, reaching for the boxes. "Two of them," she said, pulling at the paper which seemed quite wrinkled and was obviously re-taped. When she opened the box her smile widened. "Oh, how cute, a blue Teddy bear. Thank you." She opened the next box and laugh aloud. "And a pink one. Thank you. You'll have to see the nursery before you leave."

"I think I saw it. Is it that room across the hall? The one with cribs and tables and God knows what?"

"Yes," Ali answered softly. "I forgot when I sent you for the chair but I wasn't sure you'd notice."

"I noticed. There sure are a lot of things in there."

"It takes a lot of stuff to get ready for two babies."

"And, I haven't helped," he said.

"You will now?

"You bet," Morgan said with a wide smile.

"Put these Teddy bears on the bureau with that stupid little pillow. I can't image why I thought it would hide this great lump I'm carry around. I must look just huge and ugly to you."

Morgan slipped from the chair to his knees next to Ali's bed. Grasping her hand, he said, "You look prettier than ever, Ali-Baba. I mean that. And that 'great lump' is our future, so don't go saying nasty things about it. You really are beautiful, sweetheart." His voice broke with emotion.

"Honey, there's something I should have done long ago," he said, his hand holding the tiny box out of sight. "I told you I loved you but I meant to say more and was waiting for a special time to do it. I think now is the time."

"What...?" Ali, asked.

Morgan brought the box up so that Ali could see it and her face turned from curious to astonished. She opened her mouth, not to speak but to gasp for air.

"Ali," Morgan said, "I've loved you from the day we met. I want to spend the rest of my life loving you, caring for you and being everything you need. Sweetheart, will you marry me?" He opened the box.

Quivering with emotion, she felt tears of excitement and joy, not like the earlier tears.

Morgan didn't know what to do. "Will you marry me?" he whispered again.

She nodded, wiping her eyes with one hand as he slid the ring on the finger she extended.

"It's beautiful," she said softly, again wiping her face with the damp cloth.

There was a brief pause as they looked at each other, holding hands, the little box lying on the bed cover between them.

"Does that mean 'yes'?" Morgan asked.

"It means 'yes,' my darling," Ali said, stretching forward to put her arms around him, pulling him to her. *My darling,* she thought. *It's been so long since I've used those words.* Their lips met and this time the kiss was passionate, covering all the hurt, all the confusion and all the uncertainty of the wasted time. "We'll be a wonderful family," she whispered in his ear.

Leaning back she extended her hand, twisting it back and forth so the light could catch the diamonds. "It's really beautiful."

"Not nearly as beautiful as you are."

"Silly," she said, then gasped. "My mother. I have to tell Mom."

***

Later that day, Karen carried a tray into Ali's room. "I'll let you two have your supper in here."

"Where else, Mom? Here's where I live right now. But you join us, okay?"

"No, I'll have mine on the terrace. You two need to be together."

"Oh, please join us, Mrs. Waterson," Morgan said, standing.

Karen smiled. "No, this time I'm going to eat on the patio. Next time we'll all eat together. Maybe Ali will be off partial bed rest then."

"Please," chorused Ali and Morgan.

She smiled at the two holding hands, grinning from ear to ear. She'd been waiting a long time to see such happiness on her daughter's face.

Her heart had sung with joy when Ali called for her this afternoon. One look at the joyous faces of both of them told the story, but she listened quietly as they told her of the plans, flashed the ring and chatted excitedly about the birth of their children.

"I plan to be here for the birth, Mrs. Waterson. I'll talk to my boss when I go in tomorrow."

"We haven't set a date for the wedding. I hope you understand, Mom, but I don't want to get married...like this," she said, rubbing her tummy. "After the babies are here we'll make plans. Are you upset?" Ali frowned for the first time in hours.

"I'm not upset at anything, honey. As long as you're happy," she looked meaningfully at Morgan, "as long as you are happy," she repeated "then I'm happy for both of you."

She was touched when Morgan reached for her hand. "I'm so grateful for all you've done, Mrs. Waterson. Things I should have been doing. I've apologized to Ali and I apologize to you."

He looked at Ali, still gripping her hand, and heard her say, "And, I've forgiven him, Mom. Isn't that what you said a long time ago?"

"When you first came home? I guess I did, honey." Karen squeezed Morgan's hand. "Our Lord has forgiven us time and time again, it's the least we can do for each other."

She stood looking at her daughter and the man she loved "Okay, I'll join you."

"Let me help," Morgan said, jumping up. "I'll get the other tray and help you carry things, if that's okay, Mrs. Waterson?"

Two tray tables were set up next to the bed with a special bed tray for Ali.

"It's just a light snack, I'm afraid," Karen said, opening her napkin. She and Morgan faced each other. Tuna sandwiches, a small plate with celery and carrot sticks with a dab of dip and a piece of apple pie graced each tray.

"It looks wonderful, Mrs. Waterson," Morgan said, hoping no

one else heard his growling stomach. "Oh," he laughed. "It must be apple pie day."

"Do you like apple pie?" Karen asked, anxiously.

"I sure do. I had apple pie at the Dilly Dally Café on the circle before I came here. I'd gotten to Gadara too soon and was killing time. I was so nervous about coming here, I told Ali I was afraid of being late and I arrived way too early."

Karen smiled at him. "Well, everything turned out well."

"Yes, Jack said it would."

"Jack?" Karen and Alice said at the same time.

"Yes, he's someone I've met recently. He seems to pop up every now and then. Of course, I've only seen him in Miami but here he was, on a Sunday morning, in Gadara, right where I was killing time. Strange."

Karen and Ali looked at each other, mouths agape, eyes wide. "Jack? Tall? With a beard? College professor?"

"Yes, do you know him?"

"Well, I think, if it's the same man, he apparently is spending the summer in Gadara. I've seen him several times. In fact, I've spoken to him at the library and in the park when I go there to think," Karen said. "He's interested in local history. He's a good listener."

"And I've seen him around, before I was confined to home, and saw him at the high school," Ali added. "We chatted."

"Well," Morgan laughed. "We have a mutual friend and didn't know it. I don't know what his business in Miami was but twice he and I shared dinner. You're right, he is a good listener."

42

The Lord looked down from heaven upon the children of men, to see if there were any that did understand and seek God.
Psalms 14:2

On Monday morning, heat waves wafted like mini vapors over the pavement as Morgan hurried to work. Not only did he not mind the heat, he didn't even notice it. For the past two weeks his weekend visits with Ali played over and over in his mind, every word and emotion etched into his brain and heart. They were going to be together forever. Anything and everything else didn't matter and disappeared from his thoughts.

Every Saturday morning he rushed northward to Gadara. With another strange turn of events, Ali's mother suggested he stay at the Twin Oaks in town. "We'd love to have you here, Morgan, but the twins have taken our spare room."

Upon checking into the bed and breakfast he discovered his friend Jack also stayed there. He was becoming a shadow no one wanted to avoid. Nevertheless, Morgan checked in early Saturday morning and checked out after breakfast on Sunday. He looked forward to seeing Jack on Sunday morning and wondered why he had been at the Dilly Dally Café the morning of his first visit to Ali. Shrugging, he brushed off the series of coincidences as just that, coincidences.

"Twins," he whispered as he waited for the elevator.

Edgar Faraday moved to stand next to him. Edgar was a fixture in the lobby of the building where the entire sixth floor was Littman & Littman. Edgar could be found there from eight o'clock until well after everyone in the building left. He didn't seem to have a job other than greeting everyone with a smile and checking late visitors as they came and then left. Not a doorman, certainly not a courier, they were much younger, Edgar always seemed to be there, neat in his tan uniform with the brown stripes down the trousers, thin strips of gray hair carefully combed across his balding head, his demeanor always pleasant.

They both stared at their reflections in the highly polished metal doors. "Hot today," Edgar said, his voice tinged with acceptance. "Well, it's the end of summer and we're in Florida. Tropics, you know?"

"I didn't notice, Edgar. I think it's a beautiful day." Morgan's smile was irrepressible, stretching as far as his lips would allow.

The doors opened and he stepped inside the elevator box while Edgar moved back a step. "Have a good day, Mr. Muldorn," Edgar said with a three finger salute brushing his forehead.

To his surprise, Morgan stepped out of the elevator and grabbed his hand. Edgar felt the young man's fingers grip his. "And a good day to you, Edgar," Morgan said, sliding quickly back between the closing doors. "You have a good day, too," his voice squeezed between the doors as they clicked into place.

On the sixth floor, Morgan looked around to see if anyone else was in yet. He knew it was early but there was no use in staying in bed or at home any longer so he'd showered at five o'clock and paced the sidewalk at his bus stop forty-five minutes earlier than his usual time.

He tossed his jacket over the back of his chair, fiddled with the empty in-basket on the corner of his desk and then having absolutely nothing to do, hurried to the break room. Maybe someone was there, hopefully the coffee was made and the Danish and donuts from Baker's Dozen had been delivered. Pushing the door open he smelled the coffee and saw the box of goodies on the counter.

Marie, stirring her coffee with a plastic stick turned to greet him. "Wow, I think this is a record, never seen you here this early before." She smiled at him. She'd almost given up getting noticed by the young hunk she'd been watching for three summers while he interned himself into favor with the big shots. Still, a smile never hurt. "You okay?"

"Never better, Marie. Never better," Morgan said, pulling his mug from the cabinet and filling it with hot coffee. "Starved though," he added, selecting a prune Danish and balancing it on a napkin as he navigated the chairs and settled into one at the second table.

Marie frowned. Was he humming? "Mind if I join you?" she asked, not waiting for a response and sitting opposite him. "I'm usually alone for my first cup. This is nice."

"Yeah." Morgan bit into the gooey part of the Danish, savoring the sticky sweetness on his tongue. "Boy, this is good."

"Same old, same old," Marie said, picking a small piece of donut from the plain ring she'd chosen. "Just carbs and calories but it's all part of the ritual. Do you ever wonder who started these things? I mean, do we have to have coffee as soon as we get here? And those sticky, sweet things aren't good for anything except pounds on the hips and bad teeth." She smiled, watching Morgan devour his pastry.

"Can't be all that bad, Marie. Everyone pretty much does the same thing and your teeth look good to me." He laughed. The sound seemed loud in the small room.

The door opened and two girls from the outer office came in. "Hi, Marie," one said, surprised to see Morgan sitting at the table with her.

"Hi," the other one echoed, going directly to the cupboard for a mug and getting her coffee. She smiled a knowing grin. She'd been privy to many of Marie's hopes and wishes when it came to Morgan.

"We're not staying," the first one announced, hurrying her companion out the door.

Marie sighed, happy to have Morgan to herself for a little while. But the sigh turned to a grimace when Dave pushed the door open and exclaimed, "Hold the presses. Morgan Muldorn is in the office thirty minutes before opening? It's news, that's what it is. What happened? Lose your lease? Get evicted?" He filled his mug, swung his legs over the chair next to Marie and reached for a chocolate donut.

"Nothing like that," Morgan said, wiping sugar from his lips. "Hey, reach over there and get me another."

"What kind?" Dave asked, twisting in his chair. "Another? Gone off your diet, have you?"

"Any one will do. Never been on a diet. Thanks."

Dave studied his friend. "Something's up. For the past two weeks you have been insufferably pleasant, almost to the point of sickening elation. I haven't seen that smile since two summers ago when you met that gal in college."

Marie stood. "Well, I guess I'll get to my desk. Have a nice day, you two," she said, her face not matching the pleasant words.

Dave looked up to wink at her but decided she didn't look receptive to a wink. In fact, her face had taken on the thunderous look of a bad storm brewing.

"What's with her?" Dave asked after the door swung closed.

"She was okay until you got here. Must be you," Morgan said around another bite of the donut Dave had handed to him.

"Okay, two donuts..."

"One donut and one Danish," Morgan corrected.

"Two goodies, then you're here forty minutes early at least and the smile. Something's up, my man. Spill."

"I'm just happy."

"You haven't been happy since you got here in May."

"Things are changing."

"Like what? Come on, man. Share."

Morgan sighed but the sigh didn't erase the smile. "Got some good news. Great news I'm savoring, is that okay?"

"That's it. That's all you're going to say?"

"For now," Morgan said, standing. "I have to talk to Junior as soon as he comes in."

"You're not leaving us," Dave said, his teasing disappearing into an expression of concern.

"No. I'm not leaving the firm. But things are changing, my man. Things are changing." He stood, squeezed from behind the table, poured himself another cup of coffee and pushed the door open.

"That's all? You owe me. I've been trying to cheer you up for three months."

"I'll tell you later. When I can," Morgan shouted through the closing door.

At exactly nine-fifteen, Morgan sat in one of the plush chairs facing the desk in the office of Samuel D. Littman, Jr.

He'd been rehearsing what he was going to say all the way home from Gadara and had hashed it over on the bus into the city. He'd tell Mr. Littman about Ali, about the babies and how he needed to be there when they were born which seemed to be scheduled for September. When Morgan asked about the due date Ali had sighed and said, "They think it will be fairly early in September. They can come any time now. I'm sure ready." Since all this was so new to him, he wondered why the date was vaguely 'fairly early in September'. He remembered girls at college talking about specific times and when he questioned Ali, she said, "there was some question as to when I got pregnant and now with twins it's a little hard to pin down."

He'd also mention a wedding in the future. *What could Littman say? I've been getting good quarterly reports since I was an intern, three years now.*

Nevertheless, even with all that confidence, Morgan laced his fingers together, licked his lips and was about to speak when Mr. Littman shuffled a few papers on his desktop, cleared his throat and said, "I'm glad you came in so quickly, my boy. I'd asked Marie to send you in as soon as you arrived."

Morgan frowned. Hadn't he asked for the appointment? He'd checked with Marie to see if Mr. Littman was free early this morning. She hadn't said anything but, "Sure. He's free at nine-fifteen."

He felt a flush sweep over his face and stared across the desk. Something was not right.

"You've been a valued part of Littman and Littman for," he paused, looking at some notes on his desk, "three years internship and now since May of this year." He leaned back, his leather chair creaking with the change of position.

"We have some great news for you, son. The quarterly seminar for the National Association of Investment Brokers is being held in San Francisco this month. Usually this conference is in September but because of some scheduling difficulties, it has been moved up to August fifth, sixth and seventh. My partner and I have reviewed your activities and your faithful participation with our firm and have decided you are to be our representative. The fall meeting is pretty cut and dried, no bi-law changes or anything like that. They are always done at the spring meeting when the Directors are all present.

"You'll be leaving for California on Thursday. Since it's Monday I'm sure you can make whatever arrangements are necessary. If you'd like Wednesday off for personal reasons, just let personnel and Marie know.

"For three nights and four days you will be our representative. You'll be required to attend all the meetings and seminars I've checked on the program. Everything is in this package. I suggest you look it over carefully. Your tickets and reservations are also in the folder."

He leaned forward, pushing a large green folder with a black strap toward Morgan. "I guess I don't have to explain that in choosing you to represent us is a feather in your cap, young man. We are relying on you to make yourself known, take part as indicated and bring back a wealth of information to be shared at our next Board meeting, which," he glanced at the calendar on the corner of his desk. "which will be in October."

He stood and extended his hand. Morgan rose in a trance. He automatically gripped Mr. Littman's hand. His throat constricted around the words he'd wanted to say, instead he heard himself saying, "It's an honor, Mr. Littman."

"As I said, if you have personal arrangements to make, Muldorn, you may take a day off prior to your leaving Miami. We are putting a lot of faith in you, young man. We expect great things of you one day." His eye twitched, not a wink but an indication of something unsaid.

Morgan backed away from the table. "Thank you, sir," he said, turning and fleeing to the safety of his little office.

In his office, Morgan slumped in his chair, legs sprawled, hands laced behind his neck his body the consistency of a badly used rag doll. He leaned forward to check his calendar. First client wasn't until ten o'clock. He returned to the rag doll position only to be brought up short by Dave's voice.

"Okay. Out with it." He closed the door, something almost

never done unless clients were in the offices, and threw himself into one of the client chairs, sending it scooting across the floor several inches. "Smiles, smiles and exorbitant cheerfulness and now a visit to Boss Number Two? Out with it. Haven't I been your best buddy from the minute you stepped across the hallowed doorstep of Littman and Littman?"

Morgan thumped forward, elbows on his desk, his face cradled in his hands. "I don't know, Dave. I just don't get it."

"You get fired?"

"Far from it. You know that conference they have four times a year. The NAIB thing?"

"Yeah, I know about it. Went to one, it was incredibly boring but depending on which city it's scheduled for, you could make a weekend of it, if you know what I mean. Unfortunately the one I went to was in Philadelphia. Now, New Orleans or Vegas..."

"How about San Francisco."

Dave straightened. "You're going to Frisco? You lucky dog, you. So what's with the long face? You should be dancing in the aisles."

"There's other stuff."

"Aha, that's what you've been mooning over. Don't tell me it's a woman. I've tried to prod you towards some pretty hot dishes and got zero. Found one on your own?"

Morgan shook his head. "No. I mean, yes, but...remember the girl I had in college?"

"The one you were stupid-silly over? Yeah. Since you were so down in the dumps when you came here full-time and never mentioned her, I figured she'd dumped you. I was trying to get you over that, my man, but you didn't bite."

"It's her, Dave. I've made a real mess of things and I thought I had it all straightened out. I've been seeing her every weekend for the past three weeks."

"The reason for the untoward merriment," he said, sitting back, grinning from ear to ear. "So what's the prob?"

"The prob is she's pregnant and about to present me with twins."

Dave shot out of his chair as if it had suddenly become electrified. "Twins! Man-o-man, you don't do things half way, do you?" He paced across the small space between the desk and window wall, adjusting the blinds so that it wasn't quite as easy to look in.

"So what's the story? When is she due?"

"That's the prob, as you put it. We aren't sure when the babies are due. The closest they can come, apparently, is early in September."

Dave threw himself back in the chair. "When's the conference?"

"August fifth, sixth and seventh, come back on Sunday the eighth. I leave this Wednesday, on the fourth."

"Sorry, but I don't see any trouble with that. You'll be back a month before the kids are due to show up. While you're away, you can keep in touch with her by phone. Come on man, four days away. Think what it will do for your future." He paused and looked intently at Morgan. "You didn't turn the opportunity down, did you?"

"Of course not. Don't you think I know how important it is to keep the job? God, man, I'm going to have four mouths to feed. That's scary."

Dave stretched his long arms wide and then folded them behind his head looking like a huge bird tucking his wings away. "I don't see a problem. Go to the conference. Make points. It'll help you down the line."

"You're right. It's just I abandoned Ali for months. Now I've promised not to leave her and what do I do? Three weeks after making these promises I'm dashing off to San Francisco."

"She'll understand, man. It's business, money in the pocket, money for baby food and diapers."

Morgan stood and paced. "I know you're right, but somehow I have this uneasy feeling."

"It's sympathy pains."

"Where'd you hear that?"

"My sister. She has a kid every two years. Five of them now. I've been through this."

"I haven't."

"It'll work out. Whew. You had me worried. Listen, don't make a mountain out of a mole hill, something my mother used to tell me when I went off half-cocked. You'll explain to your lady love and she'll understand. Look, she must know how important your job is now."

"I'm sure she does, yet..."

"Yet, nothing. Just do what you have to for good old L&L and you'll be back in time for the blessed event. Geez, I thought you were going to chuck the job for some bimbo and here you are being Mr. Goody Two Shoes." He stood and thrust his hand at Morgan. The two men gripped hands. "It'll work out," Dave said, giving Morgan a hearty thump on the back. He opened the door and began to leave. "Listen," he said, "if I can help, you let me know. Even though Patty and I don't have kids, yet," he said, crossing his fingers, "I know a lot about that stuff. Sister Lou, remember? See ya'." He loped along the hall to his office.

It'll work out, he'd said. Just like Jack said. I sure hope they know what they're talking about. Morgan picked up the green folder, slipped the strap off and began to go through the papers inside.

Tonight he'd call Ali and explain why he had to leave. Only for four days, purely business. Surely she'd understand. He flipped through the information but he had to re-read most of the things he'd already looked at so he shoved the papers back in the green folder. *I'll look at them tonight,* he thought and then looked up to see his clients standing at Marie's desk.

43

Therefore my heart is glad,
and my glory rejoiceth:
my flesh also shall rest in hope
Psalms 16:9

Wednesday morning, Ali buried her face in the pink teddy. Was she fooling herself or did the little bear really smell like baby powder?

"You're going to have them worn out before the kids get here," Karen said from the doorway.

"I just love them, Mom. I can't wait to put them in the cribs with the babies. Gosh, I'm so sick of being pregnant. Is this normal? Do other mothers-to-be feel like this?"

"I think so, honey. But it won't be long now."

"Another month," she moaned.

Karen left and returned a few minutes later with a tray for Ali. "Here comes breakfast in bed."

Ali rose up and peered at the tray. "Skim milk and cereal. Thanks, Mom. I'm not hungry but I'll drink some of the milk."

Karen sat in a chair next to the bed. "You feel okay?"

"Uh huh. My back hurts. In fact it has all night."

"You're not upset about Morgan going away, are you?"

"No. At first I thought, 'Oh, no', but then I realized it's part of his job. I'm so proud of him being chosen to go to this thing. He must be doing a great job. I know he always liked his internships during the summers. At first I just thought it was because he didn't have to go home for the summers. You know," she said, sipping the milk, "Now that I know what was going on, I understand why he never really wanted to go home much."

"It must be sad to be in a family that...well, I shouldn't judge. I'm sure his feelings are justified but I pray he can put the hurt behind him and go on," Karen said.

"I think he has put it behind him." Ali pushed the tray away. "I can't eat any more."

"You didn't eat a thing."

"I'll do better later today." She slid down under the covers. "Morgan promised he'd call me every chance he gets. He read me the conference schedule of events and he's going to be very busy." Her eyelids drooped.

"You're tired," Karen said, tucking the covers around Ali's shoulders. "Take a nap, honey. You didn't sleep much last night. If you need me, the little bell is right on the corner of the nightstand."

"Thanks, Mom," Ali whispered.

Karen tucked the covers around Ali's shoulders and tiptoed out of the room. At the doorway she stopped and looked back. *It's as if she were still my little girl, me tucking her in. All this will end when she and Morgan set up their home in Miami. I'm going to miss her—and the babies, and they aren't even here yet. Nothing stays the same, but that doesn't mean it's bad, or at least that's what I'm going to convince myself.* She closed the door only half way so she could hear the bell if she was needed.

Karen took her Bible out of the drawer and laid it on her pillow. After a quick shower she'd do her morning devotions. "I have so many things to be thankful for," she murmured, walking into her bathroom, "I'm ashamed when I let little 'sorry for myself' ideas creep in."

***

Wednesday afternoon, Morgan stood next to the floor to ceiling windows at Miami International Airport.

"I fly home Sunday, sweetheart," Morgan said, standing with his cell phone to his ear. "I miss you already. It's one thing being three hours away and another going clear across the country."

"I'll miss you too. I've grown to like these weekend visits."

"Well, it won't be long and they won't be visits. I've done some investigating with the help of my friend, Dave, and there are a couple of houses we'll have to check out when you're able to come down here. Good neighborhoods."

"You know, I don't know when that's going to be. I'm worried about that. We need a place of our own but I won't be able to just jump up after the babies are here and tear down to Miami. Maybe not for...several weeks," she said. "Everything is so up in the air. When are the babies arriving? How long before we can uproot them? And I know Mom's not real happy we're all going away. She's been looking forward to having the twins right here. It's going to be an adjustment for her, too."

"I know, honey. But, together we'll work it all out. I don't want your Mom hurt any more than you do." He sighed.

"Well, we can't worry about that now until we know what's what. I wish the babies were here already."

"Me, too."

"Not as much as I do."

"You're okay, aren't you? You'll tell me if anything happens."

"Happens?"

"Well, I don't know..."

"No one does. We'll just have to play it by ear. I don't want you worrying while you're away. Have a good time and enjoy the conference. I know what an honor it is for you. I'm so proud of you."

Morgan felt his heart swell, not with pride but with love. "You're the best, Ali. I love you." He paused, something had been niggling at his thoughts for several days now. "You know, I've been thinking. Maybe it's too soon to talk about this, but have you any thoughts about names for our babies?"

Ali laughed. "I have for months, but nothing has come to me. Mom and I talked about it..." she hesitated. "Before you, ah, came back. I didn't like her suggestions and she didn't like mine so we let it drop. They've been just the babies or the twins but you're right. We have to decide and we can't wait forever." Again, Morgan heard her laugh. "We don't have forever."

"I don't have any suggestions, only I sure wouldn't want our son to be named after me."

"Why not?"

"Because my name is fake. Remember, I was named for a grandfather who wasn't mine and as for my last name, well, I'm stuck with it."

"I think, Morgan Muldorn is a very distinguished name, honey, but I understand. When you get back we'll do some serious thinking. In the meantime, see what you come up with. Just remember, I love you and we'll be here when you get home."

"I love you, too. Call me when you can. I'll have my cell with me all the time. I'll have to put it on vibrate when I'm in meetings though. Oh, they're opening the gate. Gotta go. Love you," he listened to Ali say goodbye and then hurried to the gate. Already counting the days to his return, he still admitted he was looking forward to this adventure. *And it'll mean good things with L&L, I hope,* he thought, handing his boarding pass to the uniformed clerk at the gate.

Later that evening in San Francisco, Morgan followed a porter who carried his suitcase and garment bag. Opening the door to room 398, he turned to Morgan, "Your room, sir. Can I get you anything else?" He hung the garment bag in the closet area and put the case on a luggage rack and turned to give Morgan the plastic entry card, every move with calculated experience.

"Nothing else, thanks," Morgan said. "Looks like a very nice room. I'm here with the NAIB. I guess all the meetings and things are held right here." He knew he was babbling but the young man just smiled.

"Yes, sir. We're looking forward to making this stay pleasant for everyone."

"My wife is going to have twins," Morgan blurted out.

Again the young man smiled. "That's very good news, sir." He paused a moment and Morgan suddenly realized why. Reaching into his pocket he pulled out the first bill his fingers closed around. "Here, you've been very helpful," he mumbled, pushing a five dollar bill into the hand of the porter.

"Thank you, sir. My name is Arnold and I'll be on duty until eleven o'clock tonight. Ask for me if you need anything." He turned and exited, the door automatically closing behind him.

Morgan threw himself across the king-sized bed. *What an idiot! I told him my wife is having twins. Where did that come from, and why did I think he needed to know?* He sat up and caught his expression in the mirror. "I said wife," he grinned. "I said wife, and it sounded great." He glanced at his watch and pulled his cell phone from the clip on his belt. He dialed Ali's cell phone number and listened to it ring three thousand miles away.

"Hello."

"Hi, it's me. I'm in the hotel and I have a great room. The hotel is huge; I'll need a map to get around." His heart raced in his chest and he pictured her in her bed, blonde hair spread across a pink pillow.

"I'm glad you called."

"You okay?"

"I'm fine. In fact, I'm looking at the pink and blue Teddies. I keep hugging them. Mom says I'm going to wear them out before... Have you thought of any names? I thought on the plane ride you might have time to think about that."

'I did. Listen, you can just say no if you don't like this, but," he turned away from the mirror, "when I was a kid, I always wanted to be called Robert. You know, Bobby at first then Bob when I got older. Nice neat names, there aren't any nicknames for Morgan. But, look, if you don't like Robert we can keep thinking."

"I like Robert. I hadn't thought about it but I think that would be perfect. Now we just have to come up with a name for Bobby's sister."

"If you're sure. We can always change our minds, we have time yet."

She laughed. "We have time. I'll keep thinking."

"Well, if we do choose Robert, then you should choose the little girl's name."

"I'll try."

"You sound tired. Are you?"

"Yes, I am tired. Thanks for calling. I'll talk to you tomorrow."

"Let me call you, sweetheart. I'll have to call between meetings or at lunch, but I'll call you as soon as I can."

"Don't call early. I may decide to sleep in a little."

"Okay. Talk to you tomorrow. Love you."

"Love you, too." Ali was reaching to put her phone on the night table when Karen came in.

"Here, let me help you. I think we should move the table forward a little. It will be easier for you. Did someone call?"

"Yes, Marla called while you were at the store, and that was Morgan. He sounded excited. I think he's going to like this trip. Kristi and Marla wanted to come over this evening but I told them to call tomorrow, I was too tired."

"You look tired, honey."

"I am. I feel beat."

That night Ali complained more and more about her back ache. "There isn't a comfortable place to lie," she moaned, twisting against her pillows.

"I think we should call the doctor. You haven't seen any more blood, have you? I don't like your blood pressure going up."

"It didn't go up much."

"It's been creeping up for the past week and that's why they're having me take it every day and calling them at the end of the week. I'm not a nurse, hon, but I really think we should call the doctor."

"I don't know. I feel good except I have this heavy feeling like my stomach is filled with lead and sliding down my body and my back aches more. But I keep looking at it and it seems to be in the same place, just huge."

"I think I'm going to call the doctor in the morning. It can't hurt to tell him of these things."

"I guess, but we have a month to go. What can he do?"

Karen laughed. "He's the doctor, he'll tell us."

44

Wait on the Lord: be of good courage,
and He shall strengthen thine heart:
wait, I say, on the Lord.
Psalms 27:14

The next morning, which was Thursday, Karen left a detailed message with Dr. Perez's staff. Then she paced the kitchen waiting for a response. Now she listened to his nurse who had called back.

"Dr. Perez wants Alice to be in the hospital for complete bed rest. He doesn't want her walking at all, so we're arranging for medical transport. Call us when you're ready to leave the house. You might want to pack a bag, some toiletries and things like that. There's no hurry as long as she remains off her feet completely. Do you have a bed pan? Or Depends?"

"No," Karen stuttered, her mind going madly through what was going to happen in the next few minutes.

"Then don't wait too long," the nurse said, a hint of humor in her words.

Karen hurried down the hall to Ali's room. "Well, I've spoken to Dr. Perez's nurse, Jennifer. You remember her?"

"Yep. So what's up?"

"He said you have to be hospitalized, honey." She paused, watching terror take over Ali's expression.

"No!" she shouted.

"Yes, I'm afraid he's ordered complete bed rest, at least for now. We have to get ready as soon as possible because he doesn't want you on your feet at all."

"But I haven't taken a shower, washed my hair," she moaned, pushing herself up higher on the pillows.

"There's no way you can do that," Karen said, pulling one of the pillows from behind Ali. "And, I think you might want to lie a little flatter, and on your side, honey. That's what she said. They'll take care of bathing at the hospital so don't worry about that."

"I don't believe this. The twins aren't due for a month. You mean I have to be in the hospital for a month?" she whined.

"Maybe. Who knows, maybe after a week or two you can come home."

"Did Jennifer say that?"

"No. But we can't jump to conclusions, and you know how good Dr. Perez is. You like him."

"I did," Ali said, her mouth twisting with frustration.

"What do you want to take, honey, besides your toiletries?"

Ali looked around the room. "My cell phone and the charger so I can call Morgan, and...and Mom, please, Morgan is not to know where I am. He can call me but I'm not telling him this while he's away." She looked around the room. "And I want the Teddy Bears," her voice broke with emotion.

Forty-five minutes later Ali was being transported to the hospital in an ambulance without all the lights. An anxious Karen followed in her car, her mind racing through what might lie ahead. *I have to let Bill know,* she thought. *And Kristi and Marla, they'll help cheer Ali up, but I'm going to wait until I talk to Dr. Perez to make those calls. Jennifer said he would see Ali at the hospital around noon today.*

The next couple of hours were hectic to Ali and Karen but routine to the hospital staff. Efficient and caring, it wasn't long before Ali was settled in Room 467- Maternity- East Wing, bathed and in a gown, an IV drip in her left arm and a blood pressure cuff on her right.

"That wasn't so bad, was it?" Karen said, sitting in one of the comfortable chairs next to Ali's bed. The room was decorated nicely and everything looked new and clean.

"It's the first time I've had a bath in bed. How embarrassing."

Karen sighed, thinking of what lay ahead for her daughter. She smiled. "You can't worry about being embarrassed, honey. The nurses and doctors have to do what's best for you and the twins."

"Morgan says we have to come up with names and not keep calling them babies or twins."

"He's right. Have you thought of any?"

"No. He's going to think and so am I. When he comes back we'll get together and come up with something. He doesn't want our son to be called Morgan, though." Ali suppressed the suggested name of Robert, somehow holding the information to herself as being too private or too new to share.

"Oh?"

"He says it's a fake name since he never had a grandfather and that's who he's supposed to be named after. I told him I like his name."

"I understand his feelings. He's still got a lot to deal with and it looks like he's finally got his ducks in a row."

Ali laughed. "Speaking of ducks, did you bring the Teddies?"

Karen jumped up. "They must still be in the overnight case. Let me get them."

"Put them on that shelf there so I can see them, please."

"I think this is for flowers," Karen said, pushing the Teddy Bears onto the shelf. "There, how's that."

"Fine, and don't go getting me flowers, Mom. I won't be here that long. When Dr. Perez comes in to see me I'm going to tell him I feel a lot better."

"Do you?"

"What?"

"Feel better."

Ali bit her lip. "Well, no, but I don't see what the fuss is. I'm big and awkward so naturally I'm going to have back pain."

"Let's not jump to conclusions until he sees you, okay?"

Ali looked away. Her mother could convey vast messages with her *look,* as Ali called it when she was being reprimanded as a child. She wasn't in the mood to deal with reprimands or anything else. She just wanted to go home. Fighting tears, she said, "I don't mean to be rude, Mom, but right now I'm not very happy."

Karen stood and moved to her bedside stroking her daughter's hand. "You should be happy, honey. You're in the best place for you and the doctor will be in soon, then you can talk to him and see exactly what he thinks is best. Best for you and your babies. Nameless, but wonderful babies," she smiled. "Want to watch some television?"

"No, thank you."

"Should I go down to the gift shop and get you a magazine or book? I forgot to pack anything for you to read."

"No, thank you. I'll just rest," she said, closing her eyes, trying to shut out the sterile room and the terror she was hiding.

Karen sat down again. Her heart ached for her child and she watched her in silence, quietly praying that everything would be okay. *After the doctor comes in,* she thought. *Then we'll know what's going on.*

The silence in the room was only broken by the inflating blood pressure cuff. Karen watched the slow drip, drip, drip of something disappearing into the long plastic tube affixed to Ali's arm. She, too, closed her eyes. "Please, God," she whispered to herself.

At twelve-thirty Dr. Eduardo Perez breezed into the room, a chart in his hand and a stethoscope around his neck. "How's my patient?" he said, leaning across the bed.

"Unhappy," mumbled Alice.

"Well, we can't have unhappy mothers, can we?" he said, folding back the sheet. "Let me listen to these two trouble makers." He placed the stethoscope on Alice's stomach, moving it from place to place. "Now let's listen to Mommy." When he had finished the examination he smiled. "Everyone seems happy at the moment."

"Then why am I here?" Alice asked, her eyes going to her mother.

"You're here because when you called in your symptoms I thought complete bed rest would be best for you and those little guys. Let me clear things up for you.

"First, you aren't in any danger and neither are the babies. But we want to keep it that way. Your blood pressure is elevated and you seem to be retaining fluid. Not unusual in a pregnancy like this. You're carrying twins and it's your first pregnancy.

These factors have to be taken into consideration." He smiled at her and at Karen who was sitting on the edge of the cushion.

"At all costs we want to prevent preclampsia which is serious. Blood pressure that gets out of control and too much fluid are warnings and we are going to take care of them right here and right now in order to prevent that happening. I've ordered complete bed rest and you have to be here for that to work. You also must be monitored for blood pressure and fluids. I've also ordered medications for both those problems. And we'll monitor the babies. I have to tell you, though, there is a possibility of the babies delivering early and a possibility for the need of a Cesarean section."

Ali's mouth sprung open and her eyes widened. She looked at her mother and then back at the doctor. "Cesarean? I thought you said I could deliver naturally."

"I did, but pregnancies are like books, once you turn a page something you didn't think would happen is right there. It's getting there in time that counts.

"You and your babies are going to get the best care possible so relax and let all these lovely people wait on you hand and foot. It's like a vacation in a plush hotel, right?" he asked the nurse who stood at the foot of the bed.

"Right," she said, smiling broadly. "Only the view isn't as good as Diamond-head."

"And the food, while good, isn't exactly gourmet. That, too, will be monitored." He squeezed Ali's hand and then addressed Karen. "Any time you have questions you just call the office. I'm on twenty-four hour call so you can always reach me. Smile," he said. "Grandmothers should always smile."

It seemed as if he was there one moment and gone the next, the nurse following him out the door.

Karen moved to Ali's side and took her hand. "It's going to be okay, honey. I'm so glad we came right away."

"I'm scared, Mom," Ali said.

45

The Lord is my light and my salvation;
whom shall I fear?
The Lord is the strength of my life;
of whom shall I be afraid?
Psalms 27:1

For Ali, the following two days dragged and then alternatively sped by in a kaleidoscope of sounds, scents, and touches. The food was bland but okay, the sounds at night scary, and the touches and handling were not only embarrassing but invasive. At all times of the day and night she seemed to be vulnerable to people she didn't know. She cringed at phrases such as, "Let's take a look at this," by an intern, or, "Time for meds, hon, your doctor has ordered a change." Dr. Perez came twice a day, usually around seven o'clock in the morning and then nine o'clock at night. Knowing his schedule at his office and factoring in hospital births, Ali and Karen wondered when he took time off to eat or sleep.

Kristi and Marla came in the afternoon, bringing her stuffed toys and flowers. Once they brought a body splash but the nurse put it on the shelf with the Teddy Bears who were now sharing their space with two kittens, two small rabbits and two windup music boxes, one with a ballerina spinning around on top and the other with a whimsical clown. The music boxes were from Jocelyn who was working crazy hours and couldn't visit. She called twice.

"No perfumes," the nurse said, smiling and then pulling the sheets down so she could position a monitor on Ali's stomach.

Karen arrived each day at nine o'clock and stayed until eight in the evening. "Mom, you don't have to be here all day. They do wait on me hand and foot and all places in between," Ali said with a laugh. "I have a thousand hands taking care of me and a buzzer to get help if I need it. Kristi and Marla will be here around two. Go home and get some rest. I'm going to need you after Bobby and sister arrive." But Karen shook her head and perched in a chair near the bed, reading or watching television with her daughter. Ali loved the company but felt guilty just the same.

One thing she loved was using the name Morgan had given to their son and she had picked out just the name for their daughter but didn't want to use it in case Morgan had some objection, which she thought highly improbable. Her choice—Rebecca or Becky.

"Becky and Bobby, don't you think that's just perfect?" she asked her mother and then Kristi and Marla and several nurses who were poking or prodding her. They all agreed, still it was Bobby and his 'sister' until she spoke to Morgan.

He had called yesterday. "How's the mother-to-be," he'd said, his voice light and without the usual tension Ali was accustomed to hearing.

"I'm fine and you must be doing well, I can tell by your voice."

"Oh, yeah? Well, I've been spinning from seminar to seminar, some of them interesting and others boring. But the best part is just meeting the other men, some of whom are in my boat, intern last year and associate this year, all hoping for a step up the ladder. There are a lot of summary papers to fill out after each class so I've been busy. Haven't left the hotel yet so I guess I won't be seeing much of San Francisco. We'll come and visit the Golden Gate together."

"That sounds great. I'm so happy you're enjoying the conference."

"I am, but I wish I were closer so I could slip away and see you."

Ali laughed, "That will be the day, when Gadara hosts a convention. And it looks like you're busy enough without slipping away to see me. I'm fine, honey." She sighed.

"Still tired?"

"Yes, I guess it goes with the territory." She covered the

phone as a nurse approached her bed. "Can you come back in two minutes, phone call," she whispered desperately, her hands holding the phone away from her face.

The nurse smiled, nodded and pushed her med cart out into the hallway. Karen had left a few minutes earlier so Ali was alone in her hospital room.

"Ali? Hello? Are you still there?"

"Yes," she laughed softly. "I almost dropped the phone."

"Your voice sounds funny, like you're in the bottom of a barrel."

"No barrel, just bed as usual. Must be the connection."

"Well, I have a 'Greet and Meet and Repeat' thing to go to in a few minutes. I think it's kind of a rehashing of what has happened so far. Tomorrow is the final breakfast and then I have a very important flight to catch."

"Have fun, darling. I miss you. See you late tomorrow?"

"Yeah. My flight lands at MIA at 1:45. I'll head up to Gadara right after that. I've already made arrangements to have Monday off. I explained to Marie, the gal at the front desk. She'll tell my boss, but she checked with personnel and that's okay with them. It's called a 'family emergency day'. I explained you were expecting twins at any time and I guess that counts as a family emergency. I'm sure glad it *isn't* a family emergency, but Marie apparently thought your pregnancy was. She sounded shocked," he said with a laugh.

Ali drew in a deep breath. *I think being hospitalized might count as a family emergency but I can't tell him. It just wouldn't be right and I'm really not in any emergency situation,* she thought. "Well, whatever they call it, I'm glad you have the day off. See you tomorrow, have a safe trip. I pray for you every night, did you know that?"

"I didn't, but that makes me happy. You know, I never was much for prayer. Didn't have that in the family I lived with. Sometimes my friends' parents took me to Sunday School with them or to Bible School and Camp in the summer. But, you know, lately I've been praying. It's something Cliff and Millie suggested. I don't know if I'm doing it right."

Ali smiled. "Oh, honey, there is no right or wrong way to

pray. Maybe if you pray for the wrong reasons, but then they surely wouldn't be answered anyway. Prayer is just a conversation with God. That's what my mother taught me. I'll be glad when I can meet Cliff and Millie since they seem like such good people."

"You're right, Cliff and Millie are good people and they actually don't live too far from Gadara. We'll go to visit them someday. And I'm beginning to love your mother, too."

"She'd like that, I'll tell her..." Ali grimaced, she'd almost said when she comes in tomorrow, but as far as Morgan was concerned she was at home and her mother was near at hand. "She'll like that," she finished.

"Good night, sweet."

"Good night, hon."

Ali closed the phone and slid it onto the tray table.

When the nurse came back a few minutes later, she sorted out the pills and injections Ali was to have. "Last poke for the night," she said. "Talking to your husband?"

Ali hesitated a second. "Yes, he's away on a business trip. He doesn't know I'm here. We thought it best not to tell him. He couldn't rush back anyhow and I'll be fine. And the babies are okay. Right?" she asked.

"As far as I know, you three are doing just fine. Did Dr. Perez stop by tonight yet?"

"Not yet. Maybe he won't come tonight. It's getting late," Ali looked at her watch. It was a little after nine and already the hospital was quieting down. Now she could hear the squeak of the nurses' shoes as they hurried down the hallways following the soft clatter of the meds carts.

"Oh, no. He'll be here. I've seen him come in at eleven o'clock at night and if there's a delivery during the night he just sleeps on a cot and begins his morning rounds before going into his office."

"When does he have time for a life?" Ali joked.

"You and your babies are his life. I've never seen a more dedicated doctor. Every baby he brings into this world is like another child of his."

"Does he have children?"

"He had a wife and three children, two boys and a girl, five, seven and ten. They were all killed in an automobile accident about four years ago. Somewhere up in Maine. His wife had taken the kids for a ski trip and they never made it back."

Tears sprung to Ali's eyes. "How awful."

"He's a treasure to every pregnant woman who comes to him because he is so devoted to her and her baby. I count myself as blessed just knowing him. I had my children thirty years ago and I wish I'd had a doctor like him."

She turned and pushed the meds cart out of the room. "Do you want the door closed?"

"Yes, please," Ali said. "I'll watch some TV but I'll probably fall asleep."

"Good night, then," the nurse said, pulling the door closed behind her.

I told her I was talking to my husband and if felt so right. It won't be long and that's what he'll be...my husband.

She turned the television on and began flipping through the channels choosing the food channel, but before the first dish was in the oven she was asleep. Her last thoughts, *Morgan will be here soon. I'll tell him about Becky and that I called him my husband.*

46

But that on the good ground are they,
which in an honest and good heart,
having heard the word, keep it,
and bring forth fruit with patience.
Luke 8:15

Karen checked her makeup in the hall mirror, grabbed her purse and opened the door to the garage. A single rather than two car garage, she was getting used to the size change and glanced at the stack of unopened cartons holding things that had fit nicely into the garage back at the house. *Most of that stuff will have to be discarded,* she thought, touching the button and watching the door close behind her. *There's just no room in here and the boxes are probably full of things we can very well do without.*

Deciding to skip church this morning and go to the hospital, she backed out of the driveway. In fifteen minutes she'd be hoping to find a decent space that didn't entail a five minute walk. "Being so early should help," she said, exiting Windham Lakes.

At eight-thirty, Karen stepped out of the elevator on the fourth floor and hurried to Ali's room.

A breakfast tray rested on the tray table stretched across Ali's bed. "Good morning, honey. What did you have for breakfast?"

"A little cereal with watered down milk, applesauce and weak tea," she responded. "What did you have?"

"Seven grain toast with marmalade and coffee."

Ali sighed. "I'll be back on real food someday soon, I guess."

"Anything new?" Karen asked, putting a new magazine on Ali's bed. "I brought you a copy of the newest Parenting Magazine."

Ali laughed. "You're determined to make me the mother of the year, aren't you? Thanks, Mom. I appreciate everything you're doing for me and everything you've ever done. Lying here for so many hours has given me lots of time to think about the past as well as the future. I have to say, I've had a wonderful past and it's mostly because you were such a good mother. Daddy helped, too, but it seems like it was you who did so much. Frankly, motherhood is frightening, but I'll be able to look back and say, 'What would Mom do?'"

"Thank you, dear. That was very nice," Karen said, patting her daughter's arm. "Has anyone been in yet today? How do you feel?"

"I feel okay. Sometimes it feels as if I have to go, but then I don't."

"Did you tell the nurses?"

"Yep. I'm getting to be such a hypochondriac I tell them every twitch I feel."

"That's not being a hypochondriac. That's being smart in the situation you're in."

"Dr. Perez hasn't been in yet. I guess he sleeps in on Sundays," Ali laughed.

"Let's watch one of those television church services since we didn't get to go this morning." Karen pushed the t.v. on button and began to flip through the channels.

"I haven't been in weeks."

"You couldn't. God understands."

"I hope so, I feel as if I need Him more than ever these past three days."

"He's always there for you if you talk to Him."

"That's what I told Morgan last night. He was afraid he wasn't praying right. I told him what you told me. He'll be here later today."

"You'll have to tell him where you are. We don't want him coming to an empty condo."

"He's going to call me when he lands in Miami. I can tell him then."

"I have his cell phone number, right?"

"Yes, but I'll call him."

Karen pulled her chair nearer to Ali's bed and they watched a television church service together, sometimes singing softly with the choir and sometimes interrupted briefly by nurses and technicians who moved with a quieter reverence this morning.

At eleven o'clock, Dr. Perez came in, wearing a light green shirt and khaki pants.

As usual, a broad smile accompanied him.

"Sorry to interrupt your services."

"It's almost ended and we were just happy to be able to watch what we did," Karen said, moving her chair away.

"I don't often get to church myself, but I try to record a service every week. Of course, sometimes I don't get to watch it until the next week is here." He pulled his stethoscope from around his neck. "Let's listen to the terrible two and then you, my dear, and then we'll talk."

Ali blew a puff of air she had been holding. "Talk?" she said, softly.

Dr. Perez didn't answer; his stethoscope was in his ears and moving across her belly. He straightened up and pulled the ear pieces out, and with one foot he hooked a chair closer to the bed and sat down. He and Ali were face to face. "There are things we need to talk about this morning. Don't be afraid," he said when Ali's face registered instant anxiety.

"The monitors have shown one of the babies is in a breech position. Also your blood pressure and fluid retention are not responding to the medications I have requested as I hoped, so there are several indications that a C-Section is advisable. Now, as I say, there is no immediate danger but there are signals for problems and what we don't want to do is get into the position of an emergency. The babies are a good weight and since we are unsure of your actual gestation period, I feel this is the best procedure to follow."

Karen stood and moved closer, her face a picture of grave concern.

Dr. Perez looked at her and then back to Ali. "I am recommending a C-Section. I've ordered some medication to be administered intravenously which will help the babies' lungs to function better at birth. There are other medications which should be taken prior to this procedure and we'll be discontinuing the meds you are on now. So there are changes that need to be taken care of before the C-Section. Believe me, a C-Section is not uncommon in twin births and especially if it is a first pregnancy.

"There are always risks but I see no immediate dangers and feel this is the best course of action. As I said, I don't want to wait until it becomes an emergency and that could very well happen. I'm not trying to upset you or scare you, but I always like to be truthful with my patients." He squeezed Ali's hand, and he stretched across the bed to grasp Karen's hand. "Any questions?"

"I guess not. If we do have any, we'll ask," Karen said, looking to Ali for confirmation.

Ali nodded. "I read about some of these things in the book you gave me, but I didn't think I'd be doing this. I'm scared, Dr. Perez. Are the babies going to be all right?"

He smiled. "I'm going to take care of everything. You just rest and do what we say and we'll be okay."

Then he whirled through the doorway and Karen and Ali listened as he hurried along the polished hallway floor.

"Mom," Ali said, fighting tears, "Now I'm really scared."

"You heard Dr. Perez. He's thought this through carefully, dear. You're in good hands. Let's just let Dr. Perez and God take care of things." She bowed her head and Ali knew she was praying. Ali closed her eyes and in the quiet of the hospital room, both women beseeched God's help.

Several minutes later a nurse came in and adjusted the IV. "Changing the meds. Your doctor has made some changes so you'll be ready for a C-Section when Dr. Perez schedules that."

Ali watched her, then said, "Do you know when the C-Section is scheduled?"

"No, dear. He'll keep monitoring things and then let you know."

"Is it usually a day or two or is it longer?"

"It depends. He'll let you know," she repeated, adjusting the sheets. "Lunch should be along any time. In fact, I think I hear the cart now."

Karen stood at Ali's bedside. "Nurses are always cautious about medical instructions, Ali. Don't worry. But, you'll have to tell Morgan, hon. You can't let him rush up here and find this out. He needs to hear it from you."

Ali bit her lower lip and gazed at the window for several moments. "Mom, I don't know if I can tell him. I'm afraid I'll cry and get him all upset and then he'll be driving like crazy to get here. That's not good."

"You can't *not* tell him, Ali," Karen said sternly. "It wouldn't be fair. You'll have to stress you and the babies are okay but the doctor thinks a C-Section would be best. You can't fall apart. Let him know the surgery is not scheduled yet. You have to be strong."

"Like you," she said and sighed. "I know, Mom. I know you're right. Let's see, it's just after nine o'clock in San Francisco. I think his flight is scheduled for around ten forty-five because he said he'd be in Miami around one forty-five. I'd better call him now."

"I'll wait outside," Karen said, walking to the door. She paused, her hand on the doorknob. "I'm very proud of you, honey." She pulled the door closed and Ali reached for her cell phone.

***

Morgan stood at the front desk, his luggage on a carrier behind him.

"Thank you, Mr. Muldorn, I hope you had a pleasant stay," the woman said, handing Morgan the receipt for his expenses at the conference. "Have a safe trip home."

"Thank you," Morgan said, sliding his papers into his briefcase. "I'm headed back to Florida and I'll be..." The sentence was interrupted by his cell phone. He was going to tell her about the twins on the way but instead he smiled and pulled the luggage cart with him. "Hello."

"Hi, it's me. I hope I haven't interrupted anything important." Morgan thought he detected a hint of strain in the breezy easiness of Ali's words.

"Hi, Ali Baba. No, as a matter of fact I just checked out and I'm standing in front of the hotel waiting for the courtesy bus to take me to the airport. Is everything okay? I can't wait to see you."

Ali hesitated and Morgan's heart skipped a beat.

"Everything is okay, isn't it?"

"Yes. I'm okay and the babies are fine. But," she drew in a deep breath and Morgan's heart shrunk a tiny bit more.

"But what? What?" he demanded.

"Oh, don't panic, dear. I'm not telling this well. Dr. Perez was in a little while ago and he feels it might be best to deliver the babies by C-Section rather than wait full term. You see, I've had some signs that something...well I'm calling you from the hospital. I've been here three days and..."

Morgan sank onto the bench, his knees too weak to hold him upright. "Three days! I think you'd better tell me everything."

Ali stuttered her way through the information finishing with, "I'm not sure when the C-Section, the surgery, is scheduled for."

Morgan held his breath. *Surgery?*

"We have to wait to see what all the tests show and how the medications are reacting. I'm not sure of anything but I didn't want you to just show up and find me in the hospital and not know what was going on."

Morgan ran his fingers through his hair. "You've been there for how long?"

"Three days."

"And you didn't let me know?"

"I didn't want to worry you. I didn't think it was serious. I thought I'd be home before you came back. I'm sorry. I thought it was best to just let you concentrate on your conference." She listened to him sigh and waited for a response. When none came, she said, "Morgan, don't be mad at me. I thought I was doing what was best."

"You are okay, though? The babies are all right?"

"Yes, honey. We're okay and Dr. Perez is doing everything to keep things that way. I know it sounds scary. I'm scared, but

Mom is here and you'll be here later today." Her voice drifted off with insecurity. "I need you."

"I'll be there as soon as I can get there."

"Don't drive too fast getting here. I didn't want to tell you but Mom insisted."

"I knew I loved her. I'll be there as soon as I can," he repeated. "The C-Section isn't scheduled yet?"

"No."

Morgan thought for a moment. "I'll get into Miami at about 1:45. I'll see if I can get a commuter flight to Tampa and rent a car. Tampa is closer than Miami and it might be quicker. If that's not possible and I drive from Miami I should get there after five o'clock depending on how quickly I get my car out of the parking garage and traffic. Either way, I'll call you before I leave Miami."

"Please drive safely. We need you," Ali said, her voice finally breaking.

"Don't cry, sweetheart. I'll be careful. I have some very important people to see when I get to Gadara!"

"You do?" she stuttered.

"Yes, you and two little kids who need a daddy."

A small smile poked at the corners of Ali's mouth. "You mean Bobby and Becky?"

"Becky?"

"I chose the name Rebecca for our daughter. Is that okay?"

"It sounds like a winner. Bobby and Becky. Great. You take care and do everything the doctor says. One way or another I'll be there as soon as I can. The bus is here. I'm on my way, sweet."

Ali said goodbye and placed her phone onto the tray table. Then she turned her head into her pillow and sobbed.

Karen, hearing the conversation end and her daughter's sobs, hurried to her side. "Don't cry, Ali. Please. What did he say?"

"He said," Ali said through gasps for breath, "He said he's on his way and he likes the name Rebecca."

Karen smiled.

47

Incline your ear, and come unto me; hear,
and your souls shall live;
and I will make an everlasting covenant with you,
even the sure mercies of David.
Isaiah 55:3

At nine-thirty that night, Dr. Perez hustled into Ali's room. "How's Mommy and company," he said. He looked from Ali to Morgan, who was standing next to the bed. "Ah, I see we have another visitor."

"Dr. Perez," Ali said, "This is Morgan Muldorn, the babies' father and my future husband."

He didn't miss the pride and happiness in his patient's voice. Stretching across the bed and grasping Morgan's hand, Dr. Perez said, "Nice to meet you, young man. Has the little mother brought you up to speed on what's going on?"

"Yes, sir, not that I understand all of it," Morgan said, smiling down at Ali.

"Well, let's see if I can put this in a nutshell for you. Ali has had some difficulty with blood pressure and retaining fluids. For the past three days we've tried to alleviate these conditions with medications and diet but I'm not happy with those results. Neither she nor the babies are in trouble but we want to forestall any problems and it is my diagnosis a C-Section is advisable. She is currently getting meds through the IV to assist the babies' lung functions at birth. The estimated birth weight for both babies is five pounds or more and that is excellent given these conditions. After tomorrow's results are in, we can schedule the surgery. None of these conditions are extraordinary in a multiple birth situation or for a first time pregnancy. Any questions?"

"Phew. No, sir. Only, how long can I stay tonight?"

Dr. Perez laughed. "Well, I could see if we can have a cot put in here but I don't think that's really necessary. You can stay until ten or so and then come back in the morning after eight. Nothing is going to happen tonight."

"Thank you, sir," Morgan said, returning the broad smile on the doctor's face.

Dr. Perez listened to Ali's belly and then her chest, flipped his stethoscope around his neck and said, "I understand you've been away for a while, young man, and traveling all day. So you two get caught up, but remember, Ali needs her rest. See you in the morning." With a wave of his hand he was gone.

"He always bursts into the room and then disappears in a cloud of dust. I never saw anyone move around so fast," Ali said, clinging to Morgan's hand.

"I like him."

"I do, too. Mom says he's the best and I think she's right."

Just then a nurse poked her head into the room. "Dr. Perez said to ask you if you'd eaten anything. If you want a tray I can get something for you," she said, speaking to Morgan.

"Oh, no, thank you. I'm fine."

After she'd left he turned to Ali, "What a nice gesture."

"Have you had anything to eat?"

"Not exactly. I had a bag of nuts and a Coke on the plane."

"Oh, Morgan, that's not eating. Why didn't you tell her you needed a tray? They're so good here."

"I'll get something when I leave."

"Nothing's open in Gadara after nine o'clock."

"There's a filling station on the highway. I saw it when I came in. I'll get something there. I called Ms. Hamilton at Twin Oaks and she's got a room for me. The same one I've been getting on weekends. She wanted to know where I was this past weekend," he laughed. "I guess everyone keeps an eye on you in Gadara. If you don't show up, they mark you absent."

Ali laughed with him. "You look better than when you arrived. I'm sorry you were so worried. I told you I was okay."

"I didn't believe you until I saw you. Gosh, sweet, that trip seemed to take days instead of hours."

"Well, you're here and tomorrow we'll find out more of

what's to happen." She yawned.

"You're tired. I should go."

"No. Please. Stay a little while longer."

Morgan pulled a chair closer to her bed and continued to hold her hand. For several minutes the only sounds were noises that seeped in from the hall. When he felt Ali's fingers go limp in his palm, he carefully withdrew his hand. Watching her sleep for a few minutes, he tiptoed out of the room, closing the door behind him.

As he walked down the hall to the elevators, his heart seemed to pump with a steady rhythm for the first time since he'd been sitting outside his San Francisco hotel. *Seem's like an eternity has passed since then*, he thought.

Later, a package of Twinkies in his pocket, he let himself into Twin Oaks through the unlocked front door. Walking softly up the staircase he was startled to hear, "Mr. Muldorn."

He turned and standing next to the first step was Sarah Jane Hamilton.

"Is everything okay with Alice?"

Morgan smiled. "Yes, thank you. I'm sorry if I woke you," he said, noting the robe and slippers.

"Oh, you didn't wake me. I was watching television. Knew you'd be along soon, visiting hours at the hospital being over," she said. "See you in the morning. Would you like breakfast earlier? Say eight o'clock?"

"That would be very nice, Ms. Hamilton."

"Sarah Jane," she said, disappearing into the shadows.

Morgan shook his head. *Does she miss anything? Living in Gadara must be an experience. A pleasant experience. No wonder I love Ali and her mother so much. They come from...they come from good roots.* The words were tinged with sadness as he put his case in the closet and pulled the covers back. He couldn't remember being this tired, or this happy. Ali was okay, his children would soon be here and he was with them. "Thank you, God," he whispered, unbuttoning his shirt.

***

The next morning the news in the Dilly Dally Café was that Ali's C-Section would be later today.

"You ain't sure, so why are you saying that," Sandy said, her fire red pony tail wagging with authority.

"'Cause Dr. Perez has cancelled all his appointments this morning," said the mother-in-law of the sister of Dr. Perez's scheduling clerk.

"Well, he might have other surgeries scheduled," Mildred said, arranging the pieces of her pastry on the plate in front of her. She never ate anything she hadn't cut into bite-sized pieces.

"I'll bet a dollar to donuts, it's Ali Waterson's babies he's seeing to. There's two of 'em, you know," Harry Alders said, snapping his suspenders with confidence.

"Well, that young man, who I guess is the father," Mildred said, echoing the doubts of several patrons, "he showed up late last night. Hadn't been here for the weekend like the past weeks."

Jack sat at the counter. "You know, we might know later on what's actually going on. It's kind of a waiting game, isn't it?"

Several heads nodded in agreement. "He's right, you know," Sandy said, swishing her way to the kitchen to pick up a couple of *Cracker Breakfast Specials* for Officer Hinders and his partner.

***

At Twin Oaks, Morgan sat at a table in the dining room. Earlier, when he was dressing, he'd glanced out the window and thought he'd seen Jack just leaving.

Sarah Jane put a plate of scrambled eggs, toast and grits in front of Morgan. "Sure you don't want sausage or bacon?"

"No, thanks, Ms. Hamil—Sarah Jane. This is fine. I want to get to the hospital as soon as I can."

"Well, let me fill that coffee cup for you," she said, taking a pot from the sideboard.

"Did I see Jack leave earlier?"

"Yep. Said he had some things to do. Says he won't be here much longer. I guess school will be starting at that college before long. I'll miss him. Never had a guest stay that long or be that nice."

"I like him, too. He seems to be everybody's friend, doesn't he?"

"You can say that again. At first, I thought he was just nosy, but he's right interested in everything. A.J. says he stops by every other day to make sure he's okay. Not many young men, present company excluded, care about folks like he does."

"Oh, I don't know about *present company*, Sarah Jane. I wish I was that caring. Something I have to work on, I guess."

***

When decisions about a C-Section are made in a hospital an amazing number of people ready themselves for action. The surgical nurses, the anesthesiologists and neo-natal staff including the technicians who are experts on lung functions, are put on alert. A tentative time for the surgery is set up and an operating room is reserved. When all bases are covered, the patient is prepped.

At nine-thirty, Dr. Perez told Ali, Morgan and Karen the C-Section would be performed later today. "I'm happy to report that all the tests and reports show a C-Section is indicated. In other words, all systems are 'go'," he said with his usual smile. "You're going to have some folks stop by, Ali, and they will explain what they do and why and will answer your questions. Don't be afraid to ask questions." He patted her hand and turned to leave.

"Wait," Ali called and he turned back. "Who's coming by?"

"Anesthesiologists, neo-natal techs, all the people who will be assisting me. Great bunch. Really know their stuff. You'll be in good hands, Ali. Not to worry."

He was gone.

They looked from one to the other, then Karen said, "I'm sure if they're working with Dr. Perez they're all experts. I don't think we have a thing to worry about."

Ali scrunched into her pillow. "I'm scared."

"So am I, sweetheart. But this is what's best for Becky and Bobby, and you," Morgan added. "Keep remembering that," he said, trying to swallow the lump in his throat.

"He's right, dear. Just think, in a few hours you'll be parents," Karen said, looking from Morgan to Ali.

"I feel as if I've been pregnant for years," Ali said, her voice small, her eyes large.

Just as she finished the sentence a motherly looking nurse in blue scrubs entered the room.

"Okay," she said, "First there are two too many people in the room right now. Your husband and..."

"My mother."

"Mom, Hubby, give us a few minutes, okay?" she said.

Karen and Morgan headed for the door. "We'll be back... whenever," Morgan said.

The nurse in blue faced Ali. "Dr. Perez has scheduled your C-Section. Do you know what's going to happen?"

"No. I mean, I looked at some of the stuff in the book Dr. Perez gave me but I didn't really look at C-Sections. I didn't think I was going to need one."

"A lot of multiple births end up CS's," she said, taking what looked like a small menu from her pocket and settling into a chair pulled close to Ali. "In a little while an anesthesiologist will come in to explain what she does and then you'll get a spinal. That's an injection in your lower spine. This will cause you to be numb from the rib cage down. Then you'll get some chalky stuff to drink which will neutralize your stomach acids. You'll get a catheter and an IV. Well, you already have the IV," she said, looking up from her notes. "After that, it's on to the operating room. Your hubby can suit up and come with you. Any questions so far?"

Ali shook her head.

"Good," the nurse said, "Now in the operating room a curtain will be pulled across your midsection so that in addition to not feeling the proceedings, you won't see them either. With so many of your senses out of commission, you may find yourself listening hard. You will hear some activity in the far half of the room, a scrub nurse, another nurse or two, the anesthesiologist and someone from neo-natal will probably be there since these babies are preemies."

"Will I feel the babies being born?"

"You might but you'll hear them and you'll see them." She smiled.

A good sign, Ali thought. She'd seemed so stern up to this minute.

"Sometimes these things are so routine to us we forget the exciting part. Yes, my dear, you'll hear them and see them and then they'll be put in a warmer to keep their body temps steady. Have you picked out names?"

"Yes, do we need them right away?"

"No. But, it gives you and Daddy something to talk about until the babies are all cleaned up. After the births, you may feel nausea or shaky, it's normal and nothing to worry about. You'll spend about an hour or so in recovery. You'll wear a heart monitor and have an oxygen monitor on one of your fingers. Feeling will come back to your legs, sometimes it's slow and sometimes it comes in spurts and after the feeling comes back you might be itchy. If anything bothers you or you have questions, you ask. Any questions now?"

"I wish I'd taken notes."

"You don't need notes, honey. Just relax and let us do our thing. In a little while you're going to have a couple of kids." She stood and smiled warmly, suddenly looking more like a grandma than a drill sergeant.

"I think I do have a couple of questions."

"Okay, shoot."

"Morgan can be in the operating room with me?"

"Daddy will have to be gowned and masked. Anything else?"

"Yes, how long will I stay in the hospital after their births and will the babies come home with me?"

"You'll be here about three days. As for the babies, that depends on the doctor and the neo-natal techs. Don't worry about that now." She patted Ali's shoulder. "You're going to do fine and you have the best doctor in the universe as far as I'm concerned."

She turned to leave, calling over her shoulder, "I'll let Daddy and Grandma in now."

48

For with God nothing shall be impossible.
Luke 1:37

"Did you hear them?"

"I did."

"Bobby is bigger than Becky, but they're both okay, Morgan, they're both okay! I was so scared."

"I know," Morgan said, sitting next to Ali. The sides were up on the gurney in the recovery room so he looked at her through the protective bars. "Bobby is five pounds, four ounces and Becky is five pounds. And you're okay, too. I'm so proud of you, sweetheart. I'll never forget this day as long as I live."

"Neither will I. I was frightened and then everything went smoothly. It was over in no time and there they were—two squirming little bundles of baby. They felt so soft." She closed her eyes. "I wished it would be over quickly and now I'm sorry."

"Don't be. We'll always have those two little reminders of the miracles that happened today."

"Miracles. You're right, hon. They are miracles and it's a miracle you came back."

"And a miracle you forgave me," Morgan said, kissing Ali's hand.

"You're going to be a great daddy." She sighed and closed her eyes.

"Are you okay?"

"Yes, silly. I'm just tired and happy. So happy."

"I am too. I never thought I'd ever be this happy. One thing is sure though, sweetheart. No one is ever going to try harder to be the best father who ever lived. Even though I have nothing to relate to..."

"Don't even think about that. It's in the past. We're here

now, and our children are in warm beds, one with a pink cap and the other in blue. Did you see those cute little caps they put on the babies?"

"I did." Morgan smiled at her. "You know, I can't wait until we're married."

"Why?" asked Ali, twisting to look directly at him.

"Because I want to tell everyone you're my wife."

"I want to tell them you're my husband. You know, when I was talking to you on the phone when you were in San Francisco the nurse asked me if I was talking to my husband and I said 'yes'. It was so strange but it felt, like, so right."

Morgan laughed. "While I was away I referred to you as my wife and I had the same feelings."

"It's meant to be, honey," she said, reaching for his hand.

The following morning, Morgan pushed Ali in a wheel chair to the nursery where the babies were. Karen walked behind them and they stood in front of a large, curtained window. There were several other couples and visitors waiting, too. Invisible and at the back of the group were Jack Coursky and his mentor, Samuel.

When the curtain was pulled aside there was a collective aah as the tiny bassinets were viewed.

"There they are," Ali called, pointing to two bassinets on the far left.

Karen crowded forward looking at her grandchildren. "Oh, they're beautiful. Look, Bobby is trying to suck his thumb and Becky is sound asleep."

"Dr. Perez said that Bobby has a small birthmark on the back of his right hand. Did you see it, Morgan? It almost looks like yours, only yours is more tan than red. Bobby's is red but they said it would fade and might even go away. It's not anything we have to worry about."

Jack moved forward, staying behind them. He watched as the tiny child waved his fist across his face trying to find his thumb.

Look, Jack said to Samuel. *Remember I told you about the birthmark on both A.J. and Morgan. Well, the little kid has one, too. You know what that means?*

It means you have come to the end of your journey. One thing remains, Jack. Get A.J. here to see the birthmark. After all, I've left you on your own for quite some time now. You don't need me anymore. Just get this done and we're off to the Promised Land, Samuel replied.

Easier said than done. How am I going to get that old man to come to the hospital, and into the maternity ward yet?

You've done fine so far. Go get him. It's your last challenge.

Samuel left him and although Jack knew he wasn't visible, he felt very vulnerable and he, too, hurried away, muttering to himself that some tasks seemed impossible even to a herald

Jack burst through the doors at Sylvan Hall and headed to the hallway leading to A.J.'s room. He was several rooms away when he began calling, "A.J., hey, A.J. Where are you?"

He paused at the open door but quickly saw his friend wasn't in his room. Turning, he looked down the wide hall. A.J. was nowhere to be seen. Jack ran to the small dining room. He saw someone who he thought he recognized and rushed up to him. "Have you seen A.J.?"

The old gentleman studied Jack. "I seen you in here before."

"Yes, I'm a friend of A.J. Handley. Know where he is?"

The old man wound his fingers around his suspenders. "Seems like he might be in the card room on the other side of the building. There's a gin rummy tournament tomorrow and some of the guys are playing there. You can take that hall..." He didn't finish because Jack was loping along the hall he was pointing to. He shrugged, "Some people just don't know how to wait until a sentence is done."

Jack found the card room and looked inside. There was A.J. sitting at a table with three other men. "A.J.," he said, bounding into the room. "You have to come with me."

A.J. looked up at Jack. "Hi. What's so urgent?"

"You have to come with me. It's important."

"I can't come now. See? I'm playing cards. Big tournament tomorrow. I'm gonna win or at least they'll know they've been in a battle." He laughed. "You were right, Jack. Here's where I belong." His smile erased years of loneliness.

"I know, but you have to come with me right now."

"Can't it wait until another day?"

"No. It can't."

A.J. picked up the cards dealt to him. "Make it another time and I'll be glad to go with you." He sorted his cards.

"Listen. You have to come now. It's important. You'll be glad you did." Jack put his hand on A.J.'s shoulder. "Please, come. I need you to do this. Not just for me but for you, too."

A.J. twisted around, studying Jack's anxious face. "Never saw you so het up about anything. What's so important that I have to come with you right here and now?"

Jack squatted down next to his chair. "I'm telling you. It's important. To you, A.J." He watched as the man hesitated.

"Well..."

"I have a taxi outside. You'll be back in no time."

The three card players were studying A.J. and Jack, cards clutched in their hands, blinking as their eyes went from one to the other as if they were watching a tennis match.

"You have a taxi waiting?"

"I do."

A.J. looked at his companions. "Get George to take my place. I'll be back soon," he called as he rose and followed Jack from the room. The card players, openmouthed at the turn of events, watched them disappear around the corner.

"I don't know what's so all-fired important that I have to just up and come with you. In a taxi yet. You got money to burn?" A.J. grumbled as they sped along the street. "Where are we going anyhow?"

"The hospital."

"Oh, no, you don't. Has that sawbones got you to get me in there for another test? Oh, no," A. J. said reaching for the door handle.

"Wait. Don't do that, you'd kill yourself if you fell out of a moving vehicle. This doesn't have anything to do with your doctor or any tests. Believe me, it's just something you need to see. So sit back and settle down. This won't take much time and you'll be glad you came, believe me."

"I can't think of a thing at the hospital that would make me be glad I came. Haven't been in a hospital since…well, I don't know when the last time was. Decades ago."

Jack breathed a sigh of relief as the taxi pulled under the canopy at the front of the hospital. He leaned forward and pressed two twenty dollar bills into the surprised driver's hand. "Keep the change. Wait for him, he'll be out in a little while," he whispered, keeping his voice low so A.J. wouldn't hear him. He extended his hand to A.J. who was still not moving. "Come on."

"This better be good because I don't go inside a hospital for anyone."

"Just come with me."

Jack almost pulled A.J. along the long, wide hallway, past the little chapel and the cafeteria to a bank of elevators. Pressing the button, the doors slid open. Inside, he pressed number four and both men watched the numbers light up on the panel as they passed the other floors.

When the doors opened on the fourth floor, A.J. stepped out and stared at the wall in front of him. "Maternity Ward" he mumbled. "What the…?"

Jack took his elbow, urging him down the hall. "This way. I hope we're not too late."

"Too late for what? Jack, I'm getting pretty upset. This isn't like you." They hurried to the nursery. The curtain was pulled across the wide window, a small sign indicated the curtain would be opened at 10:00 a.m., 2:00 p.m. and 7:00 p.m. "I need help, Sam," Jack muttered, looking around for Samuel. "Help me out, you miserable old man, where are you?" There was no response.

Jack knew he was on his own.

"Sit here and wait for me," he said to A.J. "I have a surprise for you. I'll be right back."

A.J. looked at Jack with jaw-dropping disbelief. "What's going on? This is crazy. I have to get back to Sylvan Halls for lunch."

"Please, sit there, A.J. I'll be right back."

Jack darted down the wide hall to the nurses' station. "Where can I find Alice Waterson?" he inquired.

The young woman in a pink plaid top and white trousers

flipped the pages on a clipboard. "Waterson? Oh, here she is. Room 467. Down that short hall, last room on the left.'"

Jack rushed to Room 467 and poked his head in the open doorway. "Hello? Anybody home?" He saw Ali in bed and Morgan standing next to her.

"Wow. Look who's here! Jack, what a surprise," Morgan said.

"Jack, what in the world are you doing here?" Ali asked.

"Heard the big news. Twins, right?" He stepped into the room, one hand brushing his beard, the other stretched toward Morgan. "Congratulations, young man. And you, Alice. You look wonderful."

"Thanks for coming," Ali said, her surprise very apparent. "How did you hear about..."

"Your blessed event? Why, at the Dilly Dally, of course. The hub of everything important in Gadara," Jack laughed.

"Well, it's so nice of you to come by," Morgan said, his puzzlement not quite contained.

"Tell you why I'm here," Jack said, moving closer to the bed. "I'll be leaving today and I wondered if I could see your children before I leave. It's something...well, I never had children of my own, just year after year of students. You know how that is."

Neither Morgan nor Ali quite knew what he was talking about but Ali smiled. She liked Jack, he'd been so receptive to listening to anything she or her mother said. "Well," she said, "you can only see the babies at certain times and the next time is two o'clock."

Jack looked at his watch. "It's just about two now."

Ali and Morgan exchanged glances. Surely time hadn't flown by that quickly but when they too looked at their watches, sure enough it was almost two.

"I have A.J. Handley down the hall. He said he'd love to see them, too."

"Mr. Handley said that?" questioned Ali. "I hardly know him. Mom, knows him from the Historical Society, but..."

"Please. I'll be gone tomorrow. I may never get back to Gadara. I've made so many good friends here and I'd just love to see your children before I leave."

Ali and Morgan looked at each other; Morgan shrugged and said, "Well, I guess it'll be okay. We'll meet you there. I have to get Ali into a wheelchair."

"Oh, thanks. You don't know what this means to me," Jack said, bolting into the hall and back to A.J. who was sitting in a chair, completely confused.

How could I have had lunch and not remember it. There's something funny going on here," A.J. thought. *Jack hustling me out of Sylvan Hall, a taxi to the hospital and then leaving me in the hallway of the Maternity Ward? How could I lose over an hour and not notice it?*

Jack almost skidded to a stop in front of A.J. "In just a minute you're going to see something you never thought you'd see."

"I'm seeing things I never thought I'd see now. Maternity Ward, ha," he scoffed, struggling out of the hard plastic chair he was seated in.

"No, wait, A.J. Here comes Alice and Morgan now."

A.J. peered down the hall, seeing a young man pushing a woman in a wheel chair. As they got closer he recognized the woman as Karen Waterson's daughter.

"Hello, Mr. Handley," she said. "They'll be opening the curtains in a moment. It's two o'clock." She smiled at the befuddled old man and Jack, who was standing behind him, smirking as if he'd just pulled off a great joke.

They all turned when they heard the curtains being pulled back. The nurse smiled and gestured to the babies, mouthing 'which bassinets?' Morgan pushed Ali to the window, A.J. followed cautiously, Jack remained behind.

Morgan pointed to the two on the far left, one held a blue capped boy and the other a pink capped little girl. Since there were no other visitors at this time, the nurse pushed the bassinets closer to the window and lifted first the little girl and then the little boy.

"Oh, look, honey," Ali said, "Bobby is still trying to get his thumb in his mouth."

"Look at his hand," Jack whispered into A.J.'s ear.

A.J. scowled. He wasn't comfortable around babies, even babies behind glass windows, but he peered cautiously at the little hand making circular motions in the air.

He frowned and pointed. "He has something on his hand."

"A birthmark, Mr. Handley. But it's nothing to worry about. The nurse said it might disappear. It's just like the one on Morgan's hand. Only his hasn't disappeared."

Morgan thrust his hand out for Mr. Handley to see.

The reaction was immediate as he blinked, trying to focus. His fingers on his left hand caressed the birthmark on his right. He looked from his hand to Morgan's and then to the little child in the blue bassinet. Could it be?

"I don't understand."

Ali saw he was distressed, pale and shaking. "Jack, get Mr. Handley a chair, he looks as if he's seen a ghost, he's so white."

Jack helped the old man sit in the chair he'd just vacated. "See?" he whispered.

"I don't believe it. There are no more ..."

"But there are," Jack said softly.

A.J. shook his head from side to side. "It can't be, but it is," he stuttered.

"Morgan, maybe we should get a doctor."

"Are you okay, Mr. Handley. Can we get you something?"

"Answers," he mumbled.

"Answers?" both Ali and Morgan said.

"Your family, son? Who were they?"

"My family, Mr. Handley? I don't know. I was adopted and never knew my family. I have no way of finding them, there's no trail. Why do you ask?"

Again A.J. just shook his head from side to side. He reached into his pocket and extracted a snowy handkerchief and patted his brow. "The birthmarks. Yours, your son's and mine," he said, and showed the back of his right hand. "It's a family mark, down through the ages, one male Handley always had this mark."

Morgan knelt down next to the old man. Disbelief written across his face, he whispered, "You must be mistaken, Mr. Handley. I have no family."

"You do now, young man. Some way, some how, you just have to be a Handley."

"But, there is no one to ask. My adoptive parents have no

way of checking back. I was..." Morgan choked back tears. "I was given to them in exchange for money. There are no records. All I have is a little wooden box with some old letters and they don't make sense."

A.J. leaned back, his head resting on the wall behind him. "My Aunt Felicity had a wooden box with her treasures in it. I don't know what happened to it."

Morgan sprang up and moved back, away from the old man in the plastic chair. He turned away, his eyes catching Ali's and then swiftly going to the little boy in the blue bassinet. The nurse smiled through the glass, pointing to the curtains and then to her watch. Morgan nodded and she began to draw the curtains across the window.

Slowly turning back to Mr. Handley, he whispered, "One of the letters in the box was signed 'Felicity'."

Jack felt Samuel's presence, felt his fingers grasp his arm. *Time to go, Jack. Your job is done. Well done.*

Together, unseen by anyone, they drifted upward. *I did it, didn't I?* Jack said. Free of any ties, weightless and fulfilled, he and Sam disappeared.

Epilogue

For He shall give His angels charge over thee,
to keep thee in all thy ways.
They shall bear thee up in their hands,
lest thou dash thy foot against a stone.
Psalms 91:11

Three weeks later on a Sunday afternoon, Karen was entertaining more people than she had in several years. A. J. Handley was seated in the wing chair at one side of the fireplace, Morgan's friends, Cliff and Millie held hands as they sat on the couch in front of the double windows. Ali, cradling Becky, sat in her father's old recliner while Morgan, holding a sleeping Bobby, sat in the matching wing chair on the other side of the fireplace. Karen's friends, Shirley and Owen perched on chairs brought in from the deck. Karen, too busy to sit anywhere, placed a tray on the coffee table, already laden with cups and saucers, napkins and plates.

"I have coffee and tea and there are slices of pound cake, Ali's favorite cookies from Kagle's Bakery, and homemade brownies, from a package," she smiled. "Who would like coffee and who'd rather have tea?"

After sorting out the coffee and tea orders, Shirley helped Karen bring the coffee decanter and tea pot in. Millie volunteered to pass the tray to avoid pedestrian confusion and Morgan took both children, one at a time, into the nursery and tucked them into their cribs.

When he returned to the living room, he paused and looked from face to face around the room. *This is my family now,* he thought, *I can't believe it.* He brushed a kiss across Ali's forehead and took his seat. Morgan looked at A.J. "I'm so glad you could join us, sir."

"I'm happy to be here. I still can't believe it."

"Neither can I," Morgan said, reaching behind him to retrieve a small box. "I have something for you, Mr. Handley." Morgan handed a cardboard box to the elderly man.

"What?" he said, watery eyes hooded by drooping eyelids.

"Open it, Mr. Handley," Ali said. "It's a surprise." She looked around the room. "We've had so many surprises lately, haven't we? "

"All good ones," offered Cliff, giving Morgan a wink.

"I'd say they were good ones, starting with a healthy son and daughter and a..." he swallowed with difficulty. "...a ready-made family."

"A blessing," Millie murmured.

A.J. held the box as if it contained something alive. "Open it," Morgan urged.

With fumbling fingers, A.J. pulled at the paper and when it fell away he held a small wooden box with a handle on top and a key on the side. He looked up at Morgan, stupefied. "This is...?"

"It's Felicity's box, sir."

All eyes were on the elderly man who seemed to be reduced in size by the big chair. His fingers trembled so much he couldn't turn the key and Morgan reached across and helped him. Slowly lifting the lid he removed a small blue ribbon. "First Place, Sawgrass Festival," he read. He looked at Morgan, then at the rest of the people in the room watching him. "I'm overwhelmed, son. These are my Aunt Felicity's things. I haven't seen them in over fifty years."

"There are letters, too."

He fingered them, pulling one or two from the box and reverently returning them. The room was so quiet they could hear his labored breathing as he closed the box. "These are yours, son; part of your heritage."

Morgan rose and knelt next to the aged man. "But they are part of your family. I've read them, Mr. Handley. They don't quite all make sense but they tell a story. A story you might understand and then help me with."

A.J. looked into Morgan's eyes. "You have Felicity's eyes," he mumbled. "I'll read the letters and then give them back to you. I don't have much time on this earth, but you and your children are a new generation. Perhaps between the two of us we can sort this out. And if we don't it won't matter. You are a direct descendant of the Handleys, who settled right here in Gadara more than a century ago." He carefully folded the paper around the wooden box.

"You see," he said, addressing the others in the room. "I always knew my aunt had done something that was kept quiet by the rest of the family. Not a good thing to do but back then…well things were different. Her secret might be in this box and then again it might never be solved." He stroked Morgan's hand as it rested on the arm of his chair. "You, young man, haven't had a family, as you told me. I was blessed with a good family but we died out. For years I thought I was the last. Now I know that isn't so and nothing could give me more pleasure than to know you and your children will carry on the family heritage."

"But not the name," Morgan said moving back to his chair.

"I've always been proud to be a Handley," A.J. said quietly. "But there is more to life than labels, son. What you do with your life is far more important than the name you carry with you. I'm happy and proud to call you a Handley."

Millie sniffed and dabbed at her eyes and Cliff squeezed her hand. "Seems to me this story has a couple of happy endings. I couldn't be happier for both of you," he said, grinning at Morgan. "See, I told you. We don't always know God's plan but He has one. We just have to be patient."

Millie murmured "Amen," and other voices joined her.

The room was quiet for several moments. Ali smiled at Morgan and threw him a kiss. Karen sat on the edge of the cushion next to Millie, beaming from her daughter to her future son-in-law. Shirley and Owen smiled and nodded in agreement.

And then the quiet was broken by a baby's cry and everyone laughed. "The next generation has decided it's time to eat," Ali said, pushing forward and rising from the recliner. "Come on, Daddy. This takes a two-man team. You'll excuse us," she said, holding Morgan's hand as they disappeared down the hall.

The room erupted in a buzz of conversation. "They are such

a cute couple," Millie said, helping herself to a brownie.

"When are they moving to Miami?" asked Owen, refilling his coffee cup.

"Will you go to Miami, too, Karen?

"Of course not. Gadara has always been my home. But I'll be wearing a path from here to Miami, that's for sure. I'm not letting those kids have all the fun. Besides, they'll need a baby-sitter, won't they?"

"What does Bill have to say?" Shirley asked hesitantly.

"He's happy. His wife, Sonoma, should be delivering their baby soon. Imagine having a baby and twin grandchildren the same year." Karen said, her voice void of any of the bitterness she had felt just a short time ago.

A.J. sat quietly listening. He was happy at Sylvan Halls but there was nothing like a family conversation. He smiled and folded his hands over his stomach, the box resting in his lap.

"Mr. Handley," Karen said. "Would you like another piece of cake?"

"Couldn't eat another bite, Karen, but I've been sitting here remembering my resentment about not having any descendants. I was kinda angry at God for that when all the time He knew better." He laughed. "I hope He forgives me."

Karen rose and sat in the chair Morgan had vacated. "I've had a difficult time coming to grips with what I thought was unfair. I blamed a lot of people for my unhappiness when I had no right to. I've forgiven Bill and..." she hesitated, then said, "...and Sonoma. I have so many things to be thankful for, holding a grudge seems so petty."

Shirley rose and pulled her husband's hand. "I think it's time for us to go, but we've been honored to be part of this reunion. And as for holding grudges, well, I think we both learned long ago that was a useless activity, didn't we, Owen?"

He smiled at her then looked at the group. "She's referring to the time we almost went our separate ways. It took a lot of prayer and a cruise to fix things but we did, and we are so blessed now. It's easy to forgive when there's love in the picture."

A.J. stood. "We are all blessed and now we can watch another generation find the good and the bad in life, but, most of the time the bad just needs a little tweaking from above," his eyes flicked upward. "Life often holds a little mystery. It's not up to us to always solve the unknown." He looked at Owen. "Could I hitch a ride back to the old folk's farm?"

"We'd be happy to take you, Mr. Handley."

"Wait," Morgan called from the hallway. He strode across the room to where A.J. stood. "Goodbye for now, Mr. Handley," he said, extending his hand.

But A.J. reached out and pulled Morgan into his arms. "We're family now. It took me a long time to find you, son. I'll read the letters and then we'll talk some more."

"Oh, yes, Mr. Handley. You'll never know how much..." his voice broke and wordlessly, his fingers patted the elderly man's back.

Ali hurried to their side. "Thanks, Mr. Handley. You've made us very happy. We'll see you soon," she said, her lips fluttering a kiss on his lined cheek.

They stood in front of the wide windows. The room became very quiet as they watched Owen help A.J. into the back seat of his car and they all waved when Owen pulled out of the driveway.

Turning back to the room, Karen said, "Speaking of mystery and unknown, do you remember that fellow, Jack? I wonder what happened to him. He just disappeared the day after the twins were born. Now that's a mystery."

"Why was he at the hospital anyhow?" Ali wondered.

"How did he know to bring A.J. to see Bobby's birthmark?" Morgan asked softly. "And how did he know there was a connection when no one else did?"

"You know," Karen said, sitting in one of the wing backed chairs. "I liked Jack. He seemed to be able to make you comfortable without actually doing anything. He made the future seem as if it was going to be good, that there was help for whatever trouble you had. Not that he used those words."

"I kind of felt that way too. When I met him at the old activity field I was pretty depressed." Ali reached for Morgan's hand. They were cuddled into the corner of the couch. "He didn't actually tell me in so many words, but he held out hope that everything would come out all right." She leaned toward Morgan and kissed his cheek. "And it did."

"Well, I was beginning to wonder who the heck he was. He just turned up in Miami, once on the bus and once on the street in front of the office building. Whatever it was he said, and I can't remember, he gave me a sense of hope, too." Morgan slipped his arm around Ali's shoulders.

"I know he was influential in getting Mr. Handley into that assisted living home. Sarah Jane told me she was so surprised because she knew Mr. Handley pretty well and she was sure he'd never agree to that. She said A.J. told her it was the best thing he ever did and he had Jack to thank."

"When did she tell you that?" Morgan asked.

"Yesterday in the Dilly Dally. She told me, in fact she whispered to me as if it was a national secret, that one morning she found five twenty dollar bills on her desk and when she checked his room it was as if no one had ever been there. She sounded as if she were relating a ghost story."

"I don't think Jack was a ghost," Ali laughed. "You know, when we get married Morgan, I'd like to ask Jack to be there with us."

"What a great idea," Karen said, her smile infectiously prodding every face to join in. "I know you two want a small wedding but even so, it would be nice to have everyone who was part of this marvelous reunion to be there with you."

Morgan squeezed her hand. "Maybe we can track down an address through the university. Whatever he was, he was a nice guy. I hope he's happy wherever he is. Still, isn't it weird? Jack played a role in each of our lives without us knowing about the other and without actually interfering. Strange, I'd say."

"Strange but maybe..." Karen stood and pulled the curtains closed. "Perhaps we'll never know, but surely there was some Devine Intervention somewhere along the way. You know, it just came to me...one of my favorite scriptures is, "For He shall give His angels charge over thee, to keep thee in all thy ways. They shall bear thee up in their hands, lest thou dash thy foot against a stone."

LaVergne, TN USA
07 January 2011
211636LV00005B/82/P

9 780981 951478